Alison Stuart ... a
legal secretary ... d
of being a write ... l
drama. She lived in London in the early years of her marriage and became fascinated by the history of its people. Her first novel, under a different name, was published in 1987. As a dedicated author she is meticulous in her research and enjoys visiting historical sites and houses. She now writes full time, and lives with her husband in Sussex. She has two children and has just become a grandmother.

Alison Stuart's previous novel, INNOCENCE BETRAYED, is also available from Headline.

Also by Alison Stuart from Headline

Innocence Betrayed

Fateful Shadows

Alison Stuart

KNIGHT

First published in 1995
by HEADLINE BOOK PUBLISHING PLC

First published in paperback in 1995
by HEADLINE BOOK PUBLISHING PLC

This edition published 1999 by
Knight an imprint of Brockhampton Press

10 9 8 7 6 5 4 3 2 1

ISBN 184186 0301

Typeset by Avon Dataset Ltd, Bidford-on-Avon, B50 4JJH

Printed and bound in Great Britain by
Mackays of Chatham PLC, Chatham, Kent

Brockhampton Press
20 Bloomsbury Street
London
WC1B 3QA

Dedicated to the memory of my dear stepfather, Nobby Edwards, who would have enjoyed lifting a glass in appreciation at both the Britannia and the Ringside.

And to the memory of my beloved father. I am after all a publican's daughter.

I toast the health of all my readers.

PART ONE

And coming events cast their shadows before.

THOMAS CAMPBELL, *Lochiel's Warning*

Chapter One

1913

'We can't all be saints, Casey. Besides, sinners have more fun.'

Casey Strong laughed at her cousin's outrageous words. It was so like Eva to say what was most provocative. She gazed at her admiringly. The three-year age gap, between her own sixteen years and Eva's worldly nineteen, had until recently seemed an unbridgeable gulf. In the sixteen months since Casey's mother, Olivia, had died of influenza as the church bells had rung out New Year's Day, 1912, Eva had become her confidante and friend.

It was Sunday and they were in her bedroom at the top of the three-storey pub, the Britannia, which was owned by Joe Strong, Casey's father. From the public bar the sound of the pianola playing 'Follow the Van' was accompanied by raucous singing. Eva stopped tapping out the rhythm of the music with her fingers and picked up a tortoiseshell hair-comb and silver-backed hairbrush. Her cupid's-bow lips set in a hard line as her work-reddened hands closed around the valuable articles on the dressing table.

Casey smiled indulgently. It seemed that Eva never tired of examining the beautiful objects that Casey was fortunate enough to possess. But then Eva had so little. Her family lived in three rooms in a dilapidated terraced house two streets away. On the few occasions Casey's father had permitted her to visit her cousin, she had been shocked at the mildewed walls. The memory of the cockroaches scurrying away into dark corners and the rat- and mice-droppings in the hallways and on the stairs made her shudder. Every piece of furniture was broken in some way. The table lurched drunkenly, one leg propped on half a brick; the horsehair in the single armchair stuck out in tufts. The rooms stank of cabbage-water, and never a slither of carbolic soap had ever touched the filthy walls or peeling paintwork.

Although used to witnessing the poverty of their neighbours, it never ceased to appal Casey. Her father had ensured that she was shielded from the worst of the deprivations of the residents in the alleyways and narrow dingy lanes of the adjoining district. The Britannia was in a street on the borders of the East End and the City of London, and her own home was as comfortably furnished as any middle-class family's – unlike so many of their neighbours. It had always puzzled her that her father had chosen to buy the Britannia, which was on the outer corner of one of London's most notorious districts known as the 'Courtyard'. Some called it the Devil's Yard, so evil was its reputation.

Eva was in a strange mood this morning. She was unusually quiet and she did not seem to be able to keep her fingers still as they kept smoothing the worn material of her ankle-length maroon skirt. To dispel her cousin's strange mood, Casey taunted, 'You're not a sinner, Eva? You're just saying that.'

Her cousin studied her reflection in the oval dressing-table mirror and twirled a displaced ebony tendril from her upswept hair. 'Am I?'

Eva gave Casey one of the closed looks which often infuriated her. Eva could act the drama queen when it suited her, and said the oddest things to weave an aura of mystery around herself. Yet sometimes the flippancy was spoken with such bitterness, it made Casey wonder whether her cousin was not quite the innocent she was assumed to be.

As though sensing her suspicions, Eva shrugged and added, 'I wouldn't want you running to your Dad with tales about me.'

The teasing glitter in her cousin's green eyes did not look that of an innocent. But Casey was impressed that Eva was taking pains to speak without a cockney accent, though she still occasionally dropped her aitches. It was the only reason Casey's father had allowed her to visit them each Sunday.

'I don't tell tales,' Casey bristled. Even though she adored Eva, she would not allow her, or anyone, to impugn her integrity.

'No, you don't.' Eva regarded her for a long moment. 'You're one of life's saints, Casey. You'd never betray a friend, would you? Or lie. Or steal.' Her lip curled. 'But then you've never had to. You're Uncle Joe's little princess. You've never known hunger or want, have you?'

A shutter came down over Eva's beautiful face, her eyes shadowed with a sadness Casey had often glimpsed before. It always disturbed her. Eva could not help her poverty. Her father, Sid Bowman, was a drunkard and a bully. He frightened Casey. There were stories that he had killed a man in a street-fight just after he had married her father's sister, Aunt Sal. And he'd certainly got meaner and more surly since Aunt Sal died when Eva was eight. A few months after Aunt Sal's death, Myrtle Plunkett had moved in with Uncle Sid. Tall, thin, with brassy blonde hair, Myrtle had a foul mouth and an equally foul temper. It was obvious from the first that she resented Eva. Although Uncle Sid and Myrtle were no longer welcome in their home, Casey's mother had always encouraged Eva to visit.

Casey stifled a sigh. Eva's life was very different from the comfort of her own. Eva had no pretty trinkets; even her clothes were second-hand, brought from the wardrobe-dealers in

Petticoat Lane. Her skirt had been turned several times at the hem, and now was short enough to display trim ankles encased in low-heeled lace-up boots. The creamy blouse had long been outgrown and stretched tightly across her breasts, emphasising their fullness in an immodest way. No wonder so many of the unemployed men, lounging in the street doorways, whistled as Eva passed. Yet for all her bold and provoking comments in private, Eva ignored any men who attempted to flirt with her.

For as long as Casey could remember, she had looked up to her older, beautiful cousin. Eva was petite, with an hour-glass figure. Her complexion was unblemished, and her lustrous black hair was inherited from her Italian grandfather, who had jumped ship in London after falling in love with her grandmother. Eva, with her flashing green eyes and heart-shaped face, was as beautiful as any of the famous stars of the silent films they saw at the Rialto Picture Palace.

Beside her, Casey, who was four inches taller and slender as a wand, felt gauche. Her brown hair, with its springy curls, was always escaping from its pins since she had started to put it up last summer. Her eyes were too large and an unexciting grey in colour, her cheekbones were too angular and her lower lip too full.

'I'd never betray you, Eva. Since Ma died your company has meant so much to me. Dad doesn't allow me to mix with the neighbours.' Casey swallowed against the ache of grief which memories of her mother always aroused.

Eva had helped her overcome her bereavement. She always had so many exciting tales to tell of her trips to fairs and up West to hang around the theatres; watching the toffs, as she called the gentry, parade in their finery. Uncle Sid and Myrtle never cared where she went or what she did. Casey knew her father did not approve of Eva as her companion. But then he did not consider anyone from the Courtyard as a suitable companion for her.

Casey watched Eva prowl about her bedroom, first caressing a pearl necklace on the table, then a pale pink silk blouse over the back of a chair. She yearned to make up for the hardships that Eva endured. 'Would you like that blouse, Eva? It's yours if you would.'

'I'd love to have it. But what's the use? Myrtle will have it straight down Uncle's. You know she pawns anything she can get her hands on.'

Eva turned away so that Casey would not see the glitter in her eyes. She hated her home life. The few hours a week she spent with Casey were her only release from drudgery, hunger and squalor. She knew Uncle Joe regarded her as a bad influence over his daughter, but she had seen the loneliness in her young cousin's eyes, and used it to her advantage. And Casey had overcome her father's reservations about allowing Eva to visit her more often.

The expression in Eva's green eyes was brittle. Casey had twisted Uncle Joe around her little finger, as only she could. Joe Strong was a cold man, an ex-boxer; he was tough and a man to reckon with in the district. All his love since his wife died was reserved for Casey alone. She was his only weakness; he could deny his daughter nothing. Not like her own father.

Hatred engulfed her as she absently rubbed her ribs where Sid had lashed out at her in a drunken rage last night. She was sick of his bullying. Twice she'd tried to leave home, but each time he'd tracked her down and dragged her back. The last time he had given her such a vicious beating that she had been unable to leave her bed for ten days. And Myrtle didn't help. The woman hated her.

'Yer deserve all yer've got coming to yer, Eva Bowman,' Myrtle repeatedly screamed. 'Ye're a selfish slut. Now get this place cleaned and yer Dad's meal cooked. And 'and over yer wages. This ain't no charity 'ome.'

Her pay-packet would be wrenched from her fingers, or

stolen from any hiding place she tried to find, and a shilling returned to her to provide for her needs for the week.

But she would escape from her father's brutality and Myrtle's cruelty. And soon. It was that thought which made life bearable.

Her gaze strayed to the window and the dingy slate roofs beyond. There was no smoke rising from the chimney of their rented rooms. Sid and Myrtle were still sleeping off last night's drunken spree. The three Polish-Jewish brothers and their whore Nan, who shared the house, were already out drinking at a pub. Her expression hardened, her figure was rigid with tension. The only person who had shown her any real affection was Casey. It had been a balm to her battered pride, soothing the pain of her father's abuse as he raged at her that she was no good. Malice glittered in her eyes as she stared at the rooftop of her home.

'Cousins should stick together,' Eva affirmed. 'I never had a sister, and you know this last year you have become dearer to me than any friend. I'll never desert you, Casey. Never.'

The possessive ring to her cousin's voice disquieted Casey, but immediately she shrugged her unease aside. She was used to jealous eyes watching her balefully when she walked down a street. Her clothes and speech set her apart from the other children and, though too fearful of Joe Strong's reputation as a prize-fighter to harm her, women often spat in the gutter as she passed. She'd also heard their comments of 'stuck-up cow', which upset her. She tried to make friends, share her sweets with the children. They had just snatched them and run off, calling her names. It was a pain Casey kept to herself. For his own reasons Joe Strong had forbidden her to mingle with the other families in the district. He had taught her that she was better than them. But she could not look down on people just because their lives had been less fortunate than her own.

By his strictness her father had made her an outcast. The

isolation had continued when she went to school. Once it was known that she lived on the borders of the Courtyard, the girls at the private academy, and then later the secretarial college she had attended, had turned against her. At first she had been asked to stay for weekends at her new friends' houses, but their parents had probed into her background and the invitations had never been repeated. After that the girls had jeered at her, calling her the 'barman's daughter' or 'tavern girl'. In their eyes, a publican's daughter was no better than a slut.

Too proud to show her pain at her ostracism, she had concentrated on her studies. At college it was a hollow consolation to put every one of their snobbish noses out of joint by achieving the highest marks of the year.

Casey joined Eva by the window and moved aside the heavy lace curtain. The yellow morning fog was lifting. Just visible to the west, the four turrets of the keep of the Tower of London dominated the grey skyline. Behind it several ships' masts jostled for place along the wharves.

But her mind was not on the scenery, it was on the injustice she had felt at the isolation inflicted upon her. Her head tilted defiantly. 'Just because Dad refused to allow me to mix with the other children, doesn't mean I think myself better than them.' Rebellion from the recent years of being kept apart from the children she had grown up with burst from her. 'I'm not a goody-goody, or a stuck-up cow. I don't make judgements on the way they thieve and beg to stay alive. They have no choice, that's the way they are. Why do they make judgements on me?'

'You are different from us. Uncle Joe made sure of that,' Eva returned without rancour. 'He didn't intend that his daughter should grow up a guttersnipe. He made you a princess amidst the squalor. Uncle Joe may be a scoundrel, but he don't want his precious daughter tainted.' Her speech roughened as envy at all the comforts her cousin had ploughed through her.

Eva took a grip on herself. She had long ago learned to hide her feelings. 'Why do you think he sent you to that posh ladies' academy in Edgware? His little princess had to have the best education he could afford. He wants you to be a real lady and marry a toff.'

Casey rounded on her in exasperation. 'I hated attending that school.'

Eva lifted a black winged brow, her expression mocking. 'Well, you came back speaking all posh, with la-di-bloody-da ways. Now you walk like you've got an iron railing up your arse.'

At seeing the stiff way Eva was holding herself, Casey guessed that her cousin was hiding some inner pain. Eva would not be human if she did not resent the opportunities that Casey had been given. 'It wasn't an iron railing,' Casey said wryly, 'but being made to walk with a book balanced on top of my head for an hour every day. You would think that with women now demanding the vote, they would have abandoned such archaic rituals.'

'A small price to pay for a bit of class, I'd say. And it ain't no more archaic than those crippling corsets you and other gentlewomen squeeze your bodies into each morning.' Eva grinned, her humour restored. 'Poverty has its compensations. You don't see me going about with me fleshy bits squashed like a sardine in a tin. And as to those suffragettes who chain themselves to railings and the like – all toffs, the lot of them. There ain't going to be no vote for the likes of us, is there? And who'd use it if there was? Got enough trouble keeping body and soul together without worrying me head about politics.'

Casey ignored her cousin's taunt about women's suffrage; they had argued heatedly about it many times. She was shocked to realise that Eva's voluptuous figure was so wantonly unrestrained.

Eva sniggered. 'That's taken the starch out of your bloomers, ain't it, me not wearing stays? Where would I get the money to buy them?'

Casey cursed her stupidity at being unable to conceive the true poverty in which Eva lived. As she regarded her cousin, she saw how pale Eva looked, and that her expression was more strained than usual. Fearing that she had hurt her feelings, she changed the subject.

'I'm surprised you're not courting, Eva. Barney Gilmore is always hanging around here on a Sunday when you visit. He's a good-looking man and doing well for himself. Always dresses smart. Got his own business, hasn't he?'

Eva shook her head in exasperation. 'You're so naïve, Casey. He's got his own business all right. Debt collecting. Doesn't bother with the bailiffs, or the like. Just goes in and breaks a few kneecaps if they don't pay up. I'm not about to encourage scum like him.'

Casey was undeterred. 'There must be a dozen men who would be suitable. Not everyone around here is a villain. You don't give them a chance.'

Eva sauntered across the room, her expression savage. 'Chance to get into me knickers or maul me, more like,' she snapped. 'Men are all the same. They're only after one thing and it isn't marriage.'

'If a man loves you, he will marry you.'

'It's more likely that he'll wed you because he's got you pregnant and ain't got no choice. Should I marry, I'll make damned sure it's to a man who'll take me away from the squalor of the Courtyard. I ain't going to end up worn out by the time I'm thirty, with half a dozen brats hanging round me skirts.'

She stopped to touch the long straight black skirt Casey had hung up outside her wardrobe for her first day at work tomorrow. Eva's fingers lingered upon the row of four jet buttons down one side of the fine woollen material. Such a garment would have cost her two months' wages where she served in Fat Sam's café. Not that she ever had any spare money for clothes. Before she died, Casey's mother, out of kindness, had given her some skirts and blouses. All had been pawned by Myrtle within a week, except for this skirt, which Eva had been wearing. The blouse she wore, she'd stolen off a washing line when she was Casey's age. It was an aspect of thieving she had perfected, encouraged by her father who expected her to bring in some money if she wanted to be fed.

Eva swallowed against the bleakness of her thoughts. Thieving wasn't her only sin. She'd been twelve when her drunken father had raped her for the first time, and he'd been coming to her room every week since. When Myrtle, now his wife, learned of it, her hatred had increased, and she found any way she could to heap humiliation upon Eva. She had even sold the mattress on her bed last week, and now Eva slept on bundles of newspapers on top of the springs of the iron bedstead. Perhaps Myrtle had thought it would stop Sid Bowman's dirty tricks. Fat chance of that.

A nightmare scene danced before her inner eye. When she had sobbed out one evening that she was pregnant, Myrtle had taken the poker to Sid, attacking him so violently that she had broken his arm. Eva had been dragged off to Ma Flaggety's, otherwise known as Bodkin Bess. The woman had terrified her. Neither her flesh nor her clothing had been washed in a year. If the stench of her body was not bad enough, her breath reeked of onions and stale porter and there was a trickle of brown-flecked mucus dripping from her hooked nose, for Ma Flaggety was fond of her snuff. When she reached out a scrawny, dirt-ingrained hand, the nails black with dirt, Eva screamed.

'Gawd, ain't she even going to wash her hands? I ain't having her touching me.'

'Quit yer bawling.' Myrtle cuffed her so hard that her head

slammed back against the wall and yellow stars danced before her eyes.

Reeling, she was dragged to the kitchen table, where Bess swept an assortment of filthy rags on to the floor. Sick with fear, Eva was thrown backwards, and her arms and legs secured by bits of washing line already in place around the four legs of the table.

'The bloody dirty cow will kill me,' Eva began to scream.

Bodkin Bess backed away. 'Shut the silly slut up. She'll have the law round 'ere. And it will be two quid, not one. Those that make a fuss are trouble.'

'We 'ad an agreement.' Myrtle rounded on Bess, threatening. Both women stood their ground. Bess small but with an aura of evil menace, and Myrtle large and puffing with fury.

'If yer don't like the terms, then 'op it.'

Eva screamed at the top of her lungs, her eyes rolling as she frantically tried to free her arms and legs from their bindings.

'At least wash yer 'ands,' Myrtle said. 'That should 'elp reassure 'er.'

Muttering profanely, Bodkin Bess shuffled into a back room. There was the sound of water slopping into a metal bowl. Eva strained to see her hands as she returned carrying a chamber-pot. At least some pink flesh showed beneath the grey.

'Now shut yer wailing.' Myrtle stood over her. 'Or I'll knock yer bleedin' teeth down yer throat. Do yer think I ain't got nothin' better to do than stand 'ere mollycoddling yer?'

Eva screwed shut her eyes. She knew now what the prisoners in the olden days must have felt when they were stretched out on the torturer's rack in the Tower of London. The old crone bent and began to probe her insides with her deadly hook. The agony had been excruciating. What followed had been even worse. For two days she had screamed and writhed in torment.

Grinding, snapping pincers tore at her womb, until finally her body relinquished the tiny, mutilated form.

She had been fourteen and still the memories haunted her, feeding her loathing for her father and stepmother. She had vowed then that they would one day pay for all she had suffered.

Aware that Casey was watching her with concern, Eva shrugged off her bleak memories. To avoid any more talk of marriage, she returned the conversation to an earlier subject. 'Being an outcast in the Courtyard ain't no hardship when you got respectability instead, Casey,' she said heavily. 'Your fine speech and manners got you that job at Hardcastle's Emporium. I hate workin' in Fat Sam's café. The men who eat there are coarse and rough. They're always trying to paw me.' Her lips thinned at her cousin's shocked gasp. 'You don't know you're born. If any man dared to touch up Joe Strong's daughter, they'd get their hands chopped off at the wrists.'

'You exaggerate,' Casey returned. 'Dad's a bit of a tyrant and men keep on the right side of him because he was a champion boxer. That's how he earned enough to buy the Britannia.'

'And the rest,' Eva scowled.

'Rest of what?' Casey asked, baffled by her cousin's manner. In recent weeks Eva had made other comments which hinted at something sinister about her father's affairs.

Eva shrugged, her expression smug with hidden knowledge. 'Of course, it's because he can use his fists.'

'It's more than that,' Casey bridled. 'What are you implying? What do you think Dad's up to?'

'Nothing,' Eva prevaricated. One day Casey would learn that Joe Strong was one of the biggest rogues to tread the London streets, but she would not be the person who disillusioned her cousin about her doting father. Their friendship would suffer, for Casey idolised Joe Strong. Better that someone else told her that he fenced stolen jewellery and was in thick with the high mobsmen, the leaders of the underworld gangs who ruled the criminals of London. Then it would be for Eva to offer her comfort at the news.

Eva paced to the window and again stared out at the row of chimneys in the direction she lived. Her eyes were glacial.

'Dad wants what is best for me,' Casey persisted, refusing to listen to the doubts which nagged at her mind. They were disloyal to her father. She plucked at the cameo brooch pinned to the white lace of her high-necked blouse and smoothed the folds of a sapphire blue hobble skirt. 'But for all his good intentions, I hate being an outcast. He buys me beautiful clothes which make our neighbours resent me when so many of them are in rags.'

'But none of them voice their feelings.' Eva glared across at her and folded her arms. Envy threatened to overtake her. 'Even the most foul-mouthed harridan wouldn't dare pass a comment upon Joe Strong's daughter. They'd pay the consequences if they did.'

'What do you mean?' Casey challenged.

Eva shook her head. She should mind her sharp tongue more when with her cousin. Casey was too quick, seizing upon the smallest details. 'Don't listen to me,' she evaded. 'I just wish I'd had the chances you have. I'd kill to wear the clothes you do.'

'Eva, you don't mean that!'

Casey looked so stricken that Eva laughed, its sound without humour. 'It's just a saying.'

To change the subject, Eva gazed back out of the window, her fingers tapping an impatient tattoo on the glass pane through the thick lace curtain. In the distance a grey line of smoke trailed away from a train puffing over the arches at the back of Fenchurch Street station. Raised voices from a family argument in the alley opposite drew her attention. A battered saucepan flew out through the open door on to the pavement, and a ragged

brimmed navy felt hat adorned with three white silk roses.

Eva studied the younger woman and was unable to stifle her envy. Casey was tall and slender, her movements were graceful and assured. Her high cheekbones and oval face were dominated by large grey, expressive eyes, and her hair, the colour of burnished mahogany, made her countenance striking. Already she was beginning to turn men's heads.

'Not the park,' Eva pouted. 'The day looks like it's brightening up. If you've got money for the fare, we could go up West to one of the exhibition halls. I'm afraid I'm skint as usual.'

'You know I don't mind treating you,' Casey replied. 'We'll get the Tube-train from Tower Hill and go up to Kensington to the Victoria and Albert Museum. Or would you rather we went to Trafalgar Square and the National Gallery?'

'Trafalgar Square. If the weather keeps fair we can walk through Green Park to Buckingham Palace. Perhaps King George and Queen Mary will drive down Pall Mall in their carriage.'

'Is it the king and queen you're so eager to see, or the handsome guardsmen on duty outside the palace gates?' Casey teased as she gathered up her gloves.

'I wouldn't want no guardsman eyeing me. He'd be looking to get his leg over and brag about his taste of East End treacle to his fine friends.'

Casey ignored Eva's belligerence. She was at her most provoking today, deliberately trying to shock her.

As they walked down the stairs the noise from the bar grew louder. Shouts for ale and quarts of porter were raised above a bawdy rendition of 'Ta-Ra-Ra-Boom-De-Ay', which brought a fiery blush to Casey's cheeks as she tapped on the glass panel of the door leading to the bar. She was forbidden by her father to enter the bar-room.

Seconds later the door opened and Joseph Strong appeared.

The smell of closely packed bodies, ale and tobacco-smoke drifted out with him. Of medium height and wiry of build, his brown eyes were on a level with his daughter's. As usual he wore a bowler hat tipped back on his thick brown hair, black trousers and a scarlet waistcoat. The sleeves of his white shirt were kept from falling over his wrists by scarlet and gold armbands. A large gold fob-watch, draped across his taut stomach, added the final touch to his dapper image. A brown moustache partially hid the scar which puckered his upper lip, a wound from his boxing days when he was the prize-fighter known as Joe 'Strongarm' Strong.

'Off out then, Princess?' His sombre eyes brightened with pleasure as he looked at Casey.

'We're off to the National Gallery,' she answered. 'We'll be back before it gets dark.'

Joe nodded, his expression forbidding as it was turned upon Eva. 'Never reckoned you were interested in paintings and things. Just mind you don't lark about. Or start eyeing up the men.' He cast a condemning glance over her tight blouse where it strained across her full breasts. 'Make sure you keep your coat buttoned. My Cassandra is a respectable woman. She'll have no man paying attention to her, unless I gives him permission.'

Eva clutched the edges of her coat together. 'I can't help the way I have to dress, Uncle Joe. You know Myrtle and Dad spend all the money I earn, usually drinking it away here. And Myrtle pawned the last blouse I managed to get, and I've no money to redeem it.'

Joe's expression did not change. His reply was lost as a loud explosion from outside the pub set the glass bowls rattling over the wall gaslamps.

'What the hell was that?' Joe charged back into the bar. The pianola halted in mid-tune and the singing abruptly stopped as everyone surged into the street to see what had happened.

'Sounded like the cannon they fire in Hyde Park on the king's birthday,' Casey said, hurrying out of the side door which was the private entrance to the living quarters above the Britannia.

The street was filled with people, everyone chattering at once. A pall of dark smoke rose from the houses in the next road.

'Heavens, that looks close to your house, Eva!' Casey cried, alarmed.

Eva did not reply; her gaze was fixed on the plume of smoke. There was the sound of running feet as the men who had sped off to investigate returned. Amongst them was the Britannia's barman, Rusty Chambers. His normally ruddy skin was bleached of all colour, showing up the freckles across his cheeks and forehead. He hesitated before Eva and dragged a large hand through his thick, wheat-coloured hair.

'Better come inside, Eva.' He took her arm gently. The affection which Casey had long suspected he harboured for her cousin was tender in his troubled eyes. 'It's your Dad and Myrtle.'

Eva turned her stunning green eyes on him, her voice taut with suppressed emotion. 'They're dead, aren't they?' Her hands swept up to her face and she swayed.

Rusty caught her to him. 'Ay, they're dead, luv. Blown to bits. Best go upstairs. I'll fetch you a brandy to help with the shock.'

There were shocked murmurs of condolences all round and, as Rusty supported the sobbing Eva through the public bar to the private quarters, Casey turned to her father.

Seeing her tears, he took her into his arms, his voice gruff. 'Whole front of the house collapsed. Myrtle must have left the gas tap on when she got up, or something. The drink has been addling her wits for months.'

'That's awful. At least Eva was spared.' Casey sobbed,

child darted out to retrieve it whilst his parents' angry shouts entertained a gathering crowd. Below on the cobbles a dozen children, mostly barefoot, danced to the music of an organ-grinder. Smiles brightened their grey, gaunt faces as they hopped and skipped. Their improvised movements were jerky as they followed the rhythm in a rare moment of pleasure. Further along the street, a boy pushed a handcart loaded with coal, which he had stolen from a passing coalcart. He kicked out viciously as another youth tried to pinch his booty. Thievery was a way of life. It was the only way most of the inhabitants of the Courtyard could survive.

'I don't intend spending the rest of my days struggling to exist,' Eva said beneath her breath. The Britannia was on the outer rim of the Courtyard, nearest to the City. It was close enough to the maze of notorious streets to be a part of the Courtyard, and a favoured meeting place of the top villains of the day who frequented it. But it was also just far enough removed from it to give the establishment a semblance of respectability.

The Courtyard was in effect a labyrinth of narrow cobbled streets, bordered on two sides by four-storey tenements, their walls leprous with age. Another boundary was wasteland, rumoured to be the old plague-pits. The last border included several decaying warehouses by a river inlet. It was an area long scheduled to be cleared of its slums, but it remained a festering pocket of wretched humanity close to the commercial heart of the City. Its community was as close-knit as it was notorious. Many criminals found sanctuary in its darkest alleys.

Amongst the wretched poverty that surrounded Eva's life, the Britannia, and especially the well-furnished rooms above it, was a sumptuous world which she yearned to be a part of.

'Are we going to Victoria Park or not?' Casey broke through her thoughts.

She was pushing a long hatpin securely through a wide-

throwing her arms around her father's neck. 'Eva will be devastated. Such a lucky escape for her. But to lose her whole family!'

Joe patted her shoulder. Uncomfortable at any display of emotion in public, he gently eased her arms from his neck. As he guided her towards the bar, she felt him stiffen and was shocked at the profanity of the oath he muttered. He never used such language in her presence.

'Bastards! Those four are from the Flower and Dean Street mob. That's Bowman's brass bedstead they're having away on their heels. After the sods, men!'

With a growl of rage, several men ran after the thieves.

'Bloody ghouls,' Joe snarled. 'Never could stomach a man who stole from his own kind. They'll pay. There'll be a right barney between the Courtyard gang and the Flower and Dean Street boys tonight. Now inside, Princess. I don't want you getting mixed up in no street-fighting. Once they start, all hell breaks loose, and no woman is safe on the streets.'

He propelled Casey into the pub. That he led her through the public bar was a sign of his own shocked and furious state. Casey had a vague impression of dark panelling, cream walls, and the ceiling brown with smoke-stains. Her heel slithered on the bare floorboards soaked with spilt beer and spittle and she clung to her father's arm to steady her balance.

'Eva will have to stay here,' Casey said, drawing on the practical to overcome her own shock.

'For a time, until she can get something sorted,' Joe reluctantly agreed as he pushed open the dividing door to their private rooms.

'Please, Dad. Let me tell her this can be her home for as long as she needs it. Don't make her feel unwelcome by giving her a deadline. She's just lost her family. She has no one else but us. She's lost everyone now. Her little stepbrother died three years ago.'

‘She’s trouble, Cassandra,’ he said thickly, his expression harsh as he paused before ascending the carpeted stairs. ‘I know you’re fond of your cousin, but I don’t trust her. She’s a sly one.’

‘You’ve listened to Myrtle’s drunken grievances for too long,’ Casey defended. ‘She never had a good word for Eva, especially after young Charlie died. Myrtle doted on that young lad, though he was spoilt and extremely naughty. He was always telling tales on Eva and she was often beaten for his lies. Myrtle blamed Eva for the accident which killed him.’

Joe’s expression remained closed, and Casey hurtled on, ‘Eva was heartbroken when Charlie died. He should never have been leaning out of that window. Eva heard his scream as he fell. She gets nightmares still from seeing him impaled on those vicious iron railings in front of the house.’

Casey pulled away from her father. ‘I’m going to her. Let me tell her this can be her home for as long as she needs us.’

Joe Strong looked into his daughter’s pleading eyes and he knew he could not bear her censure if he refused. He smothered his own qualms about Eva. The girl had not had an easy life, and she had made an effort to try and better herself. The death of Charlie had roused the meanness in Sid Bowman. He had done a stretch in Wormwood Scrubs for coshing a toff lured to a dark alleyway by Myrtle. It was a crime the couple specialised in, but this time the man had fought back. Sid had been so engrossed in beating the man’s face to a pulp that he’d not heard Myrtle’s warning to run for it. The police had caught him.

‘Go to Eva,’ he grunted. ‘But she’s going to have to pay her way if she stays here.’

‘Was everything lost in the explosion, Dad?’ Casey persisted.

He nodded. 'What didn't get wrecked in the explosion will have been pilfered by now.'

'Then she'll need some clothes. Couldn't she have some of mother's things? I put them all in the attic. I didn't like to give them away, but Eva must have clothes.'

'We ain't no charity institution,' he flared. Then shrugged resignedly. 'I don't like to think of anyone in your Ma's clothes, especially the likes of her. But I suppose she must dress respectable whilst she's here.'

As he turned to go back to the bar, Casey frowned, not understanding why her father disliked Eva so much.

The pianola was already striking up another tune. Death was too common in the Courtyard for the people to mourn for long. They came to the Britannia to escape the drudgery of their own lives and they expected to enjoy themselves.

Upon entering the upstairs sitting room, Casey saw that Rusty had lit the fire in the grate and drawn the green velvet drapes across the window. Eva was lying prone on the leather-covered chaise longue, her face covered with a hand. Rusty knelt at her side, holding her other hand as he tried to comfort her.

'Don't you fret, Eva, luv. We're going to look after you.'

He stood up as a floorboard creaked and Casey entered the darkened room. 'Best get back to my work,' he said awkwardly, his gaze tender with longing as he looked down at Eva.

'Casey, what am I going to do?' Eva sobbed as she swung her legs from the seat and began to rock backwards and forwards.

She ran to her side and held her close. 'It's best to cry, Eva. Don't hold it back. It was a terrible tragedy. You were lucky not to be home when it happened. You'll have to live with us now. Dad said it would be all right. You can even have some of Ma's clothes as you've lost everything in the explosion.'

Eva buried her head in Casey's shoulder, acting distraught.

Yet inwardly she did not grieve for Sid and Myrtle. Her thoughts were on the new life which was opening up to her. At the Britannia she would live in luxury instead of squalor and fear.

Chapter Two

Hardcastle's Emporium in Aldgate was a small establishment compared to the splendour of Gordon Selfridge's store in Oxford Street or H.C. Harrod's expanding premises in Knightsbridge. Casey stepped off the tram and looked up at the gold lettering which covered the six front windows crammed with merchandise. It read, HARDCASTLE & SON, DRAPERS OF DISTINCTION. Within the three-storey premises, they sold everything from gentlemen's ready-made suits and hats, to pins and cotton for the housewife. Casey was nervous. This was her first day as a junior stenographer. Pulling down the black fitted jacket of her work costume, she took a steadying breath. Black was the colour all office staff wore in the store, and she had added a black silk armband in deference to her uncle's death a week ago.

She nodded at the floor manager as he opened the door for her to enter. Most of the shop girls lived on the premises and slept in a dormitory at the back of the shop. The Britannia was only a twenty-minute walk away from her work but, as the late April morning had threatened rain, she had taken the tram.

After the gas explosion which had killed Eva's parents, Casey had been torn between her duty to her family and to her new employer. Last Monday was to have been her first day at Hardcastle's. Family had won. Eva had become tearful and withdrawn, her sleep broken by nightmares. Going to her,

Casey comforted her cousin. 'I ain't got no one but you and Uncle Joe, Casey,' Eva sobbed distractedly.

Eva had been given one of Casey's mother's black gowns and at the burial she had worked herself up to such a frenzy of hysterical weeping that she had been violently sick. When Casey summoned the doctor and he had ordered Eva to remain in bed over the weekend, Joe had been scathing.

'Damned woman should have been an actress,' he flared. 'There weren't no love lost in that family.'

'Sid was still her father,' Casey defended. 'And for him to die like that—'

Joe remained unmoved. 'Just remember it's not for you to wait on her, Cassandra. I've given her a home. I don't expect you to be her servant.'

'The shock has been too much for Eva, that's all.'

This morning Casey had been awoken by Eva bringing her a cup of tea and she had been touched at the way her cousin forced a brave smile.

'Time to stop moping. Won't bring them back, will it? Funny, I were never close to Dad when he were alive, but . . .' She broke off and pressed a hand to her temple, covering her eyes. 'I couldn't have coped without you, Casey. I'd be out on the streets – destitute.'

'That's not going to happen,' Casey assured her.

Her cousin wore a pink satin dressing gown edged with lace over a high-necked nightgown. Both had been Casey's mother's. Eva's ebony hair hung in a single plait over her shoulder to her waist. Perching on the edge of the mattress, she threw her arms around Casey. 'I'm so grateful, so very grateful. Uncle Joe has been so generous, letting me wear Aunt Olivia's clothes and giving me a place to live.'

Casey remembered her father's reluctance when she had suggested that Eva have her mother's clothes. He had grudgingly allowed her to make use of the bare essentials of two black blouses and skirts, necessary underwear and nightwear.

'Where else should you be but with your family?' Casey consoled.

'I don't think your father has a very good opinion of me.' Eva hung her head and wrung her hands.

'That's nonsense, Eva.'

Eva lifted misty green eyes to regard Casey. 'He doesn't think I'm good enough to be your constant companion. But I'll prove to him I am.' A fierce light replaced the sadness in her gaze, and her tone was passionate with resolve. 'I never had a chance at home. Here it will all be different. I shall make him as proud of me as he is of you.' She stood up. 'Uncle Joe will be wanting his breakfast. You've done enough waiting on me. It's my turn to wait on your family.'

She was gone before Casey could protest. A quarter of an hour later the smell of bacon cooking drifted to Casey as she finished dressing. On entering the kitchen she saw Eva working industriously over the stove. She was demurely dressed with a large white frilled apron over her black clothes. Her father sat at the table, ignoring Eva as he read the sporting pages of the *Daily News*. When Eva placed the plate of bacon, toast and eggs in front of him, he gave a noncommittal grunt and proceeded to eat in silence.

'Good morning, Dad.' Casey kissed his cheek and saw his sullen expression change. 'How kind of Eva to cook our breakfast.'

'Um.' His gaze slid away from hers, refusing to be drawn.

She sympathised with Eva, who had tried so hard to please him. But there was something odd about Eva's manner. She knew her cousin had hated Myrtle and rarely had a good word to say for her own father. Yet she was putting on an act of mourning as though they were beloved to her. Casey checked the uncharitable thought. Of course Eva mourned them. And it was like Eva to make the most of the drama if it earned her some sympathy. Eva was a child of the ghetto in a way that Casey, who had been shielded from its worst horrors, could never be.

Dismissing her disquiet at Eva's melodramatic behaviour, Casey had decided that was just how her cousin was. Now her concern was on starting her first job, and her unease at arriving at the offices a week later than arranged.

She walked along the aisle of the shop's ground floor, passing the rows of dress material and books of patterns. In ten minutes the shop opened to customers, and the assistants were busy removing dust-sheets from the merchandise, or ensuring that the shelves and displays were fully stocked. Casey hurried up the side stairs past the first floor, where men's clothing and shoes were sold, and emerged on the top floor which concentrated on furnishings and household linen. The row of offices was at the far end behind patterned, frosted-glass partitions.

Knocking on the outer door she entered.

'Miss Strong.' A lantern-faced, railing-thin woman addressed her sternly and without welcome. The black material of her dress, alleviated only by a narrow, white lace collar, made her pinched cheeks look even more sallow. Her grey hair was pulled back in a tight bun. 'You will report to Mr Gibson. He will inform you of your duties, even if they are commencing a week late . . . at great inconvenience to ourselves.'

The arctic welcome stiffened Casey's spine. Her father had sent word to Mr Hardcastle informing him of the tragedy which prevented her commencing work. She bit back a tart reply which was stinging her tongue to be uttered. Having been introduced to all the office staff at her interview, she forced a polite, 'Good morning, Miss Crabtree.'

Mr Gibson, hearing her voice, opened an adjoining door.

He was short in stature and his black frock-coat parted to reveal a waistcoat, its silver watch-chain straining over a large paunch. His thin grey hair was parted in the middle and oiled sleekly to his pink scalp. A thick thatch of a moustache overhung his upper lip. 'Miss Strong, we were sorry to hear of the tragedy which killed your relatives. It was all in the papers.'

'Thank you, Mr Gibson. You are very kind.' She warmed to the chief clerk. 'I'm sorry to have inconvenienced the company by not starting last week.'

'We are a busy concern, Miss Strong. But in such tragic circumstances it could not be helped.'

He smiled, his round ruddy face and bulbous eyes arousing Casey's irrepressible sense of humour. Even the gravity of his words could not prevent a humorous image rising to her mind. Mr Gibson reminded her of a benevolent frog sunning himself on a water-lily. She quashed the comparison, which had lifted her lips to return his welcoming smile.

'This is your desk, Miss Strong,' he informed her, pointing to one of two in a third office. 'Your duties are to take letters from my dictation. Miss Crabtree is Mr Hardcastle's secretary, and she also takes dictation from the accountant. It is your duty also to type the invoices. Should young Mr Hardcastle – Master James, that is – be in the office, and Miss Crabtree is busy, you will also take his dictation. Your speeds and grade from the secretarial college were excellent. I am sure you will have no difficulty in coping.'

A bell was rung from below in the shop, signalling that the doors were about to open. At the same time the outer office door opened and Mr Edwin Hardcastle appeared. Mr Gibson stood rigid as a sentry on guard duty, and there was a rustle of skirts as Miss Crabtree rose to her feet. Mr Hardcastle curtly nodded in their general direction and disappeared into his office.

Mr Gibson returned his attention to Casey. 'You have met

Mrs Maxwell, the telephonist and filing clerk, and Miss Warren who is your junior and carries out general office duties.'

'I have met all the staff except Mr James Hardcastle,' she replied.

Mr Gibson glanced significantly at the roman numerals on the large wall-clock. 'Mr James does not usually come into the office until later in the day. It is unlikely you will have much work from him.'

Casey heard the note of disapproval in his voice, and guessed that James Hardcastle was not as hard-working as his father in running the business.

'Miss Strong, bring your notepad into my office in five minutes.' Mr Gibson interrupted her thoughts. 'There are a dozen letters which must be given to our messenger to deliver by hand before lunchtime.'

Casey slipped off her jacket and adjusted the black silk band on her white blouse before searching through a drawer for a notepad and pencils. No stationery had been provided for her. She looked uncertainly over at Miss Crabtree, who was clattering away at her typewriter, her spectacles propped low on her hooked nose. There was an industrious air about her which censured any who had not already started their work.

'Excuse me, Miss Crabtree. Could you tell me where the stationery is kept?'

A wintry glare was fixed upon her. 'The stationery cupboard is not your concern, Miss Strong. I alone hold the key to it. Anything you require will be dispensed by me and signed for. What is it you need?'

'I have no stationery in my desk.'

'That is so that you can sign for what is provided.' She stood up and walked towards a cupboard and, selecting a key from several which hung from her waist, she unlocked the door. Casey was indignant at the way she was made to feel inferior.

'Two pencils, one notebook, thirty sheets of headed and copy paper and one sheet of carbon paper. That should be sufficient for your first day. Mistakes cost money, Miss Strong. More than three sheets of notepaper ruined, and you will be fined a farthing for every sheet wasted at the end of the day.'

'Am I to be allowed a rubber?' Casey asked stiffly, knowing that although her typing was accurate, mistakes did occur.

'You may borrow mine *when* necessary.' The emphasis implied that in her opinion there would be frequent borrowings.

Casey blanched. She had seen a dozen erasers in the cupboard. She was not going to allow this would-be tyrant to play the dictator with impunity. Keeping her voice deliberately sweet, she replied, 'I was given the impression that this was a busy office. It seems foolish to waste my time and yours by my having to walk across the room to borrow a rubber, and then return it, *should* I make an error.'

'That is our policy.' Hostility gleamed in her cold, pale eyes. 'Sign for the stationery below the list, Miss Strong.'

'I will not sign an incomplete list, Miss Crabtree. I believe I am entitled to a rubber. I should not be expected to ask your permission to use one each time.'

There was a slow handclap from behind her and a deep male voice rang out. 'At last the dragon is bearded in its den.'

Miss Crabtree reddened, and from her lethal glare as she banged the eraser down on top of the envelopes, Casey knew she had made an enemy. Dismayed, for that had not been her intent, Casey turned to see a tall, blond-haired man regarding her with amusement.

Unexpectedly, her heartbeat quickened beneath his admiring gaze. Eyes, blue as a summer's sky and just as beguiling, smiled into hers. She felt her body tingle with a new awareness. At over six foot, slim-figured, and with a neat moustache and flaring sidewhiskers refining the smooth, classical features, he was the most handsome man she had ever encountered. Yet there was something about the boldness in his eyes which disquieted her.

'So this is the new addition to our office staff. Delightful.' He smiled engagingly and lowered his voice to a conspiratorial whisper. 'Don't let the old dragon get you down. Any problems, don't hesitate to come to me for advice. I'm James Hardcastle.'

Unversed though she was in the ways of men, Casey sensed his words were as dangerous as they were enticing.

'Thank you, Mr Hardcastle.' She began to pick up the stationery to carry it to her desk, but his nearness was making her flustered. To her consternation she dropped the rubber and pencils.

Scooping them from the floor, he placed them on the top of the pile with a grin. 'Until later, Miss Strong. I can see that attending to my correspondence in future will be a pleasure rather than a chore.'

He sauntered into his father's office without knocking and, as Casey returned to her desk, she caught a malicious glitter in Gertrude Crabtree's eye. She would have thought that the older woman would be furious that James Hardcastle had singled her out for special attention. Instead there was a knowing smirk around her prim lips which caused a shiver of apprehension along Casey's spine.

Dismissing her qualms as first-day nerves, she put the stationery away in her desk and took up her pad to attend upon Mr Gibson. As she settled herself for the clerk's dictation, she heard raised voices from the next office between father and son.

'I've already advanced you this month's wages,' Edwin Hardcastle stormed. 'No more, James, until you honour your obligations and actually put some work into this company.'

'Why am I expected to work when dear brother Harold does not? He's the one who inherits all this. I'm just your dogsbody. I don't see why I should slave to make Harold's fortune for him.'

'Harold has commitments to his wife's business. As a younger son you should be grateful that I have the means to provide you with a job. If you spent less time at your club, or the races and—' The office door banging ended the conversation, and the furious tread of James Hardcastle's feet preceded the slamming of the outer door with equal violence.

Used to the constant family rows which erupted in the Courtyard, Casey shrugged off the episode, but it served to warn her as she recalled the saying: handsome is as handsome does. For all his handsome looks and charming ways, James Hardcastle had a darker side.

Eva arrived an hour late for work at Fat Sam's café close by the River Thames wharves. Sam winked at her and would have put his arm around her if she had not nimbly side-stepped.

'Good to have you back, Eva.' Sam shuffled forward, dragging his lame leg which had been crushed under the wheel of a delivery wagon when he was a child. He'd taken over the café when his father became too ill to cook. It was a dark, dingy place, providing cheap meals for the dockers and seamen.

'The men have made a collection, seeing as you lost everything. It's not a fortune but . . .' He drew a brown bag from beneath the counter and handed it to her.

Eva looked inside and on hasty reckoning guessed there was about three pounds in silver. Six weeks' wages. Eva looked around the crowded café. Everyone present wore a grimy cap. They were ill-washed men and wore ragged jackets worn through at the elbows. Their shirts were a nondescript grey from washing with cold water and insufficient soap, their trousers held up with wide leather belts. Scuffed boots, resoled or reheeled by their own hands, scored lines in the uneven floorboards. They all turned their wind-weathered faces towards her and touched their caps, acknowledging her mourning clothes.

In the two years she had been serving them she had come to hate their bawdy jokes, coarse voices and questing fingers. Yet they had been generous to her, when they had so little themselves.

'Thank you,' she said, moved by their benevolence. 'You've been very kind.'

The men, embarrassed at witnessing or displaying any emotion, murmured into their teacups and turned away to resume their conversations.

'How long you staying with Joe Strong?' Sam said as he wiped his fleshy face with a white-spotted red kerchief.

Eva tied on her apron and picked up a tray to begin collecting the used crockery.

'Don't know. Too soon to decide.'

Sam sidled against her, rubbing his hands down her thigh. 'You can move in here above the café. Wouldn't charge a pretty thing like you no rent.'

She slapped his hand away. 'You'd be wantin' payment though, wouldn't you, Sam?' She coarsened her speech to emphasise her disgust. 'You can just learn to keep your filthy hands to yourself. Or Uncle Joe will hear of it. And it don't do to be crossing Joe Strongarm.'

His piggy eyes squinted. 'You ain't no better than any other tart in the East End. For a price you'll spread your legs the same as the rest. Strongarm ain't gonna put himself out for the likes of you.'

She snatched up a grimy frying-pan, the only thing resembling a weapon close to hand. She brandished it menacingly, her eyes flashing with venom. 'Lay a hand on me and I'll floor you. Uncle Joe would mash your other leg to a pulp if he heard your dirty talk, especially since I'm living under his protection. Family is family, and don't you forget it. He's got powerful friends. And don't think you can fire me. I'll tell Uncle Joe how you get your perverted pleasure by rubbing yourself against me every chance you get. I'm not standing for it no more.'

She glowered at him with such animosity that he stepped back. The first opportunity she got she was going to quit this job. But not too soon. Uncle Joe expected her to hand over her keep each week. He would not take kindly to her having no income. Not yet anyway. She had to win his trust. She knew when she was well off, and she did not intend to lose her home at the Britannia. Didn't she already have more fine clothes than she had ever possessed before? There would be more, too. Why shouldn't *all* Olivia Strong's clothes be hers? They didn't fit Casey.

At least Uncle Joe was not taking all her wages like Myrtle had done. He was leaving her with five shillings a week, plus any tips she received. Her throat constricted at the memory of her family, not with grief at her loss, but from the painful reminder of the travesty of care and protection she had experienced under their roof. Especially from her father. He was evil when the drink was in him.

A shudder gripped her and her flesh shrivelled on her bones at the memory of the depravity and degradation he had forced upon her. That devil was dead and she was glad. She did not mourn him. Why should she? He had never loved her. It was her young half-brother, Charlie, he had loved – the son her father had always wanted. And hadn't she always tried to please her father, even at first when he raped her? She had hidden her revulsion, mistakenly believing that this was the only way he could show his love for her. It made no difference. Charlie was the favourite. Charlie could do no wrong. When he died she had thought things would change. Instead they had got worse. No matter how hard she tried, she would never win her father's love. All she had ever received was abuse.

Her eyes glittered with hatred. She'd put on an act of grief for the benefit of Uncle Joe. He might never have let her stay otherwise. Now she was living at the Britannia, she had no intention of leaving such luxury to fend for herself.

Eva threw the frying-pan into the sink, which was filled with greasy, tepid water. She hated this work. Ambition burned in her. She had plans to escape the drudgery of life in the Courtyard. The move to the Britannia was just the first step. A confident smile played over her lips. She knew that she was beautiful and that men desired her. Despite her scanty education, she knew enough to read, write and do easy sums. Casey would help her better that knowledge. Looks, cunning and determination were all it took to succeed in the world, and she had them – plus a ruthlessness engendered by years of suffering.

She glared across at Sam as she worked, her thoughts angry. I'll do that bastard an injury if he ever tries his dirty tricks on me again. No man will ever maul me, unless I wish it. I've suffered enough of men's lechery.

Shame pierced her as she remembered the hugs from her father which had turned to unpleasant touching of her body beneath the sheets. Those surreptitious caresses had quickly turned to a demonic attack, ripping away her nightgown from her shivering body, and an obscene lust was used to punish her. For seven years she had been forced to endure her father's rape. Her mind and body had been battered by his drunken invasions. Her only reprieve had been his stretch in Wormwood Scrubs.

She had suffered in silence, her hatred festering at each fresh abuse. One night Myrtle had been roused from her drunken sleep by the grunting her father made as he thrust into her, whilst Eva sobbed into her pillow. Her stepmother had hauled her father off the bed, but it was Eva who had got another beating.

'Slut. Whore!' Myrtle had screamed. 'Ye're to blame. Yer've encouraged him. Yer always trying to be Daddy's little girl. Daddy's little *whore*, more like.'

Her father had swung round and punched Myrtle in the face. 'Drunken cow. When were yer last any good to me in bed? Yer drink yerself into a stupor every night.'

Myrtle never spoke a civil word to her again and the regular nightly abuse continued.

No, she did not mourn her family, Eva reflected. Their deaths had liberated her.

Casey hurried along the darkening streets, aware of the danger of being out alone in this district. Not far from here, in similar streets twenty-five years ago, Jack the Ripper had stalked his prey. The weak gaslamps spread narrow pools of yellow light over ragged bodies hunched in doorways or sprawled in the gutter. A figure loomed above her, its arm upraised. Casey screamed, her face lifted to the light in a high window.

'Leave 'er. It's Strongarm's daughter,' a mean voice grunted. 'I ain't about ter fall foul of 'im.'

Relieved at her escape, but disconcerted by the implication that her father's reputation was so sinister, Casey hurried on. The Britannia was on the next corner, light spilling out from its windows, the merry sound of the pianola in stark contrast to the threat lurking in every shadow within the surrounding alleys.

Another figure shuffled forward and she instinctively flinched. Then a man's grinning face was illuminated in the gaslight, his hunched figure on short, bandy, spindly legs, shuffling in his pleasure at seeing her.

'Archie, you gave me a terrible scare,' she chided gently. 'I didn't see you sitting on the pavement.'

Archie Cooper grunted, saliva dribbling from his mouth as he touched his cap in greeting. Casey took a shilling from her purse and pressed it into his clawlike hand. 'Get some pie and mash for you and your mam for dinner.'

She had a fondness for the half-wit. At thirty he had the mind of a five-year-old. He had been born with a withered arm and rickets had further distorted his body. It was out of kindness to Widow Cooper that her father employed Archie to sweep the pub floors and polish the tables and brasswork. Archie's father had been his first trainer and got Joe started in boxing. He had died of consumption shortly after her father's first winning fight. Archie was slow, but as harmless as an oversize puppy. When not working in the pub, he often sat outside until his mother returned from working in the laundry late at night and took him home.

'Miss Strong, you late. Joe worried,' Archie said slowly.

'And you've been sitting here waiting for me, have you? That was kind of you, Archie.'

He nodded shyly.

'Go and get your pie and mash. Your mam won't be long now.'

'Tell Joe first you back,' he said, shuffling into the public bar.

Casey smiled affectionately after him. Archie was as much a part of the Britannia as Rusty and Bertha the barmaid. She dragged her weary body up the stairs to the parlour. The office had not closed until eight, as all the invoices and letters for the day had to be finished before they left. Now she must cook her father's supper, which he would eat during his evening break from serving in the bar.

To her delight she found the table set and a delicious smell of rabbit pie filling the upper floor. In the kitchen, Eva straightened from scrubbing the wooden draining-board and bustled forward to lift the boiling kettle from the fire, tipping the water into the china teapot on the table.

'You look done in, Casey. The first day is always the most exhausting. Put your feet up and have a cuppa.'

Casey took the proffered cup and stared at the bubbling

saucepans on the stove. 'You've been at work all day too. You must have slaved to get all this ready.'

'Rabbit pie is Uncle Joe's favourite,' Eva continued, working as she spoke. 'He's been so good to me. I thought I'd thank him this way.'

Casey saw the eagerness in her cousin's face as she checked the oven where a rice pudding was also cooking. 'This is your home now, Eva. We will share what work has to be done.'

'I enjoy cooking. I want to repay you for your kindness.'

'There's nothing to repay, Eva.'

'But I want to do it. And I think Uncle Joe would prefer it.' She smiled brightly. 'Besides, it makes me feel less of an intruder.' She blinked rapidly and a tear squeezed out of her lashes and ran down her cheek.

'Eva, don't say that!' Casey was up out of her chair and embracing her. 'We love you dearly.'

The words washed over Eva in a wave. Suddenly her control slipped and she broke down. Since her mother's death, no one had said they loved her. She clung to Casey, drinking in the scent of her hair and skin, and the fresh flowery cologne which she favoured.

'Ssh, Eva. Don't cry.' Casey's eyes were misting with tears she was fighting to control, her sympathy and love a soothing balm to all the pain and hardship in the past.

'I'm being foolish,' Eva said, clasping Casey tight to her. 'You don't know how much your friendship and affection mean to me.'

Indeed, Eva could not put into words the great emotion which was swelling within her. She basked in Casey's genuine tenderness and devotion. It seemed that all her life she had wanted to be loved and now, having won it, she did not ever want to lose it again.

Chapter Three

'How do you like working at Hardcastle's?' Joe asked his daughter on the Sunday following the completion of her first week. He had just finished cleaning the beer pumps in preparation for the lunchtime crowd at opening time. He stood at the kitchen sink with his shirtsleeves rolled up past his elbows as he scrubbed his hands free of the cellar grime. Picking up a towel, he ambled into the parlour to hear Casey reply.

'Very much,' she said enthusiastically as she watered the huge aspidistra which partially filled the sash-window. 'The work is varied and I'm kept busy. Miss Crabtree can be a dragon at times, but since that first day when I confronted her over the rubber, she does not act the tyrant with me. She's a terror with young Lil Warren, the office girl, though.'

Joe watched his daughter at her work as she moved to the mantelshelf to dust the black marble and brass clock, the two bronzes of horse soldiers and the two silver candlesticks. He chuckled as he cut a slice of fruit cake laid out in readiness for him on the table. 'Never let anyone put you down, Princess. You're as good as the next man, or woman. Where are you off to this afternoon? Though I'm sure it's disrespectful of Eva to gallivant about. She is in mourning.'

'That doesn't mean she has to live like a recluse.' Casey sprung to her cousin's defence. 'It's good for her to get out. I know she's grieving inside. She's trying so hard not to be a burden to us, or cast a gloom over our lives with her pain.'

Eva would not talk about her family, and if Casey raised the subject, a canopy came down over her cousin's eyes. Her face would set white and immobile as she stared into space; then she would rush out of the room. Grief affected people in different ways. If going out eased Eva's pain, then surely there was no harm in it.

Unwilling for her father to criticise Eva, she changed the subject. 'I thought we'd go along to the tennis club and see about joining for the summer. Then we're off to the pictures.'

'Again.' He laughed. 'You've already been this week to see that Barrymore chap. Can't see what you women see in the man myself.'

'Oh, Dad. He just sort of *smoulders* on the screen.' Casey had moved to the dresser and clasped one of the porcelain dogs against her breast. She gave a dramatic sigh as she paused in her work.

'Smoulders, does he?' Joe snorted. 'Let me catch any man smouldering near you, my girl, and he'll answer to me.'

Casey grinned. 'I'll be seventeen in three months. Most girls have gentlemen friends calling on them at my age. You'll have to accept it some day.' At his frown she laughed and, replacing the ornament on the mantelshelf, linked her arm through his. 'You're the only man in my life at the moment, Dad. I'll never love anyone like I love you.'

Eva walked in to the parlour to witness the tender scene between Uncle Joe and Casey. Jealousy knifed her. In her hand was a white carnation, and she held it out to her uncle.

'I got this for you from the flowerseller at the corner. I know you like to wear a carnation on a Sunday.' She smiled sweetly. 'Makes you look very distinguished, Uncle Joe. Shall I fasten it to your waistcoat?'

She already had the pin in her hand and stepped towards him.

'That's all right, I can do it myself,' he said gruffly, taking the flower and pin from her. Standing in front of the fireplace, he secured it in place, adding, 'Nice cake that, Princess. You've got your mother's light touch with the baking. Never tasted a fruit cake like hers, but that was close to it.'

'I didn't bake it. Eva did.' Casey willed her father to turn and acknowledge her cousin. All week Eva had worked hard to do everything she could to please Joe, but he had acted as though she did not exist.

He turned to leave the parlour and paused a moment to regard Eva, pushing his bowler hat further back on his head as he did so. 'What you after, girl?'

Eva flinched as though he had struck her. 'Nothing, Uncle Joe. You've been so good to me I wanted to repay it.' His dark eyes bored into her, no longer so antagonistic.

She seized her chance and moved closer. 'The carnation has come loose, you'll lose it.' She kept her head bowed as she adjusted the pin. As she leaned across him, her breast brushed against his arm. Beneath her fingers she felt the hard rhythm of his heartbeat. He smelt of tobacco smoke and beer, but not in the unpleasant way her father had done, for it was overladen with the pleasant scent of the cedarwood soap which he favoured. At forty-four he was lithe of body and, despite his scarred lip and broken nose from his days as a boxer, still a handsome man. Beneath his bowler, thick dark hair fell forward rakishly over his wide brow. In the long months he had been a widower, she knew he had not lacked for female company, but he had never brought a woman back to his bed at the Britannia. He was too protective of his daughter's innocence for that.

When Eva stepped away from Joe, her breast again grazed his bare forearm; as she lifted her eyes to his, she saw his pupils dilate with desire. So he was not so immune to her as he made out. The knowledge sustained her. It was a power to hold over him. Her innocence was long lost. From her daily battles to keep Sam at bay, she realised that she could use that desire as a potent weapon to get her own way. Hadn't Sam advanced her two weeks' wages last night, after forcing her up against the store cupboard wall and pawing at her breasts? Fortunately, before the matter got out of hand, his wife arrived unexpectedly at the café. It was Eva's threat to tell Sam's wife what a lecher he was that had made him thrust the money into her apron, swearing her to secrecy.

The incident had taught her a valuable lesson. She did not have to be the victim of men's lust. She could use it to her advantage.

Uncle Joe had to be handled very differently to Sam. She lowered her gaze from her uncle's and adopted a demure pose, saying softly, 'I am so grateful to you, Uncle Joe. I meant what I said, that I mean you to be proud of me. You'll never regret giving me a home.'

He cleared his throat. 'Just watch you don't bring no trouble to my door, Eva Bowman. And I don't want Cassandra mixing with the wrong sort of company.'

Casey relaxed. Her father's moods were unpredictable. But he seemed to be relenting towards Eva. After being isolated for so long from a close friendship with other females of her own age, Casey was eager for Eva to stay at the pub. In spite of her grief, Eva was an amusing companion. She was so much more worldly than Casey, and knew all the most exciting places to go.

When they sat alone at night in the parlour, sipping a hot chocolate before retiring, it was enjoyable to laugh over incidents which had happened during their outing. Together they would sigh over the handsome screen idol they had seen at the pictures. It was a new experience for Casey to have someone to confide in, though Casey was beginning to wonder why Eva never spoke of her own hopes and aspirations, or about any man that she was attracted to.

And men certainly flocked around Eva. Rusty, the barman, for one. He was besotted with her. Others found excuses to talk to them when they walked through the park, or attended the cinema. But though she laughed and flirted with them, Eva never accepted an invitation to meet them again.

'I'm enjoying your company too much to be bothered with them,' she would laughingly answer when questioned. 'Besides Uncle Joe would have my hide if he found out we encouraged their company.'

Knowing how strict her father was, Casey agreed with her cousin's sentiments. This unexpected freedom to go out more was not something to be thrown away by making an assignation her father would disapprove of. Not that she had been particularly tempted. Her interest was beginning to blossom elsewhere.

She had seen James Hardcastle again when he had come into the office to deliver some papers. He had placed them on her desk, instead of Miss Crabtree's.

'See my father gets these,' he said with a wink, then abruptly departed.

His disarming smile had made her heart race, and foolishly her dreams had begun to be filled with their next meeting.

Another three weeks passed before James Hardcastle returned to the office. He was suntanned from a trip to the South of France with friends, and he was in high spirits. He marched into his office, reappearing minutes later to throw open Mr Gibson's door.

'I have a mound of letters to get out, Gibson. I shall be requiring Miss Strong's services for the entire day.'

There was a murmur of protest from Mr Gibson, and Miss Crabtree sucked in her breath sharply. It was usually her job to deal with James Hardcastle's correspondence.

'It must be Miss Strong,' James Hardcastle insisted. 'Miss Crabtree has enough work to do with my father's correspondence. I would not burden her further.'

He emerged to nod to Casey to accompany him, and held open his office door whilst she gathered up her notebook and pencils. When the door clicked shut behind her, he whispered, 'That's put paid to the old dragon interfering. Can't stand her sour face opposite me when I'm working. I'd rather have a pretty one. There must be some pleasure to our work. And I'm sure you will not disappoint me.'

His languid blue eyes were soft and teasing, but there was something within their depths which Casey found disturbing. She clutched the notepad to her chest and sat down, her pencil poised ready for him to begin his dictation.

His gaze appraised her for several moments, his eyes sparkling, as though he seemed to be sharing some conspiracy with her. 'You must tell me if I go too fast. I wouldn't want to frighten such a pretty thing as yourself by pushing you too hard.'

'I beg your pardon, Mr Hardcastle,' Casey responded, blushing hotly. She felt as though she had been locked within the lion's den.

'With the dictation,' he explained, but there was a mischievous light in his eyes which warned her he was testing her.

'I will not hesitate to inform you if you go too fast, Mr Hardcastle,' Casey returned. Her nerves were strained and she was conscious of every movement or gesture he made.

For an hour James Hardcastle worked through his post. There were no more provocative comments, or remarks bordering uncomfortably upon innuendo. She began to relax and, when he paused to consider a letter before dictating a reply, she found herself studying him intently. The wide flaring sidewhiskers added masculinity to the classical features, and she guessed he was no older than his mid-twenties. He really was extremely handsome, tall and masculine, in a way which made her skin tingle at his closeness.

He looked up unexpectedly and, catching her gaze on him, smiled roguishly.

Casey blushed again, the fiery waves of heat flooding her face and neck. Flustered, she dropped her pencil. He rounded the desk, his hand covering the pencil just before Casey would have reached it. Her fingers briefly alighted on his, a shock-wave pulsating through her before she snatched it back. She could not look at him, knowing that her cheeks were scarlet with mortification.

'Miss Strong,' he said with such insistence she was forced to look up at him. 'You have the most incredibly expressive eyes. A man could drown in them. And that is the most becoming blush I have ever encountered.'

'Mr Hardcastle, it is improper for you to say such things.' Her voice was low and resolute despite her distress. Eva had warned her that men used flattery to make a woman more susceptible to their attentions.

He laughed softly. 'I've embarrassed you, Miss Strong. That was not my intention. But surely many men have praised your beauty.'

'They most certainly have not,' she replied with indignation. Did he think she was the kind of woman who encouraged men's attentions?

The widening of his eyes showed his surprise, but he seemed pleased at her words. 'We will finish there for the moment, Miss Strong. I've some telephone calls to make.'

'I'll have your letters on your desk shortly, Mr Hardcastle.'

He nodded absently, reaching for the ear-piece of the phone and clicking the headset to attract the attention of the operator.

Casey closed the door behind her, wondering if she had misinterpreted his remarks. They were just compliments. Had she allowed her naïvety in dealing with men to make her overreact? With relief she noted that Miss Crabtree was not at her desk. The erratic pounding of her heart made her flustered, and she needed several moments to regain her composure at the way she had reacted to James Hardcastle's touch. To her alarm, her hands were trembling as she fed the notepaper into the typewriter.

There was a rattle of teacups as Lil Warren pushed open the office door with her hip and placed the morning tea on Casey's desk.

'You've got the old buzzard rattling her scrawny feathers,' Lil said with a giggle towards Miss Crabtree's vacant desk. 'Right put out, she was, that Mr James insisted you did his work.'

She brushed back a lock of blonde hair which had fallen forward over her brow. A year older than Casey, Lil was a plump girl with a sense of fun which often got her into trouble with Miss Crabtree. She had a round, homely face and, from their conversations, Casey knew that she was walking out with a cabinet-maker from Whitechapel.

Lil cast a look of longing towards James Hardcastle's office. 'Lucky you. He's gorgeous, isn't he? Wish my Bert were a bit more like him.' She sighed theatrically. It was obvious that Lil was half in love with their employer's son. 'But it's no good wishing for the moon, is it?' she added with a return to her usual cheery humour. 'He's not about to look at the likes of me, when he has the pick of the Gaiety girls to choose from.'

'He's seeing a Gaiety girl?' Casey swallowed her disappointment.

'Different one each month, if rumour is true. Though old Mr Hardcastle wants him to get hitched to Prunella Marshall, daughter of Hugo Marshall, who owns shops in Chelsea and Regent Street.'

The arrival of Miss Crabtree ended the conversation. The

older woman looked over her spectacles at the open pages of Casey's shorthand book. 'Gossiping, Miss Strong? Mr James will be wanting those letters before lunch.'

'They will be finished before then, Miss Crabtree,' Casey replied, giving Lil a fond smile as she picked up the empty teacup to leave. She began to type. Automatically she deciphered the shorthand squiggles and typed them without pause, but her mind was centred upon Lil's words.

James Hardcastle sounded something of a ladies' man if he pursued the performers at the Gaiety Theatre. Clearly her growing infatuation for him must end now.

In her agitation, she typed faster and hit a wrong key. She could feel Miss Crabtree's condemning gaze on her as she rolled up the paper to make the erasure. As she repositioned the letter, her fingers continuing their rapid tapping on the keys, she was determined to guard herself against her foolish attraction towards her employer's son. Men such as James Hardcastle did not pay court to office staff.

The letters finished, she collected them together. There was a disgruntled sniff from Miss Crabtree's direction.

'Is something wrong, Miss Crabtree?' she inquired.

Disapproval was etched into the lines around the older woman's prim mouth, the lips of which did not close over her protruding teeth. 'You may think you have usurped my authority by cultivating Mr James's favour. You are wrong. I am in charge of this office. I will expect your usual work completed before you leave this evening. The invoices on your desk are too important to be left.'

'I will start them in my lunch hour,' Casey placated, aware that the invoices were her responsibility.

'Then see that you do, Miss Strong. You are not the first stenographer to catch Mr James's eye. Pride comes before a fall.'

Casey controlled her anger at Miss Crabtree's spite. No

opportunity was missed for Miss Crabtree to criticise her work. It was easier to ignore the vindictive comments than to answer them. Mr Gibson was pleased with her work, and that was the most important thing.

Knocking on James Hardcastle's door, she entered at his response. He was standing with his hands thrust deep into his trouser pockets, staring out of the window to the busy thoroughfare below. The rattle of omnibuses, horse-drawn trams, and the occasional cry of a costermonger selling his wares carried to them from the street.

'The letters are ready for signing, Mr Hardcastle,' she announced. 'Did you want me to take any further dictation before lunch?'

He swung round, his face lighting with pleasure at seeing her. 'To spend another hour in the company of such a beautiful woman would be my pleasure.'

Casey shot him an accusing look, refusing to allow his flattery to soften her resolve. 'Such compliments are out of place, Mr Hardcastle.'

He regarded her archly, propping himself on the edge of his desk and folding his arms. 'All women like compliments, Miss Strong.'

'If that is your opinion, then you must think us all vain, shallow creatures. I find that insulting.'

'An insult was my last intention,' he continued suavely. 'But it is not your place to comment upon my behaviour, is it, Miss Strong?'

His arrogance angered her, but she checked it. She must not forget that he was her employer's son. Her indomitable nature nevertheless prompted a tart reply. 'My apology, Mr Hardcastle. A paid employee is not supposed to have an opinion, or answer back if their integrity is questioned. You are right, I forgot my place.'

She lowered her eyes to conceal her anger, and sat with her

pencil poised significantly over her notepad. Seconds passed in silence as she waited for him either to dismiss her, or continue with his dictation.

Feeling his stare upon her, she could not prevent a blush staining her cheeks. Why must that hateful colour always betray her? To counteract it, she lifted her gaze and held his with unflinching intensity.

His handsome features were tensed and his lowered eyelids hid the expression in his eyes. At last he spoke. 'I could fire you for impertinence.'

'If I have been impertinent, then that would be your right, Mr Hardcastle.' Casey squared her shoulders. She would not apologise further or plead for her job.

To her surprise, he chuckled softly. 'No, I will not fire you. You are an efficient worker. The hours I must spend here are gloomy enough. I find your comments refreshing.'

She gripped the pencil tightly, aware that he had issued some kind of challenge. Her gaze again lowered, refusing to rise to his remark, although her heart had begun to thud wildly. For some moments she could feel his stare burning into her, willing her to look up as he continued to study her in silence. When she resisted the impulse to obey his will, there was a rustle of papers.

'Letter to Messrs Andrews and Stoker, solicitors. *Re* Mary Harper – shoplifting . . .' His tone was businesslike but impatient. Six letters later, he pushed aside the pile of correspondence. 'That's it for this morning. I shall not return to the office until four this afternoon. If my father inquires, I've gone to the retailer of leather goods in Shoreditch recommended by Hugo Marshall. Though if anything urgent comes up, you will be able to contact me at my club. That is for your information alone, Miss Strong.'

She was appalled that he expected her to lie for him.

He smiled engagingly. 'You see I trust you to keep a confidence.'

He had put her in an untenable position, for she had no intention of lying to her employer. But she also prided herself that anything told to her in confidence would always remain so. James Hardcastle had guessed that. He did not hesitate to manipulate people to suit his own ends. He was not to be trusted. Yet when he smiled at her that way, she knew she would not betray him to his father.

'I can see that we will work very well together, Cassandra. I may call you Cassandra, may I not? So much less stuffy than Miss Strong.'

She had noticed that he called Lil and Doris Maxwell, the telephonist, by their first names. Though never Miss Crabtree. She was always 'the dragon' if he referred to her at all.

'I am not sure that Mr Gibson or Miss Crabtree would approve. They do insist on formality within the office, Mr Hardcastle.'

'Then I shall call you Cassandra only when we are in private. And you may drop the Hardcastle. Everyone refers to me as Mr James. Though to you, in private, I would be just James.'

He had turned the conversation around so that it had taken on an intimate note which perturbed Casey. She cursed her lack of experience with men. It seemed foolish to insist that he address her as Miss Strong if they had to work so closely together. She certainly would not be so familiar as to call him simply by his given name. That would be tantamount to suggesting that there was an intimacy between them.

'If there is nothing more you require, Mr James, I shall take my lunch now.'

His eyes glinted with devilment which sent a shiver of trepidation through her, but he did not reply. His look was enough to convey that any further requirements he had in mind were not of a professional kind.

The following Thursday evening, Casey and Eva visited the

tennis club for the first time. Casey had learned only the rudiments of the game at school, but Eva had never played. They had been teamed with two male players to teach them the techniques of the game. Both men had been enthusiastic, taking every opportunity to stand close behind the women and hold their arms as they demonstrated how each shot should be played. To Casey it had all seemed very innocent, although she was aware that her partner found fault with her shots rather more than necessary, so that he could again demonstrate the correct angle to hold the racket and the correct body position. At the end of the session both instructors had asked to take them to a dance on Saturday.

'We don't go out with men we've just met,' Eva retorted, her manner affronted. 'Do you make a habit of accosting every new member as you have us?'

The instructors looked sheepish, and Casey smiled to soften the rebuke. 'You have been most patient and helpful. I hope when we come next week you will partner us again.'

Eva had been silent for some time on the walk home, then burst out in indignation. 'Why do men always have to find an excuse to maul us?'

'They were not mauling us,' Casey observed. 'How else could they teach us to improve our game?'

'What game were they up to? That's what I'd like to know. It makes me so angry. Men are lechers, Casey. Never forget that.'

For several moments, Casey stared out of the window of the tram as they travelled down Commercial Street. The area was notorious for its footpads, and the better-off pedestrians could be robbed by day as well as night. They passed the gardens of Christchurch, known locally as 'Itchy Park' because of the number of vagrants who dossed down there and who used the railings as scratching posts.

Dusk was shrouding the East End in a dismal grey mantle.

The tram progressed slowly, for even late in the evening the thoroughfare was packed with vehicles. Tram bells rang, costers shouted as they wheeled their barrows illuminated by lanterns to attract their customers. Motor cars belched and chugged past horse-drawn omnibuses and hansom cabs. Careless of their safety, urchins darted out into the street to scoop a pile of steaming horse dung into a pail to sell to a council gardener for a few pence. Brassy-haired women loitered on street corners, their voices rising in abuse if their custom was rejected. A ragged man carrying a sandwich-board with the words 'Repent, the End is Nigh' was being jostled by a gang of youths. Two old Jews, their flowing grey hair and beards hanging over their long black coats, hurried on their way, heads down, ignoring the entreaty of a beggar woman carrying a wailing child.

They were sights Casey saw every day. Although the poverty appalled her, overriding the despair and menace was the bustling activity both here and in the City itself, which never failed to thrill her. It was like a heart pulsating. Throughout the poorer districts there was a camaraderie in their fight for survival, as the people united against intruders or oppressors.

Tonight her thoughts were elsewhere as she gazed at the familiar sights gradually being swallowed up by the darkness. She exhaled sharply and, at Eva's questioning glance, was driven to confide in her cousin.

'I can't believe that all men are such beasts, Eva. I'm sure that James Hardcastle is not. He's been very kind to me. I am to do all his correspondence in future, and that entails more responsibility, which is good experience. Old Crabtree is furious that I now have the authority to answer standard inquiry letters when James is not in the office.'

Eva sighed. 'You be careful of him, Casey. Don't trust him. Has he tried anything on yet?'

'No.' Casey was outraged that Eva could suggest such a

thing, but kept her voice low so the other passengers could not hear. 'He is too much of a gentleman. Though there is a way he looks at me sometimes – laughing, intimate, as though I am really beautiful, which I find disturbing and exciting. It's as though he wanted to . . .well, wanted to kiss me. He's so handsome. So charming. I know men like that don't step out with our class, but—'.

'But nothing,' Eva rasped, leaning to whisper in her ear. 'He's trouble. Men like that are evil. You are too innocent. He isn't interested in you in any other way but getting you into his bed.'

'That's unjust, Eva.' Despite her resolve to be unmoved by his handsome looks and charm, each meeting with James burrowed beneath her reserve. 'He can hardly do anything in a busy office, can he?'

'Just you take care you're never in the offices alone with him,' Eva warned. 'Charming men are no different from the filthy sods who just make wild grabs at you – they've just got more finesse. They only want one thing. Remember that, or you'll get your heart broken, or worse.'

'I'm not a fool, Eva,' Casey flashed back. 'But I can't help the way he makes me feel. I sort of glow inside when he is near. I know it's wrong, but I dream of him at night and wonder what it would be like if he kissed me.'

'Gawd, you've got it bad,' Eva said disparagingly. 'Your father was wrong to stop you having boyfriends. Life is not like the films, Casey. There ain't no dashing prince out there waiting to carry you off on his horse to his grand palace. Forget these romantic notions. Uncle Joe may have it in his head that you'll marry a toff, but men the likes of James Hardcastle don't marry publicans' daughters.'

'I wasn't contemplating marriage.'

Casey's tone was so vehement that Eva knew it must have crossed her mind. Her cousin was so young and impressionable

– so innocent. Perhaps they should stop going to the pictures and seeing all the romantic heroes and heroines on the screen. Casey had been too sheltered; she still thought love and romance could make everything come right.

Eva bit back her tart reply. A fierce protective need rose in her towards Casey. The hurt in her cousin's eyes pierced her. She was so trusting, always so open with her friendship, Eva could not bear to lose her affection. Casey could make her feel special again. She could make all the evil in her life seem insignificant. Let her cousin have her dreams. Didn't Eva regret that she had no illusions left to enable her to visualise an idealistic future? Romance could stay on the cinema screen as far as she was concerned. Quick wits and a strong nerve were what it took to get what you wanted in this life.

Chapter Four

Eva was fuming. Fat Sam had just knocked into her, and the congealing bowl of vegetable broth that he was carrying had tipped over the front of her black silk blouse.

'Stupid bugger!' she railed at him. 'Look what you've done, you clumsy sod.'

He grinned evilly. 'Bit of soap and water and the blouse will come ter no 'arm.'

'It better not or you'll pay for it,' she raged, dashing into the scullery where the washing-up was done. Sick with dread she dabbed at the silk with a wet cloth. It was useless. The greasy fluid, flecked with bits of cabbage and carrot, was ingrained in the lace. If she left it to dry it would be ruined, the dark greasy stain unremovable. Had it been one of her old blouses it would not have mattered. Why had she taken this one of Olivia's from the attic without Uncle Joe's permission?

Nothing ever went right for her. She hated this job, being stuck here whilst Casey worked in a posh office with the boss's son panting after her. Despite her warnings to her cousin, Eva would have jumped at the chance of ensnaring a man like James Hardcastle in marriage. His wealth and position would ensure that she lived far away from the Courtyard which she despised. She would not have hesitated to become his mistress, then when she got pregnant, Joe Strong would ensure that Hardcastle would marry her. She had no conscience about using that old trick. It had worked for plenty of others, why not herself? Instead she had to put up with the repellent groping of men like Fat Sam.

Eva groaned as she surveyed the damaged blouse. Yesterday Sam had made a lunge for her and two buttons had been ripped off her spare blouse. She'd had no time to sew them on, which was why she had risked borrowing one of Casey's mother's other blouses without permission. Uncle Joe would be furious, especially as it was ruined.

She could have screamed in frustration. It had taken weeks to build her uncle's trust, and she was just beginning to feel that he was softening towards her. Now this. To return the blouse in such a state would arouse all his old antagonism towards her.

Scowling, she pulled off the blouse and draped a drying cloth around her shoulders. Beneath it she wore a pink petticoat and the satin corset Casey had given her and insisted she wear. Anxiously, Eva glanced over her shoulder, fearing that Fat Sam would come in. If he saw her undressed, he would start his tricks. Holding the silk blouse under the tap, she rubbed at the greasy stain. To her horror the silk material shrank and creased.

'Sam, you bastard!' she groaned. 'Uncle Joe will kill me.'

At the click of the door opening, she swung round holding the wet blouse against her breasts. Her heart plummeted at seeing the leer on Fat Sam's face.

'Get out! You've ruined this blouse. I'd only borrowed it.'

His gaze was on the smooth flesh of her bare arms revealed by the scanty protection of the cloth she had draped over her shoulders. 'What's a blouse between friends, luv? Be nice ter me and I'll buy yer another.' His eyes were dark with lust and his breathing was laboured. 'Damn it, Eva luv. I'll buy yer several blouses. I want yer so bad.'

He reached for her and she backed away. Panic filled her.

He was between her and the door. The scullery was so small, she could smell his rancid breath, which stank of onions and rotting teeth.

'Keep away, you horny sod.' Fear made her heart race and icy perspiration broke out between her shoulder blades. 'Just you keep your filthy hands off me.'

He chuckled evilly and unzipped his fly. 'Won't do yer no good ter scream. Last of the customers 'as left and I've bolted the door. No one is 'ere to 'elp yer. Jus' yer and me, luv.'

Frantically, Eva scanned the scullery for a weapon. Everything but a few saucepans and plates had been washed and stored away. The only cutlery which remained was a meat fork. She darted across the room. As her fingers closed over the fork, the cloth was pulled from her shoulders. For a man with a lame leg, Sam could move fast when his blood was fired by lust.

'Stop acting coy with me,' he wheezed. 'Yer ain't no innocent. I heard tell Sid were pimping fer yer. 'Ow much yer charge? I'll double it.'

'Those are lies. I've never been no whore. Stay away from me.' The fork was firm in her hand as Sam shoved her forward over the workbench. The pressure of the wood digging into her stomach knocked the breath from her lungs, and his arm held her waist in a bear-like grip. His breath came in laboured grunts as he rubbed himself against her.

'Yer owe me, luv. I paid yer two quid the other day to keep yer trap shut when yer threatened to tell me missus. I don't pay good money fer nothing.'

'Get off me, you bastard!' she screamed. She twisted to strike him in her desperation to escape.

Her blood ran cold at the touch of his fat hand hoisting up the back of her skirt. Then his fingers were pulling at her bloomers. His weight pressed her into the bench, preventing her from turning and defending herself. Inch by inch his sausage-like fingers wriggled under the elastic of her drawers, pushing them down. At the touch of his fleshy hands on her naked buttocks she choked out her fury. 'Get off me, you bloody old lech. I'll do for you, Fat Sam, I swear I will.'

He grunted dismissively. 'Ye're loving it. Yer just trying to get me ter pay more. Well, I ain't.'

'Touch me again and I'll kill you.' Her palms were slick with perspiration as she forced the fork close to her chest. She was panting with the effort of trying to throw off his weight and strike at him. Nausea churned in her gut at the way he was mauling her, his repulsive fingers pinching and exploring. But she could not move. The breath was crushed from her lungs by his vicious hold. When an invasive jab of his fingers entered her, her body jerked rigid. She screamed in outrage, and was catapulted into a frenzied struggle to break free. 'You filthy bastard. No. No. Stop.'

Her screams rose hysterically. She was unable to wriggle free from beneath his vast weight. His fingers continued to violate her. Bile gushed into her throat. Her flesh was quivering with revulsion, her mind crazed with outrage. Summoning all her strength, she bucked back and ground her heel into his toe.

'Bitch!' he groaned, without slackening his hold.

Eva almost gagged on her bile. When the probing thrust of his hot penis touched her naked flesh, she began to struggle like a madwoman. Sobs wrenched from her. Tears blinded her vision. There'd been no escaping her father's lust, but she'd not suffer such degradation again. Something in her mind snapped. Her animal screams of horror scratched raw her throat. A demonic frenzy seized her. Then she was kicking, twisting, biting, clawing, the hand with the fork rising and falling in dementia.

There was a howl of pain. Another. The soft suction of steel as it withdrew from flabby flesh. More howls. She must have struck him well. The hold about her waist slackened. She whirled. Blindly, she stabbed out, the fork held like a dagger, her hand slashing wildly. Through crazed eyes she saw a face scarlet with blood. Sam was clutching his eye. His groans rose.

'Bitch! Yer've blinded me.'

The scene before her was a blur and the sound of her tortured breath whistled in her throat. Wide-eyed, she focused on the door. The way was clear to escape. Sobbing, Eva ran to it. Wrenching it open, she ran through the café, her fingers fumbling as they encountered the bolts on the outer door. Each second she feared that Sam would resume his attack. The moans from the scullery hardly penetrated her terror. Her only thought was escape.

There was a rush of cold air and the door was open. She ran sobbing into the darkened street. The blood pounded in her ears, echoing the wild rhythm of her high-heeled boots clacking on the cobbles as she ran towards the Britannia.

The frantic pounding on the street door startled Joe as he emerged from the cellar carrying a cask of port. 'See who it is, Rusty. Probably Eva has forgotten her key.'

'Good God!' Rusty shouted. 'Joe, you'd better come quick.'

Nodding to Bertha, the buxom blonde barmaid from Bethnel, as the customers called her, to look after the bar, Joe hurried through to the living quarters. Dread clutched at his throat with the fear that something had happened to Cassandra.

He paled at seeing Rusty carrying a woman up the stairs. All he could see was a black skirt. 'Is it Cassandra? What's wrong with her?'

'It's Eva,' Rusty answered. 'Looks like she's been attacked.'

'Take her into the parlour.' Joe followed them and lit the gaslamps before crossing the room to stand over his niece, who was sobbing hysterically on the chaise longue.

She was half-naked, and there was blood on her neck and across the top of her full breasts, which were pushed high by her corset. Rusty stood back, his arms hanging awkwardly.

'What happened?' Joe demanded.

The sobs became harder. Joe felt his throat go dry at the wantonness of her pose. He'd had a fling or two with Bertha since he'd taken her on three months ago, but she was forty and her figure was marred by the silvery lines from bearing seven children. Eva's smooth creamy curves were a seductive enticement.

Feeling his body respond, he checked himself with a smothered oath. Snatching an antimacassar from the back of the settee, he draped it around her.

'Rusty, have you any idea how to deal with a woman in her state?'

The barman shook his head, looking equally ill-at-ease.

Joe rubbed his moustache. 'I wish Cassandra was here. Eva looks like she's been set on. Better get her some brandy, Rusty.'

Anger was growing in him at whoever had done this to her. He had his reservations that Eva was not as innocent as she should be, but she was under his protection. Anyone who dared attack someone under his roof would answer for it.

There was no sign of her sobs abating and, feeling awkward, Joe sat on the edge of the seat and put a hand on her shoulder. 'You've had a fright. Were you hurt? Shall I send for a doctor?'

Eva shuddered and raised reddened eyes. Her face was puffy and wet with tears which had made rivulets in the smears of blood on her cheeks and neck. He could not see any cuts on her, but with so much blood anything could be wrong with her.

'I don't need a doctor.' Fresh tears erupted and, to his discomfort, Eva flung her arms around his neck and sobbed against his chest.

Hesitantly, his hand lifted to console her. He was throbbingly aware that her half-naked breasts were pressing into his ribs, and that her back was bare beneath his touch. He clenched his jaw to control the desire hardening his body, and sweat moistened his upper lip beneath his moustache. He was shocked at the force of his need for her. He must remember she was his niece, living under his protection.

Inhaling sharply, he reasoned that the poor girl needed comfort and that it was natural enough for an uncle to hold a niece if she was distressed.

'Pull yourself together, girl,' he said gruffly, wishing that the womanly scent of her would not play such havoc with his senses. She was clinging to him, her body shaking from the force of her sobs. 'Who did this to you, girl? They'll pay for it. They'll wish they'd never been born.'

'Oh, Uncle Joe,' her voice came out in jagged bursts. 'I should never have gone back there with Dad dead . . . But I needed a job to pay for my keep. It were Fat Sam . . . He were always trying to touch me whenever he could. I thought I could handle him. This last week he's got worse. He went crazy. Trapped me in the scullery . . . began pulling at my clothes . . . his hands touching . . .' She broke off, her sobs again uncontrollable.

Rusty had returned and, hearing the end of her speech, was white-faced with rage. 'Me and the boys will sort that whoremonger out.'

Joe struggled to master his fury. He needed all the facts before he was prepared to act. 'The blood, Eva? Where has all the blood come from?'

Her fingers dug in his neck and her body trembled violently. 'When I saw him coming for me I picked up a meat fork. It was the only weapon I could find. When he pulled up my skirts and started to . . .'

He waited for another wave of sobs to subside and, patting her shoulders, urged gently, 'You stuck him with the fork, did you, girl?'

He felt her nod against her shoulder. 'I kept hitting out. I heard him groan, then he let me go. I ran.'

She pulled back, her green eyes wide with horror, her voice sounding as though she were in a trance. 'I think there was a lot of blood.' She drew her hands in front of her face. They were covered with dried blood. 'When I ran into the café he didn't follow me.'

'He didn't actually . . .' Joe faltered, embarrassed at having to put it into words. 'He didn't . . .'

'I got away before he could rape me, Uncle,' she answered. Then she shuddered violently and her eyes rolled upwards.

As her body swayed, Joe caught her shoulders. Her head flopped forward like a rag doll's. Taking the brandy glass from Rusty, he gently tilted her head back over his arm, forcing a few drops of the spirit between her lips. She coughed, but did not try to sit up.

'Uncle Joe, am I a murderess? Do you think I could have killed him?'

'If you haven't, girl, he's going to wish he were dead when I finish with him.'

Tears squeezed from between her eyelids. 'I'm so ashamed. I didn't do anything to encourage him. You've been so good to me. Now I've brought this shame to your house. I'm so sorry.'

Joe turned to Rusty. 'You know what to do. Get over to the café. If he's alive make sure he's unfit to try this on another woman again.'

He picked Eva up and carried her to her room. As he laid her on the ruched-satin eiderdown he saw from the gilt bedside clock that Cassandra would soon be home. She would be able to see to her cousin better than he could.

'Cassandra won't be long.' Joe put the rest of the brandy on the bedside table. 'Drink that up. It's good for shock. I've got to get back to the bar. Shall I ask Bertha to sit with you?'

'I'll be all right.'

Eva did not want Bertha near her. Unlike Casey, who did

not enter the bar, Eva had ventured in on several occasions. She had burned with resentment towards Bertha at seeing the barmaid play up to Rusty and Joe. From the brazen way Bertha eyed Joe and giggled throatily whenever he was near, she suspected that the barmaid was Joe's mistress. She had eyed the older woman insolently, noting the deep cleavage above her low-necked blouse. Her cheeks were rouged and her dyed hair brassy, but she conceded that Bertha was still attractive in a blowsy, mature way. The provocative sway of her hips oozed sexual invitation, and in the close confines behind the bar, both Joe and Rusty were often forced to squeeze in a most intimate manner past her. The comments from the customers were bawdy, which the three took in good humour.

Eva was not amused. She hated Bertha because she knew her to be a rival.

Before Joe could depart, she reached for his hand. 'You won't make me leave because of this? It wasn't my fault.'

Her movement dislodged the antimacassar, and her breasts curved lusciously over the top of her corset. Though her beauty was marred by her tears, her black hair had come loose from its pins to fall in dishevelled tresses over her shoulders. Joe's throat dried and he averted his gaze before his desire betrayed him. The poor kid had gone through a lot in the last few weeks. And after all, she was his sister Sal's kid. Sal had virtually raised him after their parents died of the cholera. He owed Sal. After more than ten years he still missed her. It was a pity that Eva did not take after her gentle mother instead of her sly, no-good father. But he could not fail Sal. 'This is your home, Eva.'

'I love you, Joe,' she replied softly, and saw his eyes darken before he could shield his desire from her.

As the door closed behind him, Eva pulled herself upright and drank down the rest of the brandy. It revived her. The fear instilled in her by Fat Sam's attack faded. She was no blushing virgin. Sam had frightened her, but what she had endured from her father had been far worse.

Lying back on the pillows, she realised that she was still clutching the ruined silk blouse. She threw it aside. Uncle Joe had been more sympathetic than she had hoped. And she had not missed the way he had looked at her. Unlike Fat Sam's, his gaze did not repel her.

She snuggled down on to the soft mattress with its lavender-scented sheets, and sighed. As she regarded the lace curtains, the maroon velvet drapes and the pretty pink wallpaper, pleasure made her stretch languidly. The room smelt of beeswax and the fresh flowers which Casey arranged in a vase each week. The comfortable surroundings were a far cry from the pile of newspapers piled on an iron frame in a room no larger than a closet which had been her bedroom before.

Though Sam's attack had repelled and terrified her, the fear of it was ebbing. If it had won her uncle's favour, then, in Eva's eyes, it was a small price to pay. She had escaped Sam's intended violation. It gave her a feeling of power. She was not as weak or vulnerable as men believed. If men desired her, she would use it to her advantage. And it certainly would do her no harm to cultivate Joe's interest. He was a man feared in this district, and rich as well. The Britannia was now her home and this was where she intended to stay. Unless she could use her wiles to persuade Joe to move to a pub in a more fashionable and wealthy area. Then her future would be truly assured.

The next day Eva put off searching for another job. Instead she cleaned and cooked, content to be the unpaid housekeeper for Joe and Casey. Mid-morning Rusty Chambers came through from the bar to the laundry room. Eva was heaving steaming sheets from the copper and feeding them through the heavy iron mangle. Hesitantly, she smiled. 'There's cake for you upstairs; I'll be up in a sec to see to the tea.'

'No, Eva. I'll do me tea same as I've always done. What you doing out here? Joe always sends the sheets and stuff to the laundry since Olivia died.'

'Can't have him going to all that expense when there's willing hands to help.' Seeing his look of disapproval, she added, 'Besides, hard work takes my mind off things.'

'Aye, I suppose it would.' His expression was contrite as he stood awkwardly by the door, one hand behind his back. 'It can't be easy for you losing your family, then . . .' He broke off, his face darkening with anger.

Eva felt a rush of power that her company could reduce this huge, bluff man to such a state.

'I'm fine now, Rusty. Just as long as I never clap eyes on that filthy lecher again.' She shuddered and turned away. Her arms strained as she pushed the handle of the mangle. Instantly Rusty was at her side, his eyes crinkled with concern. With gentle insistence he replaced her hand with his own, and the handle turned rapidly as the sheet travelled through the two rollers on to the wooden draining-board.

'I could have killed that bastard for what he did to you,' he said as he straightened. 'But he won't be bothering you again. Me and the lads saw to that. Though you had stuck him good. Lost an eye, he had, when you defended yourself.' Rusty grinned with approval. 'If I had me way he'd have lost his balls for what he tried to do. When I think of his dirty hands on a lovely woman like you, Eva.' His gaze slid from her and he backed self-consciously to the door.

'You mean you went to see Sam?' Eva questioned. She felt no qualms that he had lost an eye, which accounted for the amount of blood on his face. 'That must have put the fear of God up him. Like all bullies who pick on women, he's a coward.'

'He won't be molesting unwilling women again. Not with his knees smashed.'

'But what if he squeals to the coppers? They'll arrest you. And all because you defended me. Rusty, I couldn't bear that.'

Comforted by the adoration in his eyes, she smothered her usual distrust of men. She knew Rusty fancied her, but he wasn't the sort to force himself on a woman. He could prove a good ally in the future.

He shook his head. 'Sam won't be squealing to anyone. He wouldn't want his missus to guess what he'd been up to. She'd throw him out, and a cripple needs looking after. Story he's been persuaded to tell is that the café were broken into by youths. And they beat him up when he tried to stop them stealing his takings.'

Rusty drew a hand from behind his back and put a small sack on to the draining-board. It clinked as its contents settled.

'That's for you. It's the takings from the café. Sam used to hide it under a floorboard in the scullery. Didn't believe in banks. Nor did he trust his missus not to get her hands on it and spend it. Near on seventy quid there. It's yours. Reckon it's small compensation for what that bleeder tried to do to you.'

'Seventy pounds!' Eva could not believe her ears. 'That's a fortune.'

'Mind you put it in a bank. It'll set you up. Give you a start in a new life, like.'

Eva's heart raced. She was rich. It was the start of the nest-egg she was determined to accumulate to get herself out of the Courtyard for good. But seventy pounds would not go far in the future she planned for herself. She wanted to become a gentlewoman, live in a grand house and wear only the finest clothes. To achieve that she would need to own some respectable business. What type she did not know. For certain she would need more money. But this windfall was a beginning.

Overcome with gratitude, she smiled at Rusty as she hauled the last sheet from the copper. 'I can't thank you enough. You're a good man.'

A flush tinged his freckled face. 'There ain't no need for you to be letting Miss Casey know about the money, like. Joe wants it kept quiet about how Sam were done over.'

Behind her smile, Eva bridled. Joe wouldn't want his precious daughter knowing the half of what he got up to. It wasn't coincidence that Joe Strong had bought the Britannia so conveniently close to the Courtyard. He had an understanding with the underworld gangleaders who frequented the pub. He was also one of London's leading fences. Not that anything stayed on the premises. Those dealings were done through a partner of his, Isaac the Yid, whose pawnbroking business in the darkest, foulest part of the rookery was a front for the stolen goods. All this Eva had learned from Sid Bowman's drunken ramblings after Joe had refused him a loan. Her father had been particularly demanding that night, laughing maliciously as he pinned her to the bed.

'Bastard Strong,' he had panted as he drove into her battered body. 'Thinks himself so grand. Bloody forced me ter marry 'is precious Sal when I got 'er pregnant. Useless bawd she were. Wouldn't thieve. Wouldn't whore fer me. Couldn't force 'er, or she'd go running to Joe, and 'e'd 'ave me bleedin' 'ide fer not treatin' 'er right.'

He grunted and slumped over Eva, the rank smell of his unwashed body cloying her nostrils. His voice slurred. 'Since 'e won't 'elp me out, yer 'ave to go on the game. Earn a fortune, yer could. I've seen the way yer get eyed in the street. No shilling-whore, either; they'd pay five bob to get between yer legs.' He sat up and shook a fist at her. 'And no refusing like yer did when I bought me mate 'ome last week fer yer. Try that again, and I'll carve yer face so good, yer'll never look in a mirror again without wanting ter puke with horror at what yer see.'

It was the last indignity she was to suffer at her father's hands. He and Myrtle had died the following morning in the explosion.

Aware that Rusty was studying her closely, she dragged her thoughts back to the present. He was clearly waiting for her response.

'I won't mention the money to Casey. But what of Sam's wife? Won't she suffer with no money coming in?' She had no intention of giving the money up, but she didn't want Rusty to think she was without a conscience.

'Not if I know her.' The barman grimaced. He lifted the sheets into the wicker basket and carried it through to the small walled garden of the pub, speaking over his shoulder to Eva as she followed. 'She's been using the house as a knocking-shop for years – got three girls working for her.'

Eva kept her thoughts guarded as she began to peg the sheets on the line. Rusty leaned against the door watching her and, when she glanced across at him, she caught his gaze lingering upon the outline of her full breasts as she reached her arms up. She frowned. It seemed Rusty was no different from other men.

Quickly he looked away and, clearing his throat, added, 'Sam's missus never cared if he used her girls, because he had to pay for it, same as the rest. What drove her to a fury was him getting it for free.'

Eva was not surprised. Nothing that happened within the evil domain of the Courtyard could surprise her. Her thoughts were bleak as she continued with her task. There were prostitutes on every corner of the rookery; some even came into the café to solicit the dockers. Sam could have had his pick of any shilling-whore. Yet he had inflicted his disgusting practices on her. He'd got what he deserved.

Rusty had gone back to work by the time she returned to the laundry room and retrieved the sack of money. She smiled as her fingers closed around it. All in all, things hadn't turned out so bad.

To take Eva's mind off the terrible events of recent weeks,

Casey suggested on the Sunday that they go to Hyde Park. The weather was sunny and mild, and it was good to get away from the oppressive gloom of the narrow streets of the Courtyard, where there was always a constant barrage of noise, angry voices raised, or hungry babies screaming in the overcrowded houses and tenements. Casey loved to stroll through the open spaces of the park, watching the gentry ride on horseback along Rotten Row. The strains of a military march were coming from the bandstand, and the grass around it was covered with deckchairs for people to sit and listen.

'Not much happening here,' Eva said, twirling the sunshade Casey had lent her with the arrogant aplomb of a duchess. 'Let's go down to the Serpentine.'

Casey had noticed that four soldiers had been following them for several minutes. Judging from their boisterous comments, they had been drinking, and Casey had no intention of being approached by them.

'We will lose ourselves in the crowd around the bandstand with luck. It will be quieter by the boating lake.'

Ten minutes later they were taking a leisurely stroll amongst the other Sunday promenaders. Casey was pleased how relaxed her cousin appeared, and how elegant she looked in the pale green dress which had once been her mother's. Since Sam's attack, Eva had refused to wear mourning, saying that it made her morbid. Humouring her, Casey had also discarded black, and today she wore a turquoise and white striped dress, her large straw hat adorned with matching ribbons. They paused on one of the low bridges which crossed the Serpentine, and watched the men rowing their families or sweethearts in boats on the crowded water.

A tall figure with blond hair caught Casey's attention on the far side of the lake. 'There's James.' She tugged at Eva's sleeve. 'Over there with that group by the trees. He's the tall blond man. Isn't he handsome?'

Eva scanned the group, which appeared to be made up of two families. 'And who is the pretty redhead with him?'

Casey frowned and shielded her eyes against the sun. James was with Edwin Hardcastle and a blonde woman who could possibly be his mother. A grey-haired man accompanied them and, hanging on his arm but gazing adoringly up at James, was a young woman dressed in a fashionable cream hobble-skirted gown, her large hat covered with silk camellias.

Intuition robbed the day of its pleasure. 'I suppose that's Prunella Marshall. The woman James's father wants him to marry,' she answered heavily.

'And she certainly seems to want him,' Eva observed. 'She can't take her eyes off him.'

'Let's go, Eva.'

'You're not going to allow this to spoil your afternoon,' Eva said sternly. 'It's time to put that man out of your head. It will lead to trouble. Those two will marry. It's what the fathers want, and your precious James is a younger son who needs to seek his fortune. Forget him, Casey. He's not for you.'

'I know that, but . . .' A heartfelt sigh escaped from her.

'Listen.' Eva grabbed her arm and drew her round to face her. 'This infatuation has to stop. I grant he's handsome. As the first handsome man ever to show you any attention, it's natural he's turned your head. But there's only one way you'll get him, and that's by getting his child in your belly. Then Joe will ensure he marries you, if Hardcastle wants to keep both legs.'

Casey snatched her arm away. 'I would never stoop to that. How could you think that I would sleep with any man who was not my husband?'

Eva controlled her exasperation. 'It isn't always as cut and dried as that,' she said more gently, aware that Casey was vulnerable. The thought that James Hardcastle might take advantage of Casey whilst she was smitten with him made

Eva's stomach churn with nausea. 'A man can use force and you can't escape him. Others will just use charm and persuasion. Either way the men are the winners and the women the losers.'

'Why must women be the losers? That's horrid. It doesn't have to be that way.' Casey glared accusingly at Eva. 'How come you know so much? Have you been with anyone?'

A cold glitter entered Eva's eyes and she walked away from the bank where James Hardcastle and his companions remained unaware of their presence. Seeing a vacant bench she sat down, her voice heavy as she took Casey's hand to draw her down beside her. 'Would it shock you if I had?'

Casey stared at her in astonishment. Only whores slept with men they were not married to. Eva was not a whore. She was nothing like the rough women who supplemented their meagre wages by prostitution in the Courtyard.

'Did you love him?' Casey voiced her curiosity.

'What do you think?' There was a hard edge to her voice.

'Of course you did. But what was it like?'

'Hateful. Disgusting. Degrading.' Eva rounded on her and gripped her hand. 'You can't escape it in marriage.' she whispered, her voice taut with pain. She let go of Casey's hand and looked down. 'Now you'll hate me. You'll think I'm no good,' she said.

Casey put a hand on Eva's shoulders. She felt her violent trembling. 'Was it Fat Sam after all?'

'No.' Eva wasn't about to tell Casey the truth about Sid Bowman. Better to lie and give her a warning at the same time. 'It were a young Irish navvy, Sean O'Reilly. I was fifteen and he said he loved me. Talk about Irish charm. The lying toad must have kissed the Blarney Stone. Asked me to marry him one night in the churchyard where we did our courting. Then like a fool I gave him what he wanted. Never saw the sod again.'

Seeing Casey's eyes widen with shock, Eva adopted a stricken expression. 'Betrayed I was. He never loved me. Just used sweet talk to get what he wanted. Then cast me off like a discarded sock. You won't tell Uncle Joe. He'll throw me out, say I'm not suitable to be your friend. But I swear, Casey, I thought Sean would wed me. You do believe me?'

'Of course I believe you. It will be our secret.'

'Promise me, Casey, don't ruin your life. Don't trust that Hardcastle bloke. He'll betray you as Sean betrayed me.'

'I won't.'

Yet when Casey slept that night and James Hardcastle entered her dreams and pulled her into his arms, the delicious fluttering of warmth which pervaded her body was nothing like the disgust Eva had spoken of. James would never force her to do anything. He was too much of a gentleman for that. Although she was a publican's daughter, hadn't her father instilled in her that she was as good as the next person? And her father did own his own pub. From the furnishings in their home, Casey knew that, even if he was not a rich man, he was as comfortably off as any middle-class shopowner. And what was James Hardcastle if he was not the son of a middle-class shopowner, albeit a wealthy one? Why shouldn't romance blossom between them?

Chapter Five

Casey had been horrified at Sam's attack upon Eva. Thank heavens Eva had been able to escape. Joe had spoken of men like Fat Sam being horsewhipped, and since that day her father had mellowed in his antagonism towards Eva. Now at least Casey did not have to worry that he would insist that her cousin leave their home.

Eva had shrugged off the incident with astounding courage, though she was frequently scathing in her opinion of men, and who could blame her? Casey admired her cousin for her resilience, and the way that she had refused to allow Sam's attack to frighten her. That had been a month ago, and the only after-effect seemed to be Eva's reluctance to take another job.

'I'm not working in a poky café again, that's for certain,' Eva declared. 'If I wasn't so shaky on adding up, I'd get a job in one of these posh shops up West. I fancy serving the gentry at Harrod's, but I missed so much schooling they'd never take me on.'

'That's easily remedied,' Casey enthused. 'I'll teach you. Within a month you'll be a regular abacus. You'll get the job easily. Haven't you taken care with the way that you speak and with the new clothes you've bought? You can't fail.'

A couple of hours every evening working on Eva's neglected schooling had paid off. Eva was starting work in the millinery department of Selfridge's the following week. Casey was delighted for her, since her cousin was so determined to better herself and had worked hard.

With Eva living at the pub, her own life had changed. Her father allowed her to go out more often, and even to a dance at the Town Hall on a Saturday evening. He always arrived to escort them home when the dance ended, even though that time of night was the busiest in the Britannia.

'I'm not having you wandering these streets late at night, Princess,' he remonstrated one night when she professed her guilt at dragging him away from the bar. 'They are too dangerous. Too many fights and too many drunks. A decent woman is not safe. Besides, there's Rusty and Bertha to deal with the customers. And it so happens I had a business call to make this way.'

'What business, Dad?' Casey asked.

'Nothing that need concern you, Princess.' The look he shot her warned Casey that he didn't like being questioned, and there was a lethal glitter in his eyes.

Casey did not protest at her father's insistence on escorting them home. Even Joe kept to the main streets after dark. The poorly-lit alleyways were notorious for the ambushing of strangers to the district, the victims left unconscious and robbed.

In recent weeks, life had fallen into a pleasant pattern. For the first time in her life, Casey had a close friend and companion in her cousin. They became inseparable. They were never short of dance- or tennis-partners. Eva seemed to enjoy flirting outrageously with them, then discouraging them with a blank refusal when they asked to escort them home.

Casey sometimes wondered whether Eva was playing a dangerous game. Some of the men became surly at her treatment, especially if they had bought her a drink during the evening, but she would flash them a ravishing smile, saying, 'Would that I could accept your offer, but my uncle, the ex-champion boxer Joe "Strongarm" Strong, will be waiting for us after the dance. He does not take kindly to men who he has not been introduced to forcing their attentions upon his daughter or his niece.'

'Dad's not such an ogre,' Casey challenged her with a laugh as they collected their coats from the cloakroom.

Sometimes it annoyed her that Eva always seemed to take charge of their outings. Yet, aware that her cousin was older and wiser in the ways of the world, Casey was usually content to follow her suggestions. Fortunately, Eva's wish not to encourage admirers echoed her own. She had met no one who could match James Hardcastle in looks or charm.

Over the weeks, Casey had fought her attraction to James in vain. Just as she thought she was armed against him, he would favour her with a beguiling smile, or praise her initiative and hard work in such a way that it undermined her resolve. When he was not in the office, which was frequent, as he pursued pleasure to the detriment of his work duties, she struggled to hide her dejection. Miss Crabtree's tongue always seemed more acid and accusing, and Mr Gibson seemed to find the most boring figure-work for her to type. No matter how many times she told herself that she was being foolish, the moment James walked into the office, Miss Crabtree's tyranny became inconsequential and Mr Gibson's complex accounts a joy to work upon.

Casey was waiting for him to return now. She glanced at the clock. It was seven-thirty and Miss Crabtree was collecting the last of her mail together and preparing to leave. The store closed at eight, but the office staff usually finished at six if all the correspondence of the day was completed. There was a stack of unsigned letters on Casey's desk, which were supposedly urgent and due to go in the late post, but it did not look as if James was going to return as promised. She had already filled in the extra time by completing several invoices which did not need to be posted out until the end of the week.

At James's insistence, Casey had been promoted to work as his personal assistant, with the authority to open his mail and answer any standard queries which she could. So efficient was she at this that she had halved his work load, but he still had to sign the letters. She suspected that this was to prove to his father that he was not shirking his work during his absence from the office.

Miss Crabtree paused by Casey's desk and sniffed with disapproval as she looked over the top of her spectacles at the pile of letters. 'It's the first of June tomorrow. Those letters will all have to be retyped with the new date on them. We cannot have letters going out of this office incorrectly dated. It reflects badly on the company.'

'Mr James was most adamant that he would return to sign them this afternoon,' she defended.

'On a glorious summer's evening like this?' Gertrude Crabtree sneered. 'He will be spending it on the river with his Society friends. It is disgraceful the way he conducts himself. And his father is such a hard-working man. I have finished for the day. You cannot wait in the office alone, Miss Strong. You will leave with me. And in future you would be better served leaving Mr James's letters undated, so that you can fill the date in at the appropriate time and not waste the company time.'

'I never date his letters until he has signed them,' Casey informed her, tersely. Did the woman really think she was so dim-witted as to give herself unnecessary work? Placing the unsigned letters in a drawer of her desk, she locked it. Then, pinning into place her straw boater, she followed Miss Crabtree outside. The older woman locked the dividing door between the offices and the sales floor. Few customers were on the third floor, and only one salesman was on duty. At the head of the stairs, Casey gasped.

'I've forgotten my purse,' she said with a tut of annoyance. 'I must have left it in my desk. I'll have to go back or I shall not have my tram fare.'

Miss Crabtree glowered at her. 'I am already late. Mother will be getting upset that her meal will be delayed. Your absent-mindedness is most inconvenient.'

'If you let me have the key, I'll go back. There's no need for you to delay leaving. I shall be in early tomorrow, I promise.'

Gertrude Crabtree hesitated. Her mother was becoming more difficult with advancing age. If the meal was late she would be complaining all evening, and she did not feel up to tolerating that.

'Just ensure that you lock up again and are here a quarter of an hour early tomorrow. If I have to wait upon your convenience before I can start work, Mr Hardcastle shall hear of it.'

'When have I ever been other than early, Miss Crabtree?'

With a tut of irritation, Gertrude reluctantly handed over the key. She had never liked the Strong woman since that first day when she'd dared to answer her back. The chit was insolent. That her work was neat and efficient only galled her further. When Mr James had insisted that Strong be promoted, it had been the final insult as far as Gertrude was concerned. She had been working here for ten years before she had been promoted to become Mr Hardcastle's personal assistant. That chit had just arrived. It was her pretty face which had taken Mr James's fancy, not her typing ability. And she knew very well to what Mr James's fancy always led. Hadn't there been more than one shopgirl dismissed for improper conduct when caught alone with Mr James? And the Strong woman would go the same way.

Gertrude concealed her annoyance at seeing Mr Parkin, the store manager, attracting her attention. She dealt with his query quickly, her thoughts still on the injustice of Miss Strong's promotion. She alone had worked for Mr Hardcastle and Mr James. She resented that her position had been usurped by a chit of a girl just out of secretarial school. It was an affront.

On the point of leaving the emporium, she saw James Hardcastle enter, whistling jauntily. Her eyes narrowed as she watched him disappear towards the stairs leading to the office.

Casey had searched her desk and had been unable to find her purse. It took several minutes before she finally discovered that it had fallen on to the floor behind her waste-paper basket.

Straightening with a sigh, she jumped violently as the office door burst open and James Hardcastle entered.

'Cassandra, I knew you would not fail me and leave. Are the letters ready for my signature?' He brought into the dowdy office the smell of sunshine and river breezes. Dressed in a fawn suit, his blond hair ruffled from the afternoon he had spent on the river, his appearance made Casey's heart beat faster.

Retrieving the letters, she placed the pile in front of him.

'My word, you have been industrious,' he said with a grin. 'And now I am keeping you from going home.'

'It is my job, Mr James,' Casey said softly. She glanced nervously towards the door, aware that they were alone in the offices and that the shop itself was rapidly emptying of customers as closing time approached.

Seeing her gesture, James's eyes twinkled with mischief. 'And extremely well you do it too.' He flashed her a winning smile.

Casey willed her frantic heartbeat to calm. With each letter signed she fed it into her typewriter and typed the date. There were twenty letters and by the time she had folded each one and placed it in its envelope, she saw that it was almost eight o'clock.

'Here let me help you with those,' James offered. 'I've delayed you enough as it is. You'll be late home for your supper.'

She shook her head. 'We eat at strange hours because of the pub.'

His interest brightened. 'I did not know that you were a publican's daughter. In what part of London do you live?'

'Not far. Just a twenty-minute walk,' she evaded, unwilling to disclose that she lived on the borders of the Courtyard.

He put his head on one side and regarded her archly. 'I bet that pub is the most popular in London with you helping behind the bar.'

She tensed. 'My father does not permit me to go into the bar. He does not consider it fitting.' Looking pointedly at the clock, she stood up. 'I really must be going. I have these to post.' She clasped the letters to her chest, as though they would protect her from the way his nearness was affecting her.

'Must you run off so soon?' He took her hand. 'I haven't had a chance to tell you how much I appreciate your hard work. Won't you allow me to buy you dinner as a way of saying thank you?'

Her heart sank. There had been a change in his manner since she had mentioned the pub, and his calculating appraisal was making her uneasy. She knew that the middle classes regarded those who lived in the East End as women of easy virtue. That he should presume the same of her made her burn with resentment. 'I do not think that would be considered proper, Mr James,' she returned icily.

'It would be considered very proper by me,' he said with a warm smile.

In spite of Casey's indignation, when he smiled like that it had the power to make her limbs seem to lose all their strength.

He went on smoothly, 'And I thought we had agreed that it would be just "James" when we are alone together.'

'My father would not consider such conduct proper.' She found the strength to utter a denial, although she would have loved to accompany him. When she tried to draw back, he did not release her hand.

'Put those letters down, Cassandra.' His blue eyes sparkled as he took the envelopes from her. In that moment she knew that he intended to kiss her. Panic filled her. She was alone on the upper floor of the building. What if Mr Parkin came upon them unexpectedly? By now he would be patrolling the building to ensure that all the staff and customers had left.

She snatched at her handbag. 'I have to go . . . James.'

He reached the door before her, but instead of holding it open, he leaned against it, a wicked smile playing across his lips. 'What are you frightened of? Surely not me.'

He was toying with her as a cat did a mouse. Despite her infatuation, that knowledge angered her. Reason asserted itself. Men such as James Hardcastle did not ask their assistants to dine, only their fiancées . . . or their mistresses.

She flushed, aware that he would never consider her fit to be his fiancée. 'Please let me pass, Mr James.' Indignation sparked in her grey eyes, and she lifted her head to regard him. 'I do not dine alone with a man who is not a relative.'

'Do you not?' The assurance in his voice made the heat rush from her cheeks.

Every inch of her slender body was rigid with outrage. 'Indeed I do not, Mr Hardcastle. And if you think otherwise then—'

'Then I'd be a fool.' The amusement in his eyes changed to thoughtful contemplation. 'You are not like the others.'

It was on the tip of her tongue to ask what others, then she immediately thought better of it. It accounted for the sly looks Miss Crabtree sometimes threw at her after she had been closeted with him for dictation. How many other assistants had he propositioned in this manner?

'My offer to dine was a token of my appreciation of your hard work,' he clipped out. To her surprise he bowed to her and opened the door without demur. 'Forgive me, Cassandra. I have inexcusably detained you.'

There was the sound of a stealthily placed footstep along the corridor. Casey glimpsed a long shadow thrown up against the wall from the setting sun through the long display window. The soft rustle she detected could only have come from a woman's long skirt.

'I trust you will not expect me to work so late again, Mr James, especially if there is no one else in the office.' She raised her voice to carry to whoever was spying on them.

James Hardcastle had followed her stare, and thought he heard a movement behind the glass office partition. His admiration for Casey increased. He had no intention of being caught again in a compromising situation with one of the female staff. The last time it had happened, in the storeroom with a pretty counter assistant from Stepney, his father had threatened to disown him.

'I am indebted to you, Miss Strong. Two of those letters were extremely urgent. Papa would never have forgiven me if I did not deliver them by hand this evening. We need an answer by nine tomorrow if we are to secure the stock.'

They stepped into the corridor. 'Be assured, Miss Strong, I will recommend to Papa that you be given an increase in your salary for your diligence and hard work.' He broke off as they reached the partition where the interloper was hidden. ''Pon my word, if it isn't Miss Crabtree herself,' James declared, looking suitably surprised. 'And there was I about to report to my father that you had left Miss Strong alone in the office. You know that is not company policy. Why, anyone could have broken into the offices, and she would be vulnerable and at risk!'

Casey glared at the older woman, realising that she must

have seen James return and had deliberately been spying on them. It could only be to cause mischief, and she could guess which kind. Jealous of her success, Miss Crabtree would relish finding her in a compromising position so that Casey could be dismissed.

For several moments Miss Crabtree's mouth opened and shut like a landed fish. Then she shot them a look of such venom that Casey almost choked in the effort not to give the woman a piece of her mind.

'Goodnight, Miss Crabtree,' James said, indicating that Casey should precede him to the stairs.

A sharply indrawn breath from Miss Crabtree was followed by her angry retort. 'Mr Hardcastle will indeed hear about the goings-on here this evening.'

Casey's temper snapped. She rounded on the older woman. 'I have done nothing wrong. I told you that Mr James would be returning to sign his letters. And you insisted that we leave. Had I not returned for my purse, these important letters would be delayed. How dare you impugn my reputation!'

The woman's sallow complexion changed to the colour of rancid cream. 'You are impertinent, Miss Strong. Impertinence is not tolerated in this office. Mr Hardcastle senior will be informed of your conduct tomorrow. If he does not sack you, then I shall hand in my own resignation. Twenty years' loyal service I have given to this company. I will not be spoken to with such disrespect.'

Casey clenched her fists in impotent rage.

'There will be no talk of Miss Strong's dismissal,' James said harshly. 'You have overstepped your authority, Miss Crabtree. You cast aspersions upon Miss Strong's reputation. She is a lady whom I hold in the highest regard as a trusted and diligent employee.'

'She's not such a lady from what I surmise has gone on here tonight.' Miss Crabtree faced him belligerently.

'Surmise is dangerous when you have no proof, Crabtree,' James retorted. 'You will apologise to Miss Strong, or I will have no choice but to inform my father that a woman of such a malicious disposition has no place in this company. Rather too many office staff have left because of your shrew's tongue.'

Miss Crabtree gasped. 'In all the years I've served Mr Hardcastle senior, I have never been spoken to in this manner.'

'And for ten of those years you have ruled the office like a tyrant,' James alleged. 'I've lost count of the office girls who have left here in tears because you make their working life a misery.'

The formidable figure shuddered, her lower jaw working with shock. 'I only demand efficient work. I have never made their life a misery.'

'Then why have so many left?'

His anger aroused, James was ruthless, but there was a pettiness to his argument which made Casey wonder if Miss Crabtree had crossed him and now he sought to pay her back. Coldly, he went on, 'Miss Strong is the only one I've known to stand up to you. And now, on the flimsiest of pretences, you would have her sacked. What is that, if not tyranny?'

Casey had no fondness for Miss Crabtree. But to see her reduced to this shocked state roused her sympathy for the lonely spinster who dedicated her life to her work and her ailing mother.

'Mr Hardcastle,' Casey intervened, feeling uncomfortable that the incident had been blown out of proportion. 'We are all tired. It's been a long day. I'm sure Miss Crabtree's words sounded harsher than she intended. And I was in the wrong for retaliating. Please, let us forget the incident.'

He looked at her with deepening respect. 'If Miss Crabtree agrees that her words were spoken hastily, and that she did not intend to imply a slur upon your reputation, then I am prepared to forget the incident.'

Miss Crabtree did not speak. The stubborn woman was too proud to back down. Casey held out the sealed envelopes. 'Miss Crabtree, you know how long it takes to sign, date and seal this many letters.'

Miss Crabtree nodded. 'I may have . . . um . . . spoken out of concern for your welfare, Miss Strong. I was shaken to hear a man's voice when I returned to the office. I had not expected Mr James. Those letters were indeed urgent. You did right to ensure that they are mailed this evening.'

The words were conciliatory, but the hostility had increased in her eyes. Miss Crabtree would not rest until she found an excuse to dismiss her.

In silence Casey held and matched the older woman's threatening glare. She had no intention of allowing a woman's malicious spite to jeopardise her job or dictate her life.

'I've been thinking that job ain't right for you, Cassandra.' Joe Strong came out of the bar as Casey entered the hallway dividing the pub from the living quarters. 'It's gone nine. It's not right that Hardcastle keeps you so late. It's the third time this week.'

A month had passed since her confrontation with Miss Crabtree. In that time James had often found excuses to keep her late, always ending with an invitation for her to dine with him. Until now she had refused. There was something about the way that Miss Crabtree looked at her after she had been taking dictation from James which made her suspect he had compromised other females on the staff. This job was important to her. She was not about to jeopardise it by allowing her infatuation for her boss to lead to indiscretion.

Her father's expression was now set in a way Casey knew meant his mind was made up. And once that happened nothing would change it. Her heart sank. His remark had little to do with the late hours. He must have learned of James's interest in her. Only Eva could have told him.

'It's a good job, Dad. And it's well paid to compensate for the long hours.'

His brown eyes narrowed. 'Well paid for doing what, I'd like to know? Hardcastle is taking too much interest in you. If that young bounder is taking advantage of you, Cassandra, I'll—'

'Whatever are you talking about?' Casey cut in. 'I worked until seven-thirty and then, as the evening was so warm, I decided to walk home. I suppose I was dawdling. I'm sorry, Dad. I didn't mean you to be worried.'

His expression remained dour, the dark slash of his moustache hiding the line of his mouth. 'I don't trust young Hardcastle. I've been making inquiries about him. He fancies himself something of a ladies' man. If he lays a finger on you, Princess . . .'

'Dad! Stop it!' she cried, appalled. 'I enjoy my job. I've no intention of leaving it. You should be proud that James Hardcastle values my work enough to promote me.'

'So you're not attracted to this young man?' he fired at her.

Casey swallowed. Eva *had* been talking. She was furious with her cousin. To her greater consternation she found herself blushing. 'I like working for him, Dad.'

'Look at me, Cassandra.'

The terse comment was one she knew better than to defy. Her father doted on her, but there was a side to his nature which even she did not risk rousing. He had a temper which could blister the air when he gave it full rein. She kept her stare level as she regarded him.

'If this man makes any improper suggestions, you're to tell me,' he demanded.

On the landing above, Eva listened to the conversation and smiled. Joe would make Casey leave the emporium, after all she had told him about his daughter's infatuation for James

Hardcastle. Jealousy gnawed at her breast. Casey had looked up to her for so long, Eva was not about to have that devotion destroyed by a man stealing her cousin's affection. Each evening it was infuriating to listen to Casey dreamily relating every word that Hardcastle had spoken to her. If Casey married, Eva knew their relationship would never be the same. They could never remain as close as they were now. It was Eva's greatest fear. It was obvious that Hardcastle was attempting to seduce Casey, she reasoned, to explain her obsession for keeping Casey at her side. Hardcastle was probably intrigued that Casey had held out for so long.

Eva's hand gripped the balustrade, her knuckles whitening. She did not want Casey hurt; she continued to justify her jealousy. The man was a philanderer, and her cousin just another conquest who was harder to win than most. The thought of Hardcastle putting his lecherous hands on Casey made Eva feel physically sick. Casey must not suffer as she had suffered for Sam's and her father's lust. She had spoken to protect her cousin.

Eva strained to listen as their voices dropped. There was less antagonism in Uncle Joe's voice after each reply by Casey. It made her burn with envy. She had done everything she could to win Uncle Joe's affection. Even though she was aware that he desired her, he remained cold in his manner towards her. Joe was a complex man who was made of steel where his emotions were concerned. His remoteness towards herself made her feel excluded from the family. And that rankled. Until she won Joe over, she would always be an interloper. He could throw her out on the streets on a whim. That was something she was determined would not happen.

Unexpectedly, Joe laughed. 'James Hardcastle would be a fine catch for a husband, Princess. You play your cards right, my girl. You're as good as the likes of him any day. And don't you forget it.'

The bar door opened and closed and Casey's footsteps were light on the stairs. Eva was shocked that Joe sounded so pleased at Hardcastle's interest in Casey. She would have thought he'd punch his lights out for daring to look at his saintly daughter. But then Joe had always wanted Casey to marry well.

Eva was also unprepared for the forceful set of Casey's lips and the angry light in her eyes when she saw her cousin. They prompted Eva to sound distraught. 'I've been so worried for you, Casey.'

'Is that why you've been telling tales on me to Dad?'

Casey accused her with such violence that Eva felt the blood drain from her face. Her cousin had never spoken to her like that before. Instantly, she was defensive. 'I would never betray you, Casey.'

'Then how come Dad has just told me that James Hardcastle would be a fine catch for a husband? Dad warned me about men like James being out to seduce me, but he told me to string him along. He said he'd soon put the fear of God into him if he tried anything out of order. What have you been telling him about James? You've made his kindness to me sound sordid. It's not like that at all.'

'What do you know of men like James Hardcastle?' Eva retaliated. Drawing a sharp breath she fought to control her temper. Casey was not as malleable as she believed. She did not want to lose her cousin's adoration. Casey's friendship was the only good thing that had happened to her in recent years.

As Casey was about to march past her, Eva burst into tears. 'I didn't betray you. When you were late I began to panic,' she gasped out between sobs. 'You mustn't trust men like Hardcastle. They are only after one thing – and it isn't your friendship. You're so innocent. Despite what Uncle Joe says, when Hardcastle weds he will secure his fortune by marrying that Marshall woman.'

Casey's expression did not soften. Eva could be provoking and over-protective. But her cousin was allowing her own experiences to cloud her judgement of all men. 'I don't want you meddling in my affairs, Eva. I confided in you because I thought I could trust you.'

Eva sobbed harder. 'I never meant you harm. I kept thinking what if he cornered you as Sam did me.' She ran past Casey into their bedroom and flung herself on to the bed, her sobs wild and unconstrained. 'I still have nightmares about Sam's attack. Men are beasts, Casey. Don't trust them.'

Casey shook her head in exasperation. Eva could be a trial at times. Often her fussing and possessiveness made Casey feel smothered. She made allowances because of her cousin's life and because Eva did genuinely worry about her. It was a shame that Eva had allowed her experiences with Sean O'Reilly and Fat Sam to distort her opinion of men.

Not all men were evil, Casey reasoned. And what sort of life would you have if you distrusted everyone?

Chapter Six

In the next few weeks Casey became self-conscious in James's company. He was charming, his interest in her plain. Yet something made her hold back whenever he suggested that he take her out for a meal after work. If he stood too close to her, she moved away. She became conscious of his every movement. Her heart raced whenever his hand inadvertently brushed her shoulder or arm. His compliments became harder to dismiss as her attraction for him grew.

She was typing an urgent letter for a new contract with Pudsey's, importers of exotic silks and brocades. James had insisted that he must have it by lunchtime, when he was dining with Albert Pudsey, the managing director of the firm.

Doris Maxwell, the telephonist, entered the office and handed Casey a slip of paper. She was smiling, her plump face animated even though she was breathing heavily. Even that small exertion had rendered her large figure short of breath.

'Mr James has just phoned. He's been delayed. You are to take Mr Pudsey's letter to the restaurant in the Strand where they are lunching. He's said for you to take the money from the petty cash for a taxicab.'

From across the room, Miss Crabtree tutted in disapproval. 'It is not for Miss Strong to run errands. Lil Warren is perfectly capable of taking a tram to the Strand.'

'Mr James was most insistent that it be Miss Strong,' Doris

returned, clearly disliking the older woman's inference that she had taken the message incorrectly. 'He said Lil would be overawed by visiting such a place. It's a posh French restaurant from the sound of it. Mr James is eager to create the right impression. Miss Strong must be there by twelve-thirty. And he said there is no need for her to return to the office as we finish at two today since it's half-day closing.'

'Did he indeed?' Miss Crabtree sniffed her disapproval. She surveyed Casey through her horn-rimmed spectacles, but was unable to fault her black suit and high-necked white lace blouse. 'Then I suppose Miss Strong had better leave at twelve. But I shall be expecting you to stay later tomorrow to clear up any outstanding work.'

Casey was thrilled at the prospect of a taxicab ride to the Strand. She enjoyed her work, but on sunny days like today she was always restless to get out into the open air. After delivering the letter, she would stroll through London's West End and spend an hour in St James's Park.

Promptly at twelve-thirty she alighted from the taxicab outside the French restaurant. A couple were just entering, the man in top hat and frock-coat, the woman in a cream silk suit, its jacket decorated with seed pearls which must have cost twice Casey's yearly wages. She looked down at her ankle-length straight skirt and tailored jacket. The lapels were piped with narrow white braid in a small maple-leaf pattern. It was smart and stylish and she was glad that her mother's large cameo brooch was pinned to the high lace collar which banded her throat.

The restaurant was filled with the scent of roses arranged in huge displays. The delicious aroma of spiced sauces and meats made her mouth water. The interior was dark after the bright sunshine, and each table was lit with candles. Many of the tables were partially secluded behind red velvet drapes, creating a private and intimate atmosphere. When the head waiter approached Casey, she smiled nervously.

'I am to deliver this letter to Mr James Hardcastle. He is expecting me.'

His stiff manner mellowed. 'Mr Hardcastle has arrived, madam. If you will follow me.'

She was led to a table at the side of the dining room. James stood up as she approached, and she was surprised to see that he was alone. She held out the letter, but it was her hand he took, not the envelope. 'Please sit down, Cassandra, and join me for an aperitif whilst I await Mr Pudsey's arrival.'

'I really should be going, Mr James.'

'Would you make me wait alone? Pudsey telephoned a few moments ago saying he would be delayed.' He held out a chair for her to be seated. 'I hate to drink champagne alone,' he said softly. 'You would not be so cruel as to desert me.'

Feeling it would be churlish to refuse, she sat down and removed her gloves. She glanced over her shoulder at the other diners, and realised with a start that the table was very secluded, the partitioning curtains shielding her from any curious gazes.

She sipped the champagne, her unease dispelling as James smiled at her. A lock of blond hair fell forward over his brow, and he brushed it back with a boyish, impatient gesture which she found endearing. 'You do not seem at all impressed by the sumptuous furnishings of the restaurant.'

'They are very fine, but I have seen better at the Ritz.'

'You have dined at the Ritz?' His astonishment was obvious.

The hot weather had made her thirsty, and she finished her glass of champagne. She felt wonderfully relaxed and, suspecting that James was patronising her, she intended to put him in his place. 'It was my fourteenth birthday treat. Mama insisted we dine there. It had been a favourite place of hers before she married my father.'

His blue eyes sharpened with interest and, refilling her glass, he said softly, 'Tell me more, she sounds a fascinating woman.'

Casey sipped the cool champagne. She was proud of her parents and what they had achieved. With an obstinate tilt of her chin, she defied James Hardcastle to mock them. 'My mother was Olivia Delaney. She was an actress. Her father was a banker. He disowned her when she disobeyed his wishes and went on the stage.'

'That must have taken courage. I can see where you get that indomitable spirit from.' James raised his glass in salute to her and smiled in a way which made her heart pound rapidly. 'She must also have been very beautiful to have such a beautiful daughter.'

Casey ignored his compliments, although they roused a delicious glow in her body. 'My mother was not beautiful, she was ravishing.' The champagne was making her speak more openly than she would normally. 'Everyone adored her. My father fell in love with her the first time he saw her. She had played several minor roles in a dozen productions in the West End before she met him. But she was disenchanted with the stage and what was expected from her by her admirers. She despised the stage-door Johnnies, as she called those who thought all actresses could be bought.'

Remembering that James had a reputation for escorting Gaiety girls, she blushed at her blunder, but remained defiant. He showed no emotion at her statement, and she wondered whether she had misjudged him by listening to gossip. 'I know how my mother must have felt. It's the same when you say you live in the East End. A certain type of man believes you have no concept of virtue because of that.'

'They could never think that of you, my dear Cassandra.' He reached out to take her hand. Disconcerted, she drew it back and looked at her wristwatch. 'It's one o'clock. Mr Pudsey will be here any moment. I must leave.'

'Please stay. I want to hear more about your family,' James insisted.

She shook her head and stood up, perplexed at the way the floor seemed to be moving around her. 'I must go.'

The head waiter materialised at her side and addressed James. 'Mr Pudsey sends his compliments and his apologies, Mr Hardcastle. An emergency at his factory has necessitated his cancelling his meeting with you.'

James looked dismayed. Then, with a disarming smile at Casey, he suggested, 'The answer is that you must join me, my dear. I simply cannot dine alone, and I can think of no more enjoyable a companion.'

'I couldn't, Mr James. It would not be right.'

'Nonsense. You are here and old Pudsey is not.'

She turned away quickly. She must go before she was tempted. To her alarm, the room spun erratically around her. The arrangements of roses danced and swirled and she felt her body sway. James's hand was on her elbow, gently assisting her to sit.

'You drank the champagne too quickly. That proves you must stay. The food will take away its effects. I can't have you walking out of here tipsy. It wouldn't be the done thing at all.'

Casey allowed herself to be persuaded. Once she was seated, the room no longer revolved – and she was exceedingly hungry. James watched her with amusement as she proceeded through the courses with relish. During the meal the conversation changed to teasing banter. Casey now drank sparingly from her wine glass, which always seemed to be full. Her dignity and poise never deserted her. When she found how easily her observations made him laugh, she began to forget the differences between them and to enjoy herself. The way he was looking at her now was making her heart flutter in the strangest way, and when he lifted her fingers to his lips to kiss them, she knew she should pull them away. But the touch of his mouth sent a tingling heat through her veins. Aware they could be overlooked, she cast a surreptitious glance over her shoulder.

Everyone was too engrossed in their own meal and conversation to notice them.

'We should do this more often, Cassandra,' James said softly.

Her eyes widened and she shook her head. She wanted so much to agree, but remained wary of his intentions.

'Don't say no,' he coerced. 'You've enjoyed our lunch. What are you afraid of?'

He was going too fast for her. 'It's rumoured in the office that you are to marry Miss Marshall. If that's true, how can you express an interest in me?'

Impatience made him frown. 'Nothing is arranged. My father may wish for the marriage, but it is you who are important to me. I can't stop thinking of you, Cassandra. You are an exciting and exhilarating woman. Look to what lengths I've been driven to get you to dine with me!'

She tensed. 'You were to meet Mr Pudsey.'

'There is no Pudsey. The letter and the lunch appointment were all a sham to get you here. You've been so aloof in the office lately. Yet I had begun to hope that you cared – just a little – for me.'

'You are my employer,' she began, clinging to her composure whilst aware that she was perilously close to betraying the joy his words evoked.

'I adore you.' His eyes were dark with passion. He took both her hands. 'You have no false wiles or coquetry. I've never met anyone like you.'

She felt herself on the edge of a precipice. Her mind was in turmoil. Common sense told her that men such as James did not marry publicans' daughters, even if her father believed she was the equal of any man in status. Eva's warnings also echoed through her mind.

'Mr James . . .'

'Just "James" when we are together like this.'

She fought her attraction to him, but his charm and consideration shredded her defences. She latched on to his words, using them to reinforce her reserve. 'Yes, I may call you James, but only in moments like this. And that's why I will not listen to you.'

She stood up and pulled on her gloves. 'I dislike deceit and double standards. I must remember my place. I am just an employee, an underling, your inferior.' Wounded pride was making her unreasonable, but she could not remain silent. 'I know my place, Mr Hardcastle. It is you who forget yours. I am your secretary. That is all I can ever be to you.'

Without looking back and with head held high she left the restaurant. She was angry and hurt. She did not feel inferior to James Hardcastle, and she did not like being made to feel so. The noise of the Strand's traffic jarred on her strained nerves as she strode purposefully towards Trafalgar Square. In the July afternoon the sun was hot in a cloudless sky. The road was crammed with horse-drawn carriages and buses, the noisier motor cars and taxicabs clattering over the cobbles. The pavement around Nelson's Column was crowded with pedestrians, the ever-present pigeons scuttling for food around their feet.

Casey slowed her pace and halted by the fountains. A fine spray of water carried on the breeze was cool on her hot cheeks. Absently, she smiled at seeing a street urchin splashing in the water, the boy ignoring an angry shout from a policeman. She watched the policeman leap into the water and haul the youth out. The boy did not give in without a fight. He yelped and kicked, flaying his arms wildly so that he knocked the policeman's domed helmet into the water. Whilst the policeman bent to retrieve it, the boy struggled free and made a dash for freedom. Some of the crowd cheered the youth, others jeered the policeman. Casey felt sorry for the man, whose trousers were drenched. He looked about her age, with a russet moustache. His face was scarlet as he climbed out of the water.

'Casey, we must talk.' She froze, disheartened at recognising James's voice directly behind her.

'I've said all there is to say,' she replied, keeping her head averted.

Her arm was taken and he gently turned her to face him. His distraught expression wrenched at her heart. 'Do you think I like the deceit our position forces us into? There's no woman to match you. I admire your pride, even though it wants to put barriers between us. Yet there need be no barriers.'

He had removed his gloves; when he touched her cheek his fingers were firm and cool. 'Do you doubt my feelings for you are sincere? Prunella Marshall is nothing to me. It's you I want, Casey. It's you who haunts my dreams at night. To win you I will defy my father. The whole world, if I have to.'

The passion in his voice touched her like a flame. He was the first man who had stirred her heart, and since he had given her no reason to doubt his sincerity, her resistance wavered. He was so handsome, her young heart could not help but respond to his plea.

James saw the capitulation in her eyes and seized upon it. With a relieved laugh he took her arm. 'Come, let us stroll in St James's Park. I will not be parted from you while the afternoon is still early.'

The enticement of his smile chased away a lingering unease. St James's Park would be full of people. What harm could come of spending an hour or two there with James?

Eva was disgruntled on returning from her own half-day's work that Wednesday to find that Casey had not arrived at the Britannia. She grew more restless as the afternoon progressed and there was no sign or word from her cousin. Eva had planned a surprise treat for Casey. She had purchased two tickets for that evening's variety show at the Coliseum after they had first dined at a Lyon's Corner House.

The pub was closed for the afternoon and there was no sign of Uncle Joe. She might as well have her weekly bath now as later. Lifting down the galvanised tub from its hook in the back yard, she dragged it into the downstairs scullery. She had lit the copper earlier, and the water was already hot. Filling the tub was tiring, but her aches and pains would soak away in the hot water. Before undressing, she fiddled with the bolt on the door, cursing the warped wood which made it impossible for the bolt to anchor securely in place. Having no watch of her own, she guessed it was about three-thirty. Uncle Joe was probably down the gymnasium run by an old boxing friend, where he spent most afternoons. He rarely returned until half an hour before opening time.

Eva poured several drops of Casey's perfume into the water, and lay back enjoying the warmth of the water and its fragrance. This was true luxury. They had not possessed a bath at home, and any washing had had to be done in cold water as there was no copper. She had sometimes had enough money, from the chance picking of a pocket, to pay for a visit to the public baths, but not as often as she would have liked. All that had changed; now she bathed weekly and Joe never complained how much hot water was used. The perfumed soap which she lavishly lathered over her body was another treat never experienced before.

She smiled contentedly and, unpinning her hair, she washed and rinsed it. She stroked the black tresses over her breasts. The weekly washing had given it the rich sheen of a raven's wing. Once it was dry she could run her fingers through it and watch it ripple like finest silk. Before it had always been snagged and snarled. Life now was indeed good.

With a sigh she closed her eyes, reluctant to leave the warmth and dress. She must have dozed. Her eyes opened and with a jolt she saw Uncle Joe standing in the doorway. His bowler hat was tilted at a rakish angle over his brow. With a gasp her hands covered her full breasts, which were revealed above the waterline, their rose-pink nipples hardened by the cool air. Joe Strong did not move. His shadowed gaze was on her naked figure. A shudder passed through him, and when his stare lifted to her face, anger replaced the desire she had glimpsed in his eyes.

'Good God, woman! Ain't you got the sense to bolt the bloody door?'

His anger was forced as his gaze was drawn again to regard her body, opaquely visible beneath the soapy water. She saw his throat work as he swallowed. Instead of the usual revulsion she felt at the evidence of a man's lust, Eva experienced an elation, a feeling of power. She was jealous of the adoration Joe lavished upon his daughter. Now she had his complete attention. And in a way Casey could not rival her.

'The lock's broken, Joe.' She deliberately dropped the 'uncle', her gaze holding his as she reached out to pick up a towel. 'I thought I was alone.'

Holding the towel before her she rose out of the water. He remained by the door, unmoving, mesmerised, as she'd known he would be. With tantalising slowness she wrapped the towel around her figure. It clung damply to her breasts and hips, and she noticed the effort it took him to drag his gaze away.

'Anyone could've barged in here,' he said hoarsely. 'What if it had been Rusty and not meself? I'll get the bolt mended.'

When he turned to leave, she said softly. 'I have never thanked you properly for giving me a home.'

A muscle pumped in his jaw, revealing the tight control he was exercising. He nodded. 'You're me sister's girl. I couldn't have you on the streets, could I? Now get dressed. Rusty's in the bar. He'll be getting ideas if he sees you like that.'

'Ideas, Uncle Joe?' Eva taunted, her eyes round and apparently innocent. 'What ideas would they be?'

'As if you didn't know.' His manner changed to a menacing challenge. 'Don't play the innocent with me, Eva. Any decent woman would have screamed at discovering a man had seen her bathing.'

'A fool I'd look screaming when it's me own uncle,' she retorted, turning her back on him. The door banged behind Joe as he left.

Eva looked at the door over her shoulder. Alarm clenched her stomach that he had so condemned her. She would have to be careful with Joe Strong. He desired her, but he would not tolerate his daughter becoming tainted with the company of any woman he suspected had loose morals. She pursed her lips, her mind reviewing her uncle's obvious desire for her. She'd be a fool if she did not use it to her advantage.

The shadows were lengthening, and Casey was surprised to discover that most of the afternoon visitors had left the park. Where had the hours flown as she laughed and talked so easily with James? They had listened to the band and taken a leisurely stroll along the pathways and through the trees. Casey had fed the squirrels and ducks with the sandwiches in her bag which she had packed for her lunch. Twice James had slid an arm possessively around her waist, but each time she had pulled away, disliking such a public demonstration of affection.

'Do you think me a bounder for wanting to hold you?' They were walking between the trees and he stopped and turned her to face him. 'I'd have to be made of stone to spend so many hours with you and not want to feel my arms around you, or taste the sweetness of your lips.'

Casey's pulse raced, but she side-stepped him, distrusting the intensity in his stare. His compliments had been lavish all afternoon, despite her attempts to discourage them. Each one had lifted her spirits, his nearness causing a glow to permeate her body. His charm was persuasive, and Casey was beginning to suspect that her infatuation was changing to something deeper and far more dangerous. Was this what it was like to be in love? When your feet felt lighter than air, and the tender expression in a man's eyes could send thrills of excitement through your veins?

Her eyes sparkling, Casey danced away from him. 'It's late. My father will worry that I have not returned home.'

'Ever the respectable secretary,' he teased. 'So prim and proper, except for the allure in your eyes. Innocence and fire: they are a provocative combination.'

She laughed and spun away from him and he ran after her. Still laughing, Casey ran behind a wide tree. Holding its trunk, she taunted, 'And you have a wicked gleam in your eye which I distrust.'

He grabbed her around the waist and pressed her gently back against the tree. They were both laughing, but as their gazes met, the laughter faded. Casey found herself holding her breath in anticipation.

When his warm lips took hers, his moustache was pleasantly abrasive on her soft flesh. It was her first kiss, and she was unprepared for the intoxication it aroused. Her senses careened, whilst a warmth spread through her body which sapped her strength. At the touch of his tongue tenderly circling the seam of her mouth, her lips parted. She tasted the wine and faint tobacco on his breath, and his kiss intensified to such sweetness that she trembled. Her knees no longer seemed to have the strength to sustain her. Her hands fluttered against his chest and her fingers curled around his coat lapels as she swayed, almost swooning against him.

Finally they broke apart and, strangely breathless, Casey leaned against the tree. She stared up at him with wonderment. The expression in his eyes was hidden behind lowered lashes; before she could speak, she was crushed once more against him. This time his mouth was no longer tender, but hard and demanding. He forced her lips apart, his tongue questing in a way which was no longer pleasant.

She twisted to free her mouth, her hands pushing frantically against his chest. Wrenching her lips away, she gasped, 'No, James.'

'Yes, my dear,' he moaned as his lips again descended upon hers. This time they were gentler, but Casey was alarmed at the harsh way he was breathing. She could not believe he was kissing her in public. Although there appeared to be few people in the park, anyone could come across them. When his hand squeezed her breast, indignation increased her struggles.

'No. Stop it. *James.*' She shoved him away from her, but his fingers were on her arms, holding her a prisoner. His face was no longer handsome as it hovered above hers; his countenance was taut with frustrated desire.

'Don't be a tease,' he groaned, his mouth again seeking hers.

She evaded it and wriggled to get free. 'James, have you lost your mind? Stop it at once!'

The force he was exerting alarmed her. The gentle, courteous lover of the afternoon had vanished. His mouth was hard, punishingly cruel on her swollen lips. As she continued to struggle, he clamped her face between his hands and ground his lips over hers so fiercely that she tasted blood as they caught against her teeth.

Outraged, she struck out. Her hand stung as she slapped his cheek with all the strength she could muster. 'How dare you?' she seethed.

He rubbed the scarlet imprint left by her fingers. 'Damned slut! What's got into you? You've been asking for it all afternoon. Bit late to play the innocent, isn't it, the way you've been leading me on?'

Casey backed away from him, her anger so great she was

not about to leave without retaliating. 'I never led you on. You tricked me into having lunch with you. Then you followed me to Trafalgar Square.'

'You knew what you were about. All coy one moment, big grey eyes wide and beguiling the next. I've never seen such a blatant come-on.'

He grabbed for her and she darted away, putting the width of the tree between them. 'Keep away from me,' she warned. 'Or I'll scream.'

The glitter in his eyes was feral and his expression was ugly with thwarted lust. 'Don't threaten me.'

Then his manner changed, his stare speculative. 'Or is this another ruse?' He ran his tongue across his lips. 'You are a surprising woman. I want you, Cassandra. You mistake me. It's not a quick tumble I'm after. I'll set you up in a place of your own with an allowance which is ten times your salary at the office.'

She swung out with her handbag, striking him in the stomach. 'Keep your money. And you can keep your office salary. I'm never working for you again.'

Her blow had bent him double. When he straightened his expression was furious. Casey backed away, glancing from side to side in growing panic. The golden afternoon was fast turning to a nightmare.

To her relief, several people were approaching on the nearest path and she ran in their direction. She guessed that James would not risk making a scene.

His parting words, shouted after her, fuelled her anger. 'Too right you're not working for me. You're fired. And don't expect any references either.'

Anger scalded her as she took the Underground train home. She emerged from Tower Hill station still simmering with fury. Eva had been right about James Hardcastle. Casey had been a fool to think he regarded her as his equal. Everything he had said to her had been lies. With every silken sentence he had been bent upon seduction and nothing more. Her gaze lifted to the crenellated battlements of the Tower of London. A cluster of tall gabled buildings was visible behind its stone gatehouse, all of them dominated by the four domed turrets of the square Norman keep.

Near to, the Tower had always emitted a sinister aura. Too many people had been tortured in its vaults and gone to their deaths from its prison cells. Yet after James's betrayal, she felt comforted by the sight of the familiar outline, which she had gazed upon so often from her bedroom window. How many of the prisoners who had suffered within those cold stone walls had been betrayed by misplaced trust in someone belonging to a class above their own?

Casey drew a jagged breath. She could not believe the change in James when she defended her virtue. Never again would she trust a man of his class. She was hurt and disillusioned, but she realised she had escaped lightly. Many a gullible woman had fallen for that seductive charm. They usually ended up abandoned, often with a by-blow child to raise. Even so, losing her job without a reference would have serious consequences. Who would employ her now?

It was another grudge she held against James Hardcastle. He had denied her a living out of spite at her rejection. The sheer pettiness of it sparked her temper. She would not be denied a reference. She would face him in the office tomorrow and demand one. She doubted he would risk his father learning of what had taken place this afternoon.

The experience had left a bitter taste in her mouth. She had learned a valuable lesson, not least that she would never allow someone to bully her into submission against her will.

Casey swept past Miss Crabtree who tried to stop her entering James Hardcastle's office. 'You can't go in there. You no longer work here. Dismissed without a reference. I always knew you could not be trusted.'

'I will see Mr James and I will see him now.' She lifted her voice so that it would carry to him if he was seated in his office. She knew that his father was not in the office today as he was visiting a new supplier in the Midlands. 'Unless Mr Hardcastle would prefer that I speak to his father when he returns.'

'I have never heard such audacity.' Miss Crabtree's thin face was a mask of contempt. 'Mr James is not to be disturbed. The announcement of his engagement to Miss Marshall is in the paper today and there is to be a banquet for them at the Savoy. You will leave at once, or I will call the floorwalker to have you removed from the store.'

'That would be most unwise, Miss Crabtree,' Casey countered. Her anger at James increased. The man had no sense of honour. He was a deceitful liar. God pity his poor fiancée. 'I intend to see Mr James now. I prefer to settle my business with him in private. However, if you call the floorwalker, I shall ensure that every customer in this store will hear the truth about my dismissal.'

The door was snatched open and James Hardcastle glowered at her, his voice clipped with anger. 'You had better come in.'

He returned to sit behind his desk, but did not offer her a seat. 'How dare you come here in this manner? But then I would expect a publican's daughter to resort to common tactics.'

His attitude reinforced her belief in the bullying arrogance of men of his class. She glared at him, despising his cavalier conduct. He could see no wrong in his behaviour, she was sure.

'I want a reference,' she said with quiet determination. 'You cannot fault my secretarial work. I was dismissed because I refused to become your mistress. I will not allow you to ruin my career out of spite, because I did not succumb to your seduction.'

He sat back in his chair, regarding her haughtily. He preened his moustache and his lips thinned to a cruel smile. 'If your career is so important to you, you should have been more accommodating. If I am not satisfied with your conduct, I do not have to give you a reference.' His stare was lascivious. 'Though perhaps I could be persuaded.'

His conceit was insufferable. Casey had heard enough. She rested her hands on his desk and leaned forward. She did not like stooping to his level to gain her own ends, but with such a man there was no choice.

'Then I will speak to your father. I am demanding only that which I am entitled to.'

'He's out of the office,' James gloated.

'He returns on Friday, does he not? I'm not afraid to tell him why I was dismissed.' Her eyes narrowed. 'All I'm asking for is the reference I deserve. If you try to ruin my career then I will serve you likewise.'

His deprecating laugh roused her fury. 'I'm not impressed with your threats. What can you do to me?'

It was the arrogance of his manner which made her resolve to carry out her bluff. He had to learn that he could not treat women this way. 'I am not threatening. I am stating a fact. Mr Marshall may also be interested to learn why I am no longer in your employ. I suspect I am not the first woman to suffer your attentions.'

He shot out of the chair as though fired from a cannon and rounded the desk. He tried to grab her and she stepped back, her eyes blazing. 'Lay a finger on me, Hardcastle, and I will scream.'

He was breathing heavily, but her expression stopped him touching her. 'Very well,' he said, 'you will have your reference.'

He returned to his desk, wrote a few lines on headed paper, and handed it to Casey. She scanned its contents, which commended her skills as a secretary.

'Thank you,' she said, turning to leave.

'This isn't the last of this, Miss Strong. I don't take kindly to being threatened.'

She faced him, raising a mocking eyebrow. 'Neither do I, Mr Hardcastle. But it would be better if you let the matter rest. I would hate to have to tell my father what happened. You may fear the censure from your family, but if you earned the enmity of Joe "Strongarm" Strong, it would not be your reputation which suffered but your health. My father can be over-protective where I am concerned.'

She saw him pale. She disliked answering him threat for threat, but his attitude deserved it. The gentry needed to be put in their place more often. She had heard too many stories of women abused by employers, men laid off for voicing an opinion on the appalling working conditions they had to suffer, to feel any sympathy for this man.

Chapter Seven

During the following month, Eva made herself indispensable in the Strong household. No task was too much trouble for her. She particularly took care to prepare Joe's favourite meals. When the pub closed and he flopped down wearily into his armchair, she was on the floor at his side, easing off his shoes and putting his feet in his slippers. His tobacco jar was always full, and his pipe laid on the table by his chair. She would ensure that his favourite supper of jellied eels or whelks was always ready for him.

At first he had ignored her efforts. Then he had accepted them grudgingly. Eventually, during the last few days, he had begun to look at her without his usual antagonism.

'Not in bed, Eva?' he asked guardedly as she placed the bowl of jellied eels on the table.

'I'm not tired. I promised Casey I would speak to you. She's worried you will make trouble at Hardcastle's because she's left her job.'

He gave her a searching look as he sat down and rubbed a hand across his brow. 'Is there more to this business than Casey said? If Hardcastle took advantage of her then—'

'No. Casey told you the truth,' Eva hastily intervened. 'And you should be proud of her the way she tackled him and insisted on a reference. Don't take that from her by going behind her back to confront Hardcastle.'

Joe smiled, his eyes soft with affection for his daughter. 'Casey is quite something. A pity Hardcastle was such a cad. She could have her choice of suitors, and I don't intend any of them to come from around here. She'll go far.'

Eva hid her chagrin at the praise. Hadn't she defended her virtue in a far more dramatic way by fending off Fat Sam. She forced a smile. A scheme had been forming in her mind for several days, and now seemed the appropriate time to voice it. Coming to live at the Britannia had fired her ambition to better herself too.

'But how far can a woman from the Courtyard go, Joe?' She no longer called him 'uncle' and he had not corrected her. 'If you want her to marry well, you should consider buying a pub in a posher area, like Leytonstone, or better still, the West End.'

'You saying I'm holding me daughter back? That I don't provide well enough for her?' Joe glared at her in a way which stripped away some of her confidence that she could manipulate him.

Undaunted, she persisted. Joe would despise timidness; she had to be bold and risk his wrath. 'No, Joe. No girl could have a more caring father. It's this district which is at fault. It will always taint Casey's future. And if you believe otherwise then you're a fool.'

His hands swept the jellied eels from the table as he jumped up. 'Fool, am I! Aye, fool to give a home to an ungrateful whelp, it seems like!'

'I'm grateful, Joe. More grateful than I can ever say. It's Casey I'm thinking of. You've always wanted the best for her. And rightly so. She's got courage, brains and looks. In that she takes after you, Joe. I hadn't meant to speak out of turn.'

Some of the ill-humour left his eyes and he nodded. 'My Princess has got courage, but her brains are from her mother. Perhaps you could be right about the Britannia. Casey's mother always wanted us to move up West. She said it made sense. But being born round here, I felt more comfortable than with the toffs and their kind.'

'You'd fit in anywhere, Joe. Aren't you famous? Everyone's heard of Joe "Strongarm" Strong. And didn't the toffs flock to watch you fight? Make the most of your fame and you'll make your fortune.'

Seeing the interest in his eyes, she pursued enthusiastically, 'A pub near the theatres with you behind the bar will be a goldmine.' She paused and added, softly and meaningfully, 'There'll be no need for your contacts who call here not to frequent the new pub. The high mobsmen prefer to move in respectable areas to cover their movements.'

Anger flashed in his eyes and his face darkened with menace. 'And what would you know about the high mobsmen and the like?'

Eva met his glare unflinchingly; only boldness would win him over, and she must risk the consequences of rousing his temper. 'Dad told me about your connections with the jewellery trade. And your fights were organised by the high mobsmen. I've seen Goldstein in the pub. He runs the protection and prostitution rackets up West. And I doubt you pay him protection. So why is he here? It must be business. But that's just between you and me, Joe. Our secret, if you like.'

He sat down in his armchair, his expression hostile. Kneeling at his feet she undid his shoelaces, watching him through half-lowered lashes. Suddenly his hand shot out and he gripped her chin painfully.

'You be sure to watch yer lip, girl. If Cassandra—'

'Cassandra worships you,' Eva blurted out. 'I'd never betray you, Joe. I owe you too much. I've always been so proud to have "Strongarm" as my uncle.'

He stared at her for a long moment. She could feel the tension in him and knew she could be in danger if she did not regain his trust. 'Joe, Casey is not the only one who adores you.' She lifted her gaze, intense with emotion, and put her hand on his knee. His stare remained guarded. 'I'd do anything for you, Joe. Anything to prove how much I'm grateful.'

She saw him swallow. From the tautness of his face muscles she knew that he had not mistaken her invitation, and was fighting his awareness of her.

'And I'm not so much of a girl as you called me,' she taunted with a smile. 'I'm nearly twenty. Almost an old maid.'

He laid his head against the crocheted antimacassar on the back of the armchair and studied her through narrowed eyes. After several moments he said, 'You're a good-looking woman. Rusty must have asked you out a dozen times and you refuse him. You've not had any young man come calling for you since you came to live here.'

'You made it clear you did not approve of men callers. You didn't want Casey meeting the wrong type.'

As she reached over to pick up his slippers, her breasts pressed against his knees and she heard his sharp intake of breath. Her smile was wistful as she regarded him and she dropped her voice to a husky whisper. 'Besides, I've no time for young men, they seem so immature compared to a man of the world like yourself.'

A light flared in his eyes before he turned his head away to open the tobacco jar and fill his pipe.

'You shouldn't cut yourself off from men. Rusty is a good man. He thinks the world of you.'

Eva sighed and she sat back on her heels. 'Rusty is all right. I like him, but . . .' A cry burst from her and she threw her arms around Joe's neck, laying her head against his scarlet waistcoat as her sobs increased.

He tensed and she could feel his chest muscles taut beneath her breasts. His thigh was iron hard against the soft curve of her hip. Her sobs became more violent as she gasped out,

'You've been so good to me, Joe. If only I could meet a man like you. I could be happy. I could trust them.'

Joe looked down at her sobbing figure. Every sinew of his body was aware of her feminine curves pressed against him. Her hair was loose about her shoulders, falling in gypsy-black curls to her waist. His throat dried at her loveliness. She wore only a thin peach satin dressing gown over her cotton nightdress, the neck of which was unbuttoned low enough to display the upper curves of her breasts. As he breathed in her scent, his body responded against his will.

After Olivia's death there had been many casual acquaintances with women, but never the common whores who lived in the Courtyard. Bertha was the latest; her husband was doing a stretch in Pentonville Prison. It was a casual affair; twice a week he'd visit her rooms in Bethnal after he'd finished at the gymnasium in the afternoon. Their affair was a pleasurable indulgence of their bodies, with no emotional entanglements. Despite her bawdy banter, Bertha was not a whore; she just missed her bodily comforts whilst her husband was locked away.

Though he had lived in the Courtyard all his life, Joe despised the coarseness of the prostitutes. His own mother had never married. Most nights, from the age of seven, he had been kicked out of the house to find shelter where he could whilst she entertained the sailors from the docks.

By the time he met Olivia, he had been fighting in the ring for several years and was famous on the circuit. He was fast on his feet and faster still with his fists. He'd never had his good looks destroyed. Women commented that his broken nose and the cut on his lip actually added to his attraction. They said it gave him a roguish air and made them feel wicked just to be in his company.

Yet women had never been that important in his life. Even Olivia. She had been beautiful and vivacious. He had been captivated by her from the moment she had refused to date him. No one said no to Joe Strongarm. He had courted her with a vengeance. Every night he had sent flowers to the theatre, asking her to dine with him at the Ritz. He had to persist for three months, but he'd won in the end. When he seduced her a few weeks later and discovered that she was a virgin, the novelty of it puffed up his pride and he had vowed to wed her. He had always respected her purity, although he'd been disappointed at her lack of interest in sex. Out of respect he'd kept his other affairs secret. It was not until Casey was born, and he had held her fragile form in his arms, that he had known what it was to truly love another person. The moment Casey had reached out a tiny hand to grip his finger, he had lost his heart to his daughter. It was to build a better future for her that he had invested all his fight winnings in the Britannia.

'Oh Joe, I wish I could meet a man who was like you.'

Eva broke through his thoughts. He closed his eyes and swallowed, fighting to control the response of his body towards her. The girl was his niece. Out of decency he must control his lust. He raised his hands to lift her from his chest, aware if he moved she would feel his arousal. Yet somehow he found his fingers began to stroke the velvet tresses of her hair.

'There, girl, don't take on so. You should be in bed. It's late. Casey will have been asleep for an hour or more. I've told you before, you don't have to wait for me to finish work. I can get me own supper.'

She lifted a tear-drenched face to meet his gaze. 'It's little enough for me to do to repay you for all you have done.'

Her green eyes were luminescent, wide and glittering. If he did not know better, he would swear they sparkled with invitation. But that could not be so. He was the same age as her father. He cleared his throat. 'Get to bed, girl. You shouldn't be here like this.'

'I don't know what to do.'

The tears ran down her cheeks. She spread her hands across his chest. It was a gesture of despair and also of seductive promise. She was a tempting piece. Grimly he suspected that she was not as innocent as he would wish such a close companion of his daughter's to be.

'I'm so ashamed. You've been so kind to me, Joe. You've given me so much. I feel tainted. You don't know what my life was like with Dad and Myrtle. I fear you have taken me in under false pretences.'

'What's all this?' He cleared his throat, not sure that he wanted to hear her confession. 'You're me niece, where else should you go? You're letting what Sam did to you upset you. You escaped him.' He tensed and his face became thunderous. 'You did tell the truth? He didn't rape you, did he?'

She burst into a fresh weeping, collapsing again on his chest. Her body quivered from the violence of her sobs as her figure moulded to the contours of his. 'It weren't Sam who raped me. It were Dad. Every week for years he used to force me—'

'Bloody hell! He did what?' Joe exploded and, taking her arms, held her away from him. Eva was like a crumpled doll, her body limp and without substance. She was beautiful, defiled and torn apart with pain.

'Say you don't hate me. Please, I couldn't bear it.' With surprising strength she launched herself into his arms, her mouth against the hollow of his neck. 'I couldn't bear for you to hate me. I love you so much.'

Somehow she had twisted and was seated on his lap. Her arms linked around his neck and her lips pressed against his throat in fervent kisses.

'I love you, Joe. You can't hate me for what was not my fault,' she gasped between kisses.

Joe was shocked by her revelation. If Sid had been alive he'd have beaten him to a pulp. Raping his own daughter – that was sick. Not that incest was unheard of in the overcrowded rooms of the Courtyard. Cousins, brothers and sisters often slept eight or ten to a room. It was just not spoken of.

Anger ground through him, but at the same time the pressure of her body was setting his blood on fire. He could not banish the image of her lying naked in the bath. Her firm young body with high, taut breasts had tormented his dreams at night, leaving him to wake feeling ashamed at the feelings those images aroused. But she was not the innocent he believed. When her mouth closed over his, the needs of his body became blind to reason. There was just the ache in his loins and the need to satisfy it.

Holding her close, he rose from the chair and carried her to his bedroom. Briefly, his conscience checked him and he hesitated at the door. She did not protest, instead her kisses deepened. Through the thinness of her nightdress and dressing gown he could feel the heat of her body, young, pliant and supple against his own.

With a groan he carried her to the bed.

Eva surrendered herself to Joe's caresses. This was what she had planned. She had not expected it to be so easy. As Joe's lover she would be special to him. He would love her as she craved to be loved. Casey's friendship and affection were no longer enough.

She was surprised at Joe's tenderness. It was easy to feign pleasure. He was an experienced lover, unlike her brutally fumbling father.

'Joe, there's no one like you,' she whispered as he slumped over her after his climax. 'I love you, Joe.'

'Better get back to your own bed, Eva,' he murmured sleepily against her hair, 'I don't want Cassandra knowing about this.'

There was an edge to his voice that Eva disliked. As she drew on her nightdress, her eyes were cold. After all she had done, it was still Casey's feelings he considered, not hers. She controlled her impatience. This was but the first time. It would not be long before Joe was besotted. Drink had often made Sid's need outmatch his ability. He had taught her enough whore's tricks to keep a man satisfied. And she was prepared to use every one to win Joe's affection.

Stooping to kiss his cheek, she whispered, 'You're real special, Joe. This will be another of our little secrets.'

He murmured an indistinct reply. His eyes were closed and, as Eva opened the bedroom door, his even breathing told her he was already asleep.

As Eva passed her cousin's door, Casey called out sleepily, 'Is that you, Eva? Are you all right?'

'I've just made myself some warm milk. I couldn't sleep. Go back to sleep.'

On entering her room, Eva lay on her bed, staring up at the moon-silvered ceiling. She was angry that Joe had dismissed her so abruptly. That must change. Once the heat of his passion was spent she had sensed a change in him. Could he be ill-at-ease with what he had done? Alarm tightened her stomach muscles. Joe was not like her father. He had a conscience and a stronger sense of morals. That would not suit her purposes at all.

The next morning Joe avoided her eyes as he ate his breakfast. Casey was excited about the two interviews she had to attend that morning for a new secretarial post, and she left early for the first one.

Eva lingered in the kitchen. The novelty of working in a West End store was fading. She disliked having to be meek-mannered and subservient to the haughty customers who looked down their noses at the sales staff. There were times when a customer was so rude to her that she felt like telling the haughty bitch to get stuffed. She had wanted to better herself, but even though she took pains to speak with a more refined accent, she was just another shopgirl. And besides, the work bored her.

How much more exciting it would be to replace Bertha in the pub, especially if Joe could be persuaded to move to the West End. A better class of establishment would attract the toffs, and who knew where that might lead an ambitious woman?

Clearing the breakfast dishes, she glanced at Joe. He was reading the *Sporting Life*. Piqued that he was ignoring her, she touched his hand. 'I don't want you to feel awkward about last night. You didn't take advantage of me, Joe. I wanted you. I know it was wrong. But you made me feel so good. I couldn't bear it if you thought I just did it with anyone. You're the first man I've ever wanted that way.'

He put the paper down, his brown eyes wary. 'I'm too old for you, Eva. I should not have taken advantage of you.'

She shook her head. 'No. I love you, Joe. You didn't take advantage. You showed me there is pleasure. That there need not be pain. Don't say it wasn't important to you.'

'It mustn't happen again,' he announced. 'You're me niece. If Cassandra found out . . .'

Eva lowered her eyes so that he would not see the fury blazing in their depths. He didn't care about her. He was just worried about his precious Casey and what she would think. Still with her eyes downcast, she knelt at his side.

'Casey won't find out if we're careful.' Only when she knew she had her anger under control did she raise her gaze to his. 'Didn't I please you?'

Joe groaned. She was half his age and temptingly beautiful. He was flattered by her attentions. But it was too dangerous. He risked too much. If he lost Cassandra's respect because he allowed his lust to overrule his reason, he'd never be able to live with himself.

'You pleased me very much, but it won't happen again.'

Eva stood up. She didn't believe him. He still desired her. That was why he was avoiding her gaze. She had no intention of losing her hold over him. She had seduced him once and she had every intention of doing so again.

Casey accepted the secretary's post at Messrs Pinion and Son, solicitors, whose offices were at the far end of Cheapside, opposite St Paul's Cathedral. She was to work for Jonathan Pinion, the son, who was in his fifties. His father Augustus was seventy-five and still came into the office every day. They both interviewed her. Neither man had a hair on his head or was taller than five foot, and each had a substantial girth. Both dressed in stiff winged collars and black frock-coats. Yet the moment she looked into their ruddy faces and saw the kindness and merry humour in their eyes, Casey knew that she would be happy working for them.

The dark offices were a shambles of disorganisation. Bundles of papers were piled from floor to ceiling and over every piece of office furniture. Even the umbrella stand had two rolls of documents poking out of it.

'We have never had a female working for us in the office before,' Augustus Pinion said with a shake of his head. 'Mr Rattigan always copied out the affidavits and conveyances by hand. Sadly, Mr Rattigan is no longer with us. He had a stroke last month. But times move on and I find it rather fatiguing now to write all my letters by hand.'

He leaned forward in a manner which invited confidence. 'Actually, Miss Strong, I like to think of myself as something of a rebel against convention. A new typewriter has been installed and we are proud to open our doors to the new vogue of female stenographers.' Both men nodded enthusiastically.

Casey hid a smile. The Messrs Pinion were the least rebel-like men she had ever encountered, but that these two staid figures saw themselves as such made her warm to them.

Jonathan Pinion spoke, 'The other staff members are Mr Hennessy, our clerk, and Nicholas Read, the young messenger boy.' Jonathan Pinion leaned forward. 'You have excellent references, Miss Strong, but why did you leave Hardcastle's after such a short time?'

This was the question Casey had been dreading. It could cost her the job. Most employers frowned upon workers who flitted from one company to another. She had only been with Hardcastle's for three months. 'It was for personal reasons I would rather not speak of, Mr Pinion. It is nothing which will affect my work here, if that is what concerns you.'

He regarded her shrewdly for several moments before nodding acceptance. 'You have an honest face, Miss Strong. I respect discretion. It is necessary in our work here.'

She was taken to meet the other staff. The elderly Hennessy was exceedingly tall, barge-pole thin, with stooped shoulders and a shock of grey hair. Nicholas Read, the 'young messenger boy' was forty if he was a day and looked much older. His pale face resembled crumpled linen it was riddled with so many lines.

'Good-day, Miss Strong,' the two men chorused.

Hennessy cleared his throat and adopted a superior expression. For a second Casey stiffened, suspecting the arrogance she so detested; instead he seemed to be having difficulty finding the words he wanted to say. Immediately her antagonism vanished, sensing that he was ill-at-ease in a woman's company.

'Ah hope has how you will be has happy in your work here has myself and young Read have been.' The way he emphasised and added aitches to his words told Casey that he was from one of the poorer districts of London and had striven to better himself.

The solicitors' offices were busy and she had never known time to pass so quickly. But she found it hard to cope with the confusion of files scattered over the office. How did anyone ever find anything? Her office was on the fourth floor, and its window overlooked the impressive dome of St Paul's. At lunchtime on fine days she strolled in the cathedral gardens, finding a quiet seat to eat her sandwiches. If the weather was chilly, she would walk back along Cheapside, past the tall column erected to mark where the great fire of London had started, and on over London Bridge to watch the ships being unloaded.

She was happy in her work, enjoying the chance she was given to use her initiative. At the end of August, Jonathan Pinion came into her office with a pile of letters he had signed.

'Good gracious me, you've made a change here in a few weeks.' He stared around the tidy room no longer cluttered with files. All had been cleared by Casey and stored on some shelves in an unused back office. So that she could find them easily, she had given each a number and listed the client against it in a record book.

'I hope you don't mind.' She had a sudden misgiving that they might see her tidying up as an interference. 'But the files were so dusty that I found I kept sneezing. When I opened one no correspondence had been written on it for eight years. I've stored them in the back office and I've kept a record.' She opened the book to show him the pages of neat writing.

'Splendid. Quite splendid. A woman's touch. It makes all the difference. You make me feel I should tackle my office. But where to begin?'

'Sir, I may be speaking out of turn, but I would be happy to sort out a filing system for everyone's files. There is room in the back office for shelves where they could be stored neatly.'

He laughed softly. 'How like a woman to keep us in order. You sound just like our housekeeper. Since Mama died twenty years ago, Mrs Moore has looked after us superbly. I never married, and without Mrs Moore there, life would have been very uncomfortable indeed.' He peered back into his office and frowned, as though seeing the mass of files and papers for the first time. 'Wouldn't it make a lot of extra work for you?'

She smiled. 'I think it would make life easier for us all. It took me over an hour yesterday to find a file for your father which was not in the pile he believed it to be.'

''Pon my word, we can't have you spoiling your pretty clothes searching through piles of dusty files,' he said, beaming affably. 'I shall engage a carpenter at once. And you will be rewarded for your hard work.'

'When would you like me to start on the files?'

'Such enthusiasm, Miss Strong,' he said, smiling complacently. 'I had forgotten how the enthusiasm of youth can be so exhausting. There is no immediate rush. Leave it a week or so until my father and I take our annual fortnightly visit to Baden-Baden for the waters. And I don't want you risking injury by carrying heavy files – young Read will assist you.'

Casey controlled her impatience at the thought that it would be nearly another month before the files were properly organised. But it was obvious Jonathan Pinion wanted no disruption to his office routine and would prefer to return from holiday to find the work done.

He added with a smile of satisfaction, 'I can see we have engaged a treasure. And don't think we don't appreciate it. Your cheery smile quite brightens our day.'

Casey guessed he was a man used to being waited on by servants, but there was nothing arrogant about his manner. He just accepted that it was a woman's place to keep his house in order. It seemed he now saw her in that role in the office. Casey did not take offence. Both Messrs Pinion were always courteous towards her. They were genuinely pleased at any improvements she made, and she found it a pleasure to get the office organised. It certainly made her own duties easier.

During the Pinions' fortnight-long holiday, Casey worked

hard to complete the storage and record system for the files. The solicitors were due back in the office this Monday morning and there was still one pile of files to sort through and number. To avoid inconveniencing her employers, she arrived at the office at six on the Monday morning. She was determined to have the work completed before the Messrs Pinion arrived. To protect her good work suit, she removed the jacket and wore a large apron over her lace blouse and skirt. By eight-thirty all the files were in place and the records complete.

Several times she had heard the lift clanking noisily up to the different floors, the metal doors clattering open and shut as people began to arrive for work in the building. She was just sweeping the dusty floor with a hand brush into a dustpan, when the largest spider she had ever seen ran across her hand. She gave an involuntary scream from the shock of it, and dropped the pan, spilling the dust back on to the floor.

At the same moment the inner office door burst open and a male voice queried. 'Anything amiss? I heard someone scream.'

Casey straightened from resweeping the scattered dust and found herself staring at a stranger. Feeling foolish that her scream had summoned him, she put down the dustpan and brush. She was annoyed to discover that a tress of hair had fallen down from her upswept curls and tickled the end of her nose. With an exasperated purse of her lips she blew it away and studied the man. He was no ordinary office worker, which added to her discomfort. The cut and cloth of his grey suit was obviously Savile Row. It fitted to perfection over his lithe figure. He was some three inches taller than her father and clean-shaven, with thick chestnut brown hair brushed back from his brow and just touching the back of his collar. His features were rugged and too angular to be handsome, but they were striking, as were the green and gold flecks in his hazel eyes. His skin was bronzed from the sun. Yet she guessed it was from a vigorous outdoor life which owed nothing to manual labour.

'I was just startled, that's all,' Casey said, self-consciously removing her apron. 'A spider ran over my hand.'

'A spider, you say.' To her astonishment he shuddered. 'Nasty things. Can't abide them myself. Don't blame you for screaming.' His voice was deep and attractively husky.

When his gaze continued to appraise her, she tensed. The memories of James Hardcastle were too vivid for her to feel comfortable subjected to such an admiring glance from a man of his position.

'They're harmless enough. I just didn't expect it to be so large. It tickled.' She laughed softly at her own foolishness and saw the offending spider climbing up the wall by the man's shoulder. 'There it is, see for yourself.'

He swivelled quickly. His jaw dropped and his complexion paled as he darted away from the wall. When he lifted his hand to straighten his tie, Casey saw that it was trembling. Her antagonism at the way he had looked at her dissolved. Clearly, spiders terrified this self-possessed man.

There was always a glass on her employer's desk beside a flagon of water. She snatched it up and trapped the spider beneath it as it began to move across the room. 'Open the window, I'll put it outside. And pass me that envelope so that I can slide it underneath the glass to stop it escaping.'

He did as she bade him, though he kept a wary eye on the spider as she walked to the window and placed it on the outside ledge. Only after she shut the window did he appear to relax and grin wryly.

'Now you know my innermost secret. I can't abide the wretched things. The other chaps in the Flying Corps rib me no end about it.'

The way he confided in her lessened her suspicion. James Hardcastle would never admit that he had the slightest weakness, and his arrogance and bullying tactics had shielded his inadequacies.

She wanted to ease his embarrassment. 'We all have something which affects us that way. With my mother it was mice. As for myself I become nauseous at the sight of a leech. If I ever had to have one of those vile creatures on my flesh to suck my blood, I'd be fit to be admitted to a lunatic asylum.' Just the thought of the bloated, black bloodsuckers made her shudder dramatically.

'Ugh. Let's change the subject,' she added with a laugh. 'I haven't thanked you for coming to my aid.'

His grin broadened with self-mockery. 'And then it was you who saved me.'

The stray lock of hair had again fallen over Casey's nose and she flicked it with irritation. 'I had better go and make myself presentable. The Pinions will be arriving at any minute and we have a client coming at nine o'clock. It wouldn't do for them to see me so dishevelled.'

'You look very presentable to me. But wait a moment.' He stepped forward and, before she realised what was happening, ran his thumb along her cheek. 'That's better. You had a smudge of dust there.'

His familiarity angered her. He was no better than James Hardcastle. Her eyes flashed dangerously as she regarded him, her spine stiffening with affront. 'I think you had better leave.'

He smiled disarmingly. 'I've offended you by my forwardness. I do apologise.'

She realised she had overreacted, but after her experiences with James she was wary about men of his class. It made her voice sharpen. 'You would not be so forward with a woman of your own station.'

'Not unless she was as pretty as you,' he parried, attempting to lighten the mood. When he saw that she was not amused, his manner changed. 'You seemed such a good sport. I didn't mean to be disrespectful. I forgot myself. I rather felt that we were companions in arms after the affray with the spider. Please forgive me.'

Casey bit her lip. Again she had made a fool of herself. With a start she realised that she also felt a comradeship between them, which had increased as they teased each other over their fears.

'It's not you I'm cross with, but someone else. I'm sorry. I behaved like a prim schoolma'am with no sense of humour.'

She walked to the door just as the lift reached their floor with a clanking of chains. She flipped open the diary and saw to her consternation that the first client was a Mr Matthew Frost representing Frost's Brewery. They were the brewers who supplied the Britannia; she had remarked on it to Mr Pinion when she'd come across several fat bundles of their files.

Mr Hennessy and Mr Read stepped out of the lift. Hennessy looked shocked to see a man in the reception. Collecting his wits with a start, he hurried forward.

'Sir, our apologies that there was no one here to attend to you.'

'But I have been attended to by this young lady.'

Hennessy shot Casey a suspicious look. He had not approved of her idea to move the files and, judging from his attitude, resented any interference or change in the running of the office. His eyebrows were raised in censure as his gaze alighted on the dusty apron in her hand. 'Miss Strong has been remiss; you do not appear to have been offered tea, sir.' He turned scornfully to Casey. 'What were you thinking of appearing before so important a client as Mr Frost improperly attired for your duties?'

'It's my fault.' Matthew Frost hastily intervened on her behalf. 'I arrived early.'

The lift clanked a second time and Jonathan Pinion stepped out, twirling his gold-topped cane and followed more slowly by his father who was stooped over and leaning heavily on his stick.

'Have we kept you waiting, Mr Frost?' Jonathan Pinion said. 'Our apologies. The traffic is horrendous today. A cart had overturned in Fleet Street, blocking the road. Ah, I see you've met our new secretary, Miss Strong. Miss Strong, may I present Mr Matthew Frost?'

Ever since joining the company, Casey had been introduced to each client as though she was part of the family and not an employee.

'We have met,' Matthew Frost responded, smiling at Casey as he extended his hand to both her employers.

'Of course you have.' Jonathan Pinion smiled in a fatherly way. 'You must know her father well. Joe Strong, the boxer. He owns the pub the Britannia, which is supplied by your father's brewery.'

'Near the Tower of London.' Matthew Frost regarded Casey with surprise. He quickly recovered, his voice smooth as he added, 'It's one of our more profitable outlets, so I believe.'

He was ushered into Jonathan Pinion's office and, before the door closed, she heard the solicitor say, 'Good gracious me, the woman is a wonder. You'd never believe it, Mr Frost, but before we left to take the waters at Baden-Baden, you could not move in here for piles of files and rolls of documents. I don't know how we would manage without Miss Strong.'

'She seems a remarkable woman,' Matthew Frost replied before the door closed on the three men and their conversation was lost to Casey.

Although she heard the door open an hour later, she kept her head bent over her typewriter, her fingers pounding rapidly on the keys. She was cross with herself for not having realised that the stranger was their client.

As she worked she could feel Matthew Frost watching her. Having learnt her lesson about men of his type from James

Hardcastle, she had no intention of encouraging his attentions.

'Good-day, Miss Strong.' He was standing by her desk and out of politeness could no longer be ignored.

'Mr Frost, I hadn't realised your meeting was finished,' she said coolly.

'Are you still angry with me?'

'Why should I be angry, Mr Frost? In any case, it is not a secretary's place to have an opinion about a client.'

He placed his hand over his heart and gave a theatrical wince. 'I really did make a bad impression. Was it my fear of spiders?'

She regarded him levelly. 'Certainly not. You should have introduced yourself so that I could attend to you as befits a client.'

'You are on the defensive, Miss Strong,' he said softly. 'I preferred the teasing companion before the others arrived.'

Her head jerked up. 'I don't like being taken advantage of in any form, Mr Frost. It must have been obvious to you that I was employed here, but then men of your position often believe that women employees are fair game.'

He regarded her quizzically. 'It was never my intention to take advantage of your position. I enjoyed your company. If some man in the past has treated you disrespectfully, then I bet you sent him away with a justly deserved flea in his ear.'

She slanted a glare at him, annoyed that he could read her so easily. He held her gaze steadily and the teasing golden lights brightened in his eyes. It was impossible to stay angry with him. Beneath his admiring but taunting gaze, her heartbeat quickened.

'Am I forgiven?'

'There is nothing to forgive.'

Tearing her gaze from his, she felt herself blush. To cover her embarrassment she shuffled the papers on her desk. He was an attractive man with a good sense of humour which she liked. His nearness was also affecting her strongly. There was a greater masculine magnetism about Matthew Frost than ever James Hardcastle had possessed, and she was not about to be drawn by it.

'I'll not keep you, Miss Strong,' he said bowing to her. 'I can see you are busy.'

She nodded, knowing that to speak would be tantamount to inviting him to linger. When she heard the outer door close behind him, she turned to regard the opaque glass. The office seemed strangely empty and her expression became wistful. Those few minutes they had been alone when they had first met had been so different from any other encounter with a man. She had enjoyed his teasing banter, and they had laughed and taunted each other as equals.

The door opened again and Matthew Frost stuck his head through the opening and grinned at her. Damn the man, it was as though he expected her to be gazing after him.

'Until we meet again, Miss Strong.' The door closed and he was gone.

Her anger flared at his presumption, but it dispelled before it could take root. When a few minutes later she found herself humming as she typed, she checked herself with a moan of frustration.

'Casey Strong, don't go allowing his devilish humour and attractive looks to deceive you. He's no different from James Hardcastle. Men like Matthew Frost are best kept at arm's length.'

Chapter Eight

Walking home from Tower Hill Tube station that evening, Casey purchased an evening paper from the ragged, grimy-faced youth at the corner of her road. It was early evening and the sun would not set for another hour. Yet it was already dark within the maze of narrow streets, where the soot-blackened houses with their slate roofs and smoky chimneys tilted towards one another. The lamplighter had already lit the two gaslamps which inadequately illuminated the street; as she passed under them they hissed like angry snakes.

A yellow fog was rolling in from the nearby river and the Tower of London was hidden from view. From the rapid way it was cloaking the chimneys and distorting the railway embankment, it was going to be a real pea-souper. Sometimes the fogs were so thick that it was impossible to see your hand in front of your face. Most Londoners cursed the choking smog, but not the footpads and sneak-thieves who saw it as a godsend to their illicit trade.

Aware of the dangers, Casey clutched her handbag closer to her body. Pickpockets lurked in black-shadowed alleys, awaiting any unsuspecting prey. Even in the fog, children still chanted skipping songs as they jumped the long length of rope in the centre of the road. Several youths argued shrilly as they tossed farthings up against the wall to see which landed closest to a piece of chalk. Those without farthings used roasted

'Hey, Archie – daft as a broom – only fit ter sweep the room.'

Casey glared at the boys, her anger rising as she saw them set on the simpleton and begin beating him.

'Ow ger-orf,' Archie bellowed as he held up his arm to ward off their blows.

'Stop that!' Casey demanded, running over to Archie's crouched figure. He had fallen on the pavement with his hands over his head. 'Leave Archie alone. He's done you no harm. Pick on someone capable of fighting back, you bullies.'

'Get lost,' the tallest and oldest at sixteen threatened, pulling out a knife. 'Unless yer want some of the same. 'Ow about 'anding over yer purse fer starters.'

'Gawd, Freddie, lay off 'er. It's Strongarm's daughter, yer idiot.'

The youth swaggered in front of his friends. 'Strongarm's reputation don't frighten me none. 'E's an old man now.'

'He can still give you a whipping, laddie,' Casey defended. 'And it's no less than you deserve, setting upon Archie like that.'

The knife flashed inches before her throat and she jumped back. 'Yer got too much lip. 'And over yer bleeding money, or I'll slice yer good.'

Casey lashed out with her handbag and hit the bully across the face. With a shout he staggered back clutching his nose. 'Get her, the cow's broke me nose.'

The boys hesitated. Archie was sobbing on the pavement. Casey's heart was pounding with fear, but she knew the only chance she had of escaping harm was braving it out. 'Get off to your homes, lads. Your mate is a braggart and a fool. You know my father's reputation with his fists. Do you really think you could stand up against him?'

The door of the Britannia slammed open and four men ran out, led by Paddy Murphy who must have alerted Joe.

Casey saw the flash of her father's scarlet waistcoat as he launched himself at the oldest boy, and she heard the sound of his fist striking bone. The other boys scarpered into the fog. Joe had picked the now-yelling gangleader up by his shirtfront, and was shaking him until the lad's teeth rattled.

'You're from the Flower and Dean Street mob. Stay out of the Courtyard and keep away from me daughter.' There was the thud of three more punches before Casey pulled on his arm.

'No, Dad. Leave him be. I'm unharmed. And Archie wasn't badly beaten. You've given him a warning. They won't come back.'

Joe shoved the boy away from him, planting a last kick on his backside to send him scuttling off. 'If I see you round here again, you won't be able to walk home.'

Casey knelt beside Archie who was trembling with terror. 'It's all right now, Archie. The bullies have gone. Come into the bar and have a drink.'

Paddy Murphy and another man hauled Archie to his feet, and Casey's arm was taken by her father. 'Are you all right, Princess? If those louts hurt you, they'll regret it.'

'I'm fine, Dad. Bit shaken, that's all.'

He pulled her under the gaslamp to study her and, satisfied that she was unhurt, nodded. 'Damn fool thing to do, taking on those boys. But you bloodied that thug's nose and I'm proud of you, Princess.'

'She's a chip off the old block,' Paddy Murphy said with a laugh.

Casey straightened her jacket. 'I hardly think street-brawling is something for a woman to be proud of, but I'd do the same again. Why must they be so cruel to Archie? He'd never hurt anyone.'

Joe sighed as he returned with her to the side entrance and led her into the house. 'That's the Courtyard for you. And I reckon it's time we moved on. This never was no place for a lady to be brought up. Your ma were always nagging me to get out of here. What a night for this to happen. We've a special visitor in the parlour.'

'Who?' she asked, aware that her skirt must be muddied from kneeling on the pavement.

'Someone you know. Come in the Daimler.'

Casey looked at him in alarm. 'It's not James Hardcastle?' She could think of no one else who would visit in such style. 'I don't know what he's got in mind, but I've no intention of seeing him.'

'Do you think I'd let that swine near you?' Joe snapped. 'If he showed his face round here, he'd leave on a stretcher.'

They had reached the first-floor landing and she halted in the parlour doorway. All three gaslamps were turned full on, their bluish flames reflecting in the polished silverware and crystal bowls and vases on the mahogany dresser. The ruby velvet curtains and red and purple Turkish carpet gave the room a cosy warmth.

As Casey pulled off her kid gloves, a figure uncrossed long black-clad legs and rose from the high-backed leather chair by the fire which had shielded his presence from Casey.

'I hope the disturbance which called you away is settled, Mr Strong,' their guest remarked.

Joe grinned. 'An incident with the half-wit I employ here. Some lads were bullying him. Cassandra was defending him.'

'What are you doing here, Mr Frost?' Casey cut in with astonishment. His lean features were highlighted by the gaslight and his hazel eyes glowed with pleasure as he regarded her.

He smiled, unabashed. 'We meet again, Miss Strong. And once again I find you defending the weak and vulnerable.'

'It was nothing.' Casey shrugged off the compliment. He had deliberately reminded her of the intimacy in the office that morning, and it caught her off guard.

peanuts purchased from Stumpy Will, the one-legged coster, whose patch was outside the Britannia, beside Paddy Murphy's whelk-and-cockle barrow.

The Britannia's lights were blazing on the street corner. They were a beacon in the thickening, murky fog. From inside someone was playing on a banjo and singing the popular song made famous by Harry Lauder, 'Roamin' in the Gloamin'. At the house entrance a gleaming Daimler was parked. Casey grimaced. One of those suspicious looking men must be in the pub. Several young boys stood on the running board and were peering into the windows. Casey shooed them away.

'And don't be sneaking back thinking you can filch anything off it,' she warned. 'I know all your names and my father does not allow his customers to be robbed.'

Only rarely was such a vehicle seen in these streets, unless passing through at a rapid pace. It disturbed her that her father had to mix with such men, whom he had known from his days on the boxing circuit. They were the leaders of the criminal underworld, running numerous protection rackets. Many ex-boxers became paid bully-boys to racketeers. Thank God her father had taken up the honest profession of publican.

Although her father had tried to protect her from the rougher elements of the Courtyard, she was too observant not to have caught the rumours and seen how the high mobsmen organised many of the youths into criminal gangs to steal for them. She suspected that they also organised much more unsavoury crimes. At least her father did not invite the high mobsmen into their home; it would have turned her stomach to be civil to men who were responsible for many of the young girls being lured into prostitution and the boys into thieving and later more violent crime.

The youths crowding around the alleyway opposite broke off from their game as a figure shuffled out of the thickening fog. One lad jeered.

'Cassandra!' her father rebuked. 'That's no way to greet a guest. Mr Frost is visiting all the pubs supplied by his father's brewery.'

'Doesn't a rep call every few months?' Her tone was suspicious. This meeting was no coincidence, she was certain.

Matthew Frost smiled engagingly, 'Usually that's so, but my father is recovering from an automobile accident. Since I have only a few weeks' leave from the Royal Flying Corps, I'm checking that everything is running smoothly and that we are meeting our orders. There were one or two legal matters also outstanding, hence my visit to Messrs Pinion and Son this morning.'

'You're an aviator?' Joe said, sounding impressed.

Despite Casey's reservations, she regarded their visitor with heightened interest. The few biplanes she had seen looked dangerous machines to trust one's life to.

Matthew Frost moved towards her and formally held out a hand. 'I was telling your father about our meeting this morning, and how delighted your employers are with your work.'

Her fingers were taken in a firm grip, and beneath their touch a tingle of awareness spread through her body. She removed her hand quickly, resenting that her body could respond in such a way to a mere handshake.

As though sensing her reaction, his smile lifted the corner of his lips. She stepped back, flustered. This could not be happening. Not again. Her attraction to James Hardcastle had been a warning. She had been naïve to believe his interest in her was honourable. She would not be so duped again.

'I've invited Mr Frost to dine with us this evening and he has accepted,' her father remarked.

He looked far too pleased with himself for Casey's peace of mind. Wasn't Matthew Frost just the type of suitor Joe wanted for her? She inwardly groaned. Joe's philosophy of life came from his boxing days; he didn't believe in pulling punches. Couldn't he see that they were being used by a rich man who was following a whim?

'Then I'd better start preparing the meal.' Her expression was closed as she nodded to Matthew Frost before leaving the room.

'Your daughter does not look very pleased that I'm staying,' she heard Matthew say. Out of their view on the landing, she paused to listen to his words. 'Perhaps I should leave. It's extra work for her. I had forgotten that your daughter started at the office early this morning.'

'I won't hear of you leaving,' Joe protested. 'Besides, her cousin will be home shortly. Casey is a wonderful cook and a chicken casserole in wine has been slowly cooking all day.'

'I smelt it as soon as I walked in,' Matthew Frost answered. 'I confess it smells delicious.'

Casey was furious at the way her father was praising her. She might as well be standing on an auction block with him selling her to the highest bidder. That's what it felt like. She was tempted to put too much pepper in the casserole, but she hated to spoil good food. She had seen too many starving children around here to ruin a meal out of vexation.

The sooner the meal was served the earlier Matthew Frost would leave. The succulent smell of herbs, wine and chicken had greeted her when she opened the street door and Eva had already peeled the potatoes and prepared the vegetables before leaving for work.

As she lit the gases under the saucepans, Casey frowned at seeing a basin covered with a muslin cloth on the back burner. It was a partially cooked Spotted Dick, her father's favourite steamed raisin and suet pudding. It only needed warming through. Sometimes Casey wished that her cousin was not so diligent in pleasing both her and her father. There was still the untouched treacle tart that she had made for Sunday tea which would have served just as well for tonight.

The front door banged shut and rapid footsteps on the stairs heralded Eva's arrival. When her cousin entered the kitchen, Casey caught a whiff of her own favourite perfume which Eva had also taken to wearing. She made a mental note to change the one she used. She had always felt that a perfume showed something of your individuality, and she resented the way Eva copied her. The thought was uncharitable. She should be pleased that her cousin took pains to better herself, but sometimes Eva tried too hard. Casey had always been self-assured in her abilities, but when Eva aped the way she dressed and now used the same perfume, she felt that she was losing some of her own identity.

'Who's with Uncle Joe?' Eva asked. 'I heard him talking to a man.'

'Matthew Frost. He's the son of the brewery owner who supplies the pub. Dad has invited him to have dinner with us.'

Eva looked displeased as she removed her straw boater and patted her upswept hair into place. 'I was hoping we could get out early to see the new Keystone Cops film. What's this bloke like?'

Casey kept her face averted as she basted the potatoes with lard and slid them into the oven to roast. 'Middle twenties. Rather good-looking in a rugged sort of way. You know the type. Charming, full of meaningless compliments.'

'He's made quite an impression on you.' There was an unpleasant edge to Eva's voice.

Casey eyed her sharply. 'Not at all. It's not the first time I've seen him. He was at the office today dealing with a legal matter.'

Eva rattled the gold-edged china plates she was taking down from the kitchen dresser. 'Don't you think that rather odd? You meet him at your work, then he turns up here. You must have taken his fancy. Didn't you learn anything after how Hardcastle treated you?'

'Don't jump to conclusions, Eva,' Casey snapped. 'He's here on business. When did Hardcastle ever put himself out to visit my home? If his intentions had been honourable, I realise now, he would have done.' At seeing the frown marring her cousin's lovely features, Casey amended, 'Mr Frost is here on business. His father is recovering from an automobile accident. He's checking that the brewery deliveries are running smoothly whilst on leave from the Royal Flying Corps.'

'A real toff then, ain't he?' Eva sneered. 'I suppose that was his posh jalopy outside?'

'It is!' Inexplicably Casey lost her temper with Eva. Too often she had allowed her comments to go without retaliation. Frequently she made excuses for her cousin's smothering affection because she had lost her family. But with each passing week, Eva was becoming more domineering and possessive of Casey's time. Casey was beginning to resent it. Eva's family had been dead for nearly four months. The time for making allowances was past.

'If I had an interest in Mr Frost then that would be my affair,' she retorted, her expression mutinous. 'Not yours, Eva. It's always the same. Whether we are at a dance, the tennis club, or out on a Sunday walk, you discourage any men from getting to know us. You say they've only got one thing on their mind. But many of them are perfectly respectable.' She struggled to keep her voice from rising as her anger mounted. 'I'm getting tired of your behaviour. I'd like a man to take me out for a change.'

Eva pursed her lips into a frigid line. 'Then don't let me stop you. Why don't you encourage this Mr Frost? He's obviously got your father's approval, or he wouldn't have invited the man to dine with us. Go out with him if he asks you. But don't come crying on my shoulder when he uses you then dumps you.'

'I just might do that,' Casey flung back. Eva's condemnation had angered her. She was tired of Eva always trying to inflict her opinions on her. Casey felt sorry for her cousin, but she was no longer going to allow Eva to manipulate her.

Her eyes blazing with a dangerous light, Casey finished the preparations for the meal. The table was set and she placed the pair of silver candelabra, each holding four candles, at opposite ends of the table. The tall, silver fruit-stand was positioned in the centre. Two small bowls of roses were placed beside the candelabra, and she folded the Irish linen napkins into water-lilies. The four cut-glass wine glasses reflected a prism of rainbow colours in the candlelight. When she stepped back she was satisfied that the table was looking at its best. Then she hurried down to tap on the bar door and ask Rusty to send up two bottles of her father's best wine. After that she went into her room to change.

It was defiance more than any intention to attract Matthew Frost that made her wear her newest gown. She wanted to show him that, although her father was a publican, their home was the equal of any middle-class citizen's.

She smiled at her reflection in the long cheval mirror. The pale turquoise watered-silk gown, with its scooped neckline and elbow-length sleeves trimmed with ivory lace, accentuated the creaminess of her skin. A five-string pearl choker was around her neck, the matching earrings were large tear-drop pearls which swayed against her neck as she moved. To complete the effect a wide silver and turquoise bracelet at her wrist was another defiant act to show Matthew Frost that they were not paupers.

'Gentlemen, dinner is ready,' she announced.

Her father raised a dark brow as he saw that she had changed, but there was a glimmer of approval in his eyes. As Matthew Frost turned to face her, his expression was of a man mesmerised. With a start he recovered himself.

'That is a lovely gown, Miss Strong, but not nearly as

lovely as the woman who is wearing it.'

'Aye, Cassandra has style,' Joe said, with pride ringing in his voice.

'Any man would be honoured to escort her.' Matthew bowed to Casey, his eyes sparkling with admiration. With a smile he turned to her father. 'I would like to ask your permission, Mr Strong, to dine with your daughter at the Savoy one evening, and perhaps take her to the theatre too.'

Joe squared his shoulders and ran his hand over his scarlet waistcoat to finger the lucky gold boxing-glove on his watch-chain. 'You have my permission, Mr Frost. That is, if Cassandra wishes to go.'

Put on the spot, Casey knew it would be difficult to refuse, even if she wanted to. The chaotic fluttering of her pulse made a nonsense of any wish to deny herself the pleasure of his company. Yet at the back of her mind was the unease of her experiences with James Hardcastle.

'I would be pleased to accept Mr Frost's invitation.'

'Then may I presume to be the one to lead you in to dine this evening?' Without waiting for anyone's approval, he took Casey's hand and placed it over his arm.

Eva, who had changed into a lilac and black striped dress with large leg-of-mutton sleeves, stood by the doorway, the low neckline revealing more cleavage than Casey thought modest. Giving only the briefest nod of acknowledgement to their guest, Eva swept forward to take Joe's arm with a proprietorial air.

'Looks like we must make the best of each other's company. Those two will have eyes for no one but each other.'

Casey glared at Eva. 'That comment was uncalled for.'

The false smile withered on Eva's lips and a brittle gleam shone in her eyes. 'Is it? I speak as I find.'

'You are embarrassing our guest, Eva,' Joe reprimanded sharply.

'Not at all,' Matthew Frost protested. 'You are a fortunate man, Mr Strong, to share your home with two beautiful women. My condolences, Miss Bowman, on the death of your parents.'

For a moment Casey feared that Eva was about to make a tart reply; then her expression changed and her smile was coquettish. 'I am fortunate to have such wonderful and caring relatives in Casey and Uncle Joe.'

To Casey's surprise her father's colour deepened. Obviously, Eva's display of affection was embarrassing him. He cleared his throat. 'The meal smells delicious, Casey. We mustn't let it spoil.'

Casey led the way into the dining room. Matthew Frost held out her chair at the opposite end of the table from her father and then seated himself to her right, facing Eva.

'How many pubs have you visited apart from the Britannia?' Eva asked pointedly as she served him a portion of the casserole from the Royal Doulton tureen which was part of the matching dinner service.

'This was the first.' He smiled at Casey.

'The other landlords did not have pretty daughters, presumably,' Eva commented.

'That's enough, Eva,' Joe broke in fiercely.

Matthew Frost laughed. 'I can see that Miss Bowman has seen through me. Having met Miss Strong this morning, I did want to get to know her better. But whilst my father is indisposed, I do have to ensure that our deliveries are not affected. I would have had to visit the Britannia within the next two weeks.'

'Yet you don't normally help run the brewery?' Casey tried to turn the conversation on to safer ground.

'No. I'm just helping out. Until last year I was at Oxford. Since then I have spent most of my time hanging around airfields. I'm fascinated by flight and I've always wanted to learn how to fly.' His voice throbbed with passion as he spoke, his expression animated.

'Flight has come a long way since the Wright Brothers conquered the air.' Casey fed his enthusiasm. 'Did you by any chance see Colonel Cody fly when he came over from America? He was the first man to take to the air in Britain, I believe.'

'Alas, no. Though I did see Louis Blériot's flight across the English Channel in 1909. It was from that moment that I knew I had to be an aviator.'

'It seems a precarious future for a young man,' Joe remarked. 'More fitting for an adventurer than a man of business. I'm not sure that I approve of Cassandra stepping out with you. We may live in a rough area, but she attended one of the best ladies' academies and has led a rather sheltered life.'

Casey blushed at her father's forthright speech.

'I have the greatest respect and admiration for your daughter, Mr Strong,' Matthew Frost said. Apparently he hadn't taken offence. 'As the youngest of three sons, I intend to make my own way in the world. My eldest brother inherits the brewery and runs the sales office. He is currently setting up a second brewery in the Midlands to expand our production and delivery. My other brother is absorbed with the manufacturing side. His pet project is trying to create an entirely different type of beer, though he has yet to succeed to his satisfaction. He's in Germany at the moment, studying their methods of production. Their beer is very different to ours. That's why I'm on leave. Mama thought it time I healed the breach with my father. He was furious when I declared I wanted nothing to do with the brewery.'

'Though its wealth enabled you to indulge your passion for flight,' Eva commented sourly, 'and provided you with a fancy automobile.'

A muscle throbbed along his jaw. 'The car is my father's.' He paused and looked pointedly at Casey. Her heart snatched.

From his expression it seemed important to him that she understood his actions.

'Contrary to your beliefs, Miss Bowman,' he went on smoothly, 'my father was so displeased when I refused to join the brewery that he cut off my allowance. I worked at the airfield to pay for my flying lessons. I also assisted the mechanics. I already knew the workings of the motor-car engine from helping out in the company garage from an early age. Engines have always fascinated me. Our brewery was one of the first to change to motor vehicles. I can now repair a plane as well as any flight engineer.'

Casey smiled, relieved he was not a spoilt rich man who'd had everything he wanted handed to him on a plate. She respected his ability to work for what he wanted. She cut in quickly before Eva could voice another tart observation. 'You sound as though you enjoyed the experience. Flying is clearly important to you, but isn't flying very dangerous?'

'It's exhilarating. A wonderful experience. Perhaps I can persuade you to fly with me.'

Vivid heat rushed to Casey's cheeks. 'I don't know . . .'

'Not scared, are you?' His hazel eyes sparkled with devilry as he taunted her.

Her head came up. 'No, I'm not scared.'

'Cassandra ain't scared of nothing,' Joe praised. 'Tonight proved that when she defended Archie. She's a plucky woman. I always wanted the best for her, but it hasn't been easy for her. The posh little madams at the academy turned their noses up when they learned she were a publican's daughter.'

'I've never been ashamed of that, Dad,' Casey assured him.

Joe raised his wine glass to her. 'I know, Princess. That's what makes you so special.'

Eva sighed dramatically. 'The Strong Mutual Appreciation Society is now in session.'

Joe glowered at her. To ease the tension that was building,

Casey smiled at their guest. 'Flying obviously means a lot to you, Mr Frost.'

'I feel very privileged to be part of the Royal Flying Corps. In time I intend to acquire my own fleet of planes carrying passengers and freight.' He laughed softly. 'The sky is indeed the limit for anyone with vision to invest in flight.'

Joe nodded thoughtfully. 'It's not so long ago that men were mocking the automobile as never being capable of replacing the horse for transport. Now they are everywhere, and the horse-drawn vehicle is in decline. Many of the manufacturers and transport-company owners are on their way to being millionaires. The same could happen to any industry connected with flight.'

'You'd not get me up in one of those devil's machines.' Eva shuddered with horror. 'If God meant us to fly he'd have given us wings.'

'Nonsense,' Casey parried, refusing to allow Eva to ridicule Matthew Frost's ambition. 'God gave us the intelligence to make our own means of flight.'

Her father and Matthew laughed, lifting their glasses in a silent toast to her. Eva was stiff-faced as she ignored them and concentrated on her food.

Casey had been rather disturbed to learn that Matthew Frost was a younger son, as James Hardcastle had been. He may have asked her father's permission to take her out, but had he felt obliged because of Joe's reputation as a fighter? Somehow he did not look the kind of man to be intimidated by her father's ability to use his fists; he had an air about him which conveyed that he was capable of handling himself in a fight. Yet the unease remained about his motives. Was he toying with convention? A man who approached the father formally, as Matthew Frost had done, would normally be regarded as having honourable intentions. Dare she hope that they were?

Affected by the admiration in his gaze, she wanted to trust

him. She liked the way he had not taken offence at Eva's rudeness. Spending time in his company would be enjoyable, but after her experience with Hardcastle, she must be careful not to allow her emotions to run away with themselves.

The rest of the meal passed in a blur for Casey. Matthew Frost was clearly at home at their table. He was interested in her father's boxing career and seemed to know a great deal about the sport. He named several of the fights her father had won.

'I was there when you pasted Kid O'Keefe,' he enthused as they sat over their coffee. 'You laid him out cold thirty seconds into the second round.'

'You're too young to remember that,' Joe said, though he was smiling broadly. 'That was back in 1904.'

'I was fourteen. As a birthday treat my brother took me to the fight. I've never forgotten it. You retired the following year and I was devastated.'

Casey did a quick calculation: that made him twenty-three.

Joe gave a crack of laughter. 'I was beginning to feel the punches and I'd been lucky. Cassandra's mother never liked me boxing after I'd bought the pub. I enjoyed the fame and fortune so I carried on. But there comes a time when your age eventually catches up with you. Besides, it's better to quit whilst you're still at the top.'

Eva giggled, her mood lightening as the conversation turned to Casey's father. 'You've got more stamina than many men half your age, Uncle Joe.'

Casey glanced at her cousin. She was used to Eva praising her father, but she did lay it on thick at times. Joe abruptly downed the remainder of his wine and stood up to bring the brandy decanter and box of cigars to the table.

Casey also rose. 'We'll leave you to your brandy and cigars.'

With Eva's help she cleared the table of the remaining dishes and, plunging them into the hot soapy water, began to wash them vigorously. 'How could you be so rude to our guest, Eva?'

'I wasn't.'

'Yes, you were. And don't say you don't know how to behave with dinner guests, because you do. Your comments embarrassed Mr Frost.'

'So you *have* taken a shine to him!'

Casey rounded on her, her eyes flashing dangerously. 'What if I have? I respect the way he became a flight engineer to pay for his flying lessons.'

'But he's a toff.'

'That's enough, Eva,' Casey warned. 'I like him. If I want to go out with him I will.'

Eva flounced from the kitchen and ran up the second flight of stairs to slam her bedroom door. Casey sighed. Sometimes Eva could be impossible. She returned to the parlour and found Mr Frost alone.

'Have you been deserted?'

He smiled at her. 'The barman called Joe down because a fight had broken out in the bar. He said he'd only be a few minutes. I can't see anybody getting one over on Joe Strongarm.'

'It pleased him that you knew so much about his fights,' Casey observed. From outside the pub rose a stream of obscene and very graphic verbal abuse from the troublemaker her father had just thrown out. She blushed with embarrassment.

'Would you like to see Father's trophies, Mr Frost?' she suggested in order to escape the obscenities carrying to them from the street.

'Very much indeed.'

'They're in Dad's den, as we call it.'

As they stepped out on to the landing, Joe appeared at the head of the stairs.

'Mr Frost would like to see your trophies,' she explained.

Joe grinned. 'Then you won't miss me while I relieve Rusty

so he can have his break. Go along with Cassandra, Mr Frost. No need for you to rush off.'

Casey inwardly groaned at her father's blatant behaviour. Had he carried a placard announcing that he approved of him as a suitor for his daughter, it could not have been more obvious that he was pushing them together.

Embarrassed, Casey led the way into the small back room where her father kept his trophies. To maintain propriety she kept the door open. When she turned up the gaslamp it illuminated four large posters with her father's name emblazoned in red at the top. One wall was dominated by a large glass display cabinet holding the fifty-four silver cups and shields in all shapes and sizes that her father had won.

Matthew Frost whistled softly, clearly impressed. 'Your father must be quite a celebrity in these parts.'

'As was my mother.' She told him briefly about her mother, and his eyes widened with interest. She wanted him to know about her background and also that she was proud of her parents' achievements. She needed to gauge his reaction.

'From such parents it's no wonder that you're such an exceptional woman.'

Casey regarded him warily, wishing that her heart would not beat so fast. She could feel her attraction for him growing with each hour they spent together. Yet her fascination for him disquieted her. She was not about to be made a fool of by a member of his class a second time. To avoid the possibility of any misunderstanding, she would force him to be honest with her.

'Mr Frost, I'm not sure how you do things in the circle in which you move, but for you to have asked my father for permission to take me out . . .' She faltered, her face flaming, so that she finished in a rush. 'Well . . . my father could have taken it the wrong way. He could believe that you are interested in me in a more serious way. And we both know that would not be feasible.'

He cocked his head to one side, regarding her sardonically. 'What do you mean? Do you suspect that my intentions aren't honourable?'

'We only met this morning. Our circumstances are vastly different.' She walked away from him to stand by an oil painting of her father in scarlet boxing shorts, his fists raised in a traditional fighting pose.

'I'm a younger son, my only prospects are those I create for myself. What is this nonsense you are talking? From the moment we met I knew I had to get to know you better. And everything tonight has confirmed that instinct. I have known enough women to realise when the right one comes into my life. You are the woman I intend to marry.'

A slow handclap came from the doorway. 'Now that's a new line,' Eva taunted.

Casey rounded on her cousin. 'How dare you eavesdrop? How dare you insult a guest in my father's house?' She shut the door firmly in Eva's shocked face and leaned against it, breathing heavily. She was shaking with the force of her fury.

'I'm so sorry, Mr Frost. I don't know why Eva is acting that way. What she said is unforgivable.'

'And what I said, Miss Strong, is that unforgivable also?'

She turned her head away, unable to meet his piercing stare.

Matthew caught his breath. She was stunningly lovely. Her anger enhanced the seductive smokiness in her grey eyes. As she fought to control her temper, the swell of her breasts rose and fell beneath the thin silk of her gown. He had never felt such intensity of desire. Aware that she was more embarrassed than himself by her cousin's outburst, he closed the gap between them and gently took her arm.

'I did mean what I said. You must think I'm mad. I've only known you for a few hours, and here I am pouring my heart out in a way I have never done to a woman before. I'm bewitched. Besotted. And quite irrevocably in love with you.'

Her stare was searching as she lifted her gaze to regard him. He saw her swallow, her voice becoming a whisper. 'You don't know me at all.'

'I know you more than you suspect. Both your employers and your father have told me much about your kindness of spirit and generous nature. I have seen for myself your beauty and your sense of humour. Also your courage in facing matters head-on.' His eyes twinkled with an engaging light. 'But I don't expect you to feel as I do, that would be presumptuous.'

Each word wrapped around her resolution, destroying by its promise the barriers she would erect between them. But were they a subtle trap to ensnare the unwary? She battled to maintain her guard by resorting to brutal honesty.

'I know what men in your position think of the women from this part of London. I'm not like that. I will not become your mistress. I have too much respect for myself for that. I will give myself to no man other than my husband.'

He was clearly taken aback by her words. Then his smile broadened to an intimacy which set her pulse capering. 'I never suspected otherwise. Your honesty is part of your charm. You do not dissemble. You are an unusual and remarkable woman. Will you accompany me to the theatre on Friday evening?'

It was impossible to resist him. 'I'd be delighted to.'

She could hear Eva banging saucepans as she put them away in the kitchen.

Matthew Frost looked over her shoulder in the direction of the noise. 'I have overstayed my welcome. It's late and I know you've had a long and busy day. Until Friday. I shall pick you up at seven-thirty.'

Casey escorted Matthew Frost to the door. Outside the fog had thickened, but it was still possible to see the end of the street.

'Take care. The fog can be treacherous.'

'I would face far more than fog to hear the note of concern in your voice.'

She laughed with exasperation. 'You've got more blarney than the Irish, Mr Frost.'

'Isn't it time you called me Matt? I do have your father's permission to call on you.'

'Goodnight . . . Matt,' she said, her teasing smile turning to a hastily stifled yawn. When she looked at her watch, she was shocked to see that it was nearly eleven. How quickly the time had flown in his company.

He placed his Homburg hat at a rakish angle on his head and smiled. 'Goodnight . . . Casey.'

The sound of her name was a blatant caress. She was pleased he had used the softer short form of her name, instead of the more formal Cassandra. A glow of happiness spread through her as she closed the door and heard the engine of his automobile crank into life.

Upstairs, Eva noisily continued to tidy the kitchen. A broom banged against the skirting board and Casey sighed. Her cousin's attitude was not to be tolerated.

She confronted Eva in the kitchen. She was scrubbing the kitchen table, her face frigid with anger.

'Gone, has he?' Eva asked scornfully. 'Good riddance.'

'I'm going to bed, Eva. I shall be seeing more of Matthew. If you are not prepared to be polite when he calls, then just ensure that you're not here when he does.'

Eva dropped the brush with a clatter and burst into loud sobs. 'Forgive me, Casey. I've acted badly. I just don't trust that man. He's another Hardcastle. I don't want to see you hurt.'

'I will choose my own friends and make my own mistakes,' she said pointedly. 'I think you are wrong about Matt. He's not arrogant like James was and he's fun to be with.'

'All I want is your happiness. He's ambitious. Where will

he get the money to start his own company, if not from marrying a wealthy heiress?' Eva dabbed at her eyes with a handkerchief. The powder and light rouge she had put on her cheeks was smeared across her face as the tears fell faster and louder.

Casey's anger subsided at the evidence of her cousin's distress. 'Don't spoil it for me, Eva. Matt is different. And I'm no longer so naïve as I once was.'

'Then you forgive me?' Eva pleaded.

At Casey's nod, she threw her arms around her. 'You are my dearest friend. Don't shut me out now you have Matthew Frost calling on you.'

So that was why Eva was playing up. She was scared of being abandoned. Casey shook her head. 'I will never do that. Isn't what we have special? Cousins together, through thick and thin – sharing joy and adversity. We'll always be there for each other, Eva. No man can come between us in that way.'

'No they won't, will they?' Eva released her and dried her eyes. 'I couldn't bear to lose you, Casey. You don't know what it's like suddenly finding yourself an orphan. Your world has no foundations, nothing solid to build on. I'm so scared of losing your friendship, I act stupidly. I'm jealous and insensitive, I know, but it's only because I care.'

Casey thought she understood. She had been devastated when her mother died. Eva had lost her entire immediate family. Was it any wonder that she was over-possessive at times? Casey rubbed her brow where a headache was forming. She might understand why Eva acted as she did, but there was something about her behaviour tonight which was disquieting. What it was she couldn't analyse.

Chapter Nine

Eva turned down the parlour gaslights and tightened the belt of her dressing gown. The drone of voices from the bar had faded and she heard Rusty call out 'Goodnight' as he entered the street.

She stretched her legs along the length of the chaise longue and imagined Joe throwing the bolts on the street door of the public bar, then walking through the now empty bar-room, turning out lamps and picking up any empty beer glasses. Perhaps even now he was folding a linen glass-cloth and hanging it over the brass beer pumps before pushing open the door to ascend the stairs. She waited expectantly for the sound of his footfall. Ten minutes later she was still waiting.

It wasn't like Joe to hang around in the bar after it was closed. She hesitated to move from the chaise longue. Posed as she was, she made a provocative picture, and that was how she had wanted Joe to find her. Casey had retired half an hour ago after returning from dining with Matthew Frost. It was their eighth date, and Casey was besotted with the man. Eva could feel her hold over her cousin slipping. It had strengthened her resolve to make Joe dependent upon her. Tonight she was determined that he would not ignore her.

She pouted as she glowered at the door. Why hadn't he come upstairs? Could he have been taken ill . . .?

Anxious now, she abandoned her seductive pose and hurried

to the bar. Through the glass portion of the door she saw a dim light. Pushing open the door, she halted, puzzled to find Joe seated at a table, staring into a large brandy goblet. Unaware of her presence, he drained the glass and poured another large drink into it.

'Joe, what's wrong?' She came forward, her voice soft and caressing. 'Have you had bad news?'

He sighed and pushed back his bowler, his fingers ruffling his dark hair, his body tense. 'Why aren't you in bed, Eva? It's gone midnight.'

'I was waiting for you. As I always do.' His words were like a slap in the face. It was nearly a month since Joe had taken her to his bed. Yet often she had turned swiftly and caught him looking at her. The hastily averted gaze told her that he still desired her.

She was exasperated at the morality that was making him hold back. What angered her most was that on several occasions she had seen him leave the pub at closing time with Bertha. She had lain awake listening for his return. It was never until dawn. How she longed to scratch that bitch Bertha's eyes out for taking Joe away from her. But she dared not show her antagonism in too obvious a manner. Bertha was too knowing. There wasn't much that bitch missed. Eva might want to control Joe by being his mistress, but she knew their relationship must remain a secret.

For that reason alone she swallowed her anger at Joe's visits to Bertha. The slut had her uses. Casey knew of Joe's visits to the barmaid and had accepted them. Eva doubted Casey would view the way her cousin had seduced her father in so charitable a light. Therefore Bertha must remain just a convenience to Joe. It was she, Eva, who would rule his emotions.

'Do you hate me, Joe? Do you think I'm cheap because of what happened? Or did I displease you?' She sank to her knees at his feet, her eyes pleading as she turned her face up to him.

'Damnit, Eva, you know that's not so.' He gripped her arm. 'But it were wrong. You're me niece.'

'It's not wrong. I love you, Joe. I don't want no one else. I want you.' She wound her arms around him and kissed him passionately. When she drew back, he was breathing heavily. 'I've missed you so much.'

Her fingers were experienced as she unbuttoned his fly and closed over the hardness of him. She opened her robe. Under it she wore a white satin corset which pushed her large breasts high and revealed the hardened buds of her nipples in the cool night air. She wore nothing else but black stockings held up with red garters.

Kneeling, she rubbed her breasts against his straining manhood. As his breathing quickened her head moved down, first teasing it with the soft tresses of her hair, then her tongue flickering and circling its tip until he groaned aloud. Triumphantly, she rose up to straddle his hips and lower herself on to him.

Each thrust of her hips was calculated to give him pleasure. She was detached from her actions, watching him through half-closed lashes. The tempo of her breathing deepened and, as he stroked her breasts and buttocks, she gasped and writhed ecstatically. When his face contorted with the explosion of his passion, she continued to move over him, prolonging his pleasure. He cried out in fulfilment, his fingers digging deep into her flesh, her own moans muffled by her passionate kisses as she bit into his shoulder.

His arms were tight around her, holding her over him as his breathing slowed.

'Joe, oh Joe. You're a wonderful lover. Did I give you pleasure?'

His expression was haunted as he opened his eyes to gaze into hers. 'It was more than good, Eva,' he said tautly. 'But . . .'

She cupped his face in her hands and kissed him ardently.

'No buts . . . I want you, Joe, and you want me. That's how it is. And it will be our secret. I'll always be here for you, Joe. Casey may marry and move away, but I never will. Not while you need me.'

There was a flicker of wariness in his eyes. Had she pushed too hard, been too vehement in declaring her devotion? She had to keep the upper hand. She was not going to allow him to reject her. Rising from his lap, she retied her robe and smiled enticingly. 'I know we have to be careful, Joe. And I'm not asking for any commitments. Or for you to give up other women. Bertha is our protection from anyone guessing our secret. I could never love another man as I love you, Joe.'

Having said all she intended, she left the bar before he could comment.

Joe watched her leave. Now that his passion had ebbed, he rubbed a hand across his brow. He had not intended to allow her to seduce him again. Eva was a dangerous woman. He did not believe her protestations of love, he was too worldly for that. But her youth and beauty flattered his pride. It felt good to have a young woman eager to pander to him, especially one who was so experienced in satisfying a man. But he did not trust her.

He shook his head and grinned despite his reservations. Eva was a scheming baggage, but she sure knew how to fuck. Even thinking of the way her mouth moved over him made him want her again. His hand shook as he refilled his brandy glass and downed it in a single gulp. The spirit was liquid fire in his throat, recalling him to his senses. If his plans for Cassandra's future went ahead, she would soon be married. He was a passionate man; the thought of Eva living with him, loving him, was a powerful temptation to overcome. He must tread with caution. Eva needed to be brought to heel.

First, he must get Cassandra settled. She was seeing Matt Frost regularly and he expected the man to propose to her. A pity he had to return to his duties with the Royal Flying Corps in a few days. He could have wished Frost had a more stable income than from flying, but he was ambitious. Matt Frost would go places – he knew the type. Beneath his charming veneer there was a ruthless streak.

Joe did not doubt that Cassandra could win Frost's family over. How could they fail to be charmed by his princess? Then, once won over, they would put up the cash to help support the couple when they married.

He frowned. In the meantime he could not risk the Frost family looking down their noses at Cassandra. He had begun negotiations to buy a second pub close to Covent Garden. He could afford it. For years he had been fencing high quality jewellery, and there was no need to lose his connections in that trade. The rooms above the new pub were larger than those here and the address eminently more respectable.

'How much longer are you going to hold out on me, my darling?' Matt demanded when he switched off the engine of the Daimler outside the Britannia.

They had seen a show and dined in the West End. The street was dark and he parked out of the ray of light from the bar-room windows. He drew Casey to him and kissed her ardently. His kisses, as usual, wove their magic, spiralling her emotions until they took wing to create a timeless aura of sensuality, a luminous interlacing of sensations which pulsated through and around her. When he caressed her breast, through the silk of her gown, she moaned softly. Her body demanded more, but her mind shrank from permitting further intimacies.

'We've only known each other three months,' Casey said softly, removing his hand from her breast. 'And for six of those weeks you've been away.'

'The Royal Flying Corps is a hard taskmaster when it comes to duty. I've missed you so much.' His lips were against her throat, the soft wafting of his breath and lips causing ripples of delight to spread through her body. Her heart was beating wildly, but still she strove to be wise and rational. Matt was becoming more demanding at the end of each evening they spent together.

'Say you'll marry me,' he whispered. 'We'll become engaged at Christmas; that's only three weeks away, and I'll be on home leave again.'

'Oh, Matt, do you mean it?' Casey stared at him in wonder. 'But what of your parents? They'll never agree.'

'When you meet them you will bowl them over.' He stroked her cheek. 'I want you so much, Casey.' His kiss was possessive, his hands sliding over her hips and lifting the hem of her skirt until his hand rested on her knee.

'No, Matt.' Casey wrenched her mouth free. She pushed his hand away, her eyes flashing with accusation as she fought to control the raggedness of her breathing.

He pulled back from her and stared out of the window. In the near total darkness she could hear his harsh expulsion of breath, his tension palpable in the confined space. 'We're going to be engaged, aren't we? Don't be a tease, Casey.'

'Tease, is it?' she flared. 'You're the one who keeps trying it on. I told you from the start I'm not that sort of woman. I thought you respected me.'

Her voice caught. She loved Matt. Couldn't he see that she wanted him, that to deny him was just as frustrating for herself. She swallowed against the cramping ache in her throat. He didn't care. His words of love were false. They were just a ruse to get her to have sex with him.

She opened the car door and stepped on to the pavement. 'Clearly our ideas of love are different. If sex is all you're after, then you'd better find yourself someone who is more obliging.'

She slammed the door shut and dived into her handbag for

her doorkey. Tears blinded her eyes and it was several moments before she could find the lock. Her heart ached with disappointment. She had thought Matt different from James Hardcastle. He was just the same.

As the key turned and the door swung open, Matt put his hand on her shoulder. 'I'm sorry, Casey. Forgive me.'

She glanced sideways at him, still wary and distrustful. 'It won't work, Matt. I think it's best if we don't see each other any more.'

'You don't mean that,' he said softly.

Her face was turned up to him, and in the light from the corner gaslamp he saw the tears glittering on her lashes. Her beauty and innocence smote him. He wanted her so fiercely, but she was stubborn. No one had yet stopped him from achieving what he wanted. Even his father had been unable to prevent him becoming an aviator. What he wanted, he prided himself, he achieved. Casey was testing his patience to the limit of his endurance. It wasn't that he didn't respect her. He loved her. And if she loved him, then especially coming from her background, he could not believe she meant to deny him.

'We love each other, Casey. Isn't it natural I get carried away when I hold you in my arms? We'll get engaged at Christmas and married as soon as we can.' He reasoned, 'I'd wed you next week if I had the money. But I have to think of the future – our future. First I have to get a plane and get my business going. I thought you understood.'

'I do, Matt. But how can you talk of our future – of us getting engaged – when I haven't even met your family? Or don't they think a publican's daughter is good enough for the brewery owner's son?'

How true Casey's words were. Matt had lost count of the arguments he'd had with his mother about letting Casey come to tea one Sunday. But he would never let Casey know that.

He had won his mother around as he always did. But her agreement had been reluctant.

He smiled to dispel any fears Casey might be harbouring. 'Until now Pa has been suffering severe headaches as a result of his accident. There has been no entertaining at our house. But they've invited you to tea on Sunday.' He took her arms, rubbing his thumbs in lazy circles over their flesh, the pressure warming through the thickness of her coat. 'Doesn't that prove that they want to get to know you?'

Casey sighed. Her anger had cooled beneath his persuasion, but her reservations remained. 'That silver tongue of yours must have been working overtime.' Her smile counteracted the sting in her words. 'From what you've told me of your parents, it's obvious you are your mother's favourite. She can deny you nothing. But will she condone you marrying a publican's daughter?'

'No one can stop me marrying you. Once my mother has met you she will adore you. Pa will be charmed too.' There was impatience in his voice and his warm breath caressed her neck. 'I can't stop wanting you, Casey, but it's only because I love you.'

He kissed her with a thoroughness that devastated her senses. His foot propped the door open and he drew her out of the street, away from prying eyes and into the privacy of the hallway. The supple warmth of his mouth moving expertly over hers sent her senses spiralling. Their pressure was demanding and her lips parted, tasting the sweetness of his breath. Caught up in the turmoil of the emotions he aroused, she clung to him. The promise of the sensual pleasure evoked by the message in his lips kindled a craving deep within her, and her blood was afire.

When they broke apart, Casey swayed against him and laid her head against his chest.

'I do love you so much, Matt. But I fear you're wrong about

your family. What if they disapprove? Do you intend to tell them on Sunday about our engagement?'

His hesitation was barely perceptible, but Casey, attuned to his moods, sensed it. It made her draw back. 'Let's leave things as they are for a while,' she insisted. 'What's the rush for us to get engaged? Most couples court for three or four years before they marry.'

'I love you, Casey,' he murmured against her ear. 'My sweet love. I've no intention of waiting so long to make you mine.'

'Oh, Matt, the waiting is not any easier for me. But I don't want anyone saying that we had to get married.' She knew that she should pull away from him before his caresses became bolder, but she was held captive by the joy his words evoked, and the magic of the spell he was weaving around her senses. Then, hearing a footfall on the landing above, they moved guiltily apart.

'Is that you, Casey?' Eva called. 'I've been so worried. You're not usually this late.'

'We lingered over our coffee in the restaurant,' Casey responded. 'I'm just saying goodnight to Matt. I'll be up in a moment.'

'I'll make you hot chocolate. Don't let it get cold.'

Matt let out his breath harshly. 'Is she always that bossy? She sounds more like a mother than a cousin who is near enough your own age.'

'It's just her way,' Casey defended, but she was annoyed at Eva's proprietorial manner.

He kissed her again with deepening insistence. Casey yielded. This time she did not push aside his hand as it closed over her breast, nor when it moved lower to caress her buttocks and draw her against his arousal. The touch of him ignited her own desire, her frustration matching his as their hips ground together.

With a choked sound she pulled back and whispered, 'Matt,

this is madness. Dad could come upon us. I think you'd better go.'

'One more kiss, Casey. It has been three weeks since I last saw you.'

'And in all that time you never wrote.'

'I'm a lover, not a writer,' he quipped. 'I've never been one for letter-writing, but for you I'll try harder. Besides, actions speak louder than words.'

He kissed her again and when Casey broke free she was breathless. 'It's just as well you can't get away from the airfield more often. If you did I would fear for my virtue.'

In the glow of the gaslight from the top of the stairs, she saw his grin. 'That's how it should be between lovers.'

Her lids seemed weighted with lead as she raised them to encounter his gaze. His stare bored deep into hers, the darkly ringed irises of his eyes smouldered with emotion. She held her breath as almost imperceptibly their bodies moved closer.

'Casey, your chocolate is ready,' Eva called.

Matt frowned and swallowed with apparent difficulty. 'I'd better go. We can't talk properly here. Until tomorrow at three, when I'll pick you up for tea with my parents.'

Brief though the touch of his lips was on hers, they caused her heart to ache with longing. Gradually the wild tempo of her heart stilled as she watched him crank the Daimler's engine into life and, with a wave, drive away. Already she missed him. The insidious yearning spreading through her body could no longer be denied. One by one the barriers she had erected against him had been peeled away until her heart was exposed and vulnerable. She loved Matthew Frost. If she wasn't careful, all her other resolutions about keeping him at bay would also be discarded.

Yet the joy of loving Matt was tinged with despair. She could not shake off the premonition that his parents would disapprove of their marriage. That love and happiness with

Matthew would be an impossible dream.

Matthew was appalled as he led Casey into the living room of his home to see that it was filled with people. This was supposed to be a small Sunday tea, with just his parents and his brothers and their wives. He had not expected the entire family to arrive in force. Even the formidable Great-Aunt Ethel was present. She was ensconced on the sofa next to Grandma Enid, and both women were studying Casey through their lorgnettes. These matriarchs had intimidated Matt in his youth. He still felt uncomfortable when their judgemental eyes fell upon him as they did now. But worse than their presence was that of Aunt Millicent and the young woman to whom she was guardian. Clementine sat stiff-backed at Millicent's side, her eyes downcast.

Anger bubbled in him. Aunt Millicent had been angling for years to throw him and Clementine together. He was aware that both Great-Aunt Ethel and Grandma Enid approved of the match. Even his mother had stated her preference for Clementine as a daughter-in-law. Clementine came into a fortune of five thousand a year when she married. But that was all she had to offer as far as Matt was concerned. She could not help being plain, but did she also have to be so boring and timid? What little personality she possessed had long ago been squashed by Millicent's domineering manner.

'May I present to you all Miss Cassandra Strong,' he said smoothly, careful to conceal his anger. If Clementine had been dragged along to remind him of his family's expectations, then they were about to realise that he would not have his life dictated to him. 'Miss Strong is the woman I have asked to marry me. Unfortunately, I have yet to get her to agree.'

Casey blushed scarlet. The aunts gasped with shock. For the first time that he could remember, his mother was lost for words. And his father's eyes blazed with fury.

There was a muffled sob from Clementine, who bolted from the chair and ran from the room. That saddened him. He had not meant to wound her feelings. He had not realised that Clementine may have wished for their marriage.

Casey was conscious of the shock and resentment in the room. Her pride came to her rescue. She tilted her head, meeting every condemning stare with the courage of a matador facing a charging bull. A plump, middle-aged woman, overdressed in a diamanté-studded sapphire dress which was better suited to an evening soirée, tutted angrily as she hurried after her ward. Drawing level with Matthew, the woman glared at Casey, though her speech was at her nephew.

'How could you be so cruel? You've just broken the girl's heart.'

'Matthew, you could have had more tact,' his mother said stiffly, her high colour showing her agitation. 'You've embarrassed both Clementine and your guest.'

She rose from her chair with a rustle of rose silk and extended a hand to Casey. At her imperious manner, Casey felt almost compelled to bob a curtsy, but controlled it and took the cool fingers. They were retracted immediately, as though their owner feared contamination.

'Matt has spoken so much about you, Miss Strong,' his mother added. 'Sit here next to me.' She sat down and patted a high-backed chair beside her. It was an order, not a request.

Casey smiled nervously. Sybil Frost was a head shorter than herself. Her hair was the colour of polished steel and, from her rigid stance, her body could have been encased in the same metal. The thin lips drew into a caricature of a smile, but ice dripped from her pale hazel eyes. Frost by name, Frost by nature, thought Casey as she made to obey the woman's instructions.

Matt stopped her movement. 'Casey and I will sit on the

window-seat. I brought her here to take tea with us, not be put on parade.'

'We are all aware of your droll humour, Matthew,' his mother replied. 'You have told us so much about Miss Strong, I should be disappointed not to have this chance to speak to her without having to shout across the room.'

Aware of the underlying tension, Casey decided it was easier to comply with Sybil Frost's wishes. She smiled at Matt and sat down beside his mother.

'I will introduce you to our family, Miss Strong. You will forgive my husband for not rising – his recent accident, you understand.'

'Yes, Matt told me.' She smiled at Edward Frost, whose mouth was indented with lines of pain.

His expression was dour. 'If you think to wed Matt for his money, you may as well know now that he hasn't any.'

'I have no need to wed for money, Mr Frost. My father will provide a comfortable dowry for me when I marry. Wealth does not interest me.'

'You can't get on in this life without money,' Sybil Frost declared. 'But then brought up in the Courtyard you'll be used to mixing with the uneducated and the unwashed. Their needs are small.'

The deliberate insult brought a fire to Casey's eyes. Inside she burned with indignation. 'I have never been allowed to mix with the people from the Courtyard. Though within their poverty-ridden homes a guest is always treated hospitably. And it is from people like them that some of your family's income is earned, supporting your life of luxury.'

Matt cut in tersely, his eyes dark with anger at the rudeness of his mother. 'The Britannia is not within the Courtyard. The street is a respectable one, mostly of shopowners.' He turned to his brother. 'Peter, you remember taking me to see Joe "Strongarm" Strong fight. He is a remarkable man.'

Peter nodded, but Matt's other brother sneered, 'A common boxer. Can't say I approve of grown men pummelling each other into a pulp.'

Casey bristled at this further insult directed at her father's career. 'My father rose from nothing to be a legend in his own lifetime. I think that's a great achievement.'

'That's enough of your sarcasm, Humphrey,' Matt flared.

'I am proud of my father.' Casey looked directly at Edward Frost as she spoke. The expression in his eyes changed. They were no longer condemning, and if she hadn't been so sure he disapproved of her, she might have thought there was a glimmer of admiration in those uncompromising depths.

'Your young lady has the courage to speak her mind,' Mr Frost commented. 'At least that's something. I can't abide sycophants.'

Matt winked at Casey, but by now she was feeling miserable despite her outward display of calm. She could not help glancing at the gilt French clock which sat under a glass dome on the mantelshelf. Had she only been here ten minutes? It felt like forever.

Sybil Frost gestured to Matt's brothers. 'These are my other sons, Humphrey and Peter. The brewery could not run without them. I am fortunate that at least two of my sons see their responsibility to their family. Matt has had his head filled with aeroplanes. I worry so about him.'

'Matt's a very resourceful man. He's quite capable of taking charge of his own future,' Casey replied, as defensive towards Matt as she was towards her own family and background. The atmosphere in the room was charged, everyone's manner stiff, their stilted speech showing their tension, as Millicent and Clementine returned.

'You've formed that impression having known him only three months.' The woman's eyes gleamed with malice. 'Whilst I his mother don't know him at all, I suppose.'

Casey did not comment.

Mrs Frost continued haughtily, 'I know him better than you. We had such hopes that he might start his own flight charter business. Marriage will put an end to that.'

Casey stiffened. 'Matthew is ambitious, and flight is the industry of the future. Besides, it is not as though we intend to wed for some time.'

The sigh of relief was audible from the older woman, but her manner did not alter. 'It still takes capital to get started. He'll not get a penny if he marries without our permission. I have to be honest and say that it was understood that he would wed Clementine. She is worth five thousand a year.'

'That has always been wishful thinking on the part of you and Aunt Millicent,' Matt cut in explosively. 'I am going to marry Cassandra. Now can we drop the subject? Or would you rather we both left the house? In which case I will not return.'

From the way that Mrs Frost lowered her gaze and breathed heavily, Casey knew that it was not the first time Matt had used that threat. So that was how he had got his family to agree to meet her. No wonder they hated her. She didn't want to cause a rift between Matt and his family. Each of the women was eyeing Casey with the same hostile glare.

She stood up. 'Matt, will you please have my coat brought to me? I will not stay where I am not welcome.'

She walked to the door. Edward Frost's voice rang out. 'Please Miss Strong, accept our apologies. Matt's announcement of your intended engagement was a shock to us. But that does not excuse our conduct.' He directed a meaningful glance at his wife, his raised eyebrow making her purse her lips in resentment.

'Please do not leave, Miss Strong,' she said in a voice which could have cracked a mirror.

Casey guessed at the effort that speech had cost Mrs Frost. She retraced her steps and Matt took her arm possessively, guiding her towards the oldest woman in the room. 'Allow me to complete the introductions. This is Grandma Enid.'

Grey, lashless eyes in a wrinkled face regarded her. 'You're no mealy-mouse, are you? Could be that you will be good for Matthew.'

Casey relaxed under that direct, assessing stare. To lighten the tension in the room, she returned the compliment. 'Matt told me that as a young widow you raised five children, and ran the brewery until you handed it over to Matt's father when he was twenty-one. It can't have been easy for you. You must have faced a lot of prejudice in such a male-dominated domain. Yet the business expanded under your management.'

'I just did my duty.'

'I think you did more than that.' Casey voiced her admiration. 'You also proved that women can be independent and have the wisdom to succeed in business. That's no mean achievement even in this day and age. Forty years ago it must have been even harder to overcome prejudice from other male brewery owners.'

Grandma Enid acknowledged the compliment with a slight inclination of her head. Casey knew nothing she could say would appease the hostility in Millicent's eyes. Instead, she smiled engagingly at Clementine. Her heart went out to the woebegone creature. It was obvious, from the number of times her gaze sought Matt's figure across the room, that she was in love with him. And clearly Millicent fostered the girl's expectations that Matt cared for her.

A maid came in with cakes and the tea service. Whilst Casey sipped her tea, she found herself deliberately excluded from the conversation as the women spoke of family acquaintances. Matt's brothers spoke quietly about brewery matters, and their wives, although casting sympathetic glances at Casey, obviously didn't dare challenge Sybil's attitude towards her. Casey sensed that they were very much in awe of Sybil, and that the woman was capable of making their lives miserable if she so wished. Humphrey's wife in particular was deathly pale, her eyes darkly shadowed, and she clutched a shredded lace handkerchief which she twisted nervously every time her husband or Sybil Frost spoke.

Twice Edward Frost interrupted his wife's comments to ask Casey a question. Each answer clearly pleased him, but she could see that he was in great pain and that speech was a trial to him.

After Sybil again engineered the conversation to exclude Casey, Edward Frost nodded to Matt. 'You must show Cassandra the hot-house in the garden. I fear that I must take my leave of you, Cassandra. It is time for my medication.'

Sybil gasped with annoyance. 'They can't go outside. It looks as if it's about to snow.'

'We'll pick up our coats on the way out,' Matt declared. As Casey passed Edward Frost's chair he held out his hand to her. When she took it he winked encouragement. 'I hope you will visit us again soon.'

Relieved to leave the censure of the room, Casey breathed deeply of the crisp December air.

'Take me home, Matt. Your mother and aunt will never accept me as your bride.'

'I've no intention of giving you up, Casey. They will just have to get used to the idea. My mother is in no position to judge you, her father was only a foreman at the brewery. Besides, Pa was taken with you. But since his accident he has allowed Mama to have her own way.'

The vehemence in his tone should have delighted her, but instead it echoed the arrogance of the middle-classes which she distrusted. Matt was used to getting his own way too. And Sybil Frost had all the malevolence of a woman who had chosen to forget her own past.

He put his hand in his pocket and drew out a small

jewel-box and held it out to her. 'There's no need to wait until Christmas. I want you to wear my ring now.'

He flicked open the lid and revealed a ring with three large diamonds in a crossover design.

Tears stung Casey's eyes at the impetuosity of his love. She was tempted to agree, but something held her back. Her pain at his family's censure of her was too raw. The arrogance he had shown in refusing to be thwarted was something she needed to come to terms with. It was a side of Matt she had not seen before.

She shook her head. 'If you feel the same when we have known each other for a year, you may ask me again.'

He stared at her incredulously. 'You're refusing me? But you love me.' The healthy colour drained from his rugged cheeks and his eyes glittered with anger. 'I'll be damned if I'll ask you again in a year. There's no reason why we can't get engaged now.'

'The way you're behaving is a very good reason.' The pain at the censure she had received from his mother burst from her at his callous manner. 'I was invited here as a guest and I have been insulted. Your mother doesn't want you to marry me. And at this precise moment, I'm not so sure I want to marry an arrogant bully who would dictate what I will or will not do.'

She saw a gate in a tall brick wall along one side of the garden and, breaking away from him, ran towards it. The snow which had been threatening all day began to fall in thick flakes. The afternoon had been a nightmare. She wanted to get away from Matt and his haughty, snobbish family. She had left her handbag in the house and also her hat, but she didn't care.

Matt called after her. Ignoring him, she broke into a run. Her heart raced faster at the sound of his coming after her. She did not want him to see her tears. She wanted to get away from him and his family who despised her.

The garden gate was locked and she struck it angrily with her fist. To her frustration she broke into sobs.

Matt's hands circled her shoulders. 'Casey, for God's sake, are you mad?' The anger was still in his voice, but there was also concern. 'You can't just run out on me.'

'Yes I can. I'm not ashamed of my background and I'm as good as any member of your family. I've got darn sight better manners, for a start. But I will not be treated as inferior because of my father's occupation or where I live.' She wrenched her arm free and stood back to glare at him. 'Is there any way this gate will open, or do I have to walk back through the house to get out of here?'

The snow was settling on her hair and face, making her blink rapidly to dispel them from her lashes. The wind had also stiffened; the snow was driving against her cheeks and running down her neck inside the collar of her coat. She had never felt so unhappy or wretched. But anger at her treatment came to her rescue and, in a fit of outrage, she stamped her foot and demanded, 'Are you going to open that bloody gate, or are we both going to freeze to death?'

'I'm not going to open the gate. You can't run off into the snow without your hat.' Matt was breathing heavily. The snow was so thick that Casey was forced to half close her eyes so she could not see him properly. 'I'll take you home, Casey. I hope you're not going to run off every time we don't see eye to eye.' He laughed without mirth. 'I don't intend to spend the rest of my life chasing after you.'

She glared mutinously at him. 'I'm not the one in the wrong.'

'But you are stubborn.' His gaze became tender. 'You may not have realised it, but you won Pa and Grandma over by standing up to them. Mama will also come round, given time.'

Suddenly she was in his arms, and he was kissing her.

'I suppose I can be an arrogant bastard at times, Casey,' he said gruffly. 'But you've seen my family. What you went through today is nothing to how they treated me when I told them I wanted to be an aviator. I've had to fight and work for what I want. And I want you.'

Chapter Ten

'You've been seeing Cassandra for several months now.' Joe regarded Matt over the port when his daughter and niece left the restaurant table in Claridges. The meal was to celebrate Joe's forty-fifth birthday. He had drunk several glasses of wine and his mood was reflective. 'I'd like to know your intentions.'

Matt wasn't surprised. 'If I had the money I'd wed Casey next week, but my parents are being difficult. And my pay in the Flying Corps just seems to disappear. I can't honestly see us being wed for three or four years.'

Joe lit a large cigar and puffed a cloud of blue smoke around him as he regarded Matt. 'That's hard on a man,' he said matter-of-factly. 'But I'd be happier if there were a ring on her finger. Get my meaning?'

'Casey is the woman I intend to wed, but she doesn't want a long engagement so she won't accept a ring until the future's settled. The attitude of my family doesn't make it easier.'

'That's what worries me.' Joe leaned forward. 'They want you to wed money. They see a publican's daughter as not good enough for their son. Especially as the pub is so close to the Courtyard. That's changing.' He inhaled on the cigar, watching Matt through narrowed eyes. 'I've been after a second pub for some time. The one I had me eye on in Covent Garden fell through. I'm buying one now in Kensington. Costing me a packet. And it will be cash on the nail. To keep your family's goodwill, I'll use Frost breweries. We should be moving come summer. If you're expecting to continue seeing me daughter after then, I expect a ring on her finger, and proper announcements in the papers. Otherwise leave her be.'

Matt sat back in his chair, his expression guarded. He hadn't missed the warning in Joe's eyes and he didn't like it. 'It'll be three or four years at least before I earn enough to support your daughter.'

'She don't want nothing grand. I made sure she were brought up proper, but she ain't a toff. And I've enough put by to buy her a small house as a wedding present. She ain't afraid to work. Besides, until any nippers come along, I couldn't see Cassandra stuck at home with nothing to occupy her mind but a bit of housework. She's too much go in her for that.' Joe's expression remained serious. 'Get it sorted, Matt, or get out of her life. She loves you and I want to see her happy. That's all I'm saying.'

Joe stood up as Casey and Eva returned. Casey frowned as she saw her father's expression. 'What have you two been discussing?'

Her father shrugged. 'Just putting the record straight, so to speak.'

'Over what?' Casey urged.

Joe didn't answer. She looked at Matt, who had the tense look he adopted when he was controlling his anger. 'Your father says if we aren't engaged by the summer, he wants us to stop seeing each other. I think he feels I may be trifling with your affections.'

'Dad, how could you?' Casey barely managed to keep her voice low so that the other diners could not hear.

'It's time the cards were put on the table, Princess. I'm just thinking of your future.'

'My future, and what I do with it, are my affair.'

His hand was a blur as it shot out and gripped her wrist.

'No it ain't, me girl. People are beginning to talk. I don't want it said you had expectations that weren't realised. If you get me meaning.'

'I don't care about the gossips.'

Joe's eyes slitted. 'I do. I like Matt, but hanging around with a toff don't do your reputation no good.'

'I've been telling her that for months,' Eva joined in.

Casey's knuckles whitened over the handbag she was carrying. 'You're as bad as Matt's family. When Matt and I marry is our concern and no one else's.'

'That's where you're wrong, Princess. You ain't twenty-one for three years. Until then, whilst you're living in my house, anything you do is very much my business. You're going down the aisle a virgin when you wed.'

Casey blushed scarlet and Matt stood up to put a possessive hand on Casey's shoulder. 'Now look here, Joe . . .' he began.

Eva felt her insides scald at Joe's blatant pride in his daughter's innocence. Dimly she saw the three figures locked in discussion, but their words were lost to her. The bitterness of her thoughts overrode everything else.

She'd been Joe's mistress for over a year. She knew she pleased him, but she had not won from him the devotion she desired.

Jealousy scoured her. Despite all she had done to discourage Casey from continuing to see Matt, it looked like her cousin had won herself a rich husband. Her future was assured. Little pampered Casey had achieved all her father desired for her. Whilst she, the poor cousin, still had nothing. And she didn't like it.

Hadn't she tried to be all Casey and Joe required of her? But Casey had proved to be more independent than she had at first thought. Her cousin had a mind of her own, and would not be led by another. Joe hadn't been won over as she had wished either. If Casey had Matt, why shouldn't she have Joe?

She smiled secretly to herself. Joe would be hers.

In a couple of months they were moving to Kensington. A posh area, and once there she was going to insist that she gave up her job in the department store and worked behind the bar.

It was work she enjoyed. When Joe was away from the Britannia, she would sneak into the bar and help Rusty. At first the amiable barman had tried to dissuade her. But she knew how to handle Rusty. Occasionally, when she was annoyed that Joe did not show her the affection she thought she deserved, she allowed Rusty to take her out on his night off. But she never allowed more than a kiss or two. He was devoted to her and she enjoyed being able to twist the big man around her finger. He had shown her how to pull pints of porter, the sweet, black beer flavoured with malt that was popular with the locals.

Bertha was another matter. She resented Eva working in the bar. When the older woman looked at her, Eva always felt uncomfortable. It was as though she knew what went on in Eva's head, and that alarmed her. Did the old biddy suspect that she was after Joe? As far as she knew, Joe no longer visited Bertha, since her husband had been released from prison last month. But there remained a jokey closeness between Joe and the buxom barmaid which Eva disliked.

Joe liked the company of women, and Eva didn't intend him to take up with another to replace Bertha. She'd striven too hard to allow that to happen.

During the next week, Eva began to plan carefully. To win Joe over, she needed to prove she would make a good publican's wife. On each of Joe's evenings off she would appear behind the bar.

'Strongarm don't want 'er in the pub,' Bertha protested at Eva's presence.

'Can't you take the competition?' Eva retorted. 'Too used to being queen of the roost in here, are you?'

'Now ladies,' Rusty intervened with a sigh. 'No need for that talk. We're busy tonight and Eva will be a great help.'

Eva smiled entrancingly at him. 'Thank you, Rusty. I hate my own company and Casey is writing to Matt. It will take her an hour. I'd hoped to go and see the new Chaplin film.'

'I'm off tomorrow night. We could go together.'

'That would be nice, Rusty.'

Bertha sniffed her disapproval. 'Ain't yer got better things to do than spend yer 'ard-earned money on 'er? She's using yer, Rusty. Yer too good for the likes of 'er.'

Rusty, who rarely lost his temper, rounded on her. 'Don't say a word against Eva. It ain't been easy for her since she lost her family.'

Eva was delighted at Rusty's defence of her. She loved being able to get one over on Bertha.

'Ain't seen much evidence of 'er mourning 'em,' Bertha returned. 'Yer a good man, Rusty. I hate seeing yer taken advantage of, that's all.'

'That's fine sentiments from a woman who's bin whoring all the time her husband has been banged up in the clink,' Eva retaliated.

'Ladies!' Rusty intervened, his freckled face flushed with agitation.

Eva smiled at him sweetly as Bertha was stopped from answering by the impatient cries for ale from the far end of the bar. 'Perhaps Bertha has her eye on you for the next time her husband does a stretch. He's never out for longer than six months before he's back inside again.' She squeezed his arm as she moved past him to serve a customer, and added softly, 'She's right, though. You are a good man, Rusty. Too good for the likes of me, that's for sure.'

Devotion glinted in his eyes. 'Don't say that, Eva. I'll do

anything for you. Anything. You know there'll be no other woman for me.'

The declaration was a trophy to her dissembling. She needed Rusty on her side. Never one to allow her power over another to wane, she blew him a kiss.

Several customers came in at once, loudly demanding drinks. It was some time before there was a lull. Eva enjoyed the social atmosphere of the pub. She would hum along to the singing when the pianola was played, and give back as good as she got if any man was cheeky or made bawdy suggestions. After giving one such man a taste of her tongue, she saw that she had shocked Rusty.

With a wink, she laughed, saying, 'Got to give the punters a bit of lip now and again. It's what they expect.'

He shifted uncomfortably. 'But you're a lady now, just like Casey.'

She laughed wickedly and slipped into broad cockney. 'Lord luv us, ain't I just the grand lady when I wanna be? But I'm a Courtyard woman, born and bred. I'm a survivor and a fighter. It's in me soul, Rusty. And yer can't change what's in yer soul.'

'But you deserve better than this.'

'And I mean to have it. There ain't no flies on me, Rusty Chambers!'

Demands for porter ended the conversation. The next customer Eva served was of special interest to her.

'Joe not here?' The man, a Polish immigrant, was shabbily dressed and unshaven. His cap was frayed and the scarf tucked into his jacket hid his lack of a shirt. Eva knew he'd done time for burglary, and his gaze darted about the pub as though he feared someone might accost him.

'He'll be back in half an hour. Can I give him a message?'

'I'll come back.' He scuttled out of the bar, his head furtively turning from side to side.

Eva smiled inwardly. In the last year she had kept an eye on Joe's comings and goings. By following him when he went out, she had witnessed men sidling up to him in the side alley of the pub and handing him their booty; a glint of moonlight on precious metal or gems had showed her it was always jewellery or silver- and gold-ware. She had also learned to whom he sold the goods. Casey knew nothing of her father's double life as a criminal and it suited Eva that her cousin remained in ignorance. It would be another secret she and Joe shared.

If Joe could afford to buy a second pub and still be able to purchase a house for Casey as a wedding present, he must have a hoard of money stashed away. As yet Eva had been unable to find out how much or where it was kept. Joe distrusted banks or lawyers. But his savings must be substantial. Any woman who married him would live in comfort all her life.

When a hush fell over the bar-room conversation, Eva glanced at the street door. Through the blue haze of tobacco smoke she saw a short, stout, clean-shaven man in a brown suit and Homburg surveying the customers. Behind him stood two heavily built men.

'Good evening, Mr Goldstein.' Eva greeted the high mobsman who had extended his protection racket to this district. She smiled sweetly, knowing that although Joe was one of the few shops or pubs who did not pay protection money to the Jew, this was a man to whom you showed respect, or you paid a severe price in broken bones. Solomon Goldstein stared at her, his black eyes wandering slowly over her figure and mentally stripping away her garments in a way which made the flesh shrink on her bones.

'You Strongarm's new dolly-mop? Got a bit of class. I like that. But great tits like yours should be given more of an airing, not shrouded in high-necked primness and ruffles.'

His coarseness, and the menace which emanated from him

as he strutted to the bar, dried her throat and touched her skin with ice. Even so, she held his leer levelly. 'Uncle Joe's not here.'

He laughed salaciously. 'Passing you off as his niece, is he? I've had a few nieces like you in my time. It's the only way you can get the girls into better-class establishments.'

Eva controlled her anger at his insinuations. Pouring a large measure of Joe's best whisky, she placed it before him on the bar. 'Have you business with my uncle, Mr Goldstein?'

'What business would I have with Strongarm?' Goldstein studied her intently. His olive skin was pitted, his hooked nose giving him the appearance of the vulture she knew him to be.

To her relief Rusty had edged closer, ready to defend her if need be. It gave her courage. She would not show her fear of Goldstein. 'How can I help you, Mr Goldstein? I take it this is not a social visit.'

His smile stretched open over dark ivory teeth. 'I think you know how you could help me,' he suggested, reaching out to touch an amethyst earring dangling from her ear.

She pulled back so that it fell from his touch, her tone reserved. 'I am Joe Strong's niece, and I think he would be offended at your familiarity, Mr Goldstein. I serve behind the bar to help out, and don't permit anyone to take any liberties.'

She wondered if she had gone too far. His eyes snapped black fire but his gaze became even more assessing. He turned to face the customers who were murmuring softly to each other. 'I'm looking for Chalky White. It wouldn't be wise for anyone here to go giving him shelter. He was foolish enough to let some of the Flower and Dean Street boys steal some property of mine.'

Rusty gently pulled Eva to the back of the bar, placing himself in front of the gangleader. 'Chalky ain't been in here tonight, Mr Goldstein.'

The mobster confronted Rusty. 'This is Chalky's local. Send

word to me if you see him.' He moved to stare fixedly at Eva's breasts. 'Maybe I could take you to dine one evening.'

She saw Rusty's fist clench and she moved quickly to put a restraining hand on his arm, a smile nailed to her face. It wasn't dining Goldstein had in mind, and her stomach churned with nausea. She only knew of one woman who had refused Solomon Goldstein, and she had ended up with her face slashed to ribbons.

'You honour me, Mr Goldstein, but my uncle is very protective of my reputation. He doesn't allow me to go out with any gentleman who has not called upon him first.'

'That's wise, but I'm not just anyone.' He tipped his hat to her and Eva gripped Rusty's arm more tightly to prevent him from doing anything foolish.

Rage ground through her as she watched Goldstein and his bodyguards leave the pub.

'I'll kill him if he lays a finger on you, Eva,' Rusty declared.

A glow spread through her at his championship. 'You'd do that, Rusty? You're a good friend, but Goldstein was just taunting you. He'll forget me as soon as he walks out of here. I'm going to take a break now.'

Rusty followed her, saying softly, 'Goldstein is trouble. I don't want to see you hurt.'

'You're making too much of it, Rusty.' She silently prayed that she was right, but her stomach still cramped with dread.

'I'll take a break meself,' he answered hoarsely.

''Ere, yer not leaving me alone to serve this bleeding crowd?' Bertha said sharply. 'Joe'll be back in 'alf an 'our. Can't yer take yer break then?'

'OK. But I need to pop out the back.' Rusty followed Eva into the hallway and paused by the scullery door which led through to the outside lavatory.

'Eva, I meant what I said about doing anything for you. I'd like you to be me girl. Court you proper-like. I've enough saved to get you a diamond ring. Nothing cheap. Not for you.'

Her heart plummeted. This was not what she had planned at all. Yet she knew she would be a fool to alienate Rusty. 'I'm very flattered, Rusty, but—'

'You don't have to give me an answer now.' He swept his fingers through his wheat-coloured hair, his expression fearful that she would give him an outright no. 'We're good together. I'll make you happy.'

His manner made it easier for her to prevaricate. 'I've always thought of you as a friend, Rusty. A real special friend. It takes a bit of getting used to that you want to be more than that to me. It don't mean we can't see each other as we have been.'

She didn't want to refuse him outright. He had proved a valuable ally.

He appeared satisfied. 'Then you'll still come out with me tomorrow?'

She nodded. It would be a free night out and, who knew, it might even make Joe jealous. It was beginning to look as though she'd have to take more drastic action to get Joe to marry her. She was uncomfortably aware that the only times she had succeeded in getting into Joe's bed were by seductive scheming on her part. Lately, sometimes even that failed.

Her eyes narrowed and her jaw stuck out with grim determination. Joe *must* marry her. He was worth a fortune from his dealings with the underworld. Why shouldn't she have that money? Hadn't she earned it by scivvying for him and allowing him her favours? She'd be rich. The idea, once formed, had become an obsession.

The weeks Matt was away from London dragged slowly for Casey. She enjoyed her work at the solicitors, and she went out with Eva twice a week, but loving Matt so fiercely it was his company she craved. It would have helped if he'd been a better letter-writer. He had warned her when he first returned to his duties with the Royal Flying Corps that he was a poor correspondent, and time had proved him right. The few letters she received sustained her, but they were far from the romantic missives she would have treasured.

'What am I supposed to say in a letter?' He shrugged off her criticism as they disembarked from the river launch which had taken them from the Tower up to Hampton Court. For mid-March, it was a rare, sunny day, and they made the most of it by avoiding the crowds and strolling along the river-bank. He went on, 'I fly most days and spend my free time earning extra money by servicing the aircraft engines. We need every penny to buy my first plane.' He brushed her cheek with his finger, his gaze tender. 'Besides, you know I love you.'

'But it's nice to hear that you miss me,' she said wistfully.

'Isn't it obvious?' Matt replied, sounding genuinely puzzled.

'Only if I'm a mind-reader.' Sometimes he could be so infuriating. She struck his arm in vexation. 'When I don't hear from you for weeks and your letter is then filled with praise for some aviator who has just broken another record, I do wonder if you've thought of me at all!'

Gold sparks of devilment lightened his hazel eyes. 'So you don't think I'm romantic enough, is that it?' His hand slid over hers as they walked arm in arm. 'Isn't this a romantic enough setting?'

He nodded to the redbrick gatehouse towers of the Tudor palace across the river. 'Over there is the palace Henry the Eighth stole from his chancellor and gave to Anne Boleyn as a token of his love for her. That was a romantic act.'

Casey gave a cynical laugh. History was clearly not Matt's strong point. 'If he gave it to her as a gift, he reclaimed it quickly enough after he chopped off her head. It's more a monument to the supremacy of a despot over lesser mortals.'

She glanced significantly at him. 'And talking of despots,

how is your brother Humphrey? He snubbed me at Pinions last week when he came in for a meeting. He is also adept at throwing his voice when he thinks the occasion warrants it. He was telling Mr Jonathan that if you were to wed Clementine, your father would buy you the plane you're hankering after. Has he made the proposition to you yet?'

'Yes. On those conditions, I turned it down flat.' Matt stopped and drew her round to face him. His expression was anguished. 'I didn't know you knew about it. It was unforgivable of Humphrey to speak out in that way. He takes too much on himself since Pa suffered that relapse in February. And Pa is being manipulated. Most of the time he's in too much pain to be aware of the conflict over our wish to marry. He was admitted to hospital last month to have an operation to remove a fragment of splintered skull which is causing the headaches. Since then he's been unable to leave his bed. His condition seems to be deteriorating.'

'I'm sorry, Matt. Your father at least seemed to be coming round to me. I suppose this bribe with the plane was your mother's idea?'

He did not reply, but the clamped set of his mouth told her that she was right. Her voice leaden with pain, she observed, 'We've never spoken of your family since I visited them. Humphrey was making sure I knew my place. He sides with your mother in disapproving of me as your bride. If we wed it will mean a rift with your family.'

'Don't talk that way, Casey.' He frowned as he stared along the footpath where a family group of several adults was approaching. 'Pa is dying,' he added, hollowly. 'He wants me to succeed in my business. He has agreed to buy the plane providing I don't marry until I'm twenty-five. That's in another eighteen months.'

There was an intensity in his gaze when he stared down at her which made her yearn to be held in his arms and be reassured that his family would accept her. She knew it was an impossible dream.

'It's you I want,' he declared. 'Forget about my family. Let's do as your father insists. Let's get engaged now.'

They stood to one side as the family passed and greeted them formally. Once their backs were to them, Matt put his arm around her waist. 'We will marry in eighteen months. Even then we won't have much money, but your father has promised us a house. Together we can achieve anything, Casey. At twenty-five I also inherit a small legacy from my grandfather's will. It will support us until my air-freight and passenger service gets established.'

He thrust his hand into his pocket and drew out the ring box he had shown her a few months before. 'Will you accept this now, my darling?'

'But Matt I—'

'No more buts, Casey. I'll go down on my knee if you insist.'

He took her hands and sank down on to the ground. 'Marry me, Casey.'

She laughed. 'Get up, Matt. People are staring.'

When he straightened his expression was serious. 'Fooling aside, I've been patient long enough. If you're not prepared to get engaged, then I'm not hanging around any longer for you to make up your mind. If you love me, then agree to wear my ring. Otherwise it's over between us.'

The threat brought her head up, but before she could speak he again took her hands. 'It's because I love you, Casey, that I want your answer. My family will have to accept our engagement once it's in the papers. It's up to you.'

His thumbs caressed her fingers in slow circles which spread a glow of excitement through her body. He was a proud man, but there was an arrogance to his demand which disturbed her. Yet could she bear to lose him? She knew that she could not. Matt's arrogance was different from Hardcastle's. And she could understand that her prevarication must be eating at his pride.

In the seconds that her thoughts spun through her mind, his gaze remained tender, but within it was a challenge. Matt would never plead. Over the months his brief and infrequent letters had shown her that he guarded his emotions well, but she did not doubt at this moment that he loved her.

'Then my answer is yes, Matt.'

She was unprepared for his whoop of delight. Suddenly she was caught around the waist and whirled round and round. Breathless and giddy, she swayed when he put her back on the ground. Ardently, he drew her against him and kissed her.

'Sir, that is no way to conduct yourself in a public place.'

As they drew apart, Casey saw a middle-aged, bewhiskered man in a striped blazer at the wheel of a motor launch, which was pulling alongside to moor on the bank. He was waving a fist at them.

Matt grinned as he stepped back from Casey. 'You are right, sir. I forgot myself. This adorable woman has just agreed to be my wife.'

The two women seated on the deck of the launch eyed Matt with interest. 'How romantic,' one of them cooed. 'And such a lovely setting for a proposal.'

'Aye, my dear,' the helmsman replied with pompous smugness. 'Built by the unfortunate chap who got his head cut off by that Cromwell chappie, I believe.'

Casey bit her lip to conceal her amusement that he had mixed an ill-fated Stuart king with a despotic Tudor one. His clothing showed him as a man of wealth and position.

The woman who had spoken frowned. 'Surely it was his wife who had her head cut off?'

'Do you question my knowledge, sister? Harrow isn't a school which gets its facts wrong. Although your governess was probably more interested in the fashions of the queens of England than in politics.'

'Conceited oaf,' Casey said beneath her breath.

Harrow might be one of the most expensive and exclusive boys' schools in the country, but she supposed even such a vaunted establishment could not be responsible if its wealthy students did not have the brains to match their riches.

When Matt winked at her, his lips twitching as he controlled his own mirth, her fears for their future melted away. Matt might occasionally show the arrogance she disliked in men of his class, but he was not pompous. He would never belittle her intelligence, and he respected her independent spirit. He was an exceptional man and he loved her. And she loved him. He was right. Together they could achieve anything.

Chapter Eleven

Yet another Sunday loomed with Eva forced to settle for her own company. Casey had gone out with that Frost fellow again, apparently uncaring that her cousin would be left alone. Why did Frost have to come on the scene? He was spoiling everything. Before Casey had started courting, they had been so close, sharing everything, always together.

Eva scowled and muttered, 'If I'm going to be stuck here I might as well help in the bar.'

'What you doing down here?' Joe demanded as she entered the pub.

'I want to help. I'm fed up being on my own.'

'I told you to stay out of the bar,' Joe added as he pulled a pint and plopped it down before the customer.

'Let her stay, Joe,' Rusty intervened whilst ringing up on the till the price of a round of drinks. 'It must be lonely upstairs without Casey. She knows what she's doing and the customers like her.'

'Please, Joe,' Eva pleaded.

A dozen separate calls for more ale gave her the excuse she needed to set to work and, by the time the orders were filled, Joe seemed to have accepted that she worked efficiently enough to stay. A quarter of an hour before closing time, Eva nearly dropped a glass of porter she had just poured as she recognised Solomon Goldstein in conversation with Joe. The gangleader glanced in her direction and flashed her a lascivious smile.

'Pretty young thing your niece, Joe.' Goldstein raised his whisky glass in salute to her.

'And niece she is – my sister Sal's girl. And whilst she lives under my roof, I'm very particular who she steps out with.'

Goldstein laughed. 'You and me go back a long way, Joe.'

Joe's hand snaked out and his fingers curled around the mobster's fleshy wrist. 'And we learned to respect each other.'

Eva gasped, expecting some reprisal from the two bodyguards flanking Goldstein. Instead the gangleader shrugged and let the matter drop. Eva's curiosity was pricked. If Goldstein backed down it was because Joe had some hold over him; or was he held back by some mutual agreement. Was Joe even more deeply involved in the underworld than she already suspected?

At least it would keep Goldstein away from her she thought, but her relief was short-lived. She was collecting up beer glasses when she turned to discover Goldstein standing immediately behind her.

'Joe's niece or not, I reckon one day you'll want something from me. And you know what payment I'll be asking.'

Of all the gall. What would she ever want from that villain?

'I don't think so, Mr Goldstein.'

His complacent grin told her that he thought otherwise. 'I'm a patient man and you're an ambitious woman. Who knows what bargains we may strike in the future?'

Eva turned away in disgust. God forbid she would ever be so desperate that she would need to turn to Solomon Goldstein for help.

An hour later Eva had just purchased a pint of winkles for Joe's supper from Paddy Murphy's barrow when she was hailed in the street by Casey.

Her heart clenched when she saw how radiant her cousin looked, and Frost appeared far too self-satisfied for Eva's peace of mind.

'Is Dad upstairs?' Casey could barely contain her happiness. 'Come hurry, Eva, we have such wonderful news.'

The cold winkle-shells dug into Eva's hands as her fingers tightened around the top of the bowl they had been tipped into. What she had dreaded had happened. Casey had finally agreed to be Matt's wife. Her stare was bleak as she watched the couple run up the stairs hand-in-hand. She felt sick with jealousy, and it was several moments before she could bear to face them in the parlour.

She stood by the door feeling as if her heart and limbs had turned to stone. Casey was flashing a diamond ring in front of Joe's nose; he threw his newspaper down and leapt out of his chair to hug his daughter.

'This is cause for celebration!' He beamed proudly. With one arm still around Casey's shoulders, he held out his other hand to shake Matt's. 'Congratulations! I've some champagne in the cellar.'

Joe glared at Eva as he passed her, his voice a whisper, 'Don't spoil it for them, or you'll have me to answer to.'

At Joe's departure, Matt had pulled Casey to him and was kissing her. Eva stepped back, unable to watch. She waited until Joe returned with the champagne before sidling into the room. Salt was rubbed into the raw wound of her jealousy to note that Casey only had eyes for Matt and seemed to have forgotten her existence.

'Champagne, Dad, that's awfully extravagant,' Casey remarked, her face aglow with love and happiness. 'I only wish Matt's family were so enthusiastic.'

'Never you mind them, Princess,' Joe enthused. 'They're the losers. Matthew loves you and he's a good man. You'll have the house I promised you as a wedding gift.'

'Dad, we couldn't accept so much. You've just agreed to buy the new pub.'

'Nonsense. Do you think I haven't made provision for me

own daughter's wedding? The house is yours and you'll have the grandest wedding ever seen in these parts. Joe Strong will send his daughter off in style.'

'Dad, you don't have to do so much.' Casey was overcome with emotion at his generosity and flung her arms around his neck. 'You always did spoil me. Thanks, Dad. I love you.'

'Hrmph.' Joe cleared his throat in embarrassment and rocked back on his heels. He fidgeted with the lucky boxing-glove charm on his watch-chain as he continued. 'It will be a couple of months before we can move into the new pub. Rusty will take over here. He's the only man I trust not to swindle me out of me takings.'

'I'll not be able to support Casey until I come into my inheritance when I'm twenty-five,' Matt said solemnly. 'My father has agreed to buy my first plane and it will take me a while before the business is profitable.'

'If you don't crash it,' Joe said with a laugh. 'I remember those crazy stunts you took us to see at Brooklands last autumn. Looping the loop and gliding with the engine turned off. Fair put the wind up me, I can tell you. It's a dangerous life.'

'So was boxing, Dad,' Casey intervened. 'But would you have given it up because it was dangerous?'

He tipped back his bowler hat and laughed. 'No. I'd no taste for being poor. Without a proper education, boxing were the only way I could better meself.'

Eva, who had been uncommonly quiet since Casey announced her engagement, butted in, 'And you became famous for your prowess in the ring, Joe. You're the hero of all the young lads around here. You've given them the dream that they too can escape the poverty of the Courtyard.'

'It's an achievement to be proud of, Joe,' Matt said, raising his champagne glass. 'And I will make Casey proud of me.'

'Just as long as you don't do those crazy stunts in the air,' Casey said with feeling. 'Or I shall never have a moment's peace with worrying over your safety.'

'They are manoeuvres we have to master. They could save a pilot's life in an aerial battle.'

'Then thank God there is no prospect of war,' Casey said with feeling.

'I'll drink to that.' Joe raised his glass. 'And to your happiness, Princess.' He turned to Eva, his expression severe. 'Haven't you anything to say to your cousin? Congratulations wouldn't go amiss.'

Eva's eyes sparkled brightly and her lips stretched into a smile. 'Congratulations.' As she kissed Casey's cheek, her voice lowered to a whisper. 'Perhaps I was wrong about Matt. I thought he was just stringing you along for what he could get.'

The words were like an icy blizzard blotting out the early evening sunshine which filled the parlour. Casey tossed her head, refusing to allow her cousin to spoil the day.

Yet Eva's words returned to plague her during Matt's next leave. Since their engagement, his family had found reasons why it was not convenient for Matt to use one of the cars when he was visiting Casey. And at Edward Frost's funeral, Casey had been snubbed by his mother and brothers.

Matt had been shocked by the suddenness of his father's death. Although respecting his grief, Casey was angered by his family's attitude towards her, but she kept her thoughts to herself.

Matt had spoken little since they had left the house after the funeral tea, but Casey agreed with his suggestion that they walk along the Thames embankment before he took her home. The July late afternoon sun was hot through her black silk gown, and Casey kept her parasol protectively over her head and shoulders as they strolled amongst the crowds towards the Houses of Parliament. The sun's rays reflected off the gilded face of the tower clock which housed the great bell, Big Ben, whose distinctive chimes rang out throughout the day. The once pale golden Parliament buildings were stained and blackened from the London smog which cloaked the city in its choking clouds every winter. Music and merrymaking from motor launches mixed with the shouts of watermen piloting the great barges along the busy waterway. From the road running parallel with the river came the clang of omnibus bells and constant cries of costers selling their wares.

Dabbing at her brow with a lavender-scented handkerchief, Casey paused by a seat under one of the tall plane trees which provided them with some shade.

'Are you tired, my dear?' Matt asked, instantly contrite. 'We must have walked over a mile. I'm sorry, I'm poor company. Let's sit a while.'

A flock of pigeons scattered as they approached the empty seat. Although Matt took her hand, his expression was far away and Casey remained silent. All around them, London bustled with life. A steady stream of promenaders strolled along the Embankment: men in pinstriped trousers and bowler hats, hurrying to catch a bus or Tube train home from work; women in formal jackets and long narrow skirts leaving the shops or offices; ragged flower-girls, even a shifty-eyed beggar with claw-like hand outstretched. Here the middle-classes were forced into the proximity of the near-starving and ill-washed, who strove to make a living from the streets.

Matt sighed. His eyes were shadowed and troubled when he turned to Casey. 'With Pa dead, I'll not get my aircraft. Mama took great pleasure in telling me that since the bequest was not stated in Pa's will, the only way I could get my income from the family was to work for the brewery. She has always been against me flying. I hadn't realised how much until now.'

Casey squeezed his hand. 'Are you saying that to spare my feelings, now that your father is no longer alive to support our marriage?'

'I won't be manipulated. It's just going to take longer to get my business started.'

'And therefore for us to marry. I don't mind being wed to an aviator and mechanic. We will have our own house. It doesn't matter if you haven't started your own business. I'll still work and we will soon save the money we need.'

'It matters to me. I don't want my wife working.'

'But until I have children I want to work.'

'And what work will you do if I'm still based at Hendon? It's not like London. Only married women from the lower classes work. It's a man's place to support his wife.'

'That's your pride talking, not common sense,' she retaliated, then bit her lip to stem any further reproaches. 'I thought what was important is that we love each other.'

The groan he uttered wrenched at her heart. 'I love you so much, Casey. You deserve the best. But all this waiting is tearing me apart.'

He stood up abruptly and, striding to the river wall, stared at a paddle-steamer manoeuvring towards Westminster Pier. When Casey joined him, he said stiffly, 'I'd better get you home. I have to leave early tomorrow for Hendon.'

The strain of the day was still apparent in Matt's stilted conversation on the Tube back to Tower Hill. When they reached the Britannia it was dusk and the day had turned chilly.

'Come in for a brandy before you travel home.'

He shook his head as he stood back for her to enter the dark hallway. 'I'd best get back.'

She looked at him with concern. 'Matt, I know we buried your father today, and naturally you are upset, but I also get the feeling that you are annoyed with me. I don't want you going back to Hendon with any bad feelings between us.'

He gave her such a long, searching look that her heart contracted with foreboding. Had his family finally beaten him down? Were they going to win and prevent their marriage?

'It's not you, Casey, it's me. I love you. Being away from you gets harder each time we part. Yet sometimes it's easier not seeing you. To have you so close – wanting you – yet abiding by your decision to wait before I can possess you – it eats at my self-control. I'd better go.'

Her own body ached with yearning for his kisses, yet she knew that kisses alone were no longer enough for him. 'I love you, Matt. I don't want to make life difficult for you, but—'

'But you're not that type of girl. It's marriage or nothing.' He laughed wryly. 'I respect that. I'm a cad to suggest otherwise. But there is no one else for me, nor will there ever be. You are right. But it doesn't make it any easier.'

As she returned Matt's wave as he paused at the corner under the gaslight, she wondered if purity and virtue were worth the pain of unfulfilled desire. Her body was tormented by frustrated passion. If Matt's family had accepted her, she doubted that her pride would have made her hold out against his persuasive lovemaking. Or was she being stubborn? Needing to prove that, although she was a publican's daughter, she was not lacking in morals.

Eva alighted from the tram and ran under the doorway of a shopfront out of the rain. The morning had been warm and sunny, and she had not thought to take her umbrella to work. She only wore a thin cotton dress. She shivered in the evening wind, her mood irritable. It was dark, cold and she was hungry. An automobile went past, spraying up water from a kerbside puddle over her skirt. Eva swore profanely, forgetting her resolution to always act like a gentlewoman.

There was a male laugh behind her, and she whirled to see Solomon Goldstein coming out of a bookmaker's. He was smoking a fat cigar and wore a thick coat with an astrakhan collar. One of his henchmen held an open umbrella over his head, as though he was royalty itself.

‘Not very ladylike language, Miss Bowman. Got caught out in the rain, did you?’

Eva rubbed her arms with her hands. ‘Looks like it, don’t it?’

‘Then I must offer you a ride home.’ He gestured to the Bentley drawn up at the kerb.

Eva shivered, this time from dread, not cold. ‘That’s all right, Mr Goldstein. I wouldn’t like to put out an important man like yourself.’

‘Nonsense, my dear.’

The henchman had opened the automobile door and Goldstein stepped inside, but the door remained open. It would be a grave insult to refuse his offer. But what could be the consequences if she accepted? Eva swallowed her panic. The consequences could be worse if she refused. Weren’t there rumours that the charred corpse found on the wasteland of the old plague pits had been Chalky White, the man Goldstein had been asking after? Sex was a small price to pay if it meant you stayed alive.

She pasted on an accommodating smile. Who knows, Goldstein might be generous. He was a wealthy man.

Nevertheless her heart was pattering as she slid on to the leather seat in the back of the Bentley. He stubbed out his cigar and the whites of his eyes gleamed sinisterly in the light from the betting-shop window.

Eva was tense, unable to relax even though she was trying to.

‘You are suspicious of my motives, Miss Bowman?’ Goldstein rapped out.

‘Suspicious?’ she queried, her voice less steady then she would have wished.

‘You think I need to pick up women on the street?’

‘No, Mr Goldstein. You are an important man.’

‘And I have a reputation for being ruthless.’

Eva wiped the sweat which slicked her palms on her skirt. 'People talk of you with respect, Mr Goldstein.'

His hand gripped her jaw, jerking her face round to meet his brittle glare. 'Respect is important, but I am ruthless if I have to be. As for my women, I like them to be willing. Rape is not enjoyable. But sometimes it is necessary for punishment.'

Terror churned Eva's stomach.

'I did not like that you refused to dine with me, Miss Bowman.'

'I am not sure my uncle would approve.'

His hand dropped to her knee. 'Need he know?'

Bile rose to her throat. 'He is my guardian. I'm not a whore, Mr Goldstein. I will do nothing to shame my uncle's name.'

'And you ain't no innocent, Eva Bowman. But you've got a bit of class. What if I was to offer you a business proposition? Come work for me.'

She stared rigidly in front of her. 'You don't need me to whore for you, Mr Goldstein. I want to better myself, not spend my life on the streets.'

'You'd be wasted on the streets.' His caress grew bolder as his hand moved along her thigh. 'What I had in mind for you was something special. It could make you richer than you ever dreamed.'

For a moment Eva was tempted. But whatever Goldstein had in mind, it was bound to be sordid. She was done with that life. She shook her head. 'Joe would never allow it.'

'You think that could stop me? But as I said, I need you to be willing. Wait until you learn my proposition.'

Like a drowning woman, she saw her life pass before her eyes. She dared not deny him. And the bastard knew it.

His hand slid beneath her skirt and along her stockings. Her flesh crawled as his fingers pushed up the elastic of her bloomers to caress the naked skin of her thighs.

'This is better,' he intoned softly. 'You ain't stupid. You're a beautiful woman. You could go far.'

When his fingers pressed painfully into the cleft between her legs, she clenched her teeth to prevent a scream. Her fingers itched to scratch his face, and it took all her willpower not to clamp her legs shut as he insinuated his finger inside her. She schooled her mind to think of the grand house where one day she intended to live. It was how she had stopped herself going mad when her father did such things to her. Over the years she had become adept at blocking the distaste from her mind. As long as he did not physically hurt her, she could bear it.

Goldstein's face was close to hers, watching her reaction. She hid her disgust and loathing. The urge to bloody him for treating her like dirt was carefully concealed when she finally found her voice. 'Aren't I worth more than a tumble in the back of a car, Mr Goldstein?'

'Know your worth, do you?' he chuckled. His expression was enigmatic as his other hand closed over her breast and squeezed it painfully. 'Nice tits. Too big for a man's hand, and firm with it.'

She could not stop herself from flinching. His kiss was as dry as glass-paper as his mouth ground over her lips. His tongue thrust against the back of her throat. He drew back slightly, his voice a malicious whisper. 'You ain't gonna disappoint me, are you, Eva? You should show them off more. Wear bright colours.'

She put her hand against his body to push away from him and felt the butt of a pistol jammed into his trouser waistband. Murder was second nature to this man who ruled by terror. Silently condemning him to hell, she forced her stiff lips to return his kiss.

Abruptly, he sat back, folding his hands in his lap. His stare remained as intense as a cat watching a bird beneath its paw. The car was slowing down; to her relief she saw that the driver had pulled over in the shadows about two hundred yards from the Britannia.

'Tonight I have business,' Goldstein stated. 'But another time we will dine together and talk over your future.' He leaned across her and pushed open the door.

She scrambled out, her hands shaking as she adjusted her clothing. She was trembling so hard that her legs almost gave way under her as she ran across the road to the safety of the pub. Goldstein had been playing with her. There had been little desire in the way that he had mauled her, but his intention was clear. When he summoned her, she must obey, or she would be punished.

'Dammit, Eva!' Joe exploded. 'You can't be pregnant.'

He glared at her with horror. Then, recovering quickly, he shut the parlour door so that his daughter, who had just gone to bed, would not hear them.

'Well, I am,' Eva answered stoutly. It was a week after Goldstein had given her a lift home. 'And it's yours.'

'Then you'll have to get rid of it.' Joe was white-faced, his hand shaking as he wiped it across his moustache.

Eva stood up from where she had draped herself across the chaise longue. Folding her arms, she faced him. 'I won't. The child is yours and you've got to face up to your responsibility. Marry me.'

'Marry you!' Joe's lips curled back over his teeth in a snarl. 'And just what do you think Cassandra will say to that?'

'I would hope she cared enough about us both to wish us to be happy,' Eva declared. There was a tremor in her voice as she blustered to counter his fury.

'It's not going to happen.'

Joe stood solid, his feet braced as though he was preparing for a boxing match. She knew he would not hit her, but his stance was defensive, and the brutal light in his eyes told her he would not change his mind. When he flung out an accusing arm towards her, she gasped and stepped back. She quailed at seeing the hostility and anger in his face.

'If you're thinking of telling Cassandra that I'm the father of your kid,' he warned, a threat emanating from every muscle, 'then I'd think again, else you'll regret it.'

He snatched off his bowler hat and thrust one hand through his thick dark hair. 'Dammit, how did this mess happen? I took care that you wouldn't get pregnant.' He glowered at her as though he'd like to throttle the life from her.

She struggled to overcome the pain and anger which coursed through her at his refusal to marry her. Keeping her voice suitably meek, she said softly, 'It were that Saturday when you'd had a few too many. You lost control.'

'I was sober enough. You had your legs tight around me, begging me not to stop. I see why now. You planned it, you scheming tart.'

She saw him swallow as he rubbed his hand across the back of his neck. That night it had taken all her wiles to seduce him. He'd been at the gymnasium and she guessed he worked off his frustration by sparring with his old mates. She'd enticed him with every trick she knew before he had succumbed.

'God, what a mess!' he groaned, but his manner remained unrelenting. 'I ain't marrying you and that's final. The scandal would destroy Cassandra's reputation. She's got enough problems with Frost's family, without me adding to them.'

Eva's eyes blazed with fury. Even now he was thinking of Casey and not herself. Hadn't any of the love she'd given him won his affection? She felt soiled as his voice lashed her.

'I'm sorry it's happened. I never meant for you to get pregnant.'

'Sorry's a great help, ain't it?'

He jammed his bowler on his head and regarded her coldly. 'If you've any sense you'll wed Rusty. He's keen on you. Get him into bed quick enough, and he'll think the kid's his.'

She began to tremble, her plans dissolving. She had no

intention of marrying Rusty. All she had endured had been for nothing. She had never enjoyed sex. She had used it because of the power it achieved over men. Joe didn't love her. It was the same old story. She'd do everything she could to please someone, and they would throw her affection back in her face.

Her eyes hardened as she imagined the tittering of the women of the Courtyard. During her year living in the pub, she had seen their envy and gloried in it. Now she was being tossed back into that life. Bile rose to her throat and she began to shake with frustrated anger.

'You've got to marry me, Joe. I love you.' She dabbed a handkerchief to her eyes.

'Get this straight, girl. I ain't marrying you. And I wouldn't try any funny business about claiming the kid's mine, or you'll be out on your ear quicker than you can blink.' He paced the room, his hands thrust deep in his trouser pockets. 'Wed Rusty and I'll see the two of you are all right. I'll pay for the wedding. Set you up with a bit of cash.'

'You bastard. You can't buy me off, Joe.' Eva choked on her anger, but still had the presence of mind to keep her voice down. She didn't want Casey to overhear them. Her cousin would be sickened to learn that her father had taken her to his bed. And, as Casey adored her father, her disgust would put the blame on Eva. That would be more than Eva could bear. It would mean she had lost everything.

Her thoughts tumbled over each other, seeking to salvage what she could from the mess she had made of things. And as far as Joe was concerned she had not yet played her last card. She could still ensure that Joe jerked to the strings she pulled.

Tilting back her head, her eyes blazed vengefully. 'It's not just the kid I could tell about. What about your business with Goldstein and old Isaac the Jew, and the jewellery thieves who come to the pub? I've seen what's going on.'

Before she could anticipate his next move, Joe had seized

hold of her arm and jerked it up behind her back. 'You ain't seen nothing, not if you know what's good for you. Be grateful Rusty fancies you. He'll be manager here soon. You've been going on about working in the pub. As his wife you'll be landlady of the Britannia.'

The pain in her arm was excruciating. Eva was close to swooning. She had not expected Joe to react so violently. She thought he had at least cared for her.

'You're a slut, Eva Bowman. And a fool if you got me into bed to get me to wed you. Thought you'd found an easy meal-ticket, did you? I ain't such a sucker as to fall for the oldest trick in the book. Marry Rusty, or get rid of the brat. Either way I want you out of here by the end of the month. I don't want your corrupting influence near Cassandra.'

He flung her away from him and she fell across the table, sobbing. At the door he turned back to her. 'For Gawd's sake shut that row up, or you'll wake Cassandra. Rusty ain't gone home yet, he's sorting out the empty kegs in the cellar for the delivery van in the morning. I'll send him to you. Might as well get it over with.'

'Bastard!' she flung at him.

He grinned. 'That's as may be, but no cheap whore ever got the better of Joe Strong.'

Eva picked up a crystal vase to hurl at him as he disappeared through the door. With an effort she stopped herself throwing it. Her mind was racing. It was just as well she wasn't pregnant. In desperation to escape Goldstein's lechery, she had lied to get Joe to marry her.

She'd overreached herself and panic welled up in her throat. In a few days she'd tell Joe she'd lost the kid, then she'd beg him to let her stay. God knows how she'd get round him. He didn't trust her now.

Joe hesitated before entering the cellar. How could he have

got himself into such a mess? Damn Eva. He had always known that she was trouble. If it hadn't been for Cassandra's insistence, he'd never have had her within a mile of the place. He rubbed a hand across his moustache. His conscience pricked him. It didn't seem right to play such a dirty trick on Rusty. He'd been a good mate. But there was no denying the barman was besotted with Eva. He never stopped talking about her. But Eva was trouble.

He groaned softly. He had to think of the child. He was too proud to want a child of his growing up in the gutter, to a life of thieving and eventual imprisonment. Rusty would make a good father; he adored kids.

'Damn Eva for a conniving bitch!' he said beneath his breath. 'How could I have fallen for her tricks? But she knew how to play on a man's weakness.' His thoughts were bleak with derision. There was nothing soft about her. Even her lovemaking had been calculated. He was too experienced not to know that she was acting a part. But the damned bitch did it so well. She knew every whore's trick to give a man pleasure. Hadn't he tried to resist her? Yet the woman would waylay him, weaving her sultry spell, and he was but human. Brought up in poverty it was second nature for him to take what was offered. Now the price had to be paid.

His eyes slitted. Even now his body glowed with the memories of her firm flesh moving against his. Yet each movement was coldly precise, a carefully controlled response. He realised belatedly she had never given herself with wild and natural passion. Perhaps if she had, he might have considered allowing her to have the kid and live with him.

He caught his thoughts up short. The woman was poison. How could he even consider concocting so many lies to explain Eva's condition to Cassandra? He took out a handkerchief and wiped the sweat which had formed on his brow. Once his blood had cooled and his passion had been sated, he found it hard to tolerate Eva's company. She was too eager to please, too false in her affection. There was something about her which made him uneasy, yet he couldn't identify it.

He was well out of the devil woman's clutches. God help Rusty!

The cellar was empty. Rusty had already gone home. Joe picked up a bottle of brandy. From his early days of training he had always been abstemious in his drinking and as a landlord he'd seen the way drink could strip a man of his dignity. Since Eva had begun waylaying him, using her wiles to seduce him, he sought forgetfulness from his lust for her in the brandy bottle. He had thought he was still in control, but clearly on one occasion he hadn't been. He should have known you couldn't play with fire without getting burned – and Eva was fire: as lethal and all-consuming. This was one night when he was going to get good and drunk to forget his problems.

An eerie keening sound brought Casey awake with a start. Goosebumps broke out along her flesh. It sounded inhuman – like a ghostly spirit in torment – and it was coming from downstairs.

Every hair on her body prickled with foreboding. Wrapping her dressing gown around her, she raced to her father's room, surprised that he had not already appeared. The bed was still made and had not been slept in. Dread curled icy tendrils along her spine. And that awful sound was growing in intensity.

'Bloody hell!' She heard Rusty groan in a voice fractured with alarm.

Casey ran to the head of the stairs. Archie was crouched over on the floor, his shaven head and bull-neck suffused dark red as he bayed like a snared animal in pain. He was rocking back and forth as he so often did when he was deeply disturbed.

'Archie, what's wrong? Are you hurt?' she called out as she hurried down the stairs.

Rusty stepped over Archie's figure and stood solid on the fourth step, barring her way. Every freckle stood out on a face which was otherwise the colour of soured cream.

'Stay where you are, Casey. I'm afraid it's your dad.'

'What's happened to him?'

Her eyes were wide and her heart pumped with fear.

Tears sprung into Rusty's eyes, spilling over on to his cheeks. 'I'm sorry, Casey. He's dead. Looks like his neck is broke. Must have fallen down the stairs. From the smell of brandy, he must have had a skinful last night.'

'But I've never seen Dad drunk – he hates excessive drinking.'

Rusty shrugged. 'We all lapse, Casey. Joe certainly weren't teetotal.'

She shook her head, denying that her father was dead. 'I heard nothing. He can't be dead.' Casey put a hand on Rusty's arm to push past him.

He held her fast. 'Best you don't see him.'

'Let me pass, Rusty. He's my father.' She stared at him, her voice quiet but insistent.

With a sigh he nodded and stepped back over Archie. 'Get up, man. Casey wants to see her dad.' The sobbing man stared up at him dumbly, clutching Joe more tightly to his chest. Pain was etched into his usually dull-witted eyes.

When he didn't move, Casey stepped over his crouched figure as Rusty had done. Putting a hand on the carved square newel-post, she jerked it back when she found the surface was sticky. Horrified, she stared at the wood. Dried blood, brown hairs and a few glutinous flecks of grey showed where Joe had struck his head during his fall. The red and gold staircarpet swirled chaotically before her eyes. The grandfather clock, ticking as loud as a tocsin bell from the corner of the hallway, echoed the sound of the blood pumping through her head.

Rusty caught her swaying figure and lifted her over the

still-sobbing Archie. The half-wit could not be moved from cradling Joe's battered head in his arms.

Casey braced herself to look down at the twisted limbs of her father. The legs were splayed at an unnatural angle – one, obviously broken at the knee, was twisted back to front. The scarlet waistcoat and white shirt were daubed with crimson. Yet as she found the courage to look at her father's face, she saw his profile was unmarked.

Rusty bent to close her father's eyes. There was blood on Archie's hands and his frayed grey shirt was smeared with blood where Joe's head rested on his chest. There was a dark stain on the carpet, and more of those awful grey flecks of brain and splinters of bone.

The pain of her grief welled in Casey's throat. It spread in searing waves through her heart and down to invade her stomach. She stood, supported by Rusty, eyes wide and staring at her father. Her body felt as though it was being slowly crushed between two immense stones. Yet there were no tears. Shock had numbed her mind. The body on the floor seemed to be viewed through a tunnel. Her stunned mind could not accept that her father was dead.

'What's that dreadful noise?' Eva demanded. Then her screams drowned Archie's guttural groans. 'Uncle Joe! No. No. Not Uncle Joe!'

Eva's screams only dimly penetrated Casey's dazed state. She saw her cousin run down the stairs still in her nightgown. Her hysterical shrieks were an intrusion into Casey's silent, rigid grief.

Weeping and wailing, Eva roughly pushed Archie out of the way, forcing her arms around the corpse. 'Not you as well, Joe. Must everyone I care for die!' The sobs were loud, gut-wrenching, her face contorted as she screamed until her voice cracked.

And how those screams grated. Casey glared at her. Why

did Eva have to be so hysterically emotional?

'See to Eva, Rusty,' Casey murmured, no longer able to abide her cousin's behaviour. It was too melodramatic, as were most of Eva's moods.

'Then a doctor had better be sent for,' she went on. 'It's just a formality. Clearly he died when he fell and struck his head on the newel-post. I just hope he didn't suffer.'

'I'll tend to everything,' Rusty assured her. 'Eva ain't gonna be much use to you. I'll phone the airfield. Matt should be able to get compassionate leave. He should be here with you now.'

Eva stopped her wailing and stood up. She dabbed dramatically at her eyes and took Casey into her arms. 'Come upstairs. Rusty will see to everything. I'll look after you, Casey.'

Casey was grateful that Eva had managed to get a grip on her emotions and take charge. Still too numb to think clearly, she allowed herself to be led back up the stairs.

Chapter Twelve

The funeral four days later was a blur to Casey. The coroner had declared Joe's death accidental. Matt was at her side holding her arm as she led the procession of mourners behind the glass-sided, horse-drawn carriage. The streets were lined with mourners from the pub to the church. Word had spread of Joe's death, and the church was filled with boxers, high mobsmen and the regulars from the Britannia. As the coffin passed, men drew off their caps and the women stood in silence. They hadn't seen such a turn-out to a funeral in the district in living memory. Joe Strongarm was respected by everyone in the community.

Even as the coffin was lowered into the earth, Casey stood as though carved from stone, unable to cry. Everything was happening as though from a distance. She could not accept that her vibrant, healthy father was dead.

Eva sobbed loudly enough for the two of them. 'Three close relatives I've buried in just over a year,' she declared. 'And Joe was like a father to me. I've no one but Casey now. No one.'

Rusty supported her sobbing figure, shrouded in a thick black veil which reached the hem of her skirt. Several mourners who had not seen Joe recently mistakenly took her for his widow. In comparison, Casey, although dressed in unrelieved black, wore only a short lace veil, draped over her wide-brimmed hat and tied under her chin. As the mourners began to gather to voice their condolences, Casey turned to Matt.

'Take me home.'

Eva looked shocked. 'You can't go yet, Casey. The people want to pay their respects.'

'You hear them, Eva,' Casey said hollowly. 'You made the funeral arrangements and everything else. You have been such a comfort. I can't face them. Besides, all are welcome to come back to the Britannia for the drink and refreshments laid on.'

Casey sat upstairs in the parlour, its windows draped with black crêpe. It was early evening and the free drink had flowed non-stop. Now the mourners were singing and dancing – a send-off Joe would have been proud of.

Jonathan Pinion stood up and cleared his throat. 'This is the time when normally the will should be read. But I fear your father died intestate. He left no will with the papers you handed to me, Cassandra. I'm surprised that the solicitors who dealt with the purchase of the Britannia, or the new pub he was buying, did not advise him to make one.'

'Dad did not hold much with legal matters,' Casey answered. 'He paid cash for the Britannia and intended to do the same with the pub in Kensington. He believed a man's word was his bond.'

'A pity, as it complicates the winding-up of his estate,' Jonathan Pinion said heavily. His plump face was strained, and Casey suspected that the sadness in his eyes stemmed from something more than attending Joe Strong's funeral. He cleared his throat several times before continuing, 'Cassandra, although you are the sole heir, probate can take a long time to complete. It could be several months before any money or property can be released to you.'

He broke off and sipped from his whisky glass. Casey gained the impression that he was stalling for time.

'There's something wrong, isn't there, Mr Pinion?'

He nodded. 'Unfortunately, after agreeing to act for your father's estate, I find myself in an embarrassing position. It would be better if you employed another solicitor.'

'But I trust you,' Casey blurted out, shocked by this revelation. It had been a comfort to know that her employers would handle all her legal affairs.

'I'm sorry, my dear, truly I am. It is a matter of conflict of interest.' He fidgeted with the papers in his hands. 'I have to consider another client. One who has been with the company for fifty years. A case for recovery of a debt has been lodged against your father's estate by Frost's Brewery. The Britannia cannot be sold until a debt of several hundred pounds is settled. Also . . .' He paused and, red-faced, wiped his handkerchief around his collar. 'There will be no further deliveries from the brewery until the debt is settled.'

'Oh terrific,' Eva spat. 'How the hell are we supposed to pay the debt if there's no income? A pub can't run without beer.'

'What debt is this?' Matt exploded. 'I can't believe my brother would act this way.'

Eva snorted with disparagement. 'The toffs always know how to kick those they consider their inferiors when they're down.'

Mr Pinion opened his briefcase and took out a sheaf of papers. 'The debt has accrued from six months' supplies of beer which were not paid for.'

'But Dad always paid the invoices at the end of every month,' Casey protested.

Jonathan Pinion looked at her sadly. 'Apparently in your father's zeal to buy the new establishment in Kensington, he used that money for a down-payment. Undoubtedly he had the means to make up the deficit, but there is no information within these papers about your father's income or savings. He has no bank account. I fear that he has entered into contractual obligations over the new establishment and that could incur further expenditure.'

Casey put her hand to her temple. She knew her father distrusted banks almost as much as he distrusted solicitors. He certainly didn't keep his money in the house. So where were the funds to buy the new pub? And also the rest of his savings?

Matt put a hand on Casey's shoulder. Through his fingers she felt him trembling with anger at the way his family had treated her. The skin was stretched taut across his rugged features. 'The case will be dropped. I will speak to my brother.'

Casey gazed at him lovingly. 'There's no point. It's your family's way of stopping our marriage. With the sale of the pub, you could have purchased an aeroplane and established your business.'

Jonathan Pinion picked up his hat and stood uncomfortably as he prepared to take his leave. 'I fear we must stand by our loyalty to a long-established client. I can't serve both your interests.'

Casey knew him well enough to understand how embarrassed this kindly gentleman was at the dilemma he had been placed in. 'To avoid any possible conflicts of interest between your company and their client, I resign my position as secretary.'

Regret shadowed the solicitor's eyes, but he was evidently relieved at her words, for his body visibly relaxed. 'We shall miss you, Cassandra. In recompense you will be paid a month's salary. I would recommend Messrs Peters and Cole of Bishopsgate to deal with your affairs.'

'Instead of the riches which should comfortably have set you up,' Eva wailed, 'your father has landed you with a thousand-pound debt. And thanks to Matt's caring family, you also haven't got a job.'

'Stop being so petty, Eva,' Casey snapped. 'I don't care about the money. Dad's dead. And I miss him dreadfully.'

'Petty, am I?' Eva paced the parlour, wringing her hands. 'Wait until you find out what it's like not to have money. Joe's made a right hash of things from the looks of it. Do you know where his money is? If you don't, we're going to have a lean time of it.'

'We'll manage,' Casey declared.

Rusty intervened. 'Stop looking on the black side, Eva. Joe would have made sure Casey was all right.'

Eva rounded on him. 'Do you know where he stashed his cash, then?'

'He wouldn't confide in me about a thing like that.'

'Then we'll end up in Carey Street workhouse.'

'Nothing like that will happen,' Matt promised. 'I won't allow my brother to get away with this. I'm going to see him now.'

With Matt and Jonathan Pinion gone, Casey needed to be alone with her grief. It was an added shock to find herself a debtor instead of financially secure. Rusty and Eva went down into the bar where the customers were still assembled at Joe's send-off.

Casey sat in front of her father's trophy cabinet, fingering the photographs of him winning prize-fights. Picking up the large cup, she hugged it close. She could still smell his spicy aftershave and tobacco smoke in the room. As the light faded she turned towards the full-length portrait of him on the wall. It was painted fifteen years ago but, apart from a touch of grey at his temples, Joe had not changed in all that time. As the room became darker, she lit a candle to avoid the harsher light of the gaslamp, and placed it beside the painting. The room would remain a shrine to his memory, and when she moved from here everything would be placed exactly as it was now in her new home.

She lifted her tear-filled eyes to regard the painted face. 'Oh Dad, what am I to do now? How could you have died that way? A stupid accident. You were so strong – so full of vigour.'

She burst into fresh weeping. Gradually, when her sobs stilled, she became aware of the drunken laughter and singing drifting to her from the bar below. Joe would have been proud of such a send-off. But she had neglected his friends and customers too long. She didn't want it said that she considered herself above her father's friends.

On pushing open the bar door, she was buffeted by the stench of closely-packed bodies, stale beer fumes and the thick fog of tobacco smoke. It stung her throat and irritated her nostrils. The noise was deafening. The pianola was playing a popular tune, but the bawdy rendition the customers were singing bore no relation to the words Casey knew. Women were cackling with laughter; glasses chinked together in constant toasts; and men were shouting to be heard above the raucous singing.

The central gaslights hanging from the ceiling cast bright pools of light over the gathering. In the darker corners she thought she glimpsed a woman's bare knee as her male companion stroked her thigh. There was a round of hooting from the far corner and the shout of, 'Come on, Florrie, give us a dance!'

A red-faced woman with a stout figure, her bodice half undone to expose the tops of her breasts, climbed unsteadily on to a table. The men encouraged her.

'Come on, old girl. Kick up them legs.'

There was a flash of greyish linen as the woman hoisted her skirts above her knees, her stockings showing several darns and holes as she wiggled her hips and began to kick her legs.

'That's it. Good ol' Florrie. Show us yer drawers. Or ain't yer wearing none?'

Casey blushed hotly, ill-at-ease and out of place amongst these people. A man with an eye-patch and no teeth, who she knew to be the same age as her father, saw her.

'If it ain't the li'l princess 'erself. Joe's precious daughter come slumming.'

Instantly Rusty was at her side. 'You shouldn't be in here, Casey. They've all had too much to drink.'

She looked straight at the man who had derided her and raised her voice so that more of the gathering could hear. 'You are all here to honour the memory of Joe Strong. You were his friends. I wanted to thank you all for coming, for giving him such a grand send-off.'

'Ain't no need to thank us. Joe was an hero hereabouts.' A surly man leered at Casey. 'He knew where he belonged. He didn't think himself better than us.'

To Casey's surprise, Bertha clipped the man on the side of the head. 'Don't yer be disrespectful to Miss Casey. Apple of her father's eye, she were. He wanted her to better herself. But she ain't stuck up. No one in the Courtyard 'as ever given 'er much of a chance. They were too riddled with jealousy that Joe protected 'er from poverty and squalor.' Bertha put her hand on her ample hips and thrust out her immense bosom. 'Insult Miss Casey and you insult Joe's memory.'

'Aye, well, she'll be moving on fast enough once she gets 'er 'ands on Joe's cash,' the man grunted.

Two coalmen with tidemarks around their necks as thick as Thames mud leaned against the bar. 'I'll 'ave another beer, Bertha, seeing as it's on the 'ouse,' one said. 'Spent enough of me 'ard-earned cash 'ere in the past – might as well get wot's going free.'

Eva confronted the drunken coalman. 'You can piss off, if that's your attitude. The drink is free to Joe's friends, not freeloaders. Anything else that goes down his throat, Bertha, make sure he pays for.'

'No, Eva,' Casey cut in and was forced to shout to make her voice heard above the din. 'Drink up. You were Joe Strong's friends and he would want you all to enjoy yourselves.'

The noise and press of bodies was making her head throb. She wanted the peace and quiet of her room to mourn her father, and this was a part of his world from which he had deliberately excluded her.

Bertha watched Casey leave and shook her head sadly. Joe's daughter was out of place in the pub. She was a lady, gentle and refined. Too gentle for this area where consideration and compassion were regarded as weaknesses. She squinted as her stare rested upon Eva Bowman. Now she was a different kettle of fish. There was nothing compassionate or gentle about that one. She was a schemer. Joe had changed since that hussy had come to live here. Just look at the way Rusty fawned over the baggage who was fluttering her eyes at him. The woman teased him by rubbing herself against him whenever she got the chance. Yet for all Eva's flirting, there was coldness in her. Bertha didn't trust her. Joe was proof the creature was no good. He was a private man who kept his thoughts to himself, but he had been troubled in the last months. And the manner of his death was so tragic that she had begun to wonder if there was more to it than there appeared to be. Joe could hold his drink. As a trained boxer he had fast reflexes and was light and agile on his feet. How could a man like him take a tumble down the stairs? It didn't make sense to her.

Hatred blazed in her eyes as she heard Eva Bowman laugh. She'd been all over Joe – cooking, mending, fussing over him; yet where was the grieving niece that had played the role so dramatically at the graveside earlier? And now the baggage was buttering up Rusty. And the kindly fool was lapping it up. He couldn't take his eyes off Eva. Bertha sighed. There was no doubt that Eva Bowman was a looker, but inside she was uglier than sin. She reckoned Myrtle hadn't been far wrong in calling her a devil-woman.

Eva saw Bertha studying her and registered the unmistakable loathing on the woman's face. The feeling is mutual, Bertha, she thought, but you've made a dangerous enemy in me. She knew Bertha could be a problem. The sooner you're out of this pub and unable to cause mischief, the better, she thought.

'Black doesn't become you, Miss Bowman,' a slick voice slithered through her consciousness, causing her throat to knot.

'Mr Goldstein.' She forced a smile. 'I didn't see you arrive.'

'Wouldn't be right for me not to pay my last respects to Strongarm.' His smooth face was a benign mask of fleshy contours, the thin lips stretched into a parody of a smile. It was his eyes, appraising and salacious, which turned the gin in her stomach to brine. There had been no word from him in the last fortnight, and she had begun to hope that he had forgotten her. He continued in a voice of poisoned nectar, 'And now you are alone, what will become of you, Miss Bowman? Joe had debts, so I hear, and little money to meet them.'

She felt the blood drain from her face. He missed nothing. Suddenly she knew that it was Goldstein who had Joe's money. There was a metallic taste of blood in her mouth as she bit her lip to stop her cry of anguish. In Goldstein's clutches, Joe's money was forever lost to them – and worse, in Eva's eyes, for without Joe's protection her life would be in peril if she dared to rebuff the gangleader's advances. Her heart thundered in panic. His gaze lowered to rest upon her heavy breasts which were rising and falling as she struggled to control her fear.

When his hand clamped over her wrist it bit into her flesh like a steel manacle. She gasped, fighting against nausea and faintness. When his free hand cupped her chin, she could no longer control a tremor of fear. The lecherous expression in his eyes changed: first it became angry, then speculative and finally amused.

'No man has called on you since you came here. It wasn't just because of Joe, was it?'

She prayed that if he suspected that she had no real liking for men he would leave her alone. Instead he grinned, his whisper taunting. 'I'll let you know when we shall dine together, Eva. For you, I have something special in mind.'

She nodded, dumbly, too terrified to refuse. His answering grin was without humour. 'You will not find me ungrateful.'

It took all Eva's willpower not to shudder as he raised his glass to her. The atmosphere in the bar was suffocating and, as she turned away, she saw Bertha's suspicious glare on her. She also saw that Bertha was holding Rusty back from coming to her rescue and confronting Goldstein.

'What did that scum want?' Rusty demanded as Eva drew level.

'Just paying his respects to Joe.' Eva looked away. Rusty couldn't help her.

'She ain't lost no time playing up to the men now Joe's out of the way,' Bertha said as she turned to pour whisky into its pewter measure and then into a glass. 'She'll 'ave bitten off more than she can chew with Goldstein. Don't get involved, Rusty. She's trouble and she's mean.'

Eva rounded on her. 'I was only being polite to a customer. We can't afford to pay Goldstein's men protection money on top of everything else. You'd better hope he's feeling charitable enough to his old mate Joe to lay off us.'

Bertha snorted and pushed pint glasses of porter into outthrust hands. Rusty fell silent, working without being really aware of what he was doing. He was sick with worry over Eva. He knew Goldstein for the villain he was. The gangleader was notorious for picking up women and discarding them after a couple of weeks. He'd seen Eva's fear and didn't know how he could help her. He was a big man and handy with his fists. Not in Joe's league, of course, but he could put a man out cold in a fair fight. But with Goldstein, if he set his thugs on you, there was no such thing as a fair fight.

'Don't be so hard on Eva,' he said when next Bertha passed him. 'She's had it rough this year.'

Bertha lifted a narrow pencilled brow. 'Bad seeks out bad in my book. She always were no good. It ain't no secret that

Sid Bowman regularly took his belt to 'er, and Myrtle 'ated her guts, blaming her fer the way young Charlie died.'

'There ain't no call to go talking like that,' Rusty defended her hotly.

'What's the old tart saying to you, Rusty?' Eva had sneaked up behind Bertha to demand.

'Bit of friendly advice, that's all,' Bertha returned. 'And I've been thinking it's mighty odd that a man as strong and nimble-footed as Joe fell down the stairs and broke 'is neck. I'd say such an accident was near impossible.'

'Come off it, Bertha,' Rusty intervened. 'Joe were pickled that night. It were a tragedy and we all miss him sorely.'

Eva's eyes were saucer-wide and glinting with malice as she thrust her face close to Bertha's. 'You've got a wicked mind.'

'Takes one to know one, deary.'

There was a volley of complaints from the other side of the bar. ''Ere you three, a man could die of thirst whilst you're jabbering. Joe would turn in 'is grave to see 'is customers parched, 'specially as we're 'ere to give 'im a grand send-off.'

Kept busy for the rest of the evening, Bertha managed to catch Rusty by himself whilst Eva was collecting glasses from the tables. 'Watch out for that one, Rusty. You're too soft. She's trouble.'

Eva saw Bertha had cornered Rusty. By the way the big man shuffled uncomfortably, she guessed the barmaid was warning Rusty not to get involved with her. Rusty was the only man she trusted. He might not be able to save her from Goldstein, but he still had his uses. The moment Rusty disappeared down the cellar, she rounded on Bertha.

'Just you keep your opinions to yourself,' she warned.

'Or yer'll do what?' Bertha faced her, her hands on her rounded hips. 'Don't think yer can frighten me. Ye're no good. Yer deserve Goldstein. Not that yer'll last any longer than 'is other tarts. Yer've been up ter no good ever since yer came here. Rusty won't sack me. And if 'e does, I'll know who put 'im up to it. You can sack me, girl, but yer can't silence me. Remember that.'

Humphrey Frost remained unmoved when Matt confronted him in what had been their father's study. Just seeing Humphrey ensconced behind the wide desk riled Matt. There was a smugness about his brother's expression that almost compelled Matt to punch his face into a pulp. Dragging on his reserves of diminishing patience, he kept his clenched fist inside his trouser pocket and battled to keep calm. Humphrey had grown from the bully of his expensive public school to a self-righteous patriarch. They had never liked each other.

Humphrey pressed his thin lips together, disapproval scoring the flaccid jowls on his jawline. 'If you've come here to beg me to waive the debt owed by Strong, save your breath.'

'I'm asking you to be reasonable. At least supply the Britannia with beer. Cassandra has promised that the debt will be paid once the pub is sold.'

'That could take months – a year even. It's out of the question. Let one debtor get away with it, and next thing no one will settle their accounts.'

'That's petty and vindictive.'

'It's business, little brother.'

'Pa would be ashamed to have Frost's Brewery stoop so low.'

'Don't tell me how to run my business, Matthew,' Humphrey bristled. 'You've never pulled your weight in the brewery. It's time you curbed your wild ways. Girls from the Courtyard are for bedding, not wedding. Marry Clementine and stop bringing disrepute to our name.'

'God, that's rich coming from you,' Matt raged. 'I've worked for my living. I even paid for my own flying lessons.'

When his brother pursed his lips disdainfully, Matt's temper soared. He'd taken enough of his brother's hypocritical, patronising attitude. 'What I've achieved I'm proud of. As for not pulling my weight in the brewery, I never took a penny out of it for all the work I did when Pa had his accident, whilst *you* have feathered your nest. I've seen the accounts. It's easy to see where the money came from for your large new house and flashy car. And what about your love-nest in Hackney? Your latest in a long line of mistresses lives in style. Don't lecture me on morals when your only child was born riddled with syphilis from your whoring. *You* may pretend your wife is dying of consumption, which is why you've just shut her away in a sanatorium. The truth is she's been infected. Poor wretch went mad from the shame of it when she learned the truth.'

Humphrey got up and crossed to the door. 'I won't listen to this. I don't have to explain myself to you. If you weren't so besotted with the Strong woman, you'd see that her father thought that because of your liaison with his daughter, the brewery could be conned out of money rightfully owed to it.'

'Joe Strong was not dishonest,' Matt defended. 'He was probably juggling his finances for a few weeks for the down-payment on the new pub. It's often like that in business.'

'Strong was one of the biggest rogues in London,' Humphrey sneered. 'I've had a man investigate that family. Your little strumpet may have won Pa over, but I know her type. The Strongs were stringing you along for what they could get.'

Matt's hand shot out and grabbed his brother's lapels. 'That's a lie.'

The thin lips curled back and Humphrey's tongue flickered over his teeth, like a snake tasting its prey. 'Strong was in thick with all the leading criminals. He was a fence for stolen jewellery. That's where his money came from. Dishonesty was second nature to him. Now do you see why his daughter is unfit to be your bride? Give her a good fuck and get her out of your system. That's all her kind are good for.'

Matt slammed his fist into his brother's face three times. Blood streamed from Humphrey's eye and nose. Matt was too angry to feel the pain in his lacerated knuckles as he stormed out of the house.

He jumped on a tram. Arms folded, he glared out of the window. He had travelled the width of the city before his temper began to cool. He would never forgive his brother for what he had said. Nevertheless, he was shocked that Joe was involved with the underworld. If his finances were tied up with those villains, he suspected they had seen the last of any investments Joe might have set up to safeguard his daughter's future.

The traffic had slowed to accommodate a Suffragette rally. As the tram rattled past, he saw the women and police officers tussling. Several windows of Hardcastle's Emporium had been broken by the militant women demanding the vote. Despite his grim mood, Matt managed a smile. Was it by chance the women had chosen that store, or was it retribution? While making a political point they had served rough justice on the owner's son who had abused the women in his employment.

The tram stopped at Aldgate Pump and Matt alighted. What he saw on the newsboy's placard made him frown:

'HABSBURG HEIR ASSASSINATED IN BALKANS.'

Buying the paper, he read that the heir to the Austro-Hungarian throne, the Archduke Franz Ferdinand, and his morganatic wife had been murdered in Bosnia by a Serbian. The Habsburgs were powerful monarchs. How would their allies react to the archduke's death?

Matt was not to be curious for long. The archduke's death proved to be a catalyst which threatened to plunge the great nations of Europe into war. The kaiser supported Austria, and his troops were marching on Serbia. The tsar had countered by mobilising his army. Britain and France were being drawn in to support their allies. And the question on everyone's lips was, Would Britain fight?

Chapter Thirteen

The summons from Goldstein came in mid-July. It pitched Eva into panic. She chose a high-necked, black gown without any adornment. Her black hair was piled high and ornamented with a curling black ostrich feather in a tortoiseshell clasp, and her only jewellery was a pair of jet drop earrings. A glance in the mirror revealed her face was devoid of colour, and she rubbed some light rouge into her cheeks and lips. It was not done to attract Goldstein. The severity of her attire was intended to crush his desire. She defied his wish that she should wear bright colours using her mourning as an excuse, but she did not want to appear pale and afraid. That would give Goldstein more power over her.

She did not mention the summons to Casey, who fortunately was visiting Archie's mother who had recently suffered a slight stroke. Eva had hoped to leave the pub unobserved, and was dismayed to run into Rusty returning to the bar from the back of the house.

'Where are you going at this hour?' he demanded.

'Just out.'

'Don't give me that, Eva.'

She couldn't look at him. 'I'm dining with Goldstein. Don't let Casey know, or that cow Bertha. I don't need her gloating about it.'

Rusty groaned. 'Don't go. I'll sort this out somehow.'

She shook her head and put her hand on his arm. 'There ain't nothing you can do, Rusty. I don't want you hurt. We ain't in no position to defy Goldstein.'

'There has to be something we can do.' His voice was fractured with pain.

'Be realistic, Rusty. He rules by terror. When he snaps his fingers, people jump or don't live to tell the tale.'

She swallowed and eyed him defiantly. He had proved a friend and she was realistic enough to know that if he tried to help her, he'd get himself killed, and probably her as well. 'I ain't no innocent like me cousin. You always treated me proper, Rusty.' She deliberately roughened her speech, reminding him of her background. 'I ain't a virgin. But neither am I a whore, so don't go thinking that. It's just one night. I can handle that. Better to put up with it than get me face carved up or the Britannia burned down.'

His shock rendered him speechless. She smiled bleakly. 'So now you know why I ain't good enough for you, Rusty.'

She left the pub before he could detain her. Goldstein's car was waiting outside for her, a gorilla of a driver the only occupant. She sat in the back and tried to blank her mind to the terror which was gripping her bowels. Dear God, let it be over quickly. Don't let him hurt me.

She was too immersed in her misery to pay heed to where they were going, except they drove through the City to the West End. A half-hour later the car pulled up outside a large four-storey house set back from the road. The only light which showed was in the stained-glass fanlight above a solid, iron-studded door. From the moon's light, Eva saw the tall Gothic decorated gables and ornate plasterwork around each of the eight large sash-windows fronting the house. It was a grotesque showpiece of a residence, demonstrating the owner's ostentation and power. It was as welcoming as a fortress.

The driver opened the car door and grunted for her to get

out. She did so, her legs trembling so violently she thought she would fall. She drew a deep breath, battling to show outward calm. As she approached the solid oak door, it opened soundlessly on oiled hinges. The hall was overlit with two large crystal chandeliers which hurt Eva's eyes. She was surprised when a frock-coated servant stepped forward to take her coat. Concealing her reluctance, she relinquished it, and was led through an archway to a dining room which already housed a dozen guests. Her breath relaxed in a rush. It was not to be an intimate tête-à-tête as she'd dreaded.

On closer inspection of the half-dozen women present, her alarm returned. Although their dresses were made of silk, taffeta or lace, they were all styled with immodestly low necklines and bodices which pushed up their breasts, so that only the nipples were concealed behind a fine ruching of material. The women were all courtesans, and the men looked wealthy. If she wasn't mistaken, at least two of them were members of Parliament and another spoke with the cut-glass accent of the nobility. With sickening dread she suspected that she was in one of Goldstein's high-class brothels.

Her head reeled. Just what did this pervert have in mind?

'My dear Miss Bowman – Eva.' Goldstein strutted over and slid an arm proprietorily around her waist. 'How good of you to join us. You will take some wine before we dine.' His expression was displeased as he noted her high-necked black dress. 'You look as prim as a nun. Though I doubt you realised how that could make some men desire you.'

'I'm in mourning for Joe,' she defended.

'But life goes on.' She did not miss the warning note in his voice and her bravado faltered. 'Since you have assumed a pious air, I shall seat you next to the bishop when we dine.'

A crystal goblet was pressed into her hand. Her heart palpitated as she drank deeply to revive her courage. The wine tasted strangely spicy to her uneducated palate.

'Drink up, my dear. It will relax you,' Goldstein urged, snapping his fingers for a servant to refill her glass. 'This is a special evening, as you will discover. And you will be the belle of the ball.'

The wine was intoxicating, melting the tension from her muscles. The gangleader was solicitous and attentive, and on receiving several malignant stares from the courtesans, Eva knew they viewed her as a rival. They could keep Goldstein as far as she was concerned, but their hatred for her fuelled her feeling of power. Goldstein had the pick of the most beautiful women in London, and he had chosen her. Thinking about it like that, it was a compliment. Even if this place was a brothel, she had never been in such a grand house. This was how she wanted to live. Her ambition was fired. One day she would own a house as grand as this.

As her glass continued to be topped up, she no longer felt so threatened. To her surprise the men were witty and charming. Could she have been mistaken? Perhaps Goldstein liked to entertain his friends and their mistresses in his home. When she found herself laughing at one of the politician's anecdotes, she no longer cared where she was. She had never enjoyed herself so much.

The room was hot and she began to wish she had not dressed so primly. The other women looked much cooler in their low-necked evening gowns. From then on the evening began to pass in a haze of pleasure. Several men bowed to her and complimented her on her beauty as Goldstein led her through to the immense dining room. A huge chandelier hung over the long table which seated a score of guests, and the ruby silk-lined walls were hung with six large mirrors which reflected its brilliant light.

Halfway through the first course, she was shocked when the bishop on her right squeezed her thigh. 'My condolences on your sad loss, but it is my duty to console you.'

As his hand moved higher, she almost choked on her soup. She didn't need the consolation this randy sod was offering. Incensed, she rapped his knuckles with a spoon and saw his eyes darken ominously.

'Have I been a naughty boy?' he whispered. 'Do I need a spanking to teach me to be good?'

'Not by me, you don't. Try a cold shower or self-flagellation. That might cure your impure thoughts, my lord bishop.'

She turned her back on him and was surprised to see that Goldstein seemed amused, although she was aware that she had insulted his guest.

The heat from the huge chandelier above the table was increasing Eva's discomfort. She had always reckoned she had a hard head for drink, but this wine was making her feel disorientated, heightening her senses in the oddest way. The rainbow colours of light refracted in the chandelier were vivid in their intensity; each dish of food was mouth-watering. Her body felt sinuous, too, and her bones without substance. She had lost her fear of Goldstein and her mood became euphoric. A servant was forever at her elbow replenishing her wine glass. Realising that she was in danger of drinking too much and losing control, she put out her hand to prevent him refilling her glass. Her fingers brushed the wine bottle, knocking it from the servant's grasp. Red wine gushed over her lap, soaking her to the skin. She leapt up with a gasp.

'Stupid oaf, look what you've done!'

Goldstein lashed out, striking the servant across the shoulders. 'Get out. You're fired. Imbecile. Get out.' He turned to Eva, who was distraught as she held her sodden skirt and petticoats away from her thighs. 'My dear, I cannot apologise enough for that fool of a servant. Go with Mrs Henderson, my housekeeper. She will tend to your needs and ensure your dress is not ruined.'

One of the courtesans sniggered, and Eva flushed with anger.

She was far too hot in her black dress and felt like an outcast – a crow amongst parrots. Goldstein guided her from the table and Mrs Henderson materialised from an unseen door. She was a reassuringly matronly figure in a brown cotton dress, with two grey plaits wound around her head.

Whisked away, Eva was led upstairs to a dressing room panelled in golden wood. There was a day bed in one corner and a cheval mirror in another.

'Slip out of your gown, Miss Bowman,' Mrs Henderson said. 'I'll get a maid to sponge and press it for you. Your petticoats as well. The maid must soak them at once or they will be ruined.'

'I can't strip off here,' Eva moaned, struggling to gather her disorientated thoughts. It was impossible. All she was aware of was the coolness of the wet material against her naked thigh above her stockings, and the heavy musk scent which filled the room. God knows what Goldstein had given her to drink, but anything that made you feel this good was fine by her. She couldn't remember why she'd been so afraid to come here. Goldstein wasn't so bad after all. It was some slap-up meal he was giving to his friends. She was flattered that he had chosen her as his hostess. But why her? She frowned, annoyed that she could not think straight. Any coherent thought was a cobweb-form, fluttering into her mind then vanishing without substance.

Mrs Henderson was smiling at her in a reassuring manner. 'Don't you worry about changing your clothes. Mr Goldstein's daughter is about the same build as yourself. She left half her wardrobe here when she married last year. There's bound to be something suitable you can wear.'

Eva was having difficulty piecing together the housekeeper's sentences as the older woman helped her out of her clothing. Mrs Henderson had barely left the room before she reappeared holding out an emerald silk skirt and matching low-cut bodice decorated with seed-pearls. It caressed Eva's skin as it floated over her shoulders and nestled about her waist. Once the lacing at the back was fastened, the housekeeper nodded with satisfaction.

'It's a picture you look, Miss Bowman. But permit me . . .' The housekeeper pulled down the neckline of the gown so that it revealed the swelling mounds of Eva's heavy breasts. 'Such beauty should not be covered. Black is not your colour. You should wear bright colours to enhance the perfection of your skin.'

Eva's spirits lifted at the blatant praise. Why shouldn't she show off her breasts? She was proud of their size and firmness. One or two of the courtesans were positively flat-chested compared to her. Especially the one who had sniggered at her when she had knocked over the wine. The gown was perfect, fitting snugly across her waist and flaring over her hips. It was only as she drifted down the stairs that she saw the outline of her legs beneath the clinging skirt. Mrs Henderson had not given her any petticoats to wear. Yet even as the thought formed, it no longer seemed to have importance. The colour of the dress enhanced her dark beauty and displayed her hour-glass figure in a way which would have every man admiring her. The knowledge of that power was as potent as the strong wine.

She glided regally into the dining room, confident that she was beautiful enough to have even Goldstein eating out of her hand. Eva floated to her seat in a languorous daze. The men's stares were bold and admiring. She was undoubtedly the most beautiful woman present, and every man here was spellbound by her charms.

The rest of the meal passed in a glorious dream. Courses of baked trout with almonds and spiced capon were followed by a refreshing sorbet to clear the pallet. Then oysters were served, puffs of pastry filled with peacock and figs, salmon and asparagus in aspic, before finally they gorged themselves on a spun-sugar confection which melted on the tongue. The meal had lasted two-and-a-half hours and they had consumed a dozen courses with four types of wine. She had never tasted food so exquisitely delicious, or wine so like nectar sliding down her throat. With each glassful her senses became more heightened, until it seemed every pore in her body was tinglingly alive.

As the final course was cleared away, Goldstein leaned towards Eva. He no longer seemed so fat and repulsive, nor did he hold any terror for her. His face was flushed and his eyes sparkled in a way which pierced the sensual torpor Eva had fallen into. 'Now the entertainment, my dear. Something special. Something I know you will appreciate.'

He clapped his hands and a curtain which Eva had thought covered a bay-window slid back to reveal a raised platform. A haunting melody played on an invisible violin and piano, and two blonde women dressed in long white Grecian robes began to dance. As they moved their garments parted, revealing shapely calves and thighs. The tempo of the music increased and the swirling skirts rose higher and higher. The women arched backwards, running their hands provocatively over their breasts and down to their abdomen. It was a dance of pure enticement, the women's faces rapt as they caressed themselves with loverlike abandonment. Eva's body was stinging with an excited heat. The music thrummed through her brain and the hedonistic movements of the women held her mesmerised. As they began to peel away layers of clothing, their breasts were visible. The carmined nipples jutted provocatively and Eva felt her own nipples tighten.

The dance was unlike anything Eva could conceive of. The women's bodies undulated and swayed. More clothing was shed until only a single diaphanous tunic remained, through which the dark triangle of their pubic hair was revealed. There was no pretence now that the dance was anything other than deliberately erotic. Eva's stomach was clenched with a bittersweet ache of arousal. Sweat trickled down her backbone and between her breasts, the tugging at her loins growing to an unbearable intensity. She had been unable to drag her eyes from the women throughout their performance, and the stirrings which set her blood on fire had been more tempestuous than any man's lovemaking had ever roused in her.

The dance did not end when both women were naked. Eva's throat dried as they began kissing and stroking each other's bodies. A glass was pressed into her hand and she gulped it down avidly. Again the pungent spiciness of it struck her. Moments later the room began to lose its dimensions and her surroundings became misty. Hands were raising her, the faces of the people were blurred as she was spun round a circle of men and women. The tempo of the music had become faster. She was floating. Laughter bubbled from her lips as they spun her from one to another. Some of the hands were gentle, others tugging awkwardly at her. There was a coolness on her limbs. When she dragged her hand down to look at her whirling figure, she was disconcerted to see that she was no longer wearing the emerald bodice, and the skirt was loose about her hips. Why that should strike her as amusing she did not know, but she could not stop her laughter.

A hand reached for her breast and snatched the silk chemise away. There was a murmur of approval from the men as the creaminess of her naked breasts glowed under the crystal chandelier. She threw back her head, delighting in their adoring gazes and feeling no shame. The knowledge that her beauty could hold men entranced was a powerful aphrodisiac.

Other hands, more insistent now, were jerking her body as they tugged at the laces of her corset. She was laughing with them. They were her acolytes and she the revered goddess. All the faces were reddened by drink, their eyes wild and mouths wide with laughter. They were tearing her clothes from her and she could not stop laughing.

Dizzy and light-headed, she was vaguely aware that the hands were no longer pulling at her. They were caressing, teasing her body to a frenzied seizure of longing. Several figures drifted past her dreamy vision in naked abandonment. There was a jarring of her spine as she was spun so fast that she toppled. She laughed, feeling liberated and free. Her body was aglow with new and wonderful sensations. Naked arms and legs writhed like snakes in a heavy mass around and upon her. When the softness of a woman's breast grazed her mouth, her lips sought it, sucking hungrily. Soft lips kissed her body until her cries of pleasure rasped raw her throat. The wild music faded into the distance, the pressure of sweating, interlocked figures folding around her.

Finally exhaustion triumphed over the bacchanal.

Eva returned to consciousness with the musky scent of sex filling her nostrils. Her body was chilled and she could not understand why she was lying naked on the floor. She pushed herself up on her elbow, the movement making her head pound and every muscle and limb ache. This was one hellish hangover. Her tongue was coated with fur and her body felt as though it had been mown down by a steamroller. With a groan she focused her eyes and recoiled in shock. Her head had been nestled in the crotch of one of the dancers.

A sadistic chuckle completed her humiliation. Her hair which was hanging loose was yanked cruelly, her head jerked back so that she was forced to stare into Goldstein's grinning countenance. 'You were the best we've ever had, Eva. I knew you'd be good. A natural. And what's more, you loved every minute of it.'

She drew her legs up to cover her nakedness. He chuckled wickedly. 'Too late for that, sweetheart, and I ain't your type, am I? It were Gloria, Esther and Annabel who had you cooing like a love-sick dove.'

He released her hand and it flopped forward, her gaze falling on three naked women lying entwined all around her. As she stared at them, she felt her blood stirring as it never had before. The knowledge did not disgust her; rather she felt a release.

'Where are my clothes?' she said resignedly. 'What time is it? I must get home.'

Goldstein laughed. 'You'll be back for more though, won't you?' He tossed several sovereigns into her lap. 'The men pay well for a spectacle like last night's. This way you get paid for doing what you like.'

Eva shrugged and clutched the money in her hand. Why not, she thought? The only woman I've ever really loved was Casey, and she wasn't of a like persuasion. This way she could indulge in forbidden pleasure and get paid handsomely for it. 'On one condition,' she bargained. 'I don't want to be recognised. I'll wear a wig and be known by a different name. And I don't want me cousin learning of this.'

'Why should she? This could be profitable for both of us.'

'And what happens when I want out?'

Goldstein shrugged. 'The show you gave us last night was sensational, because you enjoyed it and were willing – as are all the women. It ain't a long-term arrangement. My customers like variety. No matter how good you are, they may tire of you in a month – or it could be a year.'

Eva's mind was racing. 'This is fine for the time being, but I want to earn enough to get out of the Courtyard for good. I'm willing to do more for you than this. I know what Joe was up to, fencing jewellery and the like. I could take over from him. I'll be working in the Britannia from now until we can sell it.'

Goldstein's eyes crinkled. 'A woman can't run a pub. You'll have to marry the barman.'

Eva blanched. 'That wasn't in my plans.'

'Then we can't do business.' He tossed her a silk wrapper to cover herself. 'Though I'll send word when I need you again here.'

'But I want to fence the jewellery. And we're stuck at the Britannia until the debts are paid. Has anyone taken over from Joe yet? Wouldn't it be simpler to keep the arrangements as they were, but the thieves deal with me?'

He rubbed his chin as he considered her words. 'It might work, since you're so set on it. You get ten per cent of any deal.'

Eva guessed that this was a great deal less than Joe was paid. 'Twenty per cent.'

'Fifteen, and don't try to hold any of the goods back. There'll be someone watching you. Anyone who cheats on me gets a knife in their guts, and my boys make sure it's a slow, painful death.'

'I ain't going to cheat on you, Mr Goldstein.' Eva still reckoned the fifteen per cent was peanuts compared to what Joe had earned, but it was better than nothing.

'I'll notify the boys to collect any stuff from you on Sundays and Wednesdays in the alley behind the pub. First you'd better know the prices.'

For half an hour, Eva was instructed on what to pay out to the thieves and how much she could expect to keep back.

'Remember, I know everything that goes on in my patch.'

When Eva returned to the Britannia she found Rusty asleep at the kitchen table with his head on his arms. He had stayed up all night waiting for her. She hadn't expected that. Her footfall awoke him and his face showed his relief that she was safe.

'Did that bastard hurt you?' His fist struck the table. 'I've hated myself for not being able to do anything to save you.'

His concern touched her. 'This will surprise you. He didn't lay a finger on me. We dined with several of his acquaintances and then he put a proposition to me.'

'Aye, I expect he did.' Rusty's face hardened.

'Not what you think.' She let out a chuckle. 'You knew Joe was a fence, didn't you?'

Rusty nodded.

'Well, Goldstein reckoned I've enough sass to take over from him until we leave here.'

'Are you mad? He'll be setting you up!'

'It seemed the lesser evil, Rusty.' She challenged him with a fierce glare. Then, seeing his censure, her face crumpled and she burst into tears. 'Hold me, Rusty. I was so frightened. I didn't know what to do. It's only until we leave here when the debts are settled with Frost. The money from Goldstein will help towards that debt.'

His arms closed around her and he sighed wearily. 'Aye, it could've been worse. When I thought what he had in mind for you, I could've killed him, Eva. Whatever they do to me, I'm not allowing you to go to him again.'

He'd swallowed her story hook, line and sinker. Good old Rusty. She'd have to invent a new friend to cover her visits to Goldstein's place. She couldn't see Rusty approving of that, and she was going to need his friendship if any of the pickpockets and thieves caused her problems.

'I appreciate you waiting up for me, Rusty. I've never had no one look out for me like you do.'

His large hand gently wiped a tear from her cheek. 'I'll always be there for you, Eva. I don't approve of this fencing business, but I never judged Joe for doing it. So I won't you. I suppose something like that was inevitable, though I don't know why Goldstein didn't approach me. At least now he won't be asking us for protection money, which was something else I've been worried about. Just make sure you're careful. I don't want to see you end up in Holloway prison.'

Eva was satisfied that she had regained Rusty's trust. Thank God it wouldn't be necessary to marry him as Goldstein had first suggested.

Every morning, Casey scanned the paper, praying for a peaceful solution to the problems which seemed to be gathering like stormclouds over Europe. Since her father's death, one difficulty after another rose to confront her. She still had to find work, but dealing with the pub accounts and constant meetings with her solicitors had until now taken up most of her time. She must give finding a job the next priority. She needed every shilling she could earn to pay off her father's debts.

It was August Bank Holiday and as there were only a few days' supply of beer left in the pub, she decided to close it for the day. Matt had been quiet and distracted all weekend. After quarrelling with his brother, he now stayed overnight in a lodging house in Bishopsgate during his leave from the airfield. He was due to return to duty tomorrow and Casey wanted his last day to be a carefree one.

'I thought we'd go to Southend by train today,' she announced to Matt when he arrived at ten o'clock.

Eva was immediately sullen. 'Great. And what do I do, twiddle my thumbs all day on my own?'

'I meant the four of us,' Casey went on. 'You and Rusty as well.'

'If you're matchmaking again, Casey,' Eva glared at her, 'you can just stop it. Rusty is a friend. I don't want him getting other ideas.'

'It'll be more fun with the four of us. We all need the break. There has been so much gloom since Dad died. Especially with the troubles in Europe. Going by the newspapers, it looks like England could also get involved if it comes to war.'

Eva pouted. 'Men and their bloodlust. Rusty is talking about joining the army once the pub closes.'

Rusty had joined them in the parlour. 'I'd rather fight for my country than be out of work.'

'You'd never be out of work,' Eva retaliated. 'You're too good a barman. Joe would have made you manager here. Besides, how can we run the pub without you, Rusty?' She glowered at Matt. 'That's if we get any beer . . .'

Fear slithered down Casey's spine, but it was not caused by the thought of losing the pub. Any war would involve Matt. With her grief for her father still raw, the thought of Matt placing himself in danger filled her with dread.

'I forbid talk of war today,' she announced. 'A day in Southend will do us all good.'

She looked askance at Matt who was lost in thought as he stared out of the window. 'Is that all right with you?'

'Fine. Anything you say.'

He was tense and there were shadows under his eyes. He had been working too hard at the airfield, for now he was also training pilots. With the escalation of events in Europe, men seeking adventure were enlisting in the Royal Flying Corps.

'Today will be special, Matt,' she said softly. 'If war breaks out there'll be little fun for a long while. Already people are beginning to panic and buy up food-stocks.' Although she had forbidden the subject, she was compelled to add, 'It could come to war, couldn't it?'

He nodded.

She swallowed against rising panic. 'And you will be involved?'

'I'd welcome the chance to put the kaiser in his place. He can't invade Belgium and get away with it.' His expression remained taut and sombre as he studied her. 'But I fear for your future, my love. I should be here with you. My family are pursuing the debt against your father's estate.'

'So my solicitor informed me. He's confident that it won't go to court. They have too much to lose – not least the threat of scandal if it becomes common knowledge that you are engaged to me. I don't want that.'

He slid an arm around her waist. 'I could kill Humphrey for the anguish he is causing you. I will never forgive my family for their vindictiveness.'

'Don't say that, Matt.' The arrogance in his tone smote her.

'I mean it, Casey. I want nothing more to do with them.'

'But your mother, it will break her heart.' Casey did not like Sybil Frost, but Matt was her favourite son. Her manipulation was her possessive way of showing that.

'Mama is as bad as Humphrey. She is behind this. She has Humphrey under her thumb and wants me there as well. She must accept you as my wife and support my wish to start an airline company.'

She was startled that he could be so unyielding.

His lips compressed and he added stiffly, 'Let's not talk about them. It's been weeks since my last leave, and I mean to enjoy this day. I have a feeling that I may not get away from the airfield for some time.'

He kissed her passionately until she was breathless. His ardour confirmed his love, but that he could so coldly dismiss his family, even though Casey herself believed them despicable, troubled her. He saw their actions as betrayal.

As they broke apart from the kiss, he was grinning, 'A day in Southend alone with you could be very special indeed. Do we really have to go with the others?'

'Safety in numbers, Matt,' Casey answered with a smile. 'Your only interest would be getting me into the first hotel you could find. I want a day of fun by the sea.'

'Can you blame a man for trying?'

Even his usual attempt at light-hearted seduction seemed to be an effort. His face looked strained, and on several occasions he had failed to hold her gaze. And his kiss had been brief and without passion when he greeted her.

'I've been poor company this morning,' he said wryly. 'The fun of the seaside is just what we all need.'

Chapter Fourteen

The train from Fenchurch Street station arrived at Southend-on-Sea just before midday. As expected for a Bank Holiday, the seaside town was crowded with tourists. From their cockney accents, many of them were from London, all dressed in their Sunday-best clothes. As they strolled down the main street towards the beach, a Salvation Army band, playing a rousing hymn, marched down the centre of the road.

The mood of the people swung from a determination to enjoy themselves to pandemonium as the latest edition of a paper appeared on the newsstands. It was snatched and fought over by the men.

Matt had seized a paper and stopped to scan the headlines, his expression tense. 'Nothing yet,' he said, handing it to Rusty.

'Please, let's not spoil today by thinking about whether there'll be war,' Casey insisted.

She could feel the tension in Matt's figure. His mood remained distracted even as they sauntered along the promenade and stopped to listen to the military band playing. Too restless to stay still, Matt drew her to the iron railing along the sea wall. Down on the beach the tide was still a good half-mile out, the bathing machines lined up waiting for the water to rise so that they could be rolled into the water. Men and youths had rolled up their trousers and were walking over the squelching mud to paddle in the distant water. Donkeys plodded up and down the hard-packed sand with giggling children on their backs. At least the children were carefree, Casey thought, but with anticipation of the war looming in everyone's mind, this must be the gloomiest Bank Holiday ever.

Close to the pier, which stretched over a mile into the Thames estuary, a crowd had gathered around Happy Harry, the lay preacher, who was singing a hymn to drown out the hecklers. A steamer was about to dock, bringing more holiday-makers up from Gravesend or Tilbury. Casey's attention was drawn to the ranting preacher, who was now waving his arms wildly as he held a Bible aloft.

'Sinners. Look to your salvation. The end is nigh. War will be sent to strike down the ungodly!'

'The English will show the fat old kaiser a thing or two, see if we don't,' a man shouted from the crowd.

Eva and Rusty had walked ahead, drawn by a photographer who was luring customers to pose with a pet monkey. As the hecklers jostled and started to jeer the preacher, a stinkbomb was thrown at him by a youth. Matt drew Casey away. It was not unknown for such gatherings to end in violence.

'Let's have our photograph taken, Matt,' Casey suggested. She was feeling uneasy because of his mood and the threat of impending war. If Matt was posted to France to fly reconnaissance flights it could be months before she saw him again.

'If it's a portrait you want, then come to my studio tomorrow,' the photographer suggested, angling for a higher fee.

'No, we're just here for the day,' Matt replied.

'Then it will have to be against the jungle backdrop. Do you want to hold the monkey, lady?'

'I prefer to hold my fiancé,' she responded with a smile at Matt. For the first time that day, there was warmth in Matt's eyes as he linked her arm through his and removed his hat to stand in a formal pose.

'Now don't move,' the photographer instructed, and dived under the black cloth which covered the back of his camera. A hand protruded, holding aloft a T-shaped gadget which emitted a sudden flash of light together with a puff of smoke. Matt paid the photographer, ordering two prints of the photograph to be sent to the Britannia.

The seafront was crowded, shopkeepers vying with each other, chanting and crying out to attract customers.

'Picture postcards of Southend,' yelled out a ruddy-faced man from a booth.

'Boat rides,' a seaman in navy jumper and waders hollered. 'Trip round Canvey Island. Leaves at four o'clock. Get yer tickets now to avoid disappointment.'

'Have yer shoes shined, mister.'

'Get yer cockles here. Winkles, best winkles.'

The noise and press of people was unceasing. Music blared from hurdy-gurdys or organs on the carousel ride further along the beach, and Casey's head was beginning to throb.

'What shall we do now?' Rusty asked, his gaze straying to a pub where a sing-song was in progress.

'We could take the electric tramway along the pier,' Casey suggested, thinking it would be quieter.

'I'm parched,' Eva announced. 'Let's go in the pub. It looks like fun.'

Casey hadn't come to Southend to sit in a pub all day. Neither, from Matt's expression, had he. He had been less talkative than usual and obviously had something on his mind, but each time she asked him what, he would not be drawn.

'You two go,' she suggested. 'I'd like to walk along the promenade. It's rather noisy here.'

'We came together, we should stay together,' Eva declared primly.

'Let's have lunch before we decide,' Casey placated her, pointing to a poster advertising 'The Kursaal'. 'There's a menagerie, circus, theatre and ballroom. We could go there after lunch. When we passed the Elysium restaurant it looked popular from the number of people going in.'

'The Elysium it is,' Rusty agreed. 'Then the Kursaal. There should be enough entertainment there to keep Eva happy.'

After the meal, they strolled along the seafront. Casey lifted her face to the warm wind and inhaled the salty air. Two clowns, one on stilts, the other a midget, wove through the holiday-trippers shouting, 'Come see the pier concert. Lovely Sophia, the songbird of Southend, will thrill you with her songs. Caspar the amazing magician will keep you enthralled with acts of illusion. Come one and come all to the end of the pier.'

'Let's go and see Caspar,' Eva said. 'Remember how good he was when we saw him at the Empire, Casey?'

'I'd thought we'd agreed on the Kursaal. We can do the pier later,' Matt responded, his voice clipped.

'Sorry for breathing, I'm sure,' Eva said, flouncing off ahead of them.

'What's wrong, Matt?' Casey said softly.

'Nothing. I'd rather have spent the day alone with you,' he whispered against her ear. 'Eva can be a bit trying at times.'

The Kursaal was a large building with a square turret topped by a glass dome. They paid their sixpence admission and entered an arcade which led from the entrance. It was decorated to represent a street in Cairo and was lined with booths and shops. Eva was moving ahead of them, interested in all the booths and dragging Rusty along in tow. In the enclosed space the noise of the holidaymakers was heightened. Casey pressed her fingers to her temple as her headache returned.

'The noise is worse in here,' she remarked.

'Do you want to leave?' Matt suggested.

'Leave!' Eva groaned disgruntledly. She'd returned to them having just been bought a haircomb by Rusty. 'But we've just paid sixpence to get in here. I ain't got money to throw away like that.'

Matt eyed her with annoyance. 'Casey is clearly suffering from the noise. Why don't you and Rusty stay and enjoy yourselves? We'll take a walk along the prom to Chalkwell or Leigh, and catch the train home from there. There's a train just after seven. We'll be on that one and we'll travel home together.'

'I thought we were having a day all together,' Eva insisted.

Rusty intervened with a laugh. 'Come off it, Eva. You're an unromantic soul. Can't you see Matt and Casey want some time alone. We'll have a great time here and we'll meet them on the train.'

Casey sighed. Sensitive to Matt's mood, she guessed it was important that they talk. 'Eva, it isn't like that. I do have a headache. A walk along the seafront will cure it. Enjoy yourself with Rusty.'

'And so I will,' she snapped, showing her annoyance. 'Bloody boring, a walk. What's there to see at Chalkwell but children's rides, or a band playing marches and some cockle-stalls? Southend is where all the excitement is. Don't be such a stick-in-the-mud, Casey.'

'Come on, Eva.' Rusty caught Eva around the waist. 'We'll have fun together and I'll buy you that brooch you were admiring.'

For once Eva was not so easily persuaded. She sniffed her disapproval. 'I'm sure I won't stay where my company is clearly not needed. Though you had better watch your reputation, Casey. Going off alone with your fiancé in a place full of hotels.' She stared hard at Matt. 'I hope that's not what you've got in mind, just because Casey no longer has a father to protect her.'

'Eva, how dare you imply such a thing!' Casey flared, her eyes flashing with anger. Her chin came up stubbornly. 'You can be assured that Matt and I will not be visiting any hotels, but if we did, then it would be none of your damned affair. You're not my guardian.'

Eva's lips pursed with censure. 'Do what you like. See if I care. Come on, Rusty, let's go and have some fun. At least *we* know how to.' She put her arm through the barman's and marched off in a temper.

Casey hesitated, feeling she should go after her cousin.

'Let's get out of here before she changes her mind and tags along,' Matt said, taking her arm and guiding her back through the crowd to the turnstile. For the first time that day his tone was light and teasing. Casey giggled, feeling like an errant schoolgirl avoiding a teacher for whom she had not done her homework.

'That woman clings to you like a leech, Casey,' Matt said with a grimace. 'I thought we'd never get any time this weekend without her prying into our conversation.'

'She's not so bad.' Casey automatically defended her cousin, though Eva's manner did annoy her.

Matt shook his head. 'Isn't she? She resents any time you spend with me.'

'She can be a bit over-possessive, but we are all the family each other has.'

'And I know the trouble a family can cause.' His expression was bleak and he stared fixedly ahead. There was something so ominous in his words that Casey shivered as they walked out of the building into the August sunshine.

'Matt, you mustn't be so hard on your mother. She acts as she does because she loves you.'

He didn't answer, and she saw the tendons in his neck stiffen with tension. They walked back along the promenade towards the pier in silence. A concert show was being performed on a makeshift stage and they stopped to watch the Jolly Boys, as the company was called, perform a slapstick comedy routine.

Their antics eased the last of Casey's annoyance over her cousin's attitude.

Matt squeezed her arm as they sauntered on. 'Isn't this better, just the two of us?'

She smiled into his handsome face. 'And a few thousand holidaymakers also taking the sea air. But it *is* good to be with you. We've had so little time together recently.'

The tide was coming in as they passed Absalom's Floating Baths. On the beach was a washing line of wet towels and costumes which could scarcely be dry by the time they were hired out again to the bathers. Gradually, as they left Southend behind and approached the seafront of Westcliff, the crowds began to thin. It wasn't until they reached Chalkwell, twenty minutes later, that Matt guided her to an empty seat.

'How can you think I am wrong to condemn my family after the way they have treated you?' he said tersely, returning to the subject which was clearly troubling him.

'Because I know that, in time, you will regret breaking with them.'

'They don't consider me or my happiness,' he ground out. 'Despite my pleas, Humphrey is continuing the case against your father's estate. That's bad enough, but Mama thinks I can be bought. She told me that if I wed Clementine, not only would they drop the debt case but they would still buy my plane. How could they think I would abandon the woman I love?'

She hung her head. 'I hate to think this rift is all because of me.'

'It's not you who caused it. It's their vindictiveness. I never realised that my mother would stop at nothing to get her own way. We'll beat them yet.' He took both her hands. 'Marry me now. I'll get a special licence. They can't do anything once we're wed. As your father's heir you are responsible for his debts, but as my wife, any debts you have would become my responsibility. This way, I will be liable for the debt to my family. Even Humphrey won't risk a public scandal by allowing a case against me to come to court. He'll have to drop the suit.'

She shook her head. Her heart ached that she was the cause of the torment he must be feeling. 'I appreciate your wish to protect me, but it will only make matters worse between you and your family. Besides, it would be disrespectful to both our fathers' memories to marry before our year of mourning is over.'

The brim of his Homburg cast deep shadows about his eyes, but the chiselled line of his jaw was clenched tight with tension. 'Joe would rather your future was secure than that you clung to a ritual. In the circumstances my father would understand. He would be appalled at Humphrey's conduct. He would understand my need to protect you. He was not against our marriage. How could he have been when many considered that he married beneath him. Why do you care so much about my family's feelings when they are treating you so badly?'

She was surprised Matt needed to ask that question. He really could be so stubborn where his pride was concerned. 'In all honesty, there are times when I hate your family for treating me as though I'm not good enough to marry you! It confirms all my prejudices about the snobbery of the wealthy. But family are family. You realise how precious that bond is when you no longer have one of your own. It's why I put up with so much from Eva. Matt, I love you too much to cause a rift between you and your mother and brother.'

He shook his head, turning his head towards the sea. 'You are a romantic idealist, Casey.'

Sensing the strain he was under, she didn't take offence. 'Perhaps I am where family is concerned. But I am also a realist. You may resent the way your family is treating you now, but one day you will regret falling out with them. You can't deny your own blood.'

She stared at the advancing sea which was almost to the promenade wall. Small fishing vessels bobbed on the waves, their catch mostly shellfish which were cooked in the huts at Leigh-on-Sea. 'Since Dad died, I've heard the shopkeepers in our street say that he was involved in the underworld. I've always hated dishonesty, but although I was shocked, what right have I to judge him for his actions?' She went on, 'It doesn't stop me loving him. I know that everything he did was because he loved me. He wanted me to be financially secure and happy.'

Matt's expression remained on the horizon, his expression still bleak. 'That's where you and I are different. I can't forgive this insult to you.'

He swung round in his seat to face her. The sun behind him shadowed his features, but his anger was evident in the deep timbre of his voice. 'I begged Humphrey to be compassionate. I pleaded with him as I have never in my life pleaded with anyone. He deserved the thrashing I gave him. He's been an arrogant bully all his life.'

Her hand closed over his. 'Matt, why must you be so proud?'

He regarded her with the cold arrogance which had been so apparent in his mother. 'Pride is everything, Casey. For years I've fought the way my family have tried to manipulate me. Wasn't it pride which made you go and demand the reference you were entitled to after the despicable way Hardcastle treated you? Sometimes pride and our dignity is all we have left when we are fighting against injustice.'

She shivered, chilled by his words. 'Don't talk to me like that, Matt. It frightens me.'

His gaze intensified, the golden lights sparking his hazel eyes with ardent fire. 'Marry me, Casey. Joe would rather I protect you than you stick to a year of mourning. Humphrey will not pursue the case against the Britannia once we are married. Once the place is sold you can repay the debt. It seems inevitable now that England will declare war on Germany; I can't do much if I'm stuck on the airfield. But if we were married you could live close to the airfield and I could see you more often.'

She became obstinate, her own pride making her insist, 'Before we set a date, I want this debt to your family cleared.' Seeing his frown, she rushed on, 'Besides, I have to stay in London until Dad's estate is settled.'

'Your solicitors can deal with that.' His impatience sharpened his voice. 'You haven't even a job which keeps you there now. The Britannia will have to close in a few days since our brewery will not supply you with beer. If you go to another brewery, Humphrey will sue you for breach of contract. You can't repay the loan if you have no income from the pub. If you won't wed me so I can assume the responsibility of Joe's debts, then wed me because I love you. I don't want to wait any longer. I could be posted to France any day.'

'Matt, that's selfish. I have Eva to consider. Where would she live? I've collected together all my mother's and my own jewellery to sell. It will raise part of the money to pay the debt. And if I have to, I'll sell some of Dad's silver trophies.'

She stood up, determined to change the subject. 'Let's walk on to Leigh and have a cup of tea and a plate of cockles for tea. I don't want us to quarrel, Matt. Time is getting on – we mustn't miss the train. Rusty and Eva will be worried.'

'Rusty will be delighted to have Eva for longer on her own. The man's mad about the woman. If she'd wed him, that would be one less responsibility for you to worry about.' He grinned wickedly, his mood veering as he held her gaze. 'This is the first time we've been alone together since Joe's death. Eva watches over you like a hawk. Couldn't we catch an earlier train and have an hour to ourselves at the pub?'

The invitation and love in his eyes were a provocative challenge. It offered happiness and peace, when for weeks she had known only heartache and worry.

'Casey, I love you,' he breathed against her hair. 'Don't you realise how hard it is for me, loving you, but not having the joy of being able to make love to you?'

The hunger and urgency in his voice brought a blush to her cheeks and a pulsating glow of excitement pervaded her body. 'Matt, you mustn't tempt me. It's becoming so hard for me to resist your kisses.'

His eyes twinkled shamelessly. 'We've been courting for a year, Casey. Marry me and end both our torments.'

Her breathing quickened, the promise in his eyes causing her senses to swirl. The lack of privacy meant they must restrain their passion. But her lips trembled to feel the tenderness of his kiss, her body quivering with desire to go beyond the caresses she had occasionally permitted. She was beginning to suspect that chastity was not a natural state for her. There were nights when her body yearned to experience his naked flesh against her own. But she had been brought up to respect the sanctity of marriage. It was wanton to envisage the joy of Matt making love to her on their wedding night. Even the thought of it now caused her flesh to tingle with anticipation. To break the effect his nearness could arouse, she checked her thoughts with a start and stood up.

'I'll think about what you say, but I still prefer to settle the debt with your family first. How else can I get them to respect me? They may never like me, but at least they cannot accuse me of dishonesty.'

Eva laughed more at the concert than she had done in years. Before the show began, Rusty had bought her several gins as she had been so angry at what she regarded as Casey's defection. Rusty was generous with his hard-earned cash, and Eva enjoyed being the centre of his attention. He bought her the marcasite brooch she had liked, and won a china-faced doll on a hoop-la stand, which he presented to her. She did not object when his arm slid around her waist as he guided her through the crowds to their seat in the concert hall at the end of the pier.

As they laughed at the antics of the comedian, they frequently glanced at each other. When she saw the affection in Rusty's eyes, Casey's abandonment no longer seemed so important. He bought her ice-cream. He bought her chocolates. He even bought her a sprig of heather for luck from an old gypsy woman. Earlier in the afternoon he had hired a boat and rowed on the lake. They gorged themselves on jellied eels and oysters until Eva could eat no more, and after the concert he again kept her gins lined up. Throughout he praised her, but the edge was taken from his compliments as he kept returning to speaking of his worries for Casey.

'It's a crying shame the Frosts have taken so against her. Her and Matt make a grand couple.' His eyes clouded with anxiety. 'I still can't believe Joe is dead. Nor that he didn't provide for poor Casey.'

'Casey has got the Britannia.' Eva didn't want to talk about her cousin. She preferred Rusty to keep his mind on her.

'A pub without beer.' He shook his head. 'The poor girl. Best thing she can do is marry Frost. He'll look after her.'

Eva's eyes narrowed. 'All I've heard from you today is poor Casey this, poor Casey that. She ain't so poor. She's got rooms full of grand furniture and fine clothes and jewellery. She's even got Joe's trophies she can sell. Not to mention what she'll get from the sale of the pub. She's got a darn sight more than me. What have I got? Most of my clothes are Casey's mother's hand-me-downs. If I didn't have that little nest-egg you gave me after Fat Sam attacked me, I'd be destitute. Yeah, I've got seventy pounds, but I was attacked and suffered Fat Sam's foul lechery before I escaped. If I hadn't taken to my heels that fat sod would've raped me. But I don't hear poor old Eva.

I suppose you think I deserve all I get.'

Rusty's face, ruddy from a day in the sun, froze with affront. 'I never said that. No woman deserves what Fat Sam tried to do to you. You were brave to fight him and get away. I admire you for that.'

She tossed back the last of her gin, her mouth a thin line of torment. 'Always it's Casey people feel sorry for. Isn't she the one with the posh education that'll always land her a fancy job? Likely she'll marry her toff. Then she won't want to be reminded she has a cousin who was raised in the Courtyard.'

'Casey wouldn't abandon you,' Rusty began but, seeing the anger sparking in her eyes at the mention of her cousin, he broke off.

'Go on, defend her like everyone else,' Eva continued. 'I'm surprised you allowed Frost to steal her away so that they could be alone. It sounds to me as though you fancy her yourself.'

Rusty laughed. 'Casey wouldn't look at the likes of me. I sort of feel responsible for her now that Joe's gone. Joe were good to me. I owe him. And Casey is special, but not in the way you mean.' He took Eva's hand in his large calloused palm. 'You're the one who's special, Eva. You've dragged yourself up by your bootstraps to make something of yourself. That takes guts. And you're just about the prettiest woman I've ever seen. I'm proud to be escorting you today.'

For Rusty that was a long speech. Embarrassed that he had spoken his feelings, he got up and got another round of drinks. His words had mollified Eva, but she still remained suspicious. She had thought Rusty was besotted with her and only her. She didn't like to think he had a special affection for Casey.

When he returned with two double gins for her and two pints of porter for himself, she gave him her brightest smile. She had enjoyed their visit to Southend and liked the way Rusty spent his money on her, without expecting anything in return. He'd tried no funny business today, nor made any lewd suggestions. The few kisses she had permitted him on their infrequent dates had been almost chaste. Not once had he tried to put his hand up her skirt or on her breasts. Perversely, she wondered if he didn't fancy her enough. Was he more interested in Casey than her, but knew Casey was out of his reach?

Jealousy pitted her. She drank the two gins quickly. Was she again to come second-best? She'd never won Joe's affection in the way she'd wanted. Now Rusty seemed to have a deeper affection for Casey than she had realised. She didn't like it. The drink was making her head spin. She could usually hold her booze, but she'd had a dozen or more gins today and they must have affected her more than she realised. Why else should she even care who Rusty was interested in? It wasn't that she considered him in any special way. She despised men and the way they treated women. She wanted none of them.

Yet as they made their way up the hill to Southend station, she still resented that she did not have first place in Rusty's affection. It galled her. Perhaps she would be kinder to him. Hadn't he treated her like a lady today and bought her lots of presents? If Casey did marry Matt Frost, what would happen to herself? Rusty was a valuable friend. She needed him. And didn't she know how to win a man's devotion? If she put her mind to it, Rusty wouldn't know what had hit him.

With a hiss of steam, the train pulled into Leigh-on-Sea station. As the cloud of swirling smoke cleared from around the carriages, Casey was surprised that Rusty was not waving to them out of a window.

'They must have missed it,' Matt said, opening the carriage door for her to alight. He looked pleased.

'Shouldn't we wait until the next one?'

'They could have got the times wrong and caught an earlier train, I suppose. It would be silly for us to hang around for another hour. Eva will be safe enough with Rusty. You know how conscientious he is. He may have fretted that you'd closed the pub for the day and wanted to return early. Eva's not averse to an excuse to serve in the bar.'

The evening had turned cooler and in her light summer costume Casey was already chilled from their wait on the station. She'd freeze if she had to wait for another hour. And Matt was right. Eva was capable of returning early if she got it into her head to work in the bar.

The Britannia was in darkness when they reached home. With the pub closed, there was no custom for the shellfish stall, and Paddy Murphy had gone home. Even Archie was absent from his place where he often squatted in the doorway.

'Is there a sadder sight than a pub shut for business?' Casey said, heavily. 'It looks like Rusty and Eva missed the train after all. She'll be furious that we didn't wait for them.'

'But I'm delighted.' Matt chuckled and stooped to kiss her neck. 'The train was packed and I really do want to kiss you so very much. And not a chaste goodnight peck on the cheek.'

He took the doorkey from her fingers and was about to insert it in the lock, when they both saw that the door was already ajar.

'Stay there, Casey,' he warned. 'There could be someone inside. A burglar.'

'I'm not leaving you to face them alone. There could be a gang of them.'

She followed him as he crept stealthily across the hall, pausing to pick up a walking stick from the umbrella stand. With sickening dread, Casey saw her father's gold-topped cane was missing. As they approached the stairs, Casey removed the long, pearl-headed hatpin from her straw boater. It wasn't much of a weapon, but its four-inch, needle-sharp pin was better than nothing.

At the sound of movements above them, Matt motioned her to silence. The noise was coming from her father's study.

'They're stealing Dad's boxing trophies,' Casey whispered. Her anger swelled. Melted down, the cups would be worth a great deal of money. And they were the means of her getting out of the brewery's debt. Her temper flushed her cheeks, chasing away her fear. How dare they steal her father's trophies?

When a loose floorboard creaked on the fourth stair, she cursed herself for not warning Matt. There was a grunt from above, then the heavy clump of running feet.

'Stay where you are, the police are on their way,' Matt bluffed as he took the remaining stairs two at a time.

'Take care, Matt,' Casey cautioned, lifting her cumbersome skirt higher to follow him. In her haste her toe caught on its hem and she was pitched forward, banging her elbow and losing valuable seconds.

Matt was on the landing. She could hear a scuffle, and smelt unwashed bodies before she saw them. A pane of glass was smashed, and as she reached the corridor, she saw a skinny youth in a large cap toss a bulging sack out of the window. With the speed of a hare darting for cover, he was out of the window, dropping on to the scullery roof. A leap took him across the narrow alleyway to the roof of an outside lavatory in the next road. Once on the ground, he'd soon be lost amongst the maze of passageways which led into the Courtyard.

Two short but stocky men, each holding stuffed sacks, were fighting off Matt's attack. The landing was gloomy, and she couldn't see their faces, but from the green and red neckscarf of one of them, she recognised him as part of the Flower and Dean Street gang who had stolen furniture from the ruins of her uncle's home.

The largest of the men swung his sack at Matt. There was a clang as the silver cups struck the side of his head. He reeled sideways and, though he quickly recovered, his assailant made a dash for the window. Seeing her father's trophies about to disappear, Casey tore after him. Matt was still wrestling with the third burglar.

'Get out of 'ere, mate,' he yelled at his accomplice.

'Drop that sack!' Casey shouted.

Knowing the hatpin would be useless, she grabbed a large blue and white bowl holding an aspidistra and hurled it at the man's head. Her anger marred her aim and it crashed against his shoulder just as he was about to throw the sack out of the window. The china bowl shattered, but the impact was enough to make the burglar drop the sack as blood spurted from his cut neck. With a howl of pain he dived out of the window. As she ran to retrieve the silver, she heard him cursing as he rolled off the scullery roof into the gutter of the alleyway behind the pub.

Her fears were now for Matt. The constant thud of fist on flesh had accompanied her attempt to waylay the second thief. She kicked the sack so that the contents spilled out over the floor, preventing the last thief from attempting to steal that too.

Matt had pinned the third man up against the wall. The abandoned sack was on the floor between them. Both men grappled, fists flying indiscriminately. As her eyes became used to the gloom, Casey saw Matt's face was set with fury. The thief's expression was malevolent. There was a sinister glitter in his eyes which made Casey fear for Matt's life. Men of the Courtyard killed before they risked capture by the law.

Although Matt was strong, he was no match for the bulky figure who had grown up on the streets of the Courtyard, where vicious fighting was a way of life. The thief drew up his knee and, with a grunt, rammed it into Matt's groin. Casey screamed as Matt gagged and hunched over, slumping across the sack. His attacker wrenched himself free of Matt's hold and, discovering that Matt's figure prevented him from reclaiming the silver, his hand darted to his belt. The last of the crimson sunset reflected like blood on the blade as a dagger was raised over Matt.

Chapter Fifteen

'No!' Casey screamed. 'Matt, he's got a knife.' Even as she warned him, she was sidling around the attacker. The man was so intent on getting his hands on the silver, he ignored Casey. He would see a woman as no threat and, due to his fight with Matt, was probably unaware that she had already dealt with one of his accomplices.

In the second that these thoughts speeded like a steam-train through her mind, Matt had twisted and raised a hand to defend himself. Sweat moistened her palms. She inched forward. The thief's attention was absorbed by Matt and his own attempt to retrieve the sack.

The burglar lashed out with the dagger. Matt caught his wrist, his face straining with the effort to keep the deadly blade away from his throat. Casey inched forward. The blade flashed again and, as the thief's arm came up, Casey struck. The hatpin was stabbed into his hand with all her strength. Three inches of steel embedded in grimy flesh.

With a yell the thief froze, stupefied by the unexpected pain. Matt's hand shot upwards, the weight of his body following through as he smashed a fist into the man's stubbled jaw. Casey expected the thief to be knocked out cold. He merely staggered a step backwards. It was enough. Matt seized on the lowering of his guard and wrested the dagger from his hand.

The thief had the reflexes of the alley-cat that he was. He

jabbed out twice: a punch to Matt's stomach and another to his eye, with the expertise of a prize-fighter. The gymnasiums in the East End drew young lads like magnets. Not all used the skills learned there as honourably as had her father.

Going down under the attack, Matt fell again over the sack. The thief, realising that he could not escape with the silver, whirled and headed for the window.

Breathing heavily and far from defeated, Matt launched himself after him.

'Let him go, Matt,' Casey grabbed his arm. 'At least we saved two of the sacks.'

'Bloody scum,' he seethed. 'We'd best get the police.'

'Later.' She could see the blood on his hands and head and her concern was for him. 'By now he's already run for cover in the streets. Within the hour the silver will be with the fence and melted down before midnight. The police won't stand a chance of catching them.'

'You're going to let them get away with it,' Matt stormed. 'Bloody hell, Casey, you need that money!'

'Rusty might know who to get word to before the silver is melted down. If the stories I've heard are true and Dad was in the underworld, one of them might help us out of respect for him.' She grimaced. 'Somehow I don't think so, though. Whoever stole the trophies knew they had a buyer for them. They are too easily recognisable to be sold otherwise.'

She leaned forward to study the blood on his face and saw that his eyebrow was cut. The lid was beginning to swell. 'Let me see to your injuries. From the looks of it you'll have a real shiner by morning.'

'I'll live. Thank God we got back when we did.' He swayed unsteadily and Casey put his arm around her shoulders. 'You'd better sit down before you fall down. You shouldn't have tackled them, Matt. Their type are killers.'

She led him into the kitchen and lit the two gaslamps. 'Take off your jacket and shirt, I've some witch-hazel which will help the bruises. Come over here so I can see you properly in the light.'

He grinned. 'I never thought you'd ask me to take my clothes off until we were respectably married.'

'It's to tend your bruises and ensure you've no ribs cracked,' she warned him as she put the kettle on the range to heat some water. 'So don't go getting any funny ideas.'

'Making love to you, my darling, would be a matter I'd take very seriously indeed.'

Their gazes met across the kitchen and, although his tone was teasing, the ardour in his eyes made her breath snatch in her throat. She was suddenly aware that they were alone in the house. Alone and with privacy for the first time in months. Love burned in her at seeing the cuts on his handsome face. She saw again the dagger raised to strike him and was filled with terror. He had risked his life to save her father's trophies.

Her feelings must have shown on her face. His expression was soft with yearning. 'A kiss would soothe the pain,' he said huskily.

'Witch-hazel will do it more good.' She gathered her reserve. The way her body was tingling with anticipation, roused by just a look, shocked her. She was dangerously close to succumbing to his demands. She turned away to collect lint, witch-hazel, iodine and a small vial of laudanum from the medicine cabinet on the wall. 'These will help your pain.'

'I've been in torment for months with wanting you, yet you haven't shown me mercy before.'

She decided that the best way to deal with him was not to take him seriously. She tipped some iodine on the lint and dabbed it on his eye.

He winced and she eyed him meaningfully. 'And there will be no mercy now until those cuts are cleaned so that they don't become infected.'

He sighed dramatically. 'You're a cruel woman, Cassandra Strong.'

'And you're a wicked man, Matthew Frost.'

He winked at her and pulled her to him. 'That's why you love me.'

'Very likely.' She evaded his grab for her. 'But will you let me tend your cuts?'

'You've a one-track mind, Miss Strong.' He shrugged off his jacket and began to pull at his necktie. There was a challenge in his hazel eyes which made her pulse race.

'And so have you, Mr Frost.'

Her touch was gentle as she bathed his eye, her teeth catching her lower lip as she applied the iodine to his cut eyebrow and cheek. Only a slight tightening of his jaw showed how cruelly the iodine stung the open wound. When he stripped off his shirt, she saw his ribs were covered with reddish-purpling marks where he had been punched.

'Oh my love, they look so painful.'

Skilfully she applied the witch-hazel, her fingers checking to feel that none of his ribs were broken or cracked. There was no spare flesh on his body. The hours he spent working on the biplane engines had broadened his shoulders and slimmed his torso to finely honed muscle. The dark smattering of hair on his chest was potently masculine. Each touch sent a thrill of longing through her body, and with each dab of the lint she was aware of his gaze on her. As her hands moved over his chest she savoured the texture of his firm flesh and the play of his muscles as he shifted position. Most of all she was aware that he appeared to be holding his breath.

Somehow the movement of her fingers turned from efficient nursing to the wonder of a lover's caress. The heat of him seeped into her fingers and spread through her veins. At the sound of his indrawn breath, her gaze lifted to his. Black lashes fringed eyes which had darkened to honey-gold. The chiselled planes of his face were taut with desire.

'The man was a brute to do this to you.'

'The one who left here with your hatpin embedded in his hand,' he replied, the corner of his mouth tilting as his gaze fastened upon the laboured rise and fall of her breasts. 'You were like a tigress – quite magnificent, my darling.'

The beguiling promise in his stare dried her throat. A tremor started low in her stomach. She fought to contain it. Yet her body swayed towards him, and when his hands circled her waist, she moaned softly, 'Oh, Matt, they could have killed you.'

Inexplicably she burst into tears. His arms tightened around her.

'It's all right, Casey. I wasn't seriously hurt.' His breath fanned her hair.

It was her undoing. The strain of the last weeks finally took its toll. She wept for her father. She wept in fear of Matt going to war. She wept in frustration of the persecution and attitude of his family. She wept at the brutality Matt had faced. She wept for her own feelings of inadequacy, which suddenly consumed her. And she wept because once the tears had started, it seemed impossible to stem their flow.

'My darling, don't upset yourself so.' Matt kissed her hair and brow as he soothed her. His arms were a haven from the fears and uncertainty of the future. Her love for him a life-raft and her salvation.

Her face was pressed against the warmth of his chest, the vibrant rhythm of his heartbeat penetrating her misery, stirring desire which had been dampened for too long. His kisses and the strength of his arms around her worked their invading spell. Gradually, as he pressed his mouth to her eyelids, cheeks and ears, her fears subsided. The thrill of his touch spread its compelling magic. It made the blood sing in her veins and she moved against him, aware of the hardness of his chest against the aching fullness of her breasts. The musky scent of his skin was an aphrodisiac piercing her trance, hypnotic, seducing.

She clung to him. His kisses and soft words of love lulled her resistance. Attuned to a deepening sensuality, her feelings were aroused by the mastery of his lips. The touch of his mouth filled her consciousness, igniting a fiery trail as his kisses travelled with tantalising slowness along her jaw to the hollow of her throat, and a glow fanned out through her veins to encompass her entire body. Her love for him overwhelmed her. It robbed her of breath, building a clamouring deep within her to go beyond kisses, to the ecstasy promised in his experienced caresses.

He cupped her chin in his hand and raised it, slanting his head to claim her lips. His tongue traced sensual circles as he kissed her mouth. Her lips parted, receiving his kisses. They had always driven her to the limits of her restraint, now they desecrated the last of her resolve. Reason was subjugated. Modesty was conquered. Sensuality governed her responses, and desire conquered resistance.

A moan rose from her throat as she clasped him tight, her hands hungry on his naked flesh. When his hand moved from her waist to seek the fullness of her breast, she gasped. His fingers found the hardening peak and an exquisite pain of longing caused a tremor to pass through her body. Then his lips were on the pulse at her throat, and her head rolled languorously back, her breathing shallow and erratic. As his hands moved along her spine, she was aware that the buttons of her high-necked blouse had been unfastened. The silk was being drawn from her shoulders, slowly down over her arms and breasts. Her breath fractured, stilled in her throat by longing, and a pulse throbbed in her loins.

Of their own volition, her hips moved against his, and she felt his need for her. The touch of that hardness pressing against her inner thigh sent expanding shock-waves of heat through her entire being.

'Casey,' he breathed. 'Darling Casey. Don't deny me.'

She was floating on clouds of pleasure, craving him to make her irrevocably his. 'Matt, I love you so much.'

Her hand was clasped by his. With his ardent gaze compelling each step that she took, she was drawn out of the kitchen, and in a dreamy erotic haze led up the stairs to her bedchamber.

Her body tingled with a craving as undefined as it was primeval. Matt drew out the pins from her hair, running his fingers through its dark tresses as it tumbled in a shiny cascade to her waist. With infinite slowness and reverence he peeled each garment from her. Finally, unashamedly naked, she was in his arms, his caresses and kisses arching her spine, desire encompassing her in a fluid, white-hot heat. Her mind no longer distinguished right from wrong. This was inevitable, foreordained, irrevocably her fate. She surrendered unreservedly.

The muscles of his chest were firm and supple beneath her exploring fingers, the tangle of dark hair arrowing over his taut stomach. A moan of pleasure was torn from her as she moved against him. When her hand reached down between them to feel the powerful tumescence still restrained by his clothing, he groaned and eased her down on the bed. There was fever now in his kisses as he took each breast into his mouth in turn. Her breath escaped in an ecstatic sigh. She had never dreamed that her body could respond to a man with such abandon, that sex could be so cataclysmic: passion causing a maelstrom of emotions that made her writhe and moan in growing ecstasy.

Each kiss was adoring, even as it consumed her in its devouring heat. His hands were lifting her hips and his lips feathered in a sensuous path across her ribcage and the flatness of her stomach, down to the softness of her inner thigh. At the touch of his tongue flicking between the lips of her womanhood she stiffened in shock. She had not expected that.

With a groan Matt lifted his head and again kissed her mouth. She could taste the scent of her on his lips. 'I go too fast, my darling; I forget you are so innocent. Another time I will teach you the joy which you hold back from now.'

'I don't want to hold back, Matt,' she sighed. 'I want to please you.'

'You please me, my darling, more than I could have imagined.'

Her eyes were heavy-lidded as she watched him undress. His body was lithe, darker-skinned than her own and magnificent. He was smiling, his eyes dark with desire as he gathered her into his arms once more. Earlier tenderness was replaced by a ravening passion as they discovered the secrets and perfections of each other's bodies. They moulded together in a tumble of bedclothes. Each new experience transported her to breathless heights, instilling a nebulous, aching sweetness which made her cry out in her pleasure. 'Matt, oh Matt, I never realised – never expected – that loving was meant to be like this.'

'This is just the overture, the symphony has yet to begin,' he murmured wickedly as his lips and hands continued weaving their magic.

He positioned himself above her and a sharp pain inadvertently made her wince and tense. 'Relax, my darling. I will try not to hurt you.'

The next thrust parted the barrier. Her small cry caught in his mouth as he kissed her deeply, his body moving to a building rhythm, deluging her with an oscillating, swelling pleasure which expanded until it encompassed her in an explosion of fulfilment and wonder.

'Casey, my love, my love,' he rasped as his body convulsed and she felt the heat of his seed pumping into her. He clasped her to him, the tempo of his racing heartbeat matching hers.

His kisses slowed, again reverent, so that in the aftermath of her passion, her body shimmered in an exquisite glow of sensual languor. Levering himself on to his elbow, he smiled down at her.

Casey looked up into his eyes. 'I love you so much, Matt, I feel my heart is going to explode. I don't want to wait any longer. I can't go back to the way we were. We must marry soon.'

'Very soon. What we have is special, it only happens once in a lifetime.'

Eva scowled as they reached the station just in time to see the train puffing away from the platform.

'Dammit.' She stamped her foot. 'There isn't another for ages.'

'So we get longer together.' Rusty smiled at her. 'What do you want to do? Go for another drink?'

The fast walk to the station had made Eva's head start to reel. The whalebone in her corset was digging cruelly into her side and she was feeling rather ill. 'No. We might miss the next train. Let's sit over there and wait.'

The seat she indicated was at the far end of the platform, beyond the waiting room and porters' office. That end of the platform was empty, and it would be some time before it started to fill up with passengers awaiting the next London train.

She sat down and gave a mock shiver. The wind was freshening, but the drink she had consumed had warmed her.

'Are you cold, Eva?' Rusty hesitated a moment before he put his arm around her shoulders. 'Snuggle up to me, I'll keep you warm.'

She laid her head on his shoulder, wishing that the platform and the ornate ironwork supporting the roof would not dip and sway so erratically around her. 'I think you've got me drunk, Rusty. What have you got to say about that? I trusted you to keep me safe. I hope you won't try to take advantage of me.'

'Lord, Eva, I'd never do that.' Rusty sounded shocked.

She could not suppress a giggle. Rusty was so funny at times. Perhaps it would be fun to seduce him. Not the whole way, of course. But to tease him, just to see if she could break through his rigid control.

'I knew I could trust you, Rusty,' she drawled, moving her body so that her breast was pressed against his arm. Through his jacket she felt the muscles tense and she hid a smile. She shifted so that her breast grazed back and forth across his sleeve and then, putting a hand to her head and with a soft moan, dropped her head forward.

As she expected, Rusty caught her shoulders. 'Lord, Eva. Are you all right?'

She tilted back her head so that she was gazing up at him and ran the tip of her tongue over her lips. 'You're a wicked man to get a woman tipsy. But you're nice as well. I've had a lovely day, Rusty. I don't know how to thank you. Would you like to kiss me?'

She saw him swallow and parted her lips invitingly. From the distant murmur of voices, she knew that the platform was beginning to fill with passengers, but there was time for one kiss. An appetiser to keep Rusty interested. By the time they reached Chalkwell and met up with Casey, she wanted to have Rusty completely under her spell. She'd ensure his worries would be all for her in the future, and not for her cousin.

His lips brushed hers lightly. She almost groaned in frustration. Why did he have to be so respectful all the time? That was a kiss you'd give to your great-aunt under the mistletoe at Christmas. She'd show him what it was like to be kissed by a real woman. Her tongue flickered over the softness of his mouth, her lips parting as her hands slid around his neck to hold him close. She kissed him with slow, lingering passion, each movement of her mobile mouth designed to ensnare his senses. His arms tightened around her, his breathing changing and becoming harder. No longer was his kiss restrained. The pressure of his lips were demanding. When she finally broke away from him, she kept her eyes closed, sensing that he was gazing at her.

'Oh, Rusty, you ain't never kissed me like that before. I feel all weak and faint.'

'That's the gin.'

She opened her eyes and shook her head. 'No, it's not the gin.' She patted her hair and straightened her hat. 'You're quite a man, Rusty. I'll have to be careful you don't turn my head. Plying me with presents and drink. A girl could get quite the wrong idea about your intentions.'

'You know my intentions, Eva.' Rusty reached to draw her closer, but she provocatively slid away from him on the seat. 'I asked you before if you'd wed me. Does this mean you look favourably on me?'

She widened her eyes in feigned confusion. 'You're going too fast for me. Marriage is a big step. And with Joe dead so recently it would be disrespectful to consider your proposal whilst I'm in mourning. Joe was like a father to me this last year.'

To her relief, Rusty nodded. 'I'll not rush you. 'Sides, I could be out of a job with all this trouble with selling the Britannia. And you deserve the best, Eva. I'd lay the world at your feet if you were to marry me.'

She leaned forward and kissed him lightly on the lips. 'There's no one else I care for as I do you, Rusty. Just give me time.'

Laying her head on his shoulder she closed her eyes. The months ahead could be difficult until the Britannia were sold. He would be there if she needed him.

By the time the train arrived, the effects of the gin had worn off. When they left both Chalkwell and Leigh-on-Sea stations without finding Casey and Matt waiting for them, fear clutched at her heart. Casey had abandoned her. Clearly she had not thought it important to wait for them. Tears stung her eyes and she angrily blinked them away. Matt's hold over Casey was growing stronger, and Eva knew that she was losing her influence over her cousin.

Casey stretched languorously, replete and content. Her body was bathed in an aureola of sensuality which was far from saintly in its origins. Opening her eyes she stared up at Matt, who was propped on his elbow smiling down at her. He took her hand and pressed her palm to his lips.

'My love,' he said in wonderment, 'you have given me more joy this night than I thought possible.'

'The joy was all mine. Am I shameless to have loved you so well? Even now I want more of you.' Her hand reached up to caress his cheek, her heart so filled with love that further speech was impossible.

'Love is a constant journey of discovery and fulfilment. This is just the beginning.'

His kiss destroyed the lassitude of dreamy contentment; every sense was attuned to the ardour his touch evoked. She responded with unrestrained passion, eager for each new initiation, and uninhibited in her wish to give him equal pleasure.

Her only awareness of the sunset was the magnificent way its light bathed Matt's naked figure in a rosy glow. Passion again finally spent, they lay unmoving, their bodies entwined.

'Casey, are you home?' Eva's voice was shrill with her displeasure. She was furious at having missed the train. Reluctantly she conceded that she had enjoyed Rusty's company, but she felt that Casey had deliberately deserted her.

'There's a light on in the kitchen,' Rusty observed as he followed her into the living quarters. 'She must be back.'

'Or gone out gallivanting again.' Eva remained peevish. When she tripped up on the first stair, Rusty's steadying arm was about her waist. 'Damnation, I don't need your help.'

He chuckled softly. 'Too many gins.'

'I can hold my drink,' she returned, and was annoyed to find that the words slurred. 'Casey, are you there? Couldn't you have waited for us?'

She glowered when there was no reply. Though she detected a faint noise on the upper landing in Casey's bedroom. It spurred her forward, her mind conjuring images through a red haze of anger. 'I'll do for that bastard Frost if he's done anything to Casey.'

'Hold on.' Rusty gripped her arm and pulled her to a halt as she reached the first-floor landing. 'Don't jump to conclusions. And don't go saying anything you'll regret. Casey loves Matt and he loves her.'

'The lecher. If he's—'

'What's the matter with you, Eva?' he said sharply. 'They are engaged. What they do is their affair.'

In the pale light from the kitchen gaslight, her face was bleached of all colour, her eyes cavernous with hatred. Rusty gripped her shoulders and shook her gently. 'Don't interfere, Eva. Casey's been through enough. Happen she needed a little loving.'

'Not with one of his kind. He'll ditch her now he's had his way. The little fool! I thought she had more sense.'

Rusty sighed. 'She's human and in love. Don't spoil it for her. With war threatened in Europe, it could be months before she sees Frost again.'

'Precisely. He could get himself killed. Where would that leave her if he's got her pregnant?' She peered up the second flight of stairs, where movement was now audible from Casey's room. Her voice was a stinging rebuke. 'Casey!'

'I'm here, Eva.'

Casey appeared at the top of the stairs in the dress she had been wearing earlier. From the way it clung to her hips and thighs, Eva knew she had nothing on underneath it. Her dark hair waved to her waist, tousled in a way which showed that Casey had most thoroughly been made love to. Matt stood with his arm around Casey's shoulders. He wore trousers, but his shirt was unbuttoned to the waist and he was barefoot.

Eva's lips curled back. 'Your father would turn in his grave to see you behaving so shamelessly.'

'I don't have to answer to you, Eva,' Casey replied with quiet defiance.

Rusty cleared his throat. 'I feel responsible for Casey. I understood that you needed a bit of time alone together, Matt, but I think you've taken advantage of her.'

Casey felt Matt tense. She kept her stare fixed on Eva and Rusty at the foot of the stairs. 'Matt did not take advantage. I'm not ashamed of what has happened. We will marry on Matt's next leave. We didn't plan this. If it hadn't been for the burglary—'

'Don't make excuses,' Eva shrilled, too angry to listen properly.

'What burglary?' Rusty demanded, looking around. His jaw dropped as he saw the broken window-pane at the far end of the landing. 'Good God! What was taken?'

'Some of Dad's trophies. If Matt and I hadn't caught the train we agreed on, no doubt the place would have been looted by the time we got home. We caught them red-handed, but only managed to save some of Dad's trophies. One got away with his loot.'

'How many were there?' Rusty asked. 'Have you told the police?'

Matt held up a hand. 'Look, there's a lot to discuss. I suggest Eva puts the kettle on while we finish dressing.'

'Don't tell me what to do!' Eva flared. 'I'm not a bloody servant.'

Casey sighed. 'Matt didn't say that you were. This isn't easy, Eva. I'm not making excuses for myself. But it has changed my plans for the future. We have to discuss it.'

She was shocked by the fury on her cousin's face. What right had Eva to condemn her? It wasn't as though her cousin was a virgin. She'd given herself to a boy she thought she loved. Matt wasn't like Eva's feckless lover. He had been adamant that they marry on his next leave, and had cursed the necessity that he must return to the airfield tomorrow.

Chapter Sixteen

An hour later tension was high and too many harsh words and recriminations had been spoken instead of a solution being found to their immediate problems.

'In the light of the robbery, I'll move in here,' Rusty declared. 'They could come back and the women shouldn't be left alone.'

Matt shot out of his chair to stand over Rusty. 'And what of the women's reputation? I won't hear of it.'

Rusty eyed him stonily. 'If you'd cared for Casey's reputation, you'd not have taken advantage of her tonight.'

The gaslamps showed the swellings and bruising on Matt's face. He was tight-lipped with anger.

'Stop it, you two,' Casey intervened. Ever since they had come downstairs, she could see Rusty was spoiling for a fight with Matt. Rusty obviously believed Matt had betrayed her trust. She was touched by his protective manner, but he was not her father and she would not have him judge either her or Matt's morals. 'Matt didn't take advantage of me. I knew what I was doing. If that shocks you, I'm sorry. I regret nothing. I appreciate you wishing to protect me and Eva, and as manager it would be easier for you to live on the premises.'

'Or you should be moving out,' Matt rounded on Casey. 'With Joe dead this place will be seen as ripe pickings. It's no place for two women alone.'

'And where will Casey go?' Eva crowed. 'To live with your family. Over their dead bodies, I should think. Rusty is right. I'll feel much safer knowing he's here to protect us.'

Eva had been siding with Rusty, and Casey guessed it was mostly to rile Matt. From the rigid way her cousin was holding herself, it was obvious that she was boiling with anger at discovering Casey and Matt were lovers.

Matt jammed his hands into his trouser pockets, a muscle flickering in his jaw as he battled to contain his own anger. 'I won't have a man living here with two unmarried women. It's scandalous. Casey can come to Hendon and take rooms there. I'll get a special licence and we can be married next weekend.'

Eva let out a wail. 'Casey, you wouldn't abandon me and the pub?'

'Of course not,' she placated. 'I'd not shame Dad's memory by running away.'

She turned to Matt to reason with him, but before she could speak he cut through her words, his tone chillingly arrogant. 'Is that how you see marriage to me – an act of running away?'

She stared at him incredulously. 'What other solution is there?' She could not believe that Matt could be so obstinate. It was as though the man who had made love so tenderly to her an hour ago had been replaced by a stranger.

All at once the worry and the strain she had been under since her father's death caught up with her. Her temper exploded. 'It's your family which has caused this situation. I could have sold the Britannia by now if it wasn't for them, and repaid the debt out of the sale money.'

'And you're using that as an excuse not to marry me.' He stood rigid, proud and unyielding.

'Don't twist my words, Matt.' Her heart ached at his attitude, but she was too angry to back down. 'The Britannia is my home and my inheritance. I owe it to my father to stay until this mess with the brewery is sorted out.'

'But if you were my wife, my brother would drop the case against you. I thought we had agreed on that,' he announced, hauteur and outrage dripping from every word.

'Be reasonable, Matt. I can't leave Eva.'

'She'd leave you if the boot was on the other foot.'

'I'd never desert Casey.' Eva leaned forward in her chair, her eyes bright with malice. '*Never*. Do you hear? We know how to look after our own. Family loyalty is everything. That's something your family know nothing about, as has been proved by this court case.'

Casey put her hands over her ears. 'Stop it! This is getting us nowhere.'

Instantly Matt's manner changed. He put a hand on her shoulder. 'I was wrong to suggest you leave your cousin. I'm just tired of the barriers which keep appearing to prevent our marriage. Forgive me, my darling.'

'Smooth words,' Eva derided. 'To my mind actions speak for themselves. The actions of you and your family are typical of how your class believe themselves above those less fortunate than themselves.'

'That's enough, Eva,' Casey rounded on her cousin. 'I won't have Matt's integrity doubted. And I'm sick of your interfering. You take too much on yourself, cousin.'

'Sorry I spoke, I'm sure.' Eva flounced round in her seat so that her back was to Casey. 'I'm just in the way, I can see that. Don't you worry your head about me. Go off with your paramour. Set up a love-nest, for all I care. I'm sure I shall survive on my own.'

Rusty groaned. 'Now, you two, this ain't like you to be at each other's throats. Least said, soonest mended.'

Eva stood up and strode to the door. 'If Casey wants to make a fool of herself over that man, that's her affair. I'm off to bed.' She gave Rusty a long, thoughtful look. 'I'm all for Rusty moving into Joe's room. I shall certainly feel safer with a man on the premises. That's if I still have a place to stay.'

'Eva, you know I wouldn't turn you out. Can we just stop this?' Casey curbed her impulse to shake some sense into her cousin.

Rusty looked pointedly at Matt. 'I'd best board up that window, and I'll kip in Joe's room tonight. It could be risky for the women to stay here alone with that window broken.'

'They could spend the night in a lodging house,' Matt said stiffly.

'No, Matt,' Casey declared firmly. 'This is my home and I will not be chased from it.'

He dragged his fingers through his hair and paced the room. His expression was haggard, the skin across his angular cheeks pale in the hissing gaslight. 'I don't like to think of you in danger.' He looked across at Rusty. 'They need your protection, but it will be the ruin of their reputations. Eva's as well as Casey's.'

Eva's mind was racing. She could see everything she had worked for crumbling at her feet. If Casey married Matt, what would happen to her? She'd have no home. No friends. No one to love and cherish her as she loved them.

Rusty had paused by the door and she studied him through lowered lashes. He was well-built, pleasant enough looking, a pillar of protective strength. The bleak depression which had settled over her since learning that Matt had made love to Casey lifted slightly. Today had shown her that she could twine Rusty around her finger.

She sneered at Matt, allowing her hatred for him to show. 'You're a fine one to talk of reputations, after what you've been up to with my cousin tonight. For years, Rusty has been Joe's right-hand man. No one will question his staying here. I trust Rusty to treat us with honour and respect.'

Moving to Casey's side, her smile was malicious. 'Just so no one gets the wrong idea about who is sleeping in whose bed, Casey and I will share the double bed in my room.'

'There's no need to take that attitude, Eva,' Casey responded haughtily. 'Matt and I love each other. You are trying to make our love sound sordid.'

She turned to Matt and smiled. 'It's getting late, I think you'd better leave. Will I see you before you go back to the airfield tomorrow?'

It was obvious from the muscle ticking like a time-bomb along Matt's jaw that he did not like being so dismissed. Surely he didn't expect to stay the night. What had happened between them had been wonderful and she had no regrets, but she could not countenance Matt staying. It would cause too much gossip. To soften her dismissal, her smile broadened and, linking her arm through his, she drew him away from the others. 'Tonight was wonderful. I love you, Matt. But you cannot stay. It would be an insult to Dad's memory were I to permit you to sleep in my bed. And when we marry I don't want people sniggering and saying that we had to.'

His expression remained displeased, but he nodded a reluctant acceptance. 'Having made you mine, my nights will be doubly empty without holding you in my arms. I'll return early tomorrow. We can spend a few hours together before I catch the train to Hendon.'

There was a remoteness to his voice which disturbed Casey. She could feel the tension in his body. When he bent his head to kiss her, it was brief and without passion. Guilt made her feel like a discarded trollop.

'What's wrong, Matt?'

'Everything, isn't it? Why does everything have to be so complicated?'

The curtness of his reply smote her. Along the corridor she heard Rusty banging nails into the window-frame as he boarded up the broken pane. Her stomach clenched with sickening dread. It was as though he had detached himself from her. She had made love to him without reservation. But now he was treating her as James Hardcastle had done when she had fought off his advances. A disquieting thought lodged in her mind. Was he acting as he did because she had lost his respect? Having made love to her, had his interest begun to wane?

She swallowed painfully. It was disloyal to think of Matt capable of such pettiness, but wasn't it said that men never married their mistresses. 'I love you, Matt. But you seem so . . .' She paused before blundering on. 'Have you lost your respect for me because we . . .'

A spasm akin to pain flickered through his eyes. 'Do you think I'm like Hardcastle?' Then a shudder went through him and he sighed wearily, 'It's not you, my darling. It's my damned family and this threat of war.'

Matt held her face in his hands, staring down at her for several moments before adding softly, 'Tomorrow we shall set a date for our wedding. That will still any vicious tongues.'

His parting kiss was more ardent, but again Casey sensed that he had withdrawn from her. Was it his family, or was it her? She closed her eyes and suppressed the thought. Matt was not like Hardcastle. She would never believe that. It was his family, not her.

Casey felt Eva watching her as Matt left. Her head lifted in defiance. 'Don't judge me, Eva. I love Matt and regret nothing.'

'Then let us hope he keeps his promises. I suppose there's always a first time for the gentry to feel obliged to keep their word to us lesser mortals.'

'Matt is not like others of his kind,' she declared with fervent heat. She swept past her cousin, refusing to be drawn into an argument.

'Time will tell.' Eva fired her parting shot, intending that it wound Casey as she had been wounded by the way her cousin had preferred Matt's company to hers today.

Eva was too disturbed by the knowledge that Casey had

finally succumbed to Matt to sleep that night. She tossed and turned, seeking ways to secure her future. It seemed likely that Casey would marry Matt soon. The Britannia would be sold and she'd be homeless. It wasn't fair. Nothing went right for her. She had been happy here, enjoying the bar work far more than slaving in a shop and pandering to stuck-up customers. She turned over and thumped the pillow. Why did Casey have to meet Matt? She'd only been here sixteen months. She really thought she'd found a niche for herself, found a refuge from the hardships she had endured in the Courtyard. Damn Casey!

She glared at the ceiling. Her gaze travelled slowly around the room. How could she bear to give all this up? The pretty pink roses on the wallpaper, the deep pink satin eiderdown and quilt. Red velvet curtains with tasselled edges and several thick rugs scattered on a pale grey linoleum floor. There was also the walnut dressing table and wardrobe and the luxury of a soft mattress and sprung bed. A far cry from the poverty and squalor of her father's house. This was how she wanted to continue to live.

Her visits to Goldstein's place were providing her with a substantial nest-egg, and she had finally found an outlet for her sexual frustration. She did not care that men watched her performing. It was exciting. She was the centre of their attention and that gave her power over them in a way that was gratifying. Knowing that they lusted after her pandered to her vanity. She despised them for their weakness as she despised all men. No man would use her again. The tables were turned and she would use them to suit her own ends. But even so, she took care not to be recognised and always wore an auburn wig.

Yet even that triumph left a bitter taste in her mouth. The sexual pleasure the women gave her was unfulfilling, the gratification hollow without the love she craved. None of the women she had enjoyed had moved her in that way. The need to be loved entirely for herself was becoming an obsession. She felt no guilt at the secret life she was leading, but aware that Casey would be shocked and might sever their friendship, she pretended she had a friend Cynthia who lived in Bow and that they went out occasionally. That covered the nights she went to Goldstein's place.

The sound of stairboards creaking made her sit up. It was six o'clock, too early for Casey to be up. Then she remembered that Rusty had stayed the night. Rusty had appointed himself their protector. She smiled as she recalled how demonstrative Rusty had been towards her yesterday. She sat up in bed and picked up from her bedside table the marcasite brooch he had bought her. It wasn't worth a fortune, but Rusty was generous with his money. She recalled Goldstein's words that two women could never run a respectable bar on their own. And she had more ambitious plans to eventually own a hotel. What if she continued to reject Rusty's advances and the fool joined the army? He was always talking about the possibility of war.

Clearly if she was to achieve her aim and run a grand hotel, she needed a man at her side. She suppressed a shudder. At least she knew she could control Rusty, and once he was committed to a contract, he would not abandon her and Casey. It wouldn't do any harm to play up to him for a while, just to ensure that he didn't do anything foolish like enlist.

Rising from her bed, she slipped on her chamber robe. Pausing only to run a brush through the thick black tresses, so that they shone in the early morning with the bluish sheen of a raven's wing, she hurried to the kitchen.

At the door she let out a theatrical gasp and drew together the bodice of her robe as though in confusion. 'Rusty, you startled me. I'd forgotten that you had stayed over. I'd better get dressed properly. I couldn't sleep, so I came down for a cuppa.'

Rusty had lit the fire in the kitchen range and the kettle was boiling. He had a pencil poised over a sheet of paper on which he had written several columns of figures. 'You look decent to me, and very beautiful,' he said, unable to take his gaze from her. 'Have your tea.'

'Rusty, you should be ashamed of yourself. How can I sit down with you in my night-clothes? It would be the scandal of the street if anyone saw us.' She smiled beguilingly. 'And after the way you kissed me yesterday, I certainly wouldn't trust myself alone with you. Keep my tea warm, I'll be back in two ticks.'

Satisfied that she had tantalised his interest, she ran back upstairs and reappeared a quarter of an hour later. This time she was dressed in a demure high-necked white and navy striped blouse, with leg-of-mutton sleeves and a navy serge skirt. Her hair was swept up into a neat powder-puff, held in place by the comb he had bought her.

'You're an early bird, aren't you?' he said, pushing her teacup towards her. 'It's not seven yet.'

'Couldn't sleep.' She studied him archly. He was wearing new black trousers and the sleeves of his grey and white striped shirt were rolled up, displaying his muscular forearms covered in golden hair and freckles. Since taking over as manager he had started to wear a plain black waistcoat. She flicked this now with her finger. 'You look very smart. Why don't you wear a snazzy waistcoat – scarlet like Joe's?'

'No. That were Joe's trademark. And there were only one Joe. Reckon plain black is fine enough for me.'

Eva was struck by his modesty. 'Don't sell yourself short, Rusty.'

A flush of embarrassed colour stained his face as he picked up the crockery and carried it to the sink. She was there before him. 'I'll wash these up and get your breakfast started. I thought after that, if the pub's not going to open, I'll start washing down the walls in the bar. They are brown with tobacco smoke.

It will help sell it if it looks smart and clean.'

'You can't go doing that!' Rusty said, aghast. 'If it needs to be done we'll get a man in to do it.'

'That costs money. We have to go careful now.'

He shook his head. 'Not that careful. Besides, I've an idea to get us some beer. The longer we keep the pub open, the more chance Casey has of paying off that debt.'

'Frost's Brewery won't supply us, and if we sell a rival company's brew they can sue us for breach of contract. That will cause more trouble.'

'Then we shall sell Frost's beer.' Rusty picked up the sheet of paper he had been writing on earlier. 'I've worked it out. I know several publicans who Frost's supply. They were good friends of Joe's, and don't hold with the way the brewery are treating us. Each of them will sell me three or four barrels at a cost that'll make it profitable to them, but still below pub prices. That should tide us over. I can also get the odd barrel of another brew smuggled in.'

'That will only work for a time,' Eva said with a frown. 'The brewery will be suspicious we still have stocks. They're bound to have a watch put on us. And they have the right at any time to check our cellar to ensure that we don't sell other brews.'

He threw down the paper and sat down with his head in his hands. 'I hadn't thought of that.'

She put a hand on his shoulder, 'I dare say we could get away with a score of barrels to start off with. Thank God, Casey returned in time yesterday to stop the thieves stealing all Joe's cups. She'll get some money for them. Surely if a part-payment is put down on the debt, the brewery must honour its contract to supply us.'

'Aye, but it's a sin to sell Joe's cups for the price of the silver alone.'

'Then Joe should have made provision for his daughter,'

Eva snapped. 'He wasn't a poor man by any means, or he'd not have agreed to buy the new pub. Where is his money?' She played the innocent to goad Rusty, for she was convinced Goldstein had been Joe's partner in some way. But Goldstein had only laughed her suggestion aside.

'Whoever has it, ain't saying,' Rusty said heavily. 'They know we can't touch them.' He stood up. 'Joe may have had some standing with the underworld gangleaders, but now he's dead they'll not hand over his money. I'll get off and arrange for those kegs to be delivered when it's dark. We've enough to remain open until then. Casey will need every penny we can make for her.'

'It may be best if Casey doesn't know what you're doing,' Eva warned. 'She'd refuse to allow you to sell the beer, if it's not purchased through the proper channels. She'll not do anything to antagonise the Frost family. Yet they're doing their best to ruin her.'

Ten minutes after Rusty left, Casey put her head round the kitchen door. 'Did I hear Rusty go out?'

Eva kept her expression guarded. She was still put out over the way Casey had abandoned her yesterday. 'Yes, he's gone to collect his stuff. He won't be back until we open at lunchtime.'

'Then I suppose I'll have to tell Bertha not to come any more. There's so little beer left.'

'Good riddance to that scheming cow.' She vented her spleen on the barmaid she hated. 'You sack her when she finally turns up. She's not been in for two days.'

'That's not like Bertha. She's always let us know if she's been ill before.'

Eva lowered her gaze so Casey would not see the venom in her glare.

'Probably been offered a better job elsewhere, or got a fancy man to keep her company. Her husband is back inside again.

She'll earn more lying on her back than in the bar.'

'Eva, that's unfair. Bertha isn't a whore.'

'Isn't she? She were your father's bit of stuff on the side.'

Casey paled at the crudity of her cousin's speech. 'I had suspected it, but I don't want Dad spoken of like that. He deserves more respect from you.'

Eva saw her error. Casey would never allow ill to be spoken of her father. It was Bertha who was the thorn in her flesh. But not for much longer. 'Forgive me, I didn't mean to speak badly of Joe. It's just her. She can be so uppity when it suits her, and she's no better than she should be. Forget Bertha. She'll have to go anyway to save us money. But Rusty reckoned there was more beer in the cellar than he'd thought. He'll get some cheap spirits that will keep our customers happy. I'll help out in the evenings. That will save Bertha's wages. I enjoy serving in the bar.'

Casey nodded. 'Thank you. I hate to sack Bertha, but if she's becoming unreliable . . . Perhaps I'll go round and see if she's all right. She could be ill.'

'You can't go to her place. It's in a rough area that's almost as bad as the Courtyard. Joe will turn in his grave.' Eva stared at her, appalled. 'If someone has to go it will have to be Rusty, but I don't see what all the fuss is about. She's probably got a new gentleman friend. You see if I'm not right.'

She could see Casey looked stubborn. Really, her cousin could be exasperating, always thinking good of people and worrying over them. She added, 'Rusty will go. Now while he's out, why don't you have a relaxing bath. You've got time before Matt arrives.'

Casey nodded absently. There were dark circles under her eyes and Eva realised that she had slept little better than herself. Had she regretted giving herself to Matt? In Eva's opinion, she wouldn't be surprised if that was the last they saw of Matt Frost. He'd got what he wanted and, with his family putting so much pressure on him, he was bound to take off.

Eva busied herself washing up the breakfast things and mixing a suet pudding for their lunch. The doorbell rang. Knowing Casey was still dressing after her bath, she ran two floury hands under the tap and was still drying them on a towel as she opened the door. To her astonishment a telegram boy held out a brown envelope. 'Miss Cassandra Strong,' he piped.

Eva nodded and took the envelope. She turned it over and, seeing that it was not properly sealed, she glanced quickly up the stairs to ensure that Casey was not in sight, then opened it.

My darling, must return at once to Hendon
Will write soon. Love Matt.

So he'd scarpered, Eva reflected with satisfaction, just like she thought he would.

'This is for you,' she said as she entered Casey's bedroom.

Casey was in her stockings and bloomers and was struggling with the laces of her satin whalebone corset. 'Give us a hand, Eva. I want to wear the black taffeta gown and it's always been a close fit around the waist.'

Eva tossed the envelope on the bed as though it was unimportant, and yanked on the corset strings to cinch Casey's waist to a willowy nineteen inches.

'Aren't you going to open it?' Eva prompted.

'In a moment,' Casey called as she dived into her wardrobe to lift down two elegant black cartwheel hats, one decorated with white ostrich feathers, the other forget-me-nots. 'I want to look my best for Matt. Which hat? We'll probably go to one of the parks as it promises to be a fine day.'

'It's a telegram, Casey,' Eva insisted. 'Perhaps its from your solicitors, or it could be from Matt.'

Casey's mouth formed an 'ooh' of alarm. She snatched up the envelope and tore it open. Then flopped down on the mattress. 'Matt has been recalled to Hendon.'

Eva bit her tongue. To run Matt down would only make Casey more defensive towards him. 'Don't let it upset you,' she soothed. 'I'm sure it's important or he wouldn't have gone.'

There was fear in Casey's eyes as she stared at Eva. 'You don't think it's because of what happened? That he despises me now?'

Eva paused long enough to heighten Casey's doubts. 'He'd be a fool if he did. You've known him almost a year. It's not as though you jumped into bed with him the first opportunity you got. But then men can be bigoted fools where morals are concerned.'

'I didn't think Matt was like that.'

'So trust your own judgement. Things are hotting up in Europe. And he is in the Royal Flying Corps.'

Casey looked at Eva with gratitude. 'No, Matt wouldn't desert me. He loves me. There is an explanation.'

She believed she had the answer to Matt's hurried departure a few hours later. With Eva helping Rusty in the bar, she'd gone shopping to get the day's meat and vegetables. At the corner shop, four women in threadbare skirts and blouses were gossiping over the counter. They were obviously from the Courtyard and fell silent as Casey entered.

'Good morning, ladies.' She ignored the snub. Ever since she could remember, women such as these had been suspicious and unfriendly towards her, resenting her refined speech and clothes. Expecting no reply, she browsed, selecting some fruit but gradually becoming aware that a question had been directed at herself.

'I'm sorry, what did you say?'

Dulcie the shopkeeper was bursting with news. 'Ain't yer 'eard about Bertha. Poor cow fell on to the electric line just as the train were going into the station at Bethnal Green two nights ago. Must 'ave been on 'er way into work. She'd 'ad a skinful.

She were real cut up over Joe's death and 'ad started drinking again.'

Casey put her hand to her mouth as she pictured how Bertha had died. 'Poor Bertha.'

Dulcie nodded. 'If I didn't know better I'd say the Britannia had a jinx on it. There's been enough gossip about the way Joe died. Now this. As I 'eard it, she were pushed by another drunk, but there were no sight of 'im when the peelers arrived.'

'Bertha had a heart of gold,' Casey said. 'To die like that!'

Shocked, she paid for her purchases and walked down the street in a daze. As she approached the Britannia she was dimly aware of shouting from behind her. When she was jostled by a score of shouting men, she tripped and fell against the wall of a house, grazing her cheek. The pain took her attention away from Bertha's death. Why were there so many men in the street shouting and waving their caps?

'War's declared.'

'We're at war with Germany.'

Their words hit her like a shock-wave.

'Get yourselves to the recruiting station, men. Let's show the kaiser the measure of British steel.'

As they broke out into the national anthem, Casey stared after them with horror. In their wake, women huddled in doorways or called across the street, fear on their faces for their menfolk.

'Don't yer go doing nothing daft, my Alf. Yer've got five kids ter keep fed.'

'Nor yer, Bert.' Another woman grabbed hold of her husband's arm and tried to hold him back from joining the chanting men. 'Yer ain't no bleeding good ter me in Germany. I need yer 'ere. Let bleedin' Asquith fight, if 'e's declared war.'

War was the reason that Matt had left with only a telegram to explain. Relief flooded her. Of course he must put duty first. Hot in the wake of relief, alarm trammelled her elation. Matt's life was now in danger. She was uncertain of his role as an aviator in any war, as the Royal Flying Corps was newly formed, but he had boasted of the useful reconnaissance a plane could do over enemy territory. And hadn't he told her that all those daredevil loop-the-loops and aerobatics at the air displays were designed also to be used in aerial combat?

All she could visualise were the horrors and unnecessary deaths caused by a war. There were still one-legged cripples sleeping rough on the streets, veterans of the Boer War. Yet the men were jubilant as they cheered and encouraged others to join them at the recruiting office. They saw the glory and adventure. All Casey saw was a mother mourning the loss of her only son and husband, struggling to make ends meet in her old age. Or a young wife bearing a child who would never hear its father's voice. That image caused her to sway with sudden nausea. What if she had conceived from their love-making last night? And what, heaven forbid, if anything should happen to Matt? She fought the panic threatening to overwhelm her. Stop it. Don't be foolish, she berated herself. Besides, she'd heard that you couldn't get pregnant the first time.

A month passed and she had received no word from Matt, though she wrote to him three times a week. Each day saw more men in uniform on the streets, many now seen marching to the stations or docks to board the ships which would take them to France. Already the English had fought beside their Belgian allies at Mons.

'Don't worry, Casey,' Rusty repeatedly reassured her. 'You'll hear from Matt any day now. Besides, they're saying it will all be over by Christmas.'

Chapter Seventeen

This was the life, Eva reflected in a quiet moment between serving customers. Rusty had kept the pub supplied with beer and they had managed to make a small profit. But it wasn't the triumph at pulling a fast one on Frost's Brewery which made her hum a tune as she worked behind the bar. It was the bag of booty hidden in an empty barrel in the cellar. This had been the best week yet. Forty pounds she reckoned she'd earned from fencing for Goldstein. Easy money. On top of that she'd added another ten sovereigns to her earnings by lifting a purse and two gold bracelets from gentlewomen shopping in Selfridge's last week. No one expected someone as well-dressed and -spoken as herself to be a pickpocket. And it surprised her how careless these women were with their handbags.

Working for Goldstein had handsomely increased her savings. Not that Rusty would approve if he knew. It was her secret. He made enough fuss about her taking in the stolen goods from the thieves. He said it was too dangerous. He'd hit the roof if he learned what she did on the evenings she visited Goldstein's house. She felt no guilt. She enjoyed the sexual antics and they did no one any harm.

She glanced at the clock. It was five minutes before the meeting in the alleyway. The pub doorbell pinged and she looked up to see Boots Lambert amble outside. He was so named as he was fond of putting the boot in during the frequent skirmishes which broke out in the Courtyard. He was her contact.

She touched Rusty's arm and winked. 'Be back in ten minutes.'

Rusty hastily pulled a pint. The beer foamed over the top of the glass as he banged it down on the bar and followed her to the door to whisper, 'You take care. I don't like you out there alone with Goldstein's boys.'

'I earn too much for them to give me trouble. Besides, no one would be fool enough to give a fence working for Goldstein trouble. They know the Jew will stick them good.' She'd shrugged aside his fears and patted the small pistol she now carried in her skirt pocket. 'I dealt with the last piece of scum who tried. Shot the bleeder in the foot when he tried to steal the payout money away from me. Word's got round I ain't no easy target. Goldstein was impressed how I handled the thieving runt.'

Eva continued to hum the song running through her mind as she collected the sack from the cellar and sauntered into the alley to hand over the stolen jewellery to Boots Lambert. In the unlit alleyway, the red tip of Boots Lambert's cigarette showed his presence. He flicked the cigarette aside and took the sack from her. It wasn't heavy: Eva dealt in jewellery, watches, and small items of silver or gold only.

'What's owing?'

'Twenty.'

'Doing well, ain't yer?' He counted the money and handed it to her.

Eva smiled in the darkness. 'Couple of bits I added meself. Like to keep in touch.'

Without warning his hand shot out and Lambert grabbed her wrist, forcing her two middle fingers back. 'But yer ain't 'anding all the stuff over. Goldstein warned yer – no tricks.'

Eva went deathly cold. Why had she kept that mother-of-pearl snuff-box back last week?

'What do you mean?' she blustered.

'Do yer think Goldstein wouldn't 'ave yer watched and the goods accounted for? Where's the snuff-box Shifty Brown brought yer last week?'

'Wasn't it with the rest?' she bluffed. 'It must have fallen out of the sack. It'll still be in the barrel in the cellar. I'll go get . . .'

The pain of her two fingers being snapped back and broken ended her words with a scream. Gasping with pain she cradled her hand. 'I said I'd get the snuff-box.'

'Make sure it's there next week. Next time it will be more than two broken fingers if yer hold out on us. It will be a broken neck. Seems Goldstein has other uses for yer, so just this once 'e's prepared to be lenient. Dancer of some sort, ain't yer? He says to get yer hand fixed in a splint and yer can still work next Friday. Car will be at the corner at eight in the evening.'

Eva was grinding her teeth at the pain in her fingers. She staggered into the scullery and was appalled to see how fast her fingers were swelling. 'Sod him! The bloody snuff-box weren't worth that much.' Even so, she reckoned she'd be dead if Goldstein weren't so taken with her other services to him. It didn't bode well for her getting out of his parties. And though the money was good, the novelty was beginning to wear off for her.

'You've been a long time, Eva,' Rusty said from behind her. 'What you doing out 'ere?'

She turned slowly, holding out her hand. 'Christ, woman! What's that bastard done to you?'

'Goldstein thought I'd kept some of last week's goods back. I swear I didn't. It were to teach me a lesson.'

'I knew you should never have started this.' Rusty reached

for her arm and, holding it, gently examined her hand. His face was tight with anger.

'I didn't have much choice, did I?' she reminded him. 'It were a better option than what I'd feared Goldstein had his mind set on when he took me out to dine that night. Would you rather he'd made me his whore?'

'Of course not.' Rusty looked haggard. 'I'll close the pub and get you to the hospital.'

'You won't say nothing to Casey. Tell her I fell awkward in the cellar and broke my hand.'

'Reckon Casey has enough to worry about over losing the pub, without knowing what you're getting up to. One thing she can't abide is dishonesty.'

Beneath her lashes, Eva shot him a baleful glare. She was near fainting with pain and he was still protecting Casey. Was there no justice?

'It's been seven weeks, Eva. And not one word from Matt.' Casey's cheeks were pale and there were dark shadows under her eyes as she sat with her head bent over a pile of mending. 'Not even a card for my birthday last week. I know he's no letter-writer, but just a few lines would be something. I wish now I'd persuaded Dad to have a telephone installed. But you know how set he was against new-fangled gadgets.'

Eva adjusted her sling. Her fingers were healing and she hoped to have the splints off in a couple of weeks. It suited Eva that Matt had not written. The sooner Casey dropped him, the sooner they could become close again like they had been before her cousin's courtship. Still, there was no point in making her cousin defensive towards her lover.

'Matt could be in France,' Eva consoled. 'Letters do go astray.'

Casey's chin was tilted stubbornly. 'It's because I slept with him, isn't it? He despises me.'

Eva paused in ironing the frill across the front of her blouse. It needed all her concentration since she could only use her good hand. 'Men can be bastards. They pester us to have sex with them. They flatter us and declare their undying love to get their way. Then once we surrender our virtue, we're tossed aside like yesterday's dinner. Perhaps you're well rid of him. His family will never accept you.'

Casey put aside her sewing and stood up. For a moment she swayed and pressed a hand to her head.

'You all right?' Eva asked.

Casey was ashen. She'd lost weight and her black skirt hung loosely across her hips. She nodded. 'Must have moved too quickly. I feel faint.'

'You should eat more. You ain't doing yourself no good pining over Matthew Frost. And that new secretarial job at Duncan's solicitor's is long hours. You want to give it up. The man's a bloody slave driver. You do the work of three secretaries.'

'It's only while Mrs Black is off with a broken wrist. She'll be back next month.' Casey did not mind the extra workload at the solicitor's she had started at last month. The work kept her mind off Matt and why she had heard nothing from him. 'I get paid extra for the overtime I do,' Casey reminded her cousin. 'And we need every penny to pay off the debt. And Mr Duncan isn't charging for the legal work he is doing for me.'

'I should think not,' Eva scoffed. 'He ain't having much success. Humphrey Frost won't even see you to agree to a part-payment of the loan.'

Casey sighed and went to her handbag to pull out a letter. 'I had this today. It's from Jonathan Pinion on behalf of the brewery. He says that if I hand over the deeds of the Britannia, Humphrey Frost will take it off my hands in settlement of Dad's debt.'

'That's daylight robbery,' Eva choked.

'Apparently it's not a bad price, according to Mr Duncan. At least I won't have to sell Dad's cups. The dealer wouldn't give me more than thirty pounds for the lot. They are worth ten times that, but their sentimental value is priceless. I'm thinking of taking the brewery's offer. With the little money I've saved, and if I sell the jewellery, I could still buy a small house in a respectable area for us to live in.'

'Oh, Casey, you'd still have me with you,' Eva burst out, running over to hug her.

Casey looked at her in astonishment. 'Of course, Eva. You will always have a home with me for as long as you wish. We are all each other has. Matt would have written by now if he loved me. You were right. He used me. He was no different from James Hardcastle.' She blinked rapidly to dispel a rush of tears. They would not solve her problems. It had been hard to accept that Matt had betrayed her trust. But with no word in seven weeks, she had to accept that he didn't love her.

'I've instructed Mr Duncan to go ahead with the transfer of the Britannia to the brewery. We'll move out in a month.'

Casey swayed again, and this time her stomach churned with nausea. 'I think that fish I ate last night was off. I've been feeling sick on and off all day.'

'You sure it's the fish?' Eva shot her a knowing look.

Casey blanched. 'It has to be the fish.' For several seconds her expression was haunted as she stared across the kitchen at her cousin. Then her knees buckled and she fell to the floor in a faint.

'Rusty!' Eva yelled. 'Rusty, get your arse up here!'

The pub manager burst through the door, his mouth gaping at seeing Casey sprawled on the floor.

'Don't stand there gawping like a bleeding landed eel,' Eva snapped. 'Carry her into her bedroom, then get someone to run for the doctor.'

Silence stretched between the two women in the bedroom as the doctor departed. Casey was stunned. This couldn't be happening to her. It couldn't. A baby! She was carrying Matt's child.

Her mind tumbled, seeking solutions. For how much longer could she work? Thank God the Frost family would take the pub in payment of her father's debt. She'd move away from the Courtyard long before anyone suspected what had happened to her. She would not tarnish her father's name by bringing shame upon it in front of those who knew him.

'A fine mess this is,' Eva said at last.

'I'll manage.'

'The sooner you notify Matt, the better. He can't get away with this.'

'He has the right to know he's fathered a child, but I've no intention to insist he weds me. I want him to marry me out of love, not duty.'

Eva concealed her emotion from her cousin. She was almost euphoric. Casey needed her now. She'd be sympathetic and supportive. But she would be in control. Casey would be indebted to her for standing by her. They would be close, as a family should be. She saw her dream of a perfect family materialising: everyone caring, sharing the workload, needing her, loving her.

'I'll stand by you, Casey,' she declared passionately. 'I've some money put by. We could go into partnership – get a place of our own which will bring in an income.'

'What sort of business?' Casey said with a frown.

'A pub-cum-guest-house. But in a better area.' She brightened, warming to the idea. 'Rusty has a bit put by. He's said he won't stay when the brewery takes over. All three of us could be partners. We could let a couple of rooms to lodgers. I'll talk to Rusty tonight.'

'We can't involve Rusty,' Casey said. 'I won't be a burden

on anyone. I can work for a few months yet.'

'Nonsense. It's what Rusty needs. He can't afford to run a pub of his own. And he don't know no other trade. The three of us will be equal partners.'

The letter to Matt telling him he was to become a father was the hardest Casey had ever written. She loved him passionately, but having received no word from him for weeks hurt her deeply. Had he just used her? She hadn't wanted to believe that. She had been so certain that Matt was different, but without even a postcard from him in two months, her faith was tested. She could not believe that he would abandon her so callously. Not Matt. Not her beloved.

She was sitting up in bed writing, weighing each word she wrote carefully and placing no blame on him. She ended simply,

I leave the Britannia at the end of the month. If I have not heard from you by then, I will know you did not truly love me, and your child and myself will take no further part in your life.

She was resolved that she would stick to her decision. Matt had until she left the Britannia to contact her. Otherwise she would not send him her new address.

Whilst Casey wrote her letter to Matt, Eva tackled Rusty after the pub closed for the night. She was helping him wash the glasses. The bar was eerily quiet after the noise of the evening's customers. It smelt of stale beer, and a blue tobacco haze formed a canopy beneath the nicotine-stained plasterwork of the ceiling. Only the gaslights behind the bar were alight, casting the rest of the pub into deep shadow, except where a streetlamp illuminated one corner.

'What plans have you got when the brewery takes over, Rusty?'

'I've been thinking about enlisting in the army.'

Eva reeled. That was the last thing she had expected. At thirty-four Rusty was not a young man. In her mind only fools risked their lives fighting wars.

'You'd desert us as well? I were relying on you, Rusty,' she coerced.

'Not enough to marry me though.'

She saw the trap she had fallen into. Twice since they had visited Southend Rusty had asked her to marry him, and she had refused to give him a straight answer. 'I never said I wouldn't marry you, Rusty.'

'I know a brush-off, Eva.'

'That's not true.' She prevaricated, needing to keep Rusty interested without committing herself. 'It's so soon after Joe's death. Casey needs me. Even more so now. She's pregnant.'

Rusty dropped the glass he was drying. It smashed unheeded on the floor. 'She'll have to wed Matt straight away. She don't need you.'

'Chance would be a fine thing,' Eva sneered. 'She hasn't heard from lover-boy in two months. Looks to me like he's done a runner. He got what he wanted out of her. She's lost the pub to pay Joe's debts, and that's due to his family putting the boot in. She's better off without him.'

'They ain't getting away with it,' Rusty blazed, twisting the drying cloth in his hands. 'I'll go round that bloody brewery and sort them out.'

'What good will that do? Except create a scandal. It's Casey we have to think of.'

Rusty smashed his fist down on the bar top, his expression murderous. 'Bastards!' he spat. 'At least they've agreed to take the Britannia in settlement of Joe's debt. Though I could never see that Joe would put himself at risk that way. He had money.

Why didn't he pay the brewery?'

'Joe were always wheeling and dealing,' Eva shrugged. 'Likely he just overstretched himself this time.'

'The sooner Casey can put all this behind her and start a new life, the better. The Courtyard never was no place for her to live.' He inhaled several times to master his anger, but his fist was still clenched when he ground out, 'Anyway, how's she taking the news of the kid?'

'On the chin and still fighting. She's got plans. She don't want no pity and no charity.'

He shoved himself away from the bar and crossed to the door. 'I'll speak with her. I never had Matt down as a man to shirk his responsibilities. He loves Casey.'

'Got a funny way of showing it,' Eva bit out.

'I owe Joe too much to see Casey so shamed. If Matt won't marry her, and since you won't have me, I'll give her my name.'

'But you don't love her.'

'I respect her more than any woman I've ever known. And I do care for her. She's Joe's daughter. I couldn't face Joe at the Pearly Gates if I let Casey down when I could've helped her.'

Eva burst into tears. 'Oh, Rusty you can't mean to marry her. You can't. You love me.'

'But you don't love me. And if I have to, I'd be proud to raise Joe's grandchild as me own. I love kids. It's time I settled down.'

This wasn't in Eva's plans at all. It was bad enough that Joe always put Casey first. Now Rusty was doing it.

'You're just saying that to make me marry you,' she sobbed. She hugged her injured hand close to her chest in her misery.

'No. Casey needs me and clearly you don't.'

When he put his hand on the door she launched herself at him. 'I do need you, Rusty. You're the only man who's ever really loved me. I will marry you. Casey will live with us. She could pass herself off as a widow when we move to a new area.'

'You're not just saying this because you've been forced into it?' Rusty was staring down at her with incredulity and wariness in his eyes.

She was driven by a demon. Why should Casey have Rusty? She knew the barman well enough to know that within a year he would be wildly in love with her cousin if she gave him any encouragement. And Casey would never wed a man whom she would not do her best to love and honour. But Rusty adored *her*, Eva inwardly fumed. He was the only person who knew some of Eva's failings and did not judge her.

'I'll marry you as soon as the banns are read. Does that satisfy you?' Before he could reconsider, she wound her uninjured arm around his neck and drew his head down to receive her kiss. They were both breathless when they finally broke apart.

'I do love you, Rusty. It's marriage I were against. Sid and Myrtle were hardly a couple to recommend the state. But even for Casey, I couldn't sacrifice our happiness.'

'You mean it?'

Eva smiled. 'I needed the shock of nearly losing you to realise how much I loved you. But I want no more talk from you of enlisting. A man of your age should have more sense. Besides, you've too many responsibilities now if Casey and her child live with us.'

She kissed him again, satisfied at the adoration she now saw shining in his eyes. 'We won't mention this to Casey just yet. Wouldn't be very tactful in the circumstances. We'll wait until the arrangements are made. But we'll marry before we leave the Britannia.'

Rusty grinned broadly. 'Getting married in a month suits me. I'll go and look in on Casey, just to see she's all right.'

He bounded up the stairs and Eva pressed a hand to her

head. Had she made the right decision? She'd have to give up going to Goldstein's now. Married to Rusty, he would become suspicious of her visits to a friend who never showed her face in their home. She sighed. Perhaps it was time to put that side of her life behind her. The excitement had palled. It would not be so easy to find a female lover in the future, but it was certainly not impossible. Her goal now was to own the hotel she dreamed of. Everything would come to her in time. It usually did.

As she turned to cast a last look around the bar she froze. Her eyes widened with fear as she stared at a table illuminated by the shaft of light from the streetlamp. The shadows around it flickered. For a moment she could have sworn she saw a figure in a bowler hat and a glimmer of a scarlet waistcoat standing watching her. The arm lifted in accusation.

Every hair on her body prickled with terror, and with a small scream she ran out of the bar into the hall. Her limbs shook uncontrollably as she stared at the foot of the stairs where Joe's body had lain. The carved newel-post threw a long, menacing shadow. It seemed to build in substance, rounding in shape until a man's figure lay there. She tore past it and up the stairs, colliding with Rusty on the landing.

'What's the matter with you? Seen a ghost, old girl?'

Eva threw her arms around him. 'I suddenly realised how close I came to losing you, Rusty,' she explained away her need to be held and reassured.

Matt sat on his camp-bed and picked up his pen, resolving that he would write to Casey. Every day since arriving in France he had made the same promise. She was on his mind in every free moment, which were few and far between. When not flying reconnaissance flights, he was helping the overworked engineers repair the planes. Amongst the new recruits, none was his equal in expertise. Each night he fell exhausted into his bunk. He had already witnessed the horrors of war – of losing pilot friends whose planes were shot down or who crashed.

He scratched his head, searching for the words to write which would convince Casey how much he loved and missed her. Already five sheets of paper were screwed up on the floor, the written word failing him. Her letters were always tender, amusing, and she never wrote of the problems she was facing in running the pub. He could not forgive his family for what they were doing to Casey. His conscience pricked him. Her letters gave him so much pleasure and he never seemed to have the time to reply. It was unforgivable.

His heart swelled with love and pride whenever he read her words of affection. If only he could write similarly. He had never found it hard to speak of his love, but to put it on paper was beyond him. He'd choke on his own emotions, feeling foolish seeing them written down, sounding so trite. Casey knew he loved her. The only letter he had written when he had forced himself to pour out his heart, she had not even mentioned. Had it gone astray? Surely he had not offended her by writing of the joy she had given him on his last leave. It made this letter harder than ever to compose.

It was with relief he looked at his watch and saw that it was time to prepare for his reconnaissance flight. It was the tenth he would fly. The thrill and danger of flying over enemy lines was both exhilarating and terrifying. Behind him, a cameraman trained his apparatus on enemy troop movements or munition convoys. Today he had to survey the area along a river with a strategic bridge which was vital for the advance of the British army. Their commanders needed to know the strength of the enemy in the area before the attack.

It was a dangerous mission, as it meant flying low and they'd be exposed to enemy fire.

Hastily he folded the letter to Casey. He'd post it when he

returned. Then, conscious that it was far from the passionate letter she would be hoping for, he hastily scribbled, *'I love you. I always will. Forever yours, Matt'*.

There was plenty of cloud-cover, which was encouraging. He had been following the wending course of the river for several miles when his calculations showed that the bridge was just ahead. They emerged from the shielding clouds half a mile from the five-arched medieval bridge. Woods covered the river-bank on one side, cornfields the other, and clustered on both sides of the bridge were a score of cottages and a tall spired church. Around the market cross were several German vehicles. The field behind the village was white with the tents of the battalion preparing for another day's march. Adrenalin pumped through his veins at seeing the machine-guns mounted on two trucks. Derek, the cameraman, had better get the pictures first time, for there could be no circling back. The option of flying into the clouds never crossed his mind. Intelligence was unaware that the kaiser's troops were in this area.

Within seconds all hell broke loose. There was a volley of machine-gun fire from the trucks, and more from the church tower. Matt felt the plane judder as two of the wing-struts were smashed. Then pain exploded along his right arm, side and leg, blood spurting across his goggles. The bridge and river disappeared in a red haze. He shouted back at Derek but got no reply.

Everything seemed to be happening in slow motion. Wiping his goggles with his sleeve, he looked down. He could see the torn sleeve of his flying jacket and the oozing blood. Every breath was laboured. The engine was coughing and spluttering. The controls juddered in his fast numbing fingers.

Glancing over his shoulder, he saw that Derek was slumped forward in his seat. There was blood running down his face beneath his leather helmet and goggles. A second glance at his own body revealed more blood. Hell! How many times had he been hit? The pain was excruciating all down his side and leg, but the will to survive was greater.

The biplane was losing height. This side of the bridge the water was shallow; he could see the black forms of rocks below the surface. On the far side was a weir. More gunfire ricocheted off the plane's wings, and there was a burst of orange flame from the engine.

'Dear God, have mercy on me!' Matt screamed as he kept the plane on course towards the deeper water.

'Jump, Derek. If you can hear me, *jump*,' he yelled.

Thick black choking smoke spewed back from the engine. Matt's right arm was numb and his leg felt as if it had been thrust into the burning flames which were curling over the cockpit. Was he already burning, or was it the pain of splintered bones? His mind raced. He had seconds to jump. There was no parachute. He lined up the plane, which was now forty feet above the river. He'd either burn alive in the cockpit, or likely be smashed to pieces on the rocks below if the water was shallow. Better that than death by fire.

Matt's jaw clamped against the agony in his wounded arm and leg as he struggled to heave himself up out of his seat. The smoke obscured the river. The pain was appalling and he battled against unconsciousness. Somehow he managed to get his uninjured leg over the side, but the wounded right one was useless. In seconds they would crash. He banked the plane steeply to the left. The engine screamed. The force of the plane tilting pitched him out of the cockpit.

There was a brief moment where he tumbled through the air. Then the sound of an explosion as the plane crashed into the trees. A hot wind buffeted him. The river water rushed towards him. A large boulder was directly in his path. No time even to mutter a prayer. He screamed Casey's name. Then felt searing pain . . . Silence . . . Oblivion.

A fortnight later, Casey's unopened letter to Matt was amongst those belongings which were returned to his family by the Royal Flying Corps, together with a letter informing them that Matthew Frost was missing in action. His plane was reported as being shot down in flames. Sybil Frost, on reading Casey's letter, tore it into pieces and threw it into the fire. The unposted letter that Matt had written to the Strong creature had earlier been consigned to the same flames. Her voice was harsh with bitterness.

'Serves the little slut right. Good riddance to her and the bastard she carries.'

She glared across at Humphrey, holding back her tears for Matt. She refused to believe that he was dead. She would never believe that until she stood over his grave.

'If that slut is not out of the Britannia as arranged by the end of the week – evict them. I never want that scheming hussy's name mentioned again in this house.'

'She'll have to be told that Matt's plane was shot down and he's missing,' Humphrey pointed out.

'Tell her he's dead. I don't want her around when my darling Matthew comes home. It was clear from her letter to him that he had ended the relationship. She was trying to blackmail him into marrying her.'

Humphrey sighed. It was obvious that his mother would not accept that Matt was dead. Ever since his brother had walked out of the house, she had begun to act irrationally, becoming obsessed with the idea that the rift with the family was all his fiancée's fault. Sybil's love for Matt was as destructive as it was obsessive. He feared for his mother's health. All his life he had adored Sybil, but she had never shown him the love reserved for Matthew. Now he would prove to her that he was the better son. He would make it up to her for her loss. His mother might choose to believe that Matt had survived, but no one lived through a burning plane crashing.

The pilots weren't even issued with parachutes. Both his brothers and father may have fallen under Cassandra Strong's spell, but not him. The loose morals of the women from the Courtyard were well known to him. He'd had one or two of them himself when out on the prowl with male companions. He would obey his mother's wishes. If Cassandra Strong had given herself to his brother outside marriage, then how was he to know that there had not been others? This child she was carrying need not be his brother's. It was not his responsibility.

His conscience was clear as he instructed Messrs Pinion that his brother was dead.

Goldstein rubbed his hooked nose and sniffed as he regarded Eva. 'So you want out. Just like that?'

'You said I could. It was part of our agreement.'

'I don't make agreements with whores. And you're a whore just like the rest.'

'But I'm getting married. How can I work the parties for you? My husband doesn't know about them. He'd never marry me if he did.'

'Then that's your problem. Not mine.'

Eva was getting desperate. 'I'm not backing out of everything, just the parties. I've done well fencing the jewellery at the Britannia. Doesn't that count? Wherever I move to, I can do the same.'

His brown eyes glittered. 'It ain't that easy. You owe me for that little job you wanted set up.'

'I paid you for that.' The first trickle of fear iced her spine. She had thought that incident was long past.

'Ah, but then you were working for me and I did it as a sort of favour. But I have clients who enjoy watching you perform. You're quite something, Eva. I ain't ready to let you go yet.'

'I'm getting married. I can't continue.'

His stare was malicious. 'Bit late to turn respectable, ain't it?'

Her shoulders slumped. She was frightened but daren't show it. Her broken fingers were hidden under a long trumpet-shaped sleeve. They were a reminder of just what he was capable of. And broken fingers were nothing compared to the punishments he could mete out when crossed.

'How much will it cost me to get out, Mr Goldstein?'

He named a sum.

'But that's every penny and more than the money I earned working for you! What about the risk I've taken fencing the stolen stuff?'

He shrugged, seeming to enjoy her discomfort. 'That's the price. Take it or leave it. But I'd take it as a deliberate slight if you let me down when I still had need of you.'

The threat was unmistakable. Tears started in Eva's eyes and she blinked them defiantly away. 'Damn you, I'll leave it then. I haven't much choice, have I? But when we move away from the Courtyard, I won't be able to get here so often. And it's on condition that I still fence for you.'

His hand shot out, grabbing her chin and forcing her head back until she felt her neck would snap. 'I don't take orders. I give them.'

Sweat broke out on Eva's brow and back. His other hand struck her hard, sending her reeling across the room. She fell against the wall, jarring her injured hand.

A scream was wrenched from her. Protectively she cradled her broken fingers in their splint. She could feel blood trickling down her cheek where Goldstein's ring had broken the flesh.

'Understand?' he threatened.

'Yes, Mr Goldstein.'

He thrust his face close to hers. She could smell garlic and violet lozenges on his breath. 'You finish when I says so.'

She nodded, too frightened to speak.

Seeing her capitulation, he took a pair of nail scissors from his trouser pocket and trimmed a broken nail. 'Where's this new pub you're thinking of taking on?'

'Rusty's seen one in Leytonstone.'

'I've got that area pretty well covered. So you won't be needed to fence. Still, as a kindness to you, I'll take anything you can lift yourself. You've got an eye for quality stuff, and dress well enough to mix with the toffs.'

Stealing on impulse was one thing. Having to do it to order was another. Eva straightened. 'The pay-off as a fence was worth the risks. But I ain't going to be a common pickpocket. I'll just stick with the parties, seeing as I've no choice. Though I thought you always said you needed the women to be willing to put on a good show.'

Goldstein laughed. 'It ain't as though you don't enjoy it, is it? Besides we've got a few secrets between us, ain't we, Eva? Not least the bother my boys went to dealing with that barmaid who was beginning to give you trouble.'

Casey stared at the solicitor's letter. Matt was dead. Her baby would never have a father.

'Good Lord, Casey, you look awful,' Eva said, coming into Joe's old study. 'What are you doing in here? Though it is time you sorted out Joe's cups to sell. We have to leave here at the end of the week. You don't want the Frosts giving you more trouble.'

'Matt's dead. His plane was shot down in France.'

Saying the words made them real to her. She swayed and Eva caught her, helping her to Joe's leather swivel-chair. 'He's dead. He didn't desert me. He did love me. He would've married me, wouldn't he?'

Eva kept her opinion to herself. 'Of course he would. But what are you going to do now? The sooner we can make a fresh start the better. You'll live with Rusty and me. He's asked me to wed him and I've accepted. We're taking over a pub in Leytonstone not far from the Thatched House. The details are all settled. It's big enough to take in lodgers, the George and Dragon it's called.'

'That's good, Eva.' Casey's heart felt like it was being squeezed in a merciless clamp. There would be no marriage for her. The only man she would ever love was dead. She tried to rally from the despair which was fast settling over her. 'I am pleased for you, Eva. Rusty is a good man. I know you will be happy.'

'We'll make a new life together at the George and Dragon,' Eva was saying excitedly. 'All three of us. Four, once the baby comes along.'

'I'll have a little money left once I hand over the pub. I'll still sell some of Dad's trophies. I won't be a burden to you and Rusty.'

'You won't be. Didn't we already discuss something like this? You can keep the books for us and run the guest side of the business. Rusty and I will work in the bar. It will be a partnership.'

Stunned with grief, Casey latched on to Eva's words. She wanted to keep her mind away from accepting that Matt was dead. She needed to think about providing a secure future for her child. 'In a few months I shall be unable to work,' she said heavily. 'If I live with you when I have the baby, your reputation will be dragged in the mud along with mine. Too many people knew Joe. I don't want to shame his memory.'

'Blimey, Casey!' Eva could not hold back her exasperation. 'No one will know you if we move to Leytonstone. Say you're a widow.'

Casey shook her head, her eyes brimming with tears as she stared up at her cousin. 'No, I will remain Cassandra Strong. Yet I don't feel inside that Matt is dead. I feel the pain of grief, but not the emptiness I expected. What if he survived the crash? Was somehow thrown to safety?'

'There's not much chance of that. It's better for you to face the truth now. Matthew Frost is dead. You're clinging to a false dream. How many weeks has it been since you last saw him? He were no better than James Hardcastle. Not one single letter – just that telegram after he left. Forget him, Casey. He wasn't worth it.'

It was several moments before Casey replied. 'To me he was worth it,' she began slowly. 'I will always love him. I never thought him capable of deceit.'

'Perhaps normally he weren't,' Eva reasoned. 'But his family were putting pressure on him. If he'd loved you – truly loved you – wouldn't he have written?'

Casey hung her head. Eva was probably right. After the way his family had treated her, had he been torn by his conscience? Had he realised that his family were more important to him than she was? Could she even blame him if he had? Perhaps she was a fool to make excuses for Matt. Even so, hope could not be completely vanquished. He had always been a poor letter-writer.

'I have every faith that Matt was in love with me when our child was conceived. I have no regrets. But now I must think of the baby's future and security.'

An attack of nausea made Casey stagger to the sink. When she returned to her cousin, she was weak and shaken. 'I never thought being pregnant could take so much out of you. I've no energy. I thought the morning sickness would have passed by now.'

Eva studied Casey. She was deathly pale and her slim figure as yet showed no sign of thickening. She actually looked as though she had lost weight. Though strong of character, Casey was clearly suffering with her pregnancy, and Eva was worried about her health. The shock of her father's and Matt's death must also have taken its toll upon her. At the sight of Casey's weakness, a sense of fulfilment swelled in her breast. This was her chance to prove to Casey how much she cared for her.

She would look after her. Protect her. It was a pity she still felt bound to marry Rusty, but they'd need a man to give respectability to the plans she was making for the future.

'Leave everything to me, Casey,' she said with relish. 'Everything will work out for the best. We will get away from the Courtyard and start a new life in the George and Dragon. In a few years we may even be able to afford to buy a hotel. That's what I'd really like.' Eva puffed out her chest with pride. 'A hotel sounds really grand. But we bloody well won't be selling Frost's beer, that's for sure.'

Casey was again feeling too ill to protest. It was a good idea. A change of scenery. A fresh start, the past firmly behind her. Inexplicably, she shuddered, as if someone had walked over her grave. The feeling stayed with her, adding to her nausea.

'You look like death, Casey,' Eva observed. 'Go and lie down.'

'I think I will. We must start packing tomorrow if we want to leave here at the end of the week.'

The nausea stayed with her as she lay on her bed and closed her eyes. Visions of Matt haunted her sleep, making her toss and turn. Twice she heard him call to her, but when she started awake in the darkened room, she was alone and bereft.

Unable to bear the thought of lying and dwelling upon what might have been, Casey got up. The pub was in darkness and she was drawn to her father's study. The moonlight played over the poster of Joe Strong on the wall, and a rush of love and grief overwhelmed her. Sinking down on to his leather swivel-chair, tears streamed down her cheeks as she gazed at the lifelike image of the portrait.

'Did you have to leave me too, Dad? I'll never understand how you could have got so drunk to fall down the stairs. I never meant to shame you by giving my love to Matt. I was so proud of you, Dad. If we ever get that hotel Eva is so set on, it will be dedicated to your memory.'

This room was filled with happy memories which crowded her mind. How as a child she had run into the study on her return from school, and flung herself on to her father's lap when he was taking an afternoon nap while the pub was closed. He would awake with a start and grunt as she landed on him and then he would hug her close. 'What have you been up to today, Princess?'

The memory made her smile and her head flopped forward as she was overtaken by sleep.

A sensation more than a sound awoke her. The room was still dark, except for the pale moonlight glinting on the remainder of Joe's boxing trophies. She was glad she would need to sell so few of them. They would always be precious to her. The moonlight shimmered in the far corner and, still dreamy with sleep, her smile broadened as she discerned the stocky figure silhouetted by the window. His bowler hat was tipped back and she could faintly make out the scarlet of his waistcoat. She reached out to touch him before she realised she was awake and not asleep. The image vanished and was replaced with a cold sense of imminent danger.

Shocked, she stood up and backed towards the door. She shook her head, unable to shake the sensation of danger. She didn't believe in ghosts, but Joe's image – and its implicit warning – had been so real.

PART TWO

Necessity and chance
Approach not me, and what I will is fate.
MILTON, *Paradise Regained*

Chapter Eighteen

1919

Casey was sitting at her father's old desk in the room she used as an office at the Ringside Hotel. Her mind drifted from the neat column of figures in the leather-bound account book. In the months since the war ended, their takings had tripled, and they continued to rise each month. In partnership, she and Eva and Rusty had purchased the beautiful twelve-room Georgian building on the outskirts of Richmond eighteen months ago. It was the fulfilment of a dream, paid for by the success of the George and Dragon, which they had run in Leytonstone for three years after they had moved from the Britannia. Their hard work had been rewarded. Eva and Rusty had been popular, drawing crowds into the bar. Casey, as business manager, was involved in letting the guest rooms and providing meals for the residents.

Even with their success and the joy she had experienced since her daughter Josephine had been born, Casey remained unfulfilled. She wanted more purpose to her life. As the war progressed and she saw more and more wounded war veterans return to England to rebuild shattered lives, she felt compelled to do something worthwhile for the men she regarded as heroes. Too many were badly disfigured or crippled from their wounds and had no family to look after them. Often they were shunned by old friends. Josephine's birth had prevented her offering her services as a field nurse during the war, but Casey had a natural empathy with the wounded. Their wounds did not horrify her, just their despair at coping with their disability.

On her insistence, the Ringside had become a hotel primarily for war veterans who had recovered from their surgery and no longer needed medical attention. She provided them with a friendly, family atmosphere in which to recuperate. Apart from the bar, restaurant and hotel staff, she employed three trained nurses who worked in shifts, so that there was always a professional on hand to tend to any of the veterans' specific needs.

At first Eva had been against the idea. She had changed her mind when she realised that their prices were necessarily higher, geared to a more selective clientele: most of the guests were officers. Casey never told Eva that at least three of the current residents were paying only half-price, as she did not have the heart to turn away less wealthy veterans when they had need of the facilities they offered.

Workmen had just completed the eight-room extension and glass-fronted restaurant and terrace which overlooked the river. The restaurant had been expanded to cater for non-residents as its reputation grew for high-class cuisine and excellent service. There was never an empty table in the evening or at weekends. A string quartet played for the diners, and any who wished to dance did so on the polished dance-floor at the centre of the tables. In the bar on the far side of the hotel, a pianist played every night, catering for those who preferred a sing-song with their drink. It had proved a popular combination.

The hotel had been renamed the Ringside and dedicated to the memory of Casey's father. Both the restaurant and the pub were hung with photographs and posters of Joe 'Strongarm' Strong in his days as a champion.

Casey's gaze strayed to the wedding photograph of her mother and father she kept on her desk. 'I hope that me running a hotel and pub does not shock you, Dad,' she said softly. 'I know you wanted so much for me. But I'm happy here and feel I am doing something worthwhile.'

She frowned, recalling the vision of her father in his study just before they left the Britannia. It had been as though he had been giving her a warning. How wrong he had been. They had prospered. Yet five years later she still felt the chill which had settled over her that night. The night she had heard that Matt's plane had been shot down.

Unexpectedly, the pain of her loss returned. She didn't know if Matt was alive or dead. Deep in her heart she had never accepted that he had died, but obviously he did not love her. There had been no word from him, even after the war ended eight months ago. If he had wanted to find her he would have done so. He didn't even care enough to seek out his own daughter. That was what hurt so terribly. Gradually, as the war had dragged on and the months of silence turned into years, her heart had hardened. Whether Matthew Frost was alive or not, he was dead to her. Yet no other man had captured her interest in the intervening years.

To dispel the heartache of her lover's betrayal, she rose and went to the window. In half an hour she must collect Josephine from the little dame school she had special permission to attend as she was so forward for her age, and spend some precious moments alone with her daughter. The daughter who believed she was Casey's niece. To protect Josephine from the censure and ridicule of bastardy, everyone believed that Eva was Josephine's mother.

Casey hated that deception. She longed for the day when Josephine would be old enough to be told the truth. She knew Josephine loved her. Eva smothered the girl in love and affection, more so than she did her own son, Danny, who was a year younger. Yet it was always to Casey that Josephine came if she was upset, and it was Casey she asked to read her a story at bedtime.

Knowing that the accounts must be completed, Casey hesitated by the window. She was loath to return to the desk. It was such a gloriously sunny July day. Several red admiral and tortoiseshell butterflies hovered on the purple blooms of a buddleia bush outside her window. She wanted a moment to savour the pleasure she had always experienced when she gazed out at the gardens and river. The immaculate lawns were bordered by roses and lavender, and honeysuckle and jasmine sprawled over the trellis-work fences, adding their exotic scent to the summer's air through the open windows.

Mallory the gardener was trimming a privet peacock which decorated a hedge. Beside him, Archie whistled as he tended a bed of carnations. Casey had been so moved by Archie's grief over her father's death that she had kept in touch with him and his mother over the years. When his mother had suffered a fatal stroke last year, Casey had been horrified to learn that Archie had been put into the workhouse by the parish. She had rescued him and given him a home and work. In the gardens of the Ringside he had found a vocation. Everything he planted flourished and he seemed to have a natural empathy with all plants. He spent hours potting, cutting and setting seeds in the greenhouse.

Several of the veterans were sitting in cane chairs, playing cards at tables set out by the willow trees which sheltered one side of the garden. Harry O'Keefe, a one-legged sergeant, was playing his harmonica softly. A burst of laughter from the card players brought a lump of emotion to Casey's throat. That had been real laughter, which was becoming more common as the soldiers, sailors and aviators began to put the horrors of the war behind them. When they first arrived, many of them were withdrawn; others joked constantly, their humour forced and brittle, and usually self-deprecating to cover their frustration and pain. Joyful, unrestrained laughter was a sign that the mental scars were healing.

Casey was drawn to four men seated apart from the others and drinking whisky or beer. All had been here over a year. The sunshine beckoned her and she put off doing the accounts, stepping through the open casement window on to the terrace.

'Here is the woman of my dreams.' Captain Gerald Weston grinned at her. He'd lost an arm, and his torso and the left side of his face were badly scarred from shrapnel. Deep lines of pain were scored into his brow and cheeks, making him look closer to fifty than a young man of twenty-three.

'She's mine,' Bert Hodgekins wheezed, his lungs impaired by the mustard gas which had almost killed him. 'I were 'ere first. And there ain't no rank-pulling at the Ringside. That right, Miss Casey?'

'I don't believe in favourites, Bert,' Casey laughed.

'She's the darling of us all, but sweetheart to none,' Lieutenant Reginald Trent rubbed the leather strap which secured the iron hook which replaced his blown-off hand.

'And who would want us?' Captain Weston ground out. 'Our broken bodies are useless to a woman.' He was given to bouts of melancholy, his vivid blue eyes usually shadowed with bitterness.

'Speak for yourself,' Reggie Trent chuckled. 'Though I do wonder why a pretty thing like Cassandra wastes herself on us old crocks?'

'And why am I wasting myself?' she teased.

Bert Hodgekins shook his head. 'Good Lord, Miss Casey, a lovely young woman like yourself should be married and raising beautiful daughters in your own image.'

'Marriage is not for me, Bert. The war took from me the only man I shall ever love.'

Captain Weston raised a dark blond brow in scathing mockery, his cobalt blue eyes now flashing with bitterness. 'Killed, was he, or wounded? He'd not want you to see him if he'd ended up like this. My fiancée screamed and ran out of the hospital ward when she clapped eyes on me.'

It was the first time he had spoken of a fiancée, and Casey now understood some of the emotional pain which tormented him. From his unscarred profile with its aquiline nose, high cheekbones and strong jaw, he had clearly been an exceptionally handsome man. Women must have adored him.

'She was a foolish woman and unworthy of you, Gerald,' Casey said firmly. 'You received the Victoria Cross for storming the enemy trenches and knocking out that machine-gun. Your scars are healing and you are one of the nicest men I've ever known, when you don't let self-pity drag you down.'

He continued to regard her narrowly, deliberately keeping his scarred cheek towards her. The puckered skin twisted up the side of his full lips into a permanent sardonic sneer. 'It's easy to say that when you don't have to look at this horror in the mirror every morning.' He downed a whisky and poured himself another from the decanter on the table.

Casey put her hand on his to stop him from drinking the second glass. Too often Captain Weston drank himself into a stupor. His blond hair was thick and, unrestrained with oil, fell forward over his wide brow. He was exceptionally tall at six foot four, and slim in build. 'You may no longer be the perfect Adonis that once you were, but a woman would be very shallow indeed to only see your scars and not the man beneath them. When you are not feeling sorry for yourself, you are witty and amusing and have a generous nature.' She did not add that he had a voice like crushed velvet which could send shivers of expectancy along a woman's spine. With a smile she stooped to press a sisterly kiss on his scarred cheek. 'You only get bitter and bloody-minded when you drink. Couldn't you ease up on it?'

She didn't wait for his answer, for three men on crutches, each with a leg amputated at the knee or thigh, were shouting and cheering as they swung their bodies forward on their crutches and kicked a football with their good leg. She smiled at their irrepressible courage, for she knew each one of them was in pain. Turning back to Gerald, she observed, 'Don't forget the bowls tournament we have set up with the veterans from the hospital next week. And the darts team from the pub have asked for a game tonight. Can I leave it to you, Reggie, to get a team together?'

'Boyish games to keep the cripples happy,' Captain Weston jeered. He slid his whole arm around her waist, pulling her closer. 'I can think of better games to play than bowls and darts, and they don't involve teams.'

Casey firmly gripped his fingers and removed them from her waist. 'You will behave yourself, Captain Weston, or I will have to ask you to leave the hotel. Every man here has my friendship, but I will be treated with respect.'

Bert had risen from his seat and was glowering at the captain. 'Keep yer bloody 'ands off Miss Casey. She's a saint and deserves better—'

'That's all right, Bert,' Casey intervened. 'Thank you for defending me, but I can look after myself.'

Bert remained scowling. 'Anyone who lays a finger on Miss Casey, disrespectful-like, will 'ave to answer to me and the others.'

'She isn't in much danger from a one-armed cripple, is she?' Captain Weston flared and, downing his second whisky, picked up the decanter and strode off.

Casey watched him march down to the river. There was a stone seat in the shade of the willow trees, where he often sat for hours drinking and smoking when a dark mood settled upon him. Many of the veterans had mood swings and days of depression. Captain Weston could be the most caring and considerate man one moment, then without warning a devil seemed to enter him, and he would be deliberately cruel. It was as though he wanted to stop people liking him.

She did not try to fathom what went on in the men's minds. She just tried to be compassionate and understanding, allowing them space to themselves when she sensed they needed to be alone. Often at night the peace of the hotel was split with screams as a veteran relived, in his nightmares, the horrors he had seen and experienced in the war. Gerald Weston never had nightmares, but there were times, like now, when Casey felt that the demon possessing him was more lethal and destructive. It kept his horrors caged within him, and they would take longer to heal.

From the hotel the grandfather clock in the lounge struck the hour, and Casey bade the men a hasty farewell to collect her daughter from school. Today was her nephew Danny's third birthday, and she and Josephine were collecting the iced cake from the baker's this afternoon. The tricycle Casey had bought Danny was wrapped up and hidden in her office.

Arriving at the school gate, Casey felt a rush of pride as her daughter came out, surrounded by her friends. Instantly, on seeing Casey, Josephine's face lit with pleasure and, tossing back her dark ringlets, she ran headlong into Casey's arms.

'Auntie, I got all my sums right today, and I coloured this picture for you.'

To hear Josephine address her as Aunt instead of Mother always slashed like scissors through her heart. Her daughter held up a drawing which was meant to be the Ringside Hotel, with a river running along the bottom of the garden. A woman with brown hair dominated the picture, with a yellow-haired man beside her. Obviously that was herself and Rusty, and a boy with a mass of black curls was Danny. The smallest person in the picture was a black-haired woman in the background.

'Why have you drawn Mummy so small?' Casey laughed. 'She is bigger than you.'

Josephine pouted. 'Mummy was nasty. She said Danny wasn't getting a birthday present because he'd been naughty.

He will get a present, won't he, Auntie Casey?'

'Of course he'll get a present.' Casey was angry that Eva should have spoken so thoughtlessly to Josephine. Eva lavished Josephine with gifts, but towards Danny she was cold and could barely speak civilly to him. Danny was a lovable child. If, as boys do, he was adventurous and often getting into mischief, he was never wilfully disobedient. To console Josephine, she said, 'I saw Rusty bring home a large parcel from the toy shop.'

Immediately, Josephine brightened. 'Oh, goody, I wonder what he's got. I hope it's a train set. Danny wanted one.'

'Train sets can be very expensive, my dear,' Casey answered.

'They're not any more expensive than the tricycle you've bought for him and he loved that.'

Casey gasped. 'You mean the little devil has seen it! I kept that hidden as a surprise.'

Josephine looked stricken. 'It wasn't Danny's fault. You won't tell on him, will you? It was last night before you wrapped it up. Danny was upset. Mummy had hit him again. She called him a nasty, dirty boy – he'd ripped his shirt trying to get his ball when it rolled amongst the roses. He felt no one loved him. I wanted to show him that you loved him, because you had bought him the bright yellow tricycle he saw in the toy shop.'

'Of course I love him. We all love him.' Casey inwardly cursed Eva for being so hard on the boy. She had never heard her cousin scold Josephine. Not that she would have allowed it. Eva might, as far as the world was concerned, be Josephine's mother, but it had been agreed from the outset that Casey would be the one who disciplined her if need be. It was she who decided how her daughter would be brought up. Yet Eva was always buying Josephine pretty dresses and toys whilst seeming to ignore the needs of her son.

Casey decided that she would change Josephine into a cool summer dress and then they would seek out Danny who would be with his father in the garden. Rusty always played with Danny in his free time in the afternoon when the bar was closed. It also kept the boy away from Eva, who insisted on quiet and slept for an hour every afternoon.

As she entered her daughter's bedroom, Casey frowned. On the bed was a new white taffeta dress with a wide red sash. The hem was embroidered with large poppies.

Josephine groaned. 'Mummy has brought me another white dress. Now I can't play properly with Danny. I'm bound to spoil it and then she gets cross. I hate all the dresses with frills and bows she buys for me. Why can't she buy me dresses like the ones you do? They're always pretty, but they don't have all the fancy bits that keep getting torn when I play.'

Casey suppressed a smile at her daughter's practicality. In truth she did not like the frilly dresses Eva preferred either. They made her daughter look like a fairy doll, but as it gave Eva so much pleasure buying them, she hadn't the heart to tell her so. Now that Josephine had stated her own preference, it was time Eva considered the girl's choice. She would rather Josephine wore less fussy dresses so that she could enjoy herself without worrying that they got spoilt.

'Put on another dress whilst you are playing with Danny, and save this one until I take you to the park on Saturday afternoon.'

From across the hall, Casey heard Eva's voice rising shrilly. 'How could you let the boy get in that state, Rusty? Just look at him. He's filthy. It's a waste of money buying decent clothes for him. He always looks like street urchin.'

She heard the deeper rumble of Rusty's voice placating his wife, then the sound of running footsteps as Danny ran sobbing to his room. Casey hurried on to the landing just as Rusty emerged from his wife's bedroom.

'It's all right, Casey, I'll calm Danny down,' he said wearily. 'Perhaps you could make Eva see sense. It's the lad's birthday and she's just . . .' He looked world-weary. In the last four years he'd lost weight and the teasing sparkle had faded from his eyes. 'She's being unreasonable again.'

That, Casey thought, was an understatement. Eva was being downright nasty to her son. Her heart went out to Rusty. She knew that Eva and he were not happy together, and she often wondered why her cousin had agreed to marry the affable barman. Though how she and Eva would have coped without him, she also did not know. She was very fond of Rusty, who had worked hard to make the Ringside a success. She smiled reassuringly. 'I'll see what I can do.'

Rusty nodded, and Casey felt a pang of sympathy for him. Eva led him a merry dance. The arguments had started a few months after their wedding. When Eva became pregnant she did not speak to Rusty for months. To her cousin she poured out her scorn. 'If he thinks I'm enduring that sordid fumbling again, he can forget it,' Eva had raged. 'I've done my duty. If I hadn't married him, two women alone could never have run the George and Dragon or the Ringside.'

'I thought you loved Rusty,' Casey remonstrated. 'There were other businesses we could have started together.'

Eva had glared at her. 'But without my marriage your daughter would be ridiculed as a bastard.'

She'd paused significantly, and Casey burned with anger that Eva saw herself as a martyr, bartering her body to ensure that Josephine need not carry the stigma of bastardy, and to protect Casey's own reputation. She bit back a tart reply. She had wanted no sacrifices from anyone to cover the mistakes she had made. Eva had been so adamant at the time that she loved Rusty and that this was the best solution. But then Eva was in the habit of reminding the people she did favours for of their indebtedness. Clearly, Eva was discontent. But then Casey had never known her not to complain at the misfortunes life had dealt her.

Throughout her pregnancy, Eva had spoken only of giving birth to a daughter. 'A cousin for Josephine. They will be as close as we are, Casey. She will look just like me. A daughter of my own would at least make this farce of a marriage worthwhile.'

Casey's conscience pricked. If anyone was a martyr in their partnership, it was Rusty, not Eva. And he never complained. Eva had made him a poor wife. From the moment Danny had been born she'd demanded a separate bedroom from her husband. She had ignored the existence of her son, refusing to ruin her figure by nursing him and a wet-nurse had been employed. Not once had Casey seen Eva hug or kiss Danny. But in one respect Eva had got her wish. Her son was the image of her, with a cherubic, heart-shaped face and tight ebony curls.

Casey knocked at her cousin's door and entered to find her glaring at her reflection in the mirror. She brightened at seeing Casey's image appearing behind her shoulder.

'Did Josephine like her new dress? I couldn't resist it. It's perfect for her colouring.'

'Josephine is afraid of spoiling it as she wants to play with the train set you've bought Danny.'

'I didn't buy it.' Eva's lips compressed. 'I wouldn't waste good money on that ungrateful brat. Rusty spoils him, and I told him so. That boy is nothing but trouble, unlike dear Josephine. Do you know what he's done now?'

'Boys will be boys, Eva.'

'Grubbing around in the dirt like a guttersnipe, he was,' Eva snapped. 'I told him he couldn't have his presents until he learned to behave properly.'

'Eva, that's wicked. He's only three years old.'

Seeing her anger, Eva pursed her lips, then unexpectedly burst into tears. 'Oh, Casey, what have I done? I didn't mean to be wicked. But that boy is such a trial to me. Why couldn't he have been a girl? I wanted a girl so much.'

In recent years it had been common for Eva to resort to hysterics to get her own way. Casey did not understand why her cousin acted as she did. In the first year of her marriage, Rusty had worshipped the ground that Eva trod upon. And in repayment, Eva had treated him like dirt.

Eva looked up at her through tear-soaked lashes. 'I don't know what comes over me, honestly I don't. I try to be a good mother, but Danny is just like my brother Charlie. Charlie was a little sod. I hated him. He took all of Dad's love and he had none left for me. Danny is Charlie come back to haunt me. To punish me.'

'Don't talk that way.' Casey saw the bright flaring of colour in Eva's cheeks and the glitter in her eyes, alerting her to the fact that her cousin was working herself up to another fit of hysteria. They could last all day, and it would ruin Danny's birthday if his mother stayed angry with him.

'Danny is a dear child,' she soothed. 'And if you had but seen it, Charlie adored you. He followed you everywhere.'

'Don't I know it? The snotty-nosed bleeder were always telling tales on me. The number of times I felt the lash of Dad's belt because of that little sod.'

Casey hadn't realised how much Eva had hated her half-brother, and it was with shock that she perceived that deep down Eva didn't like men in general. She had no time for the veterans in the hotel, although occasionally to make Rusty jealous she would flirt outrageously with one of them. Then she would cut the poor man dead the next time she saw him.

'Danny is your son. He loves you, Eva. If you gave him one quarter of the attention you give Josephine, he would adore you.'

'No, he wouldn't. It's Rusty he wants, not me. It's always fathers and sons. Dad never had time for me, only that runt Charlie.' The face which had once been so beautiful had thinned in recent years. Lines of bitterness marred the cupid's-bow mouth and hardened her eyes. 'I know men,' she spat. 'Every one of them has betrayed me in some way.'

'Not Rusty.' It was obvious Eva was getting herself worked up to a fit of hysterics, and Casey was desperate to placate her so that Danny's birthday would not be spoilt.

'He was no better than the rest.' Eva shuddered theatrically. 'He knew I found sex disgusting. Yet he still used to try and force himself on me. I fought him off for six months. Then he got drunk and raped me. You didn't know that, did you? That's how come I fell pregnant with the brat. Rusty is like all men. Only after one thing. You should know that after the way Matt ditched you.'

'Matt's plane was shot down. It was different,' Casey defended.

Eva's eyes narrowed, her lips drawing back into a snarl. 'He didn't contact you when he got out of the hospital though, did he?'

Casey stared at her blankly. The blood roared in her ears as though she had received a blow to her head. 'Out of hospital? Then he's *alive?*' The colour had drained from her face as she stared accusingly at her cousin. 'You knew he was alive and didn't tell me? Good God, Eva, how could you be so cruel?'

Her voice broke as she struggled with the pain of Matt's desertion. She closed her eyes and heard the coercing seduction of his voice, and saw the false tenderness in his handsome face. The bitter-sweet memories of his courtship flashed like fork-lightning through her mind, striking and splintering the façade that his betrayal had killed her love. It scorched her, leaving her soul singed in its aftermath.

Beneath Casey's anguished glare, Eva lowered her gaze and fidgeted with the porcelain face-powder bowl on her dressing table. 'I thought you'd got over him. I didn't want you to be upset. I only learned of it a few weeks back from

Toby the drayman. He used to work for Frost's until this spring. Apparently Matthew Frost is living back home in the loving bosom of his family. And he's getting married at the end of the year to that wealthy cousin of his.'

Casey rode the blow, her voice hollow with pain. Holding herself stiffly, she combated her misery. 'I had the right to know. Why did you keep it from me?'

Eva was conciliatory and put an arm around her waist to hug her close. 'I didn't want you to be hurt again. Hadn't you suffered enough? Better for you to have believed that he died than that he hadn't cared.'

Casey pushed her away.

Eva fidgeted with the cameo brooch on the high neck of her cream silk blouse. 'You had built yourself a new life. You were happy here. Look at what we have achieved. We are someone now. This is your life and your home. You have Josephine and me to love you. The veterans adore you. What more could you ask for?'

'That the man I will love until the day I die still loved me,' she forced out through a throat clamped tight with emotion. 'I thought he was different, Eva. I really thought he was honourable and worthy of my love.'

Eva laughed without humour. 'Sometimes your naïvety astounds me, Casey. Forget the selfish bastard.'

Casey turned away to hide the agony lacerating her heart. She was roughly spun round.

'I did what I thought was best,' Eva responded passionately. 'Families must stick together. Look out for each other.' Again Eva embraced Casey's trembling figure. 'Didn't you tell Matthew Frost that he had to make peace with his family, or he would never be happy? His kind marry for wealth and position – not love.'

Casey drew a shuddering breath and eased herself out of Eva's arms. Her cousin was over-demonstrative at times, and she found it cloying. 'At least I know the truth now. Life goes on. I can't spoil Danny's birthday by moping upon what might have been.'

Eva smiled. 'That's the spirit. Who needs men, Casey, when we have each other?'

Chapter Nineteen

'It's time you remembered you had a son,' Rusty blazed at Eva. 'The kid needs a mother. And you make more fuss of that damned cat than Danny.'

Eva continued to stroke the smoky grey fur of the Persian cat on her lap. Salome purred and rubbed her head against her mistress's hand, seeking further attention. Rusty had burst in on Eva in her bedroom, a room decorated in pale pink and yellow. An abundance of cream lace canopied the four-poster bed; the curtains and bedspread were of ruched satin. Eva lifted Salome up and kissed the cat's head. 'I never wanted children. Danny is your son, born of your lust.'

Rusty dragged his thick fingers through his thinning wheat-coloured hair and groaned. 'Even from the start you only ever spread your legs when you wanted something from me.'

'Don't be disgusting.'

'Why did you marry me, Eva? You didn't love me. You did it to stop me giving Casey my name, didn't you? You did it so your cousin should be indebted to you, and you could have her daughter under your power. God knows, Casey would have made a ten-times better wife than you, and I'd be a darn sight happier.'

'Must you cuss? You show yourself up for the common little man that you are. You haven't tried to better yourself at all. You disgust me.'

'I don't give meself airs above me station. And I know me own worth. I've slaved to make the Ringside a success. I work eighteen hours a day and Casey does at least twelve, whilst you think yourself hard done-by doing an hour at lunchtime and two in the evening.'

'I have the children to look after.'

'Aye, you've time enough for Josie. Don't think I don't know how you bribe her with toys to get her away from Casey. Only Josie, even though she's just a nipper, won't take anything from you unless you've got something for Danny. Got a heart of gold that girl. Like her mother. Whilst you . . .' His eyes slitted. 'I were a blind fool thinking you were something special. Joe tried to warn me once. Said you were trouble. I never believed him, and for a time he seemed to mellow towards you, so I reckoned he'd changed his mind.'

Eva smiled maliciously. 'Oh, he did more than mellow, Rusty. He was my lover. He were a real man. He knew how to please a woman. The only one I've known who has.'

'Now why doesn't that come as a surprise to me? It explains why he were drinking heavily when he died. Once you get your fingers in a fella you don't let up. What were you after . . . marriage? Thought you'd get your hands on Joe's money. You were very keen to learn bar work. Was it to show him what an asset you'd make as a wife? Only Joe didn't fall for it, did he?'

Her lips curled back and she pushed Salome on to the floor. 'He was the same as the others. Joe, me own dad, Fat Sam, Goldstein. They all used me, every one of them. They all took what I could give and flung it back in my face.' Her rage was icy and venom-tipped. 'Still, I survived . . .'

Rusty felt tentacles of fear wrap around his heart. There were times when Eva scared him. Now she seemed so full of hatred and resentment he could almost taste it in the air.

'Aye, you survived, like a viper in our bosom. If it weren't for the boy, I'd leave you.'

'Found someone else, have you? Someone who don't mind your great clumsy hands pawing them. Have your peccadillos, Rusty. I don't care, but you ain't leaving me. We need a man here to make the Ringside respectable.'

'I ain't staying for you, Eva. But for Danny. He needs his mother, though little good you do him. And I'm weary of your threats and your grand airs. If you want to reap the rewards of Casey's and my hard work, you can work the same hours.'

'Don't you dictate terms to me!' Eva raged. 'I made you what you are, Rusty Chambers. You were nothing but a common barman when I met you.'

'And by your own admission you were anybody's cheap whore.' To her astonishment he grabbed her by the throat, one hand circling it, squeezing tight as he forced her up out of the seat and on to her toes. 'Over the years I've had me belly-full of your grand airs and whining. No longer. You treat the boy right or I'm taking him away. And if Casey has any sense she'll throw you out and keep Josie safe from your evil clutches. Whatever you touch goes rotten. Joe rarely drank until he got enmeshed with you. Good God, even your parents never had a decent word to say for you, and Bertha weren't no fool.'

He stopped abruptly, every freckle standing out starkly on his ashen face. 'They're all dead. Even your little brother – dead!'

Eva picked up a flower vase and hurled it at her husband's head. He ducked and it smashed against the wall. 'Haven't I suffered enough without you dragging up how wretched my life has been? I've lost everyone. Everyone who could have cared for me. Dad was a weak fool; he loved me, but Myrtle was jealous and turned him against me. Joe was a real man, but he didn't want my love. I'll never know what he saw in that fat cow Bertha. And even you, you would have married Casey to save her reputation. You didn't really love me, you never understood me. You accuse me of –' she began to weep

– 'the vilest things. You say I don't love our son. Three days I was in labour with him. He nearly killed me. When I look at him, all I see is the terror and pain I suffered. And then I remember how you held me down on that bed and raped me.'

Rusty stared at Eva with loathing. The beautiful, provocative woman he had married had turned into a shrew and harridan. Her voluptuous curves had disappeared as she'd become gaunt through discontent and nerves. He shook his head. 'I demanded my rights as a husband because even then I seldom got them. You're a selfish bitch. The child was not to blame for how he was conceived. As God is my witness, you drove me to act as I did, unnatural wife that you are. Danny is not responsible for the agony his birth caused you. It's just an excuse.' He lumbered backwards, his expression dark with loathing. 'You ain't human the way you treat me and the kid. But as from now, things will change. One thing you can be sure of, I ain't never coming to your bed again. And don't expect me to go without either.'

Her laughter followed Rusty as he stormed out of the room and slammed the door. His face was winter-bleak and horror enclosed his heart. Why hadn't it struck him before? There had been an uncomfortable number of deaths of people close to Eva. Her brother, father, Myrtle, Joe, even Bertha. By her own admission, Eva had voiced her antagonism at the way she had been treated by all of them. Was she responsible for their deaths? Rusty reeled as from a blow. No, she couldn't be. She was hard-hearted and self-centred – but murder, that was too far-fetched.

Eva glowered at the water stain on the wall from the smashed vase. Several red rose-petals clung like huge splashes of blood. She wished it was Rusty's blood, and that it was him lying crushed and broken on the carpet instead of the flowers. Rusty was the bane of her life. He had changed from a doting slave she could manipulate to a demanding lover. The more she had found pleasure at Goldstein's parties and the touch of women, the harder it had been to tolerate his touch. Getting pregnant had been the last straw. After the birth she had no longer bothered to hide the loathing roused in her by the touch of hard male muscle beneath her fingers, instead of the pliant soft curves of a female form. Even his smell of musky sweat, hair-oil and shaving soap made her want to gag. How much sweeter was the bouquet of subtle seduction emanating from female lovers: lavender, rose-water; their own unique essence, provocative and enticing.

She felt her stomach muscles tighten as her imagination conjured up the smell of her latest companion. Felicity was a sculptress, the daughter of a fashionable Edwardian artist. She had separated from her husband, an Austrian composer, a month after the wedding. She supported herself by her work and lived in a secluded cottage ten minutes' walk from the Ringside. They had met at the parish fête six months ago. Felicity had immediately declared that she must model Eva's face for a bronze statue of Venus she had been commissioned to produce for a Scottish lord.

Flattered, Eva had posed. On the second visit, Felicity had suggested that the length of silk that had been draped Grecian-fashion around her body should be removed, and she had reclined naked on the studio couch. Felicity never stopped praising the perfection of her body. Although Eva felt that she was now too thin, she revelled in the compliments. At the end of the sitting, they became lovers.

Felicity was the fourth lover Eva had taken since finally leaving Goldstein. When she had been pregnant she was certain that Goldstein would release her, but the perverted guests he entertained got an added thrill out of watching a woman heavy with child being made love to by other women. Her wages had doubled in the last three months of her pregnancy. But as the weight fell away from her after the birth, Goldstein told her she was too skinny and too old to be attractive to his guests. They, in their hunger for novelty, wanted the new excitement provided by young girls barely into puberty.

Free at last from Goldstein's clutches, she had been resentful of his insults. If he had not been so powerful, she would have made him pay for them.

During the next two years it had not been so easy to find lovers. In the end she had joined the Women's Social and Political Union which campaigned for suffrage. Although the suffragettes had halted their lobbying of Parliament during the war, they were still active in rallies demanding women's rights. From amongst these new friends she had found an occasional lover, but had never been in love with any of them. Once the relationship ended, she had no interest in them as friends either.

Already the piquancy of her relationship with Felicity was beginning to pale. Eva had been unable to dominate her, and that had always been the main attraction with her female lovers in recent years. It was power over another which stimulated her. Sex remained the means to that end. She had not seen Felicity for a month, as the sculptress had sailed for America, where recognition for her work had led to a major exhibition. It would be another month before she returned and Eva hadn't even missed her.

Only with Josephine did she experience the power over another that she craved. Casey had always been too independent, but Josephine was young and malleable. The girl's fondness for Casey was disturbing. Casey was beginning to hint that it was time that Josephine should be told the truth of her parentage. Eva shuddered. Josephine was the joy in her life. She was the daughter of her heart, if not her body. She did not want Casey taking that away from her.

So far she had persuaded Casey that Josephine was too young. If she became confused, she might blurt out the story at school, and that would undo all the careful work they had done to protect Josephine from being ostracised by the families of other children. Bastardy was something to be ashamed of. It would be far better to wait until Josephine was a young woman before she was told. Casey must be made to realise how much she owed to Eva for the protection her love and friendship had given both her and Josephine.

Eva smiled as she contemplated the next dozen years with Josephine, her adoring daughter, and Casey, her devoted companion.

Matthew Frost stared across the grass airstrip at the biplane he owned. A ray of sunlight had broken through the hazy cloud and illuminated its wings in a golden glow. Painted in scarlet across its sleek body were the words Frost's Flying Company. It was the fulfilment of a dream which had lain dormant through the war and the long months of his convalescence. From the moment he had been wheeled out of the hospital ward to return to his home, his mother had insisted he take an interest in working for the brewery. He had refused. He couldn't shake the feeling that something important was missing from his life. The powerful pain-killing drugs had been hard to decrease; for months he had battled against pain and depression. Eventually in desperation his mother had spoken of his love of flying and dream of starting a flying company. Like everything else since the crash, even that ambition was something he needed to be prompted about and to rediscover.

He leaned heavily on his cane and bent his leg to ease the aching muscles from the exhausting walk from the hangar. Those three hundred yards had felt like several miles. A feat which would have been impossible even six months ago.

A year before that he had still been confined to a wheelchair. His right hip and thigh bone had broken in several places from the bullets which had torn through the plane before it crashed. For years his leg had been unable to bear his weight, the muscles wasted from the bedridden inactivity in France, about which he had little recollection. Slowly images were returning. One in particular, of a woman with hair the colour of burnished mahogany, and smoky grey eyes which crinkled with laughter or tenderness. Yet who she was he had no idea. Like so many aspects of his past, her identity eluded him. Even his family could shed no light on her identity.

'You were ill so long, my darling,' his mother reasoned. 'Perhaps it is the woman who rescued you from the river when your plane was shot down. She was the wife of the doctor who was on leave from the Front. He patched up your wounds, although he could do nothing for your head injury. Don't you remember her at all?'

'She was blonde not dark.' Matt could vaguely recall her, though his years as an invalid were clouded by the pain, morphine and other drugs the French doctor and his wife had given him. 'Her name was Yvette. The woman I see is dark.'

'Then of course it is Clementine, your fiancée,' Sybil insisted. 'Your mind is playing tricks with you. It's all those drugs. It took months for you to come off them.'

Matthew did not argue with his mother. There was no point. But he knew the woman he saw was not Clementine. Neither, he was certain, was she a figment of his imagination. The vision of her stirred an aching in his breast. Yet everyone he questioned in his family denied knowing her. And none of his old friends and confidants from the Flying Corps were alive. Except Basil Armitage, who was still convalescing in some seaside town after losing both his legs. He had written to him but never received a reply.

His frustration at not being able to piece together the years he had been in France, or indeed so much of his past, made him feel disorientated, loath to meet people. When they first shipped him back to England, he hadn't even recognised his mother when she came to see him in the hospital.

The lost years of his memory disturbed him. Returning to his home he was relieved to discover that the rooms were familiar to him, although he could not have described them before entering them. Slowly images from his childhood returned. But nothing of being shot down, his father's death, or his engagement to Clementine. There was a blank from leaving university and the early years of the war. Even the last two years hiding in France were shrouded in mystery and half-remembered glimpses of reality. There had been so much pain, not only from his leg but from the head wound. Drugs had kept him alive. Yvette had mothered him like the child she had never had. And he had been like a child. He'd had to learn to eat again, and how to talk and tie up his shoelaces.

A year ago, a surgeon had drilled into his skull, saying it would remove pressure from his brain. Since then the headaches had eased and were becoming less frequent. Slowly jigsaw pieces of memory came to him but as yet they didn't fit together.

The plane had been a present from his mother when he finally set a date for his wedding to Clementine. It still perturbed him that he felt no more than fondness for the woman. Her timidity irritated him, and he could not believe he had once been attracted to so plain and dull a creature.

'You brought her alive with your love, Matthew,' Sybil Frost explained. 'Her spirit broke when we were told that you were dead. But I never gave up hope. I prayed every day that you would be returned to me. Clementine stood by you. You cannot abandon her now. It would be too shameful. Her reputation would be ruined if you broke off the engagement.'

The only honourable thing he could do was marry her as agreed before the war. Even so, he would not be badgered into an early wedding. First, he insisted that he would not marry until he could walk down the aisle instead of being wheeled in his chair. Having learned to walk, he had set the wedding for the end of the year. Yet still he felt trapped in a situation which did not feel right. Perhaps he could have accepted it more easily if the dreams of the unknown woman had not returned with greater clarity.

'Are you sure you do not know this woman?' he repeatedly asked his mother. 'I see her so clearly in my dreams, but when I awake it is as though her shadow hovers just out of my reach.'

For the first time since his return to England, his mother had lost her temper with him. 'Forget this creature of your imagination. You are honour-bound to Clementine. Would you break the poor girl's heart after she's waited for you all these years?'

To try and remember brought on the vicious headaches which crippled him for days. The more he forced himself to piece together the past, the more it eluded him. The doctor had assured him that his memory would return in time. How much time? It was nearly five years since his plane had been shot down. The doctor had given short shrift to his impatience. 'You are lucky to be alive after those injuries. God knows how you weren't crippled for life. All your energy has been concentrated on recovering from the brain haemorrhage which crippled you for so long. Once the body is healed, then the mind will follow. All your strength must be used to recover from your physical wounds.'

Matthew rubbed his shoulder and upper arm where the scars from his bullet wounds had long healed, but still on a crisp morning like this they could give the odd painful twinge. There were further scars on his back where his flying jacket had caught fire before he jumped out of the burning plane. At least his face had been spared disfigurement. The scars from his fractured skull and operations were hidden under his hair. All that was visible was a two-inch line which cut across his brow and lifted an eyebrow. It was little short of a miracle he'd survived the plane crash. From what he'd been told from the surgeons who had been apprised of his injuries by Yvette, his body had been carried downstream by the turbulent waters when he jumped from the plane. She had found him caught up by his revolver belt in the low branches of a tree overhanging the river. He was half-drowned and unconscious from a deep gash above his ear where he had been buffeted against a rock. It was dusk when she found him as she searched the river-bank for the rare herbs she used to make poultices and tisanes for her husband's patients. She had heard that a plane had been shot down at the bridge a mile up-river in the morning. Neither she nor her doctor husband had expected him to live. When, days later, he regained consciousness, he had no memory, and no feeling in his injured leg and arm. Speech was difficult. Even in English there were so many objects he had forgotten the name of. Blood from his head wound had flooded his brain; it had been a long haul to slowly recover from the haemorrhage.

He wiped a hand across his face, his jaw clenching. It did no good to dwell upon the war years. He had survived, albeit with an impaired memory. Others had suffered a great deal worse. Each day he was getting stronger. One day his memory would return, as his physical wounds had healed.

To blot out the disquieting vision of the lovely dark-haired woman from his mind, he spent hours each day exercising the crippled leg. Sweat would pour from his brow as he struggled to stand and then start the painful, slow, lengthy process of walking again.

Most nights his dreams were of the dark-haired beauty. Last night the dream had been more vivid than usual. He had been exuberant after taking to the air again for the first time since his crash. The excitement had crackled like machine-gun fire through his veins, but the effort to remember who the dream woman was, or where he knew her from, had exhausted him before he fell asleep. As the pink glow of dawn filled his bedroom, he had begun to stir, free from pain, relaxed. The smiling face formed, laughing, enticing, swelling his heart with a painful longing. She wore long robes draped around her slender figure, and some kind of hat which looked like a Roman helmet, and she appeared to be holding a warrior's spear. Waves crashed around her feet and he realised it wasn't a woman. It was a mythical female. It was Britannia floating in a barge down the Thames past the Tower of London.

Britannia! He catapulted upright in bed and groaned as agony shot through his head. The pain was crippling as he willed his memory to return. He drew up his legs and sank his head down on to his arms folded over his knees. The image was clear but its meaning evaded him. And why should he have seen the Tower of London with its infamous Traitor's Gate so clearly revealed?

The dream returned to Matthew now as he stood on the edge of the airfield. Its vividness stabbed like needles through his brain. The flight he planned was forgotten. He was consumed by an overwhelming impulse to return to London. Somehow the Tower of London held the key to the woman in his dreams. He had to go there. He was driven by a force beyond reasoning. However slender the thread of memory he had regained, it must be pursued.

Three hours later, he limped along the cobbled path by the river lined with ancient cannon, and gazed disconsolately at England's greatest fortress. The four turrets of the White Tower and surrounding crenellated battlements with its great gatehouse were familiar. But nothing further nudged his memory. Traitor's Gate yawned before him, and he stared bleakly at the water slapping its steps. It was a forlorn place, permeated with the fear of the prisoners who had ascended those steps as a prelude to ending their life on the scaffold. Why did he get the feeling that he was no less a traitor, had betrayed some force that had been an integral part of him?

He lifted his gaze again to the domed turrets of the keep, scanning the outline of towers and the clusters of tall gabled buildings within the outer walls. The image was not right. Familiar – but not what he was seeking. He decided to view it from a different angle. Slowly he traversed the battlemented wall until twenty minutes later he was again approaching Tower Green. This time the outline struck a chord within him. He surveyed the road and nearby streets, again uncertain. People spilled out of the Underground station of Tower Hill. It seemed a natural starting point to pursue his search.

Matt tried not to analyse which way he should walk or why. As soon as he tried to think which street he should walk down, his mind became a blank and he had ended up in a cul-de-sac flanked by warehouses. Retracing his steps to Tower Hill station, he walked to the corner. The stone horse-trough seemed an old friend and, allowing his footsteps to take him where they would, he trusted to gut certainty that they would lead him in the right direction. A piece of stone carving over a building doorway seemed familiar, as did the outline of a church tower and its gilt weather-vane. They assured him that he was on the right track.

Doubt returned as the streets became shabbier, windows smashed and doors swinging on broken hinges. Ragged urchins played in the street. It was a far cry from the wealth of his own home, and he could not believe the woman of his vision lived amongst such squalor. Disconsolate, he turned right, appalled by the decay of the buildings. He halted at the entrance of an alleyway which looked menacingly dark. Out of the shadows came the cries of undernourished infants, and the shrill arguing of drunken adults. The drone of flies was incessant as they swarmed over a dead cat whose sunken flesh already heaved with writhing maggots. He turned left, the road forking towards Aldgate. Here the skyline of gables and tenements triggered flashes of memory.

He halted again, faced with a warren of alleyways converging on a courtyard. Men scowled at him from doorways, several moving towards him, clearly intent upon robbery. With relief he spotted the domed helmet of a policeman ahead and hurried towards him. No one followed. His leg was on fire, unused to such harsh treatment. He stopped to massage it and, as he straightened, his eyes widened. Blinking rapidly to clear his vision, he was partly convinced he had imagined what he had seen. He was several yards from a pub across the road. A faded painting of Britannia on the pub sign creaked in the breeze.

Matt stood transfixed, jostled by passersby, unaware that the man who bumped into him had stolen his fob-watch.

Yellow lettering had proclaimed the pub sold Frost's Finest Ales. His elation faded. Obviously he'd been here before. Humphrey had told him he had helped out with the sales side of the business when his father was ill. Again he studied the pub sign. It was Britannia all right, but the face was not the one from his dream.

The reek of beer fumes hit him as he pushed open the door and entered. The bar was half empty, and several drinkers eyed his expensive dark grey suit suspiciously. The portly, red-faced landlord looked at him blankly.

'Bit out of yer way, ain't yer, Mister?'

He was about to introduce himself, then held back. 'Used to come here before the war. I'll have a pint of Frost's bitter.'

'Ah, that were before my time,' the landlord grunted. 'Bin here a year, I have. Took over from Alf Williams, who departed rather sudden-like with the law after 'im.' His eyes shadowed suspiciously. 'You from the brewery?'

Matt shook his head. 'You sell Frost's beers. Do you own this pub or are you a tenant?'

'Tenant. Brewery owns it. Some years back it were owned by the champion boxer "Strongarm" Strong. Heard of 'im?'

An image of a large poster with a boxer posing on it flashed into Matt's mind. 'Dark man, was he?'

The landlord grunted. 'Never met 'im. Got drunk and fell down the cellar steps and broke 'is bleeding neck, or somethin' like that. That were before the war.'

The smell of an unwashed body assailed Matt's nostrils as a woman sidled up to him. She was swaying drunkenly; her bright red hair hadn't seen a brush in ages. 'Buy us a drink, Mister. I'll make it worth yer while.'

Matt ignored her.

'Tight git, s'pose yer think yer too bloody good to drink with me,' the woman jeered. Her face was close to his, her breath reeking of porter. 'Well, I knew Strongarm. Quite a celebrity 'e were. Me cousin Bertha used ter work 'ere. 'Er and Strongarm 'ad a thing going for a time. After 'is death the poor cow got pushed under a train. Some reckoned it were drink and she fell. I says she were pushed. Cursed, this pub is. First old Strongarm dies, then her. Within a couple of months, Strongarm's family were kicked out by the bleeding brewery or somethin'. For debt.' The woman snorted. 'We all thought Strongarm were worth a mint. He were buying another pub before 'e snuffed it. Yet 'is family got thrown out. That stuck-up cow of a daughter got nothing. And the bitch of a cousin got even less. 'Eard tell she 'ad to marry the barman 'cos she were up the spout.'

Matt took a florin from his pocket and flicked it to the landlord. 'Fill up her glass.' He turned to the woman but took a step back to distance himself from the fetid stench rising from her clothing. 'Strongarm was the landlord here before the war,' he prompted. 'And he had a daughter, you say. What was her name?'

The woman downed half her porter and smacked her lips before answering. 'Kate. Kathy. Somethin' like that.'

Matt racked his brains. Kate Strong. Kathy Strong. Katherine

Strong. Nothing clicked, though the image of the boxer returned. Strongarm Strong. Joe Strongarm Strong. A shadowy figure in a scarlet waistcoat and a bowler hat pushed back over dark hair was resurrected in his mind.

'What was the cousin's name?' he persisted.

The woman banged her glass down on the bar and stared at it significantly. Matt nodded for the landlord to fill it up.

'A scheming cow, that one. No better than she should be. Bertha had no time for 'er, I remember.'

'Her name,' Matt rapped out impatiently.

The woman blinked, her eyes glazed with drink, and hiccuped in his face. ' "The bitch", Bertha always called her. Reckoned she were after getting 'er claws into Strongarm even though 'e were 'er uncle. Ethel, her name were I think. Or was it Gena? Long time ago, it were.'

'It weren't Ethel, you stupid cow,' another woman snorted. She was no cleaner than the first, and there were several patches sewn on her brown dress which was several sizes too large for her emaciated figure. 'Eva Bowman she were. Parents died in that gas explosion which demolished their 'ouse in the Courtyard.'

The second woman peered short-sightedly at Matt. 'Do I know yer? Ain't from round 'ere, are yer?'

'I don't believe we've met.' The smell of the two women was making Matt queasy. He glanced round the pub and was surprised it was owned by his family. Paintwork was peeling off the central pillars that supported the ceiling. The cream walls and plasterwork ceiling were mid-brown from tobacco smoke, and several of the glass bulbs of the gaslamps had been broken. Though they supplied beer to pubs all over London, the few he knew his family owned were in select, wealthier districts and kept immaculately clean. This one was a disgrace. Almost like finding a skeleton in the family cupboard.

He winced as a sharp pain shot through his skull. His leg

was aching intolerably. The thick tobacco smoke, beer fumes and the stench of the two women cloyed at his nostrils and throat. For a dreadful moment he thought he would faint. He pressed a hand to his eyes and, as he rubbed them, the image of the boxer landlord appeared. Beside him was the laughing face of the woman in his dreams. The air was oppressive and, concerned he might faint, he hurried outside. Leaning back against the pub window, he closed his eyes and inhaled deeply. When he opened them again, he expected to see Murphy's whelk stall and a chestnut brazier by the kerb, also a slack-witted young man squatting in the gutter. The whelk stall was there with a stoop-shouldered lad of about eighteen tending it. 'Murphy's Shellfish' was written in faded blue lettering across its front.

'You're not Murphy. Not the one I remember before the war, anyway,' Matt remarked as he paid for a half-pint of winkles.

'I took over after me dad went off to war. 'E came back shell-shocked, sits gibbering in the chair all day. Broken wreck 'e is. Can't work. Can barely feed himself.'

Matt had heard of many such cases, and nodded sympathetically. It was another dead end. 'Was there a half-wit who used to hang round this pub.'

'That would be Archie. That's going back some. 'Is mum died and they wanted ter put 'im in the workhouse, but Miss Casey got 'im out.'

The buildings around him swayed crazily. He staggered as floodgates opened and memories gushed like a torrent through his mind. Casey Strong. Cassandra. His Casey. The details of his past returned with harrowing intensity.

Casey, dear God, where are you? *She* was the woman who had haunted his dreams. Fury at his family's deceit ground through him. His mother had lied to him. He had never been engaged to Clementine. It was Casey he'd been going to marry.

And they had made love so gloriously . . .

A groan of anguish was torn from his throat. The whelk man eyed him narrowly. ''Ere, ain't yer Matt Frost? The bloke who were gonna wed Miss Casey. Blimey mate, we thought yer were dead.'

'Do you know where Casey is? I've been trying to find her.'

The whelk seller looked at his walking stick and the yellow sunken cheeks with sneering contempt. 'Oh yeah, after the way your family treated 'er I don't know 'ow yer've got the gall. Took this pub from 'er, they did. Left 'er with nothing.' He spat in the gutter and turned his back on Matt.

'I was shot down over France,' Matt explained. 'Got pretty smashed up. Lost my memory.' Seeing the stiff censure in the man's tense body, Matt grabbed his arm in desperation. 'I loved Casey. I was going to marry her. My family were always against it. All I've heard is lies since I returned to England. Have pity, man! Where is she?'

He slumped back against the wall, emotionally exhausted. Horror and disgust at what his family had done turned his skin to prickling gooseflesh. The wound in his head hammered viciously. The muscles along his jaw bunched and he swallowed convulsively, his throat working against the agony of betrayal from his family. His mother had deliberately manipulated him, whilst professing to love him. Anger gouged him. There had been so much injustice against Casey by his family, how could she ever forgive him? More harrowing still, she might hate him. Or be married. Had he lost her forever?

'I beg you, tell where I can find Miss Strong.' His voice cracked from the agony of what he had discovered.

The whelk seller rubbed his chin. 'Me dad thought the world of Miss Casey. I wouldn't like to see 'er hurt any more.'

'I want to make everything up to her,' he rasped. 'I still love her. And I know she loved me.'

The antagonism faded in the man's eyes. With a shrug he turned to serve a customer and said over his shoulder, 'They took a small pub in Leytonstone. Can't remember the name of it, but it weren't far from the Thatched House.'

Matt thanked him, reaching for his watch to check the time, and cursing when he discovered it had gone. His hand flew to his inside pocket and he sighed with relief that his wallet was still there. He'd get a taxicab to Leytonstone and start the search for Casey tonight.

Inside the vehicle he counted his money. His mother had been generous to him and there was twenty pounds inside. It would keep him if he lived frugally for a while. He did not want to see his family again. He'd return there only to collect his belongings once he had found Casey.

Chapter Twenty

Eva tutted with annoyance as she drew back the bolts on the bar door. She hated serving during the first hour when it was so quiet. Rusty had taken Danny over to the park on his tricycle after she had snapped at the brat. He also intended to treat the boy by taking him to a teashop for a cake. He wouldn't be back for another hour.

She scarcely gave a glance to the three men grouped outside. Her angry glare centred on Archie, who was fussing over the window-box of geraniums and marigolds. A cat had used it to sun herself in the morning and the flowers were squashed and broken. He was busy ripping them out and replacing them with blooms from the greenhouse.

'Oh, you stupid man,' she groaned. 'That should have been done an hour ago, before the customers arrive.' She gave him a hard shove. 'Get on with it quickly, it looks a mess.'

She stomped back into the pub. She had never approved of Casey employing the half-wit. But then her cousin was too soft-hearted. Any hard-luck story had her dipping into her purse, or employing some crippled war veteran to do odd jobs. They might own the posh hotel she had always dreamed of, but she hadn't envisaged it cluttered with cripples. She had wanted to cater for the élite of society. But Casey had been adamant it would be for the benefit of wounded men who had no family to care for them. It had cost Eva dear to back down and she still resented it. At least she didn't have to mix with the veterans often. Casey could pander to them all she liked; she had better things to do with her time.

At least the bar was run to her satisfaction. She sniffed with approval that there was only a faint lingering smell of stale beer and tobacco smoke. The cleaner had polished all the wooden tables in the bar so that they gleamed. Four large flower arrangements also dispelled the unpleasant staleness which pervaded all pubs.

She served the three regulars and began to realign the bottles of spirits along the back of the bar. It was more to check that the cleaner had not shirked in dusting behind them than her desire for tidiness: servants could be so unreliable. If she was paying someone's wages, she expected only the best from them.

'Good afternoon, Eva.'

She froze at recognising the deep, husky voice, despite the slight inflection of a French accent. Her hand clenched to stop it shaking, and when she turned to face the customer, her stare was brittle with loathing.

'There isn't anything good about an afternoon that brings you with it. Five years late, I'd say.'

'That's the welcome I'd expect from you.'

'If I never saw you again, Matthew Frost, it would be too soon.'

'Is that how Casey feels?'

'Of course.'

It was spat with such venom that Matt was momentarily taken aback. He sighed. 'Circumstances prevented me from returning before.'

'And you can just leave again. You ain't wanted here.'

'I'm not going until I speak to Casey.'

'So you can break her heart again.' Eva sucked in her lips in disgust. 'What have you come for? To give her an invite to your wedding that's all set for the end of the year.'

Matthew paled. 'There is going to be no wedding. I don't have to answer to you. Please tell Casey I'm here. When my plane crashed I suffered a brain haemorrhage as well as other wounds. It affected my memory. It's only just returned. I came as soon as I could find out where she had moved to.'

'A likely story.' She leaned forward over the bar and lowered her voice to a spiteful hiss. 'Sod off. You ruined Casey's life.'

'I'm not leaving until I see Casey.'

Eva turned to the three men who were watching the proceedings with interest. 'There's free drinks for you if you throw this man out.'

Matt straightened, taking his weight from his walking stick. 'That won't solve anything and you know it, Eva.'

The men moved forward in anticipation of a fight. She saw from the stubborn gleam in his eye that Matt was capable of hanging around the pub all week to catch sight of Casey. She was tempted to tell him that she was not here – that she had moved away. But it would be too easy for him to check. And Casey would never forgive her if she found out.

Reluctantly she waved the three men back, her eyes bright with malice. 'If she's got any sense she'll tell you to piss off after the way you treated her. I wouldn't want to deprive her of that satisfaction. Go through the bar to the garden. Usually at this time of day she joins the men. They dote on her.'

Matt tipped his hat to her. 'You are as gracious as ever, even in defeat,' he mocked.

Eva clamped her mouth tight, her teeth grinding with fury. If Matt had come searching for Casey, it was likely his silvery tongue would win back her love. All she had worked for would be for nothing.

'She'll give you short shrift after five years and you jilting her. Casey isn't the sweet innocent she was then. She's had to look after herself.'

'But she didn't marry, did she?' Matt queried.

Eva did not answer, but the feral glitter in her eyes told him that Casey was still single. It was as if a great boulder had been lifted from his chest. His greatest dread had been that Casey had married.

His heart was thudding as he approached the garden. The afternoon was overcast but still warm, and four men were seated around a wrought-iron table. Another man was sitting on a stone seat by the river's edge. Matt was speared with jealousy when he recognised the woman at the man's side was Casey. She was gazing up at him, her attention rapt on what he was saying.

The sight of her took his breath away. Her brown hair had been cut in a fashionably short style, swept over on one side. A style he usually disliked on women, still preferring long hair, but on Casey it gave her face a softer, elfin quality, enhancing the slant of her large eyes. His throat dried and would not form the words of greeting. Was this man someone special to her? She seemed very absorbed in what he was saying. And the blighter was handsome enough to turn any woman's head.

His hand tightened over the handle of his walking stick. He hated having to rely on it. In the last few days, in his search for the pub in Leytonstone which Casey and Rusty had purchased, he had walked miles. Tension made his limp even more pronounced as he moved forward, his eyes fastened on her lovely, expressive face.

She laughed at something her companion said, and at the same time looked in his direction. Her laughter cut off with a sob. Every trace of colour drained from her face. Her eyes widened with shock. Then a look of intense pain registered before she keeled over and slid to the ground.

'Casey!' he groaned, stumbling forward, cursing the weakness in his leg.

Her companion had already knelt at her side and was

cradling her head in his lap in such a tender fashion that Matt raged, 'Take your damned hands off her.'

The man looked up in surprise, the blue eyes challenging with anger. It was then that Matt saw the disfigurement on the cheek which had been turned away from him.

'The devil, sir. Who do you think you are?' The voice rang with the cutting authority of an officer used to giving commands. 'Don't just stand there, get someone to fetch a doctor.' The man moved helplessly, as though it had been his intention to lift Casey, and Matt saw that he only had one arm.

A soft groan from Casey had both men bending over her. 'Give her air, man,' the officer ordered.

At a disadvantage, Matt stepped back, his face strained with anxiety. He had not expected Casey to faint at setting eyes on him. Her eyelids flickered and he found himself holding his breath as her eyes opened to gaze up at him.

'Matt,' she whispered.

He nodded and attempted to lighten the moment. 'Rather late for our date, I fear.'

For an instant her eyes blazed with love for him, then slowly the light faded to suspicion and hurt. 'Five years too late.'

Slowly she stood up, taking a moment to brush the grass from her lavender, calf-length dress. He sensed she needed to recover her composure. When she lifted her head, her face was devoid of any emotion.

'It's even later for excuses. The war has been over for nearly a year.'

The scarred man had moved protectively closer, irritating Matt intensely. He did not want to explain himself in front of a stranger, but he was compelled to, or risk Casey sending him away unheard. 'Can we go somewhere and talk? When my plane was shot down I suffered severe head injuries as well as those to my body. It affected my memory.'

'For five years, Matt? You've been back with your family

for at least a year, according to a drayman who used to work for the brewery. And aren't you supposed to be marrying Clementine?'

Matt looked at the stranger. 'Could you leave us to speak alone? I intend Casey no harm.'

'What do you say, Casey?' The officer placed his hand protectively on her arm.

Matt saw the hesitation in her face before she nodded, 'Will you excuse us, Gerald?'

The man inclined his head and shot Matt a warning glance which stirred his jealousy. Whether they were lovers or not, this man would protect Casey with his life. As he left them alone, Casey regarded him coolly.

'You may have your say, Matthew. I think I am owed an explanation at least.' She nodded to the stone bench. 'Sit down.'

Casey was battling against the emotions which were raging through her. Uppermost was the joy that he was alive. Her first instinct had been to throw herself into his arms. That was ruthlessly curbed. Suspicion lingered from five years of heartache. Hope would not be crushed. Love threatened to overwhelm her, stamped down behind a mask of distrust.

Traitorously, her heart clamoured with anticipation. There was a livid white scar from his hairline to his brow which added to the ruggedness of his handsome looks. It also made him seem less approachable. Also the French accent in his speech made his voice that of a stranger, emphasising the distance of time which had separated them. He was no longer clean-shaven; a moustache covered his upper lip. It made him look older and sterner. Illness had stripped the flesh from his face, and he looked very like his father.

As Matt lowered himself on to the seat, the muscles of his face contorted, his jaw tightening with pain at the effort it cost him. His dark grey suit was new and impeccably tailored, but it could not hide from her the thinness of his body. Once he was settled, she put two feet of space between them, which was as much as the bench would allow. Even so, his nearness was like a fire touching her flesh, searing through her constraint.

Somehow she kept her voice dispassionate. 'From the dates I was given, your plane was shot down and you were believed killed seven weeks after I had last heard from you. A long silence from a man who professed to love me so deeply. I know you hated writing, but you could have managed a line or two.'

He rubbed a hand across his brow. 'My memory is still patchy over small details. But I do remember starting a letter to you before my last flight. Even so, you knew I loved you. How could you doubt my love after what happened on our last evening together?'

Heat torched her face to scarlet embarrassment. 'You got what you wanted from me. It had been a long pursuit.' She could not look at him, but stared unseeing at a family of swans gliding along the river.

There were a string of French oaths which made her glance at him sharply. The Matt she had known never swore.

'Obviously if that letter was amongst my possessions at the airfield which were returned to my family, my mother did not forward it to you.'

'I received no letter. The only communication with your family was through the solicitors over my father's debt to them.'

'My mother has much to answer for. How dare she keep that letter from you?' His eyes hardened. 'But then in the last week I have learned of the depths to which she would go to manipulate my life.'

He spoke low and urgently, explaining everything that had happened to him since the plane had been shot down. Most of it, he admitted, was as it had been told to him, as he still could not recall most of his years in France. He made no attempt to touch her as he spoke of his slow recovery.

'I was like a child, I had to learn to speak again. During my time in France I spoke only French. It seems more natural to me even now than English. A year ago I was still confined to a wheelchair; the doctors believed I would never walk again. It was then my dreams became more frequent. Dreams of you, Casey. Only I had no recollection of who you were. But you were there, strengthening me, encouraging, spurring me to overcome the pain.'

Casey gripped her hands together, wanting to believe him. From working and living with the veterans, she knew that so many of them would carry the mental scars of what they had suffered in the war to their graves. She had heard of memory loss when they blotted out the worst of the horrors. She also knew enough of head injuries to understand that if the brain became flooded with blood it could damage the cells, could even leave a man paralysed for life. It had the same effect as a stroke. Yet it was hard to take so much in. One part of her yearned to take Matt into her arms, hold him and whisper that everything was all right. But another part held back, needing to be certain that this was not another ruse, another way of gaining her sympathy to use her again for his own ends.

Still staring at the swans on the river, she gave him no sign of encouragement as he related how he had relied on his family to fill in details of his past, for only snatches of it came to him.

'But always I knew I was searching for something that was missing in my life,' he ended. 'Three nights ago I had a dream and I saw you again, but in the guise of Britannia floating down the Thames on a barge past the Tower of London. I knew then this was a sign. That the Tower of London held the key.'

Tears streamed unnoticed down her cheeks as he told her of his search for her in the last few days. 'I may not have been able to name you or remember who you were, but I knew that my love for you was deeper than memory. It was ingrained so deep it was an integral part of me. It was that love which gave me the strength to recover from my injuries. I have so much to make up to you for. When I learned how my family had treated you over the Britannia I was so angry and ashamed. My father would have been disgusted at their conduct. He approved of our wedding. He knew that you were the right wife for me. But then he was an exceptional man. I wish you had had the chance to know him better.'

He broke off sharply. 'I'm rambling on about inconsequential things.' He turned and took her hands. The warmth of his touch was like rediscovering a safe harbour in a storm. The forces of her emotions made her tremble, and she could not see him clearly through the tears of joy blurring her eyes.

'All that matters is that I have found you,' he continued. 'I love you, Casey. Dare I hope that there is a chance for us? Tell me what I must do to prove my love for you, to make up for all you suffered at my family's spiteful hands.'

'The greatest hurt your family did me was to withhold your letter. The rest is unimportant.'

'Does that mean you still care?'

'I've never stopped loving you, Matt.'

His hand tightened over hers, his thumb sliding across her knuckles as he pressed it close to his chest. 'I do love you, Casey. I've come to beg you to forgive me. To allow me a second chance.'

As he spoke their bodies leaned closer, drawn inexorably, by bonds stronger than any intervention of fate. Casey could smell the unique scent of him, feel the warmth of his breath on her cheek. He was gazing at her mouth, his own parting and only an inch from touching her lips. Then the voices of the soldiers on the lawn behind them reminded her of their lack of privacy.

She pulled back and stood up. 'I've missed you, Matt. And

if what you tell me is true, what have I to forgive you for?'

He rose and with a relieved smile drew her behind the sheltering branches of the willow trees. Tenderly he placed his hands on her shoulders as he stared down at her. There was no mistaking the love shining in his eyes. With a hoarse moan he crushed her to him, his lips adoring upon her brow, meandering to her lids, her cheeks and, with each touch, re-initiating her into a sensuality long denied but never forgotten. When his lips claimed hers, his kiss was more heartfelt than any words of love: all-consuming, tantalising and promising. She lost sense of time and place, revelling in the mystique of the sensual ecstasy he was creating. She moved so that she could feel the muscular strength of his body against her own. His kiss changed, deepening with passion; until with a groan he breathed against her ear, his arms enfolding her, 'Casey, my darling.'

Aware of the restraint he was placing upon his ardour, she said softly, 'Let's go to the hotel where it is more private.'

The snapping of twigs broke them apart before Matt could reply. Casey heard him mutter, 'Damn that blasted woman!'

She suppressed a groan at seeing Eva bearing down on them. Behind her came Rusty carrying a bottle of champagne and four glasses.

'Well, you two certainly seem to have resolved your differences,' Eva said with unexpected warmth. 'I sent Matt out to you when he came into the bar.'

Casey doubted that Eva had been so accommodating, but Matt had not mentioned it. Now her cousin was looking Matt up and down without her smile faltering. She guessed from the way Rusty was watching Eva closely that he was responsible for her present manner. 'I have to say it was a shock to see you in the bar, Matt. It made me speak rather hastily.'

Rusty stepped forward now and held out his hand to Matt, saying, 'It's good to see you. Eva told me you'd lost your memory after your plane crashed.'

Matt shook his hand, but his smile was for Casey. 'I must be the luckiest guy in the world that Casey didn't marry in the meantime and has a heart large enough to forgive and understand.'

'So when is the wedding?' Eva cut in sharply. 'I suppose you will first have to inform your current fiancée that you're jilting her.'

'I never asked Clementine to marry me,' Matt stated. 'My mother and aunt told me that we were engaged before the war. That the match had been agreed for years.'

Eva smiled placatingly, 'Casey always has had a magnanimous heart. I'm surprised she wants to have anything at all to do with your family after the way they've treated her.'

'Eva, Matt is different from his mother and brothers,' Casey announced.

At the condemnation in her tone, Eva spread her hands wide. 'I'm sorry, Casey. I've never found it easy to forgive anyone who betrayed my trust. But what is important is that you're happy. And if you're satisfied with Matt's answers . . .'

'I am satisfied.'

Eva nodded in acquiescence. 'Is there to be a wedding?'

Casey blushed. 'We've hardly had time to discuss the future.'

'Do you think I'd let this adorable woman out of my sight again?' Matt said with a laugh. 'I'll get a special licence and we shall marry next week. That's if Casey agrees. Then we shall live in Kent, close to the airfield where I keep my plane.'

'But Casey can't just up and leave,' Eva protested. 'She's a partner in the Ringside. She runs the hotel and restaurant. There's no one trained to take her place, and besides . . .'

Rusty popped the champagne cork, halting her speech. 'No besides, Eva. We will sell up. A small pub by a canal somewhere would keep me happy. I can still do a bit of fishing.

We'll get a good price for the Ringside. And as my equal partner, Casey will get half of the sale price. That should amount to a few thousand pounds.'

'I'm not moving to a pokey inn by a stinking canal.' Eva rounded on him, her face growing red. 'If you think I'll stand by and let—'

'Eva. Rusty. Please,' Casey broke in. 'I don't know if I even want to sell the Ringside. It means a lot to me. It's dedicated to Dad. So stop arguing. Today I want to celebrate, not fight over what might not happen.'

'Hrmph! Well, either way your future is rosy again, isn't it?' Eva snapped. Then she burst into tears. 'Forgive me, Casey. I didn't mean to say that. Of course you owe me nothing for the sacrifices I have made on your behalf. They were in repayment for the kindness you and your father showed me when you gave me a home after Dad and Myrtle died.'

She snatched the champagne bottle from Rusty's hands. 'Hold those glasses straight, man. We don't want to waste any of this. Casey is right. This is a day of celebration. Drink to today and the future can look after itself.'

The air in the garden crackled with tension as Eva tossed back her glass. She added, 'I have work to do. Josephine will be home from school shortly and Rusty and I have matters to discuss.'

Turning on her heel, she strode back to the hotel, her calf-length dress flapping around her thin legs.

Casey felt a twinge of guilt. Eva was upset. And rightly so, as Rusty had spoken of selling the Ringside. It had shocked her. She had been too overjoyed at Matt's declaration of love to have given any thought to anything else.

Rusty sighed. 'I'd better go after her. Will you be picking Josie up from school, or shall I?'

'I will,' Casey said, suddenly awkward that Matt knew nothing of his daughter's existence. Since he had not mentioned the child, she presumed that her letter had arrived at the airfield after his crash.

'You'd think Eva could pick her own child up from school today, wouldn't you?' Matt blurted out. 'She always did put on you too much.'

Casey didn't answer. She didn't want to tell him outright that Josephine was his daughter. Things were moving too fast. Even Matt's proposal to get married by special licence. They needed time to get to know each other again.

'So an afternoon making love comes second-best to picking up your niece from school.' His irritation was obvious. 'Lord, Casey, have you no idea how much I want to make love to you.'

She laughed to lighten her words. 'As ever, your mind is on carnal matters. There is so much we've got to discuss.'

Impatience hardened his features. 'I'm rushing you. I'm sorry. But you cannot believe my feelings have changed. I love you. I'd marry you tonight if I could.'

They were walking across the lawn towards the lane. Several of the veterans were watching them curiously, and she gave them a wave. Her mind was too full of the last hour's events to consider introducing Matt to them.

'We'd have been married before the war if it hadn't been for your prevarication. Haven't I waited long enough to become your husband?'

'There's more to marriage than becoming a husband. There's becoming a father . . .' she said hesitantly.

He threw back his head and laughed. 'A natural progression from the joy of possessing you, my love. So, you are eager for children? And I, too, in time. But selfishly I want you all to myself at first. I hear husbands take a second place in a woman's life once the children start demanding her attention.'

'You would never take second place, Matt, but I have to disappoint you if you want me all to yourself.' She took a deep breath and studied him intently. 'Josephine is my child. Our daughter.'

He stopped dead. 'Our daughter!' A look of anguish pitted his eyes. 'Dear God, Casey! To think what I must have put you through.'

Casey's heart lurched. Matt was not pleased. He seemed distressed at the news. Of course it was a shock, but she had not expected this reaction.

They walked several yards in silence along the road until Casey could no longer bear it. 'You're displeased.'

Matt's throat was working furiously. When he turned to her, she saw the reason he had not spoken was that he was struggling to master the tears of joy in his overbright eyes. 'I hadn't even considered there could have been a child. It takes some getting used to. But how could I not be pleased that we have a child? You named her after your father, I presume. Is she like you?'

'She has your colouring and eyes and I think is a little like me in temperament.'

Again he struggled to master his emotions. 'I don't deserve this happiness.' His expression sobered as he continued, 'Did my family know of the child?'

'I never told them. Pride, I suppose. But I had written to you. It's possible the letter was amongst your possessions if it arrived after the crash.'

Matt lifted her hand to his lips, his expression flayed with remorse. 'How you must have suffered. Damn them, Casey! I've finished with them.'

They were approaching the school, and other mothers or servants were ahead of them in the road. Unwilling that they should be overheard, Casey stopped and drew Matt on to the hedgerow bank at the side of the lane. 'It's Josephine I don't want to hurt. She believes that I'm her aunt and that Eva is her mother. It's a deception I agreed to until she was old enough to understand the truth. I didn't want her young life blighted with the stigma of bastardy. Children can be so cruel if they have a weapon to use against one another. I will introduce you as a friend just for now. Once we are married she will be told the truth. We shall move out from here and start a new life, the three of us.'

Chapter Twenty-one

Matt saw a petite, dark-haired girl with shoulder-length ringlets detach herself from several friends and run pell-mell towards them. Her arms were flung wide and her hazel eyes danced with merriment as Casey stooped to catch her and swing her in the air. The girl giggled with delight and, throwing her arms around Casey's neck, kissed her. Then she drew back and frowned.

'Aunt Casey, you didn't bring Danny. I thought we were going to the tea-shop today.'

'Rusty took Danny earlier. And I have a special friend I want you to meet.'

When Josephine turned her gaze upon Matt, he felt a surge of love and tenderness more profound than anything he had experienced before. He smiled at his daughter. 'Casey, you didn't tell me the young lady who was going to join us at the tea-shop was so beautiful.'

Josephine laughed and, when Casey lowered her to the ground, she put one hand trustingly into Matt's, the other into her mother's. The touch of those small fingers curling around his own again aroused an emotion so intense that it was all he could do not to crush the child to him.

His throat was tight with emotion as he looked at Casey over the child's head. 'Josephine is a credit to you. You must be very proud of her.'

Unused to young children, Matt feared he would be tongue-tied in the child's company. That didn't prove to be the case. Josephine was full of questions, her easy laughter stealing into his heart until he was besotted with his vivacious daughter. There was so much he needed to say to Casey which had to be delayed until they were alone. The hour in the tea-shop was both a joy and a strain.

On returning to the Ringside, Josephine ran into Eva and Rusty's private suite calling out, 'Mama, Dadda, Auntie Casey took me to the tea-shop.'

Hearing her address others as 'Mama' and 'Dadda' was like a knife slashing at Matt's heart. Then guilt pierced him. Every day Casey had had to tolerate the agony of her daughter regarding another as her mother.

'It must be so difficult for you witnessing Eva parading as Josephine's mother,' he said softly.

Casey shrugged, but her eyes were shadowed with pain. 'I'm with her for most of the day when she's not at school. I'm the one who cares for her. Her bedroom is next to mine and I go to her if she wakes in the night. Eva is her mother in name only, for appearances' sake.'

They entered Casey's own suite of rooms which overlooked the river. The sitting room was decorated in a restful pale green, and several plants softened the edges of the dark furniture. Two armchairs faced each other across a cream Indian carpet. Through an open door Matt saw the lilac silk hangings draped around a four-poster bed. Another door was open on to a Wedgewood blue and white tiled bathroom.

Still troubled, Matt ventured less certainly, 'And now the scandal must come out when we leave here. How will Eva take that?'

'She will hate being apart from Josephine. As for the scandal, Eva will be shown in a favourable light. Hasn't Eva taken her wayward cousin's illegitimate child and reared her as her own?'

There was a tautness to her voice which spoke of the anguish she had endured, and Matt tensed. His wounds were aching, but the pain was light compared to the agony which tore at his heart. 'Is that how you see it?'

For a long moment, Casey stood immobile as a statue, her arms locked tight across her breast. Her eyes were misty with remembered pain. 'I hated all the deception.' Then the rigidity left her like shedding a heavy mantle, and her voice became a husky whisper. 'But I have no regrets. She was your child.'

With a groan, Matt pulled her into his arms. Her lips were warm and yielding beneath the pressure of his own. Her perfume encased him, a sensual aura pervading his senses. When they broke apart he was trembling and Casey was breathless.

'Josephine has been my comfort and joy,' she assured him. 'I knew I would never marry, for I still loved you. I always wanted a large family, and Josephine was a part of you no one could take from me.'

'And now all three of us have a life to build together.'

His words made her frown.

'What's troubling you?' Matt probed.

'I owe Eva and Rusty so much. If I sell my share in the Ringside it will set them against each other. You heard Rusty say he wanted to buy a smaller place in the country. Eva would hate that. And their marriage is already under strain. I don't know why she married Rusty. She never loved him.'

Matt held back from telling Casey what a coldly calculating bitch Eva could be. Casey was always so stubbornly loyal, he wanted nothing to spoil their reunion. 'Eva would have had her reasons,' he observed. 'She likes to manipulate people.'

Casey stiffened in his arms. 'Without her help I would have been ridiculed as wanton. I owe Eva a great debt.'

'She did it for herself, not you, my darling.' His restraint snapped at Casey's fervent defence of her cousin. 'It kept you and Rusty in her power, didn't it? Or rather you. That woman is obsessive where you are concerned. It isn't natural.'

'I was all the family she had left,' Casey retorted. 'She's had a hard life.'

Matt fought to control his anger. Casey was too precious to him to risk losing her over an argument about her cousin. He knew Eva was a manipulator, but Casey was too tender-hearted to see it. Yet what did he know of the tribulations Casey had suffered in his absence? He was not about to let their differences of opinion over Eva ruin this moment. Even so, the need was strong to warn Casey not to trust her cousin so implicitly. He forced lightness into his voice. 'I doubt in recent years you've had an easy life yourself. Yet where adversity has made you stronger and more sympathetic towards others less fortunate, Eva is the opposite. I was never comfortable in her presence. There is a coldness about her which is almost malignant.'

'You two just never hit it off.' Casey again wound her arms around his neck. 'Let's not go into the past. Both Eva and your mother were against our marriage. They were both jealous. But we are together now.' Her voice was seductive. 'Together after so long.'

'Casey, my love.' Her name was a hoarse rasp, his eyes smouldering with desire.

The ardour in his gaze swelled her heart with love, her breathing becoming shallow and ragged. Her fingers traced the line of his jaw, their touch lightly skimming his moustache. 'This makes you look like your father, but also sterner.'

'And you've cut your glorious hair.'

'It will grow again.'

'I'll shave off the moustache.'

The words were inane, but hinting at the permanence of the years that lay ahead. Every pore of Casey's body was aware of the controlled passion in Matt's muscles. Standing so close, with only her fingertips touching him, sent ripples of shock-waves between them which built up to an unbearable yet exquisite vibrancy.

In silence their gazes devoured each other as they noted the changes the years had wrought. Features subtly changed, moulded by experiences, lines of laughter and suffering; contours refined with maturity and now softened by the rediscovery of their love. The stillness was charged with a gathering tension, crackling and explosive, until Casey's entire being pulsated to the expectant thud of her heart. When their lips touched, desire was cataclysmic.

There was a savage urgency to their need as they entered the bedroom, not even troubling to disrobe as they lay entwined on the bed. The momentum of their passion raged like a furnace out of control. When she cried out in pleasure, the sound was muffled by Matt's kisses as they climaxed together.

As their breathing slowed to normality, Matt eased back from her and tugged impatiently at his tie. 'Forgive me, Casey, that was no way to show you how much I love you.'

'If it lacked finesse, my darling, you made up for it in ardour.' She smiled up at him enticingly. 'I hadn't realised I could be so wanton. I've been starved of your love too long to hold back.'

Her eyes widened as she felt him harden again inside her. She gasped and lifted her hips to heighten the sensations again building within her, glorying in his passion. Matt kissed her ear, his voice low and throaty with promise. 'This time I will show you how much I adore you.'

Gently he withdrew from her, then slowly he began to undo the buttons down the front of her dress. Laying back the material, he kissed her throat and breasts as he removed her clothing. His tongue feathered across her ribcage, the soft hair of his moustache sensually abrasive as his lips caressed her stomach and inner thighs. As her flesh responded to the mastery of his touch, Casey had never dreamed that such sensuality existed.

'This is how it will always be between us,' Matt vowed as

he removed the last of his clothing and rolled on the mattress so that she was lying on top of him. The hunger of his mouth parted her lips in a long, searing kiss. She moved above him, an avid pupil, willingly shedding the last of her innocence as she copied the caresses which had given her so much pleasure. Her reward was the gruff moan of ecstasy every touch evoked. Exaltation blazed through her. Each caress received and given conveyed more profoundly than speech the joy of loving and being loved in return.

When she discovered the knotted scars from the bullet wounds down the right side of his body, she gasped. Laying her head against his chest, her voice cracked with anguish, 'Oh, my darling, how you must have suffered!'

'Do the scars repel you? They are not a pretty sight.'

'Nothing about you could repel me.' Casey kissed each puckered ridge of flesh in turn, moving from his shoulder down to his thigh and calf, then slowly back upwards along his inner thigh until her mouth closed over his erect member and he moaned with pleasure.

'I'll have no strength left to leave this bed,' he teased, and surprised her by raising her chin so that she held his gaze.

There were bruising circles of fatigue beneath his eyes. 'How could I have forgotten you have so recently regained your strength from your wounds? I'll never forgive myself if you have a relapse,' she said.

He smiled provocatively. 'It's nothing that a glass of champagne won't revive. Didn't I notice a bottle and ice bucket in the sitting room? I bet Rusty put it there for us.' He sprang out of the bed with a vigour which belied any show of tiredness and, unmindful of his nakedness, padded into the sitting room and returned with the champagne and glasses. Once back in the bedroom he crossed to enter the bathroom. There was a cough of water from the hot water tap, then the splattering of the bathtub being filled.

Feeling abandoned, Casey wrapped a sheet around her and approached the open door. Matt was examining a row of bottles and lotions on a small pine dresser. He was thinner. A slight indentation of his ribs showed through his flesh, but his body was still magnificent: broad of shoulder, slim-hipped, the muscles firm from his hours of rigorous training to rebuild the strength in his limbs.

Assuming that he intended to bathe before he left her, her voice was heavy with disappointment. 'Are you leaving so soon, Matt? I thought we would at least dine together, and that's not for another two hours.'

Seeing her uncertainty, he grinned. 'I've no intention of leaving.' He tested the water's heat and swirled it around with his hand. 'This is luxury. We haven't got hot water laid on in the bathroom at home.'

Turning off the two brass taps he lowered himself into the water and looked expectantly at Casey. 'Not too shy to join me, are you?'

She blushed. To her surprise, after all the intimacies they had shared, she was overcome with modesty. 'Matt, it seems rather decadent.'

He lay back against the rim of the tub, the dark hair at his neck and temples curling up in the steam. 'And so much fun. Don't stand there wrapped up like an Egyptian mummy. If you don't intend to join me, you can wash my back.'

He tossed a dripping sponge to her, striking her cheek. Provoked, she launched it back. At the same time she stepped forward and her foot connected with a bar of soap which had fallen from the rack. She pitched headlong and was saved from banging her shoulder on the side of the enamel bath by Matt's arms going around her. It was a false reprieve. The sheet had fallen away as she'd tried to recover her balance. Matt grinned wickedly, and with a twist of his body pulled her down on top of him in the water.

'You must learn to restrain yourself more; throwing yourself naked at a man like that could get you into trouble.' He picked up the champagne bottle from the floor.

'This is absurd, Matt.' Despite her words of censure Casey was laughing. The water lapped warm and sensuously around them, and she was potently aware of his arousal against her leg. The champagne cork hit the ceiling and landed in the water between them. She had forgotten about this playful side to Matt, and now realised it was one of the things she had missed most.

His expression became serious. 'Is it? Tell me if you think it is absurd in half an hour's time.' He leaned forward and pressed a glass of champagne in to her hand. 'To us, my darling. To the future. To our happiness, and to further such absurdities where I can show you how much I love you.'

They drained their glasses and Matt soaped the sponge and began to massage Casey's shoulders and the swell of her breasts above the water. She gasped, her head lolling back at the delicious sensations he evoked.

'Is that absurd?' he taunted. 'Or this?' He bent his head to kiss each breast, his tongue flicking across each hardened nipple until she moaned, lying back in the water. 'And what of this?' His fingers slid across her stomach to bury themselves in the curls between her thighs, dipping inside the heat of her. Her internal muscles pulsated and clenched around him and, again roused to a fever of desire, she reared up and impaled herself on him. Her hands were braced on the side of the tub as she pushed down, deepening the penetration. It was like velvet encasing steel, a myriad of sensations unfurling, as explosive as firecrackers, expanding to pitch them into shuddering fulfilment.

With an ecstatic sigh, Casey sank down into the water and laid her head against Matt's shoulder.

Tenderly, he wiped the sheen of perspiration from her brow.

'Like Aphrodite, or was it Venus? Greek mythology was never my strong point. You are a goddess of love, rising from the water.'

'And you are a wicked satyr, seducing and corrupting.' She kissed him tenderly, their hands languid in their caresses until the water became cool and they returned to the bedroom draped in towels.

Casey flopped down on to the bed and rolled on to her side to make room for Matt. 'I never thought I'd be happy like this again. There was never anyone else.'

He held her close, sighing with contentment. 'There is so much to plan for. When I came here this morning, I had never dared hope that the day could end like this. I feared that you might send me away with a flea in my ear after not hearing from me for so many years.'

She put a finger to his lips. 'No more talk like that. I admit I was hurt and for a time I felt betrayed. But I could not stop loving you. This is like a dream to me. So many times I have visualised you appearing, saying that you loved me. And now I feel ashamed that, even for a moment, I allowed myself to doubt you.'

He cupped her face in his hands, his eyes serious and searching. 'I'll make everything up to you, Casey. I swear. At least now I have my plane and can support us. But we will have to live close to the airfield in the country,' Matt stated. 'I'd hate our marriage to be the cause of putting Rusty and Eva in a difficult position over the Ringside. The money you invested in it will also provide us with an income. To keep the Ringside on, all Rusty needs to do is employ a business manager to take over your duties.'

Casey frowned. 'Rusty and Eva aren't happy together. I think he's had enough of her tantrums. We'd get enough from the Ringside's sale for him to set himself up in a smaller pub, and also provide for Eva's future.'

'I can't see her being paid off without causing problems.'

'And then there are the veterans and Archie to consider. This is their home. They need a place of stability to live in to fully recover from the war.'

The joy went out of the afternoon. Casey shivered, inexplicably feeling cold. She rolled on to her stomach to regard Matt with a serious expression. 'There are so many problems to find answers to. And Eva idolises Josephine. It will break her heart to be separated from her.'

Green flecks sparked in Matt's hazel eyes. 'She's your child. Our child. I don't like to think of her under Eva's influence.'

'We don't have to settle everything at once.' Casey felt acute unease. Eva could be so highly strung, almost to the point of being unstable when she was crossed. She had seen it too often when her cousin's will had been crossed by Rusty.

'I'm not putting off our wedding,' Matt warned. 'It will be in ten days' time. Time enough to make arrangements. We can have the reception here. We will honeymoon for a week in Paris. For a month or two after the wedding, until you can employ and train someone to take over here, you will live here. I shall stay as often as I can. It will take that long to buy a house near the airfield. By then Eva should have got used to the idea.'

Casey sat up and rubbed her brow. 'Eva is not the only problem. Your family must be told.'

Matt's face hardened. 'I've finished with them this time. What my mother did was unforgivable.'

Casey shook her head. 'It was vindictive. But you are her favourite son. You will break her heart if you shut her out of your life. Besides, would you have Josephine brought up without knowing her grandmother?'

'Her grandmother wanted nothing to do with her.'

'That was before she was born. Once Sybil sees her, and sees her likeness to you, she will feel differently. That is human nature. We must at least try to heal the breach. And you must also consider Clementine's feelings. You cannot just jilt her. She does love you. Sybil and Millicent probably bullied her into pretending that you had been engaged before the war. The poor woman would have done anything to have married you.'

Matt lay with one arm behind his neck and stared up at the ceiling before replying. 'I'll go back there tonight and return here tomorrow. I will speak to Mother and Aunt Millicent and be as kind as I can to Clementine.' His hand thrust through his hair. 'When I think that I could have married her if my memory had not returned, I feel little charity towards any of them. I would have lost you for good and they would have felt no compunction over that, or cared that I was unhappy with a woman I clearly did not love.'

Casey swallowed a feeling of panic that threatened to overwhelm her. Sybil had so nearly succeeded. But fate had been kind to them. Matt's memory had returned, and now that they were reunited she could be forgiving. 'That didn't happen. We are together. We must be reconciled with your family.'

Matt's eyes crinkled at the corners. 'You're a saint, Casey.'

Casey sat back on her heels. 'I'm far from that, Matthew Frost, or I would not be here with you now. Besides, I remember Eva saying once that sinners have more fun.' She gasped as he leaned over to kiss her breasts. 'And she was right.'

The clock on the mantelpiece struck six o'clock and Casey sat up with a start. 'Matt, the time. It's almost Josephine's bath-time and I always read her a story when I put her to bed.'

'Can I read it tonight? It takes some getting used to, this father business, but I want her to accept me. It will be hard for her when we tell her the truth. She must know that she is our daughter when we marry. When we move to Kent there will be no scandal attached to her name. It will be a new start for us all.'

Casey was delighted that he wanted to read to Josephine, and she realised how she had wronged Matt. Hadn't it been his consideration and generous spirit that had attracted her to him? It was inconceivable that the man she had fallen in love with was capable of ignoring the existence of his child. She should have known that he had never received her letter, and that his mother would have kept the information from him if she had known.

'Yes, read to Josephine. She'll like that. But I think we should leave telling her that we are her parents for a few days. At least until you have spent more time with her. Tonight we'll announce our wedding plans. Josephine will be excited at being our bridesmaid.'

The announcement that Casey and Matt were to marry so quickly and live near the airfield in Kent pitched Eva into despair. Somehow she managed to keep smiling and say all the things that were expected of her. Inside she was raging. Jealousy slashed through her. Casey was glowing with happiness. Matt couldn't take his eyes off her. Rusty had never looked at her that way, with such open adoration. After all the sacrifices she had made for her cousin, Casey was turning her back on her and leaving. Worse, she would be taking Josephine with her. The child was dancing around the nauseatingly happy couple, babbling with excitement that she was to be a bridesmaid.

'Do keep still, Josephine,' she snapped.

Casey shot her a condemnatory glare, reminding her that *she* was the mother, not Eva. Eva felt the blood rush to her head. Her heart was torn in anguish. Casey was already asserting herself in her new role. In a day or two she would tell Josephine the truth about her parents. The blood roared in Eva's ears, and a feeling of slow suffocation almost overwhelmed her.

It took all her willpower to draw a shutter over her emotions. Her face was an emotionless mask as she murmured expressions of polite interest in the wedding plans. It was a relief when Casey left to bath Josephine and put her to bed. When Matt left the room with them, her distress magnified. When she heard the three of them laughing, she nearly choked on her jealousy. That laughter was an ominous and frightening sound. It was the death-knell to her own need to be with the child.

Later, she was unable to stop herself peeping through the crack in Josephine's bedroom door. Her rage boiled up at hearing Matt reading the bedtime story. Josephine was not in bed but sitting on his lap. There was such tenderness and love in his expression as he smiled at his daughter that Eva saw her future crumble.

She had accepted that the love she felt for Casey would never be returned in the physical way she would have cherished. That they lived and worked together was enough. With the need to keep secret the truth of Josephine's birth, Eva had believed that she had gained ascendancy over Casey. How could her cousin leave her when everyone believed that Josephine was Eva's daughter? Yet, disconcertingly, Casey had remained very much her own woman. She had agreed to the deception over her daughter's parentage merely to spare Josephine the taunts her bastardy would bring upon her. Even within their working partnership, it was Casey who was in control. It was Casey to whom Rusty deferred and listened to for advice.

Envy burrowed through Eva, bringing two bright spots of colour to her cheeks. Why was it always Casey who won people's love and not herself? Hadn't she always tried so hard to please? Always her love was thrown back in her face. But they had all paid the price for their betrayal.

Her eyes narrowed with cunning. After her marriage, Casey would take Josephine with her. How could she live having lost them both? She would not allow it to happen. She would not lose Josephine. The girl was hers. The child believed that *she* was her mother, not Casey. A fever mounted in her mind. A plan formed. Scheming was second-nature to her.

'Damnit, Eva. You haven't heard a word I've said.' Rusty's terse voice penetrated her thoughts. 'We might as well get this settled now.'

Misinterpreting his remarks, she answered vaguely, 'Oh, Casey will organise everything about her wedding and engage any extra staff we need if she wants the reception here.'

'I wasn't referring to the wedding. I was referring to *us,*' he added coldly.

She rounded on him, her eyes flashing with venom. 'You can forget about selling the Ringside. I won't permit it.'

Rusty regarded her sourly. 'I'm sick of what you'll permit and what you won't. I've kept me silence in the past because I prefer a quiet life. I reckoned if you were happy you'd be a better mother to Danny. Fat chance of that. You hardly look at the boy. You don't want me as a husband and you don't want the kid. So I've decided to sell up and make a fresh start for the boy and meself.'

'That's what you think,' she blustered. She could not believe the docile man she had manipulated for so long could turn against her.

'It's what I'm going to do, Eva. So you had better get used to the idea. There's nothing you can do to stop me. The deeds for the Ringside are in Casey's and my name only. Of course I'll make sure that you are provided for. But I've had enough of this farce of a marriage. I want out.'

Eva put her hand to her head. There was a ringing in her ears as the blood pumped through her veins. She couldn't think straight. Everyone was deserting her. She drew a deep breath, striving to remain calm. The sound of her heartbeat slowed and her voice sounded flat as she answered, 'What do I need with a husband? But your freedom won't come cheap.'

Rusty reckoned he had pushed Eva far enough for the moment. He was adamant he would not budge from his decision, but he hated confrontation. At least she had not resorted to screaming hysterics. Perhaps she would see reason. It was not as though she'd be a pauper. She could either live modestly or use the money to set herself up in business in a tea-shop or the like.

He watched her pour two large measures of whisky from the crystal decanter and offer one to him. To his surprise, she tossed her one back. When they'd first been married, Eva had begun to drink like a fish, but in recent years she had abstained altogether. He suspected that she disliked losing control. That she was knocking it back now showed her agitation. Eva was up to something. She'd capitulated too easily for his peace of mind. If she agreed to a separation, she probably meant to screw every last penny she could from him. He sighed. He just wanted shot of her and enough put by to support himself and his son. She could have the rest. And good riddance to her. The biggest mistake of his life had been to marry her. Joe had been right. She was trouble.

He rubbed the back of his neck, his thoughts on the dead boxer. Recalling the sight of his broken body at the foot of the stairs, he shuddered. That wasn't the way for a fine man like Joe to go. His thoughts took a morbid turn as he dwelt on the past. He'd miss the Ringside. He was proud of how they had made it a homage to Joe. And he enjoyed the company of the veterans, many of whom regarded him as a friend. He'd miss them. If it weren't for Eva he could be content here.

He paced the room, disquiet growing within him. He positioned himself by the fireplace, preparing to confront his wife.

'Are you going to be reasonable over this matter?' he demanded.

She topped up his glass with whisky before answering. 'I'm always reasonable, but I won't be the subject of scandal.' Her lips were pursed and her eyes glittered in the gaslight, warning Rusty that she was not going to make it easy for him. Since there was no point in antagonising her more than necessary, he tossed back the whisky, inwardly grimacing as it burned his tongue and throat. He'd always preferred porter to spirits. Too restless to sit down, he remained standing and began to fill his pipe with tobacco.

'I won't suffer the shame of having my husband abandon me,' Eva continued. 'I'm your wife.'

'You've been more of a wife to that perverted creature along the lane than you have to me,' he jeered. Seeing her mouth drop open, he gave a bitter laugh. 'You didn't know I knew about those goings-on, did you? Did you take me for a fool? You only ever used sex to get something you wanted from me. The rest of the time my touch disgusted you. You hate men. But you don't hesitate to use them when it suits you.'

'And you think I haven't been used?' Her voice began to rise. Again to his surprise she checked it. Histrionics were her favourite trick to get her own way. Eva poured herself a third whisky and drank it straight down. When she faced him, she was shaking, and her anger spewed forth.

'You were no different from the others. Just like me dad. And Joe. Well, I showed them, didn't I?' Her snort of derision made the hairs at the back of Rusty's neck rise. The room was suddenly cold – a malevolent, evil chill entering it. Again he saw Joe's twisted body at the foot of the stairs, the reek of brandy on his body. But Joe had been as agile and sure-footed as a mountain goat.

'How did you show Joe? What did you do?'

Eva smiled enigmatically, her stare unflinching. 'Like the others, the bastard got his come-uppance.' The words began to slur and run together. 'He were going to throw me out. He were quick enough to fuck me when he wanted me, and he wanted me night after night.'

Her crudeness was deliberate, calculated to shock him, and his senses began to swim at these revelations. With a feeling that his knees were going to buckle he gripped hold of the mantelshelf, whilst Eva spared him nothing in her tirade.

'I was in his blood. I was more than a wife to Joe. I cooked for him, mended his clothes, knew more whores' tricks than any of his other mistresses. I did things to him that no wife would have tolerated. And how did he repay me? By threatening to sling me out when he got bored with me.'

Rusty's guts churned with nausea. His temper exploded and, before he realised what he was doing, he had lifted his hand to strike Eva's vindictive sneer from her face.

'Go on, hit me!' she taunted.

His fist clenched and his hand fell to his side. Dear God, the woman would goad a saint. No wonder her father and Joe had turned on her. It was all lies, of course. Evil lies. Joe wouldn't have used her so ill. 'You've a foul mouth, woman. I'm not talking to you whilst the drink's in you. We'll discuss this later.'

There was a rap on the door and Rusty sighed with relief when Matt stepped into the room. 'I'm off now. Casey is insisting that I tell my family about the wedding. I'll be back about midday tomorrow.'

Eager for an excuse to leave Eva, Rusty accompanied Matt and Casey to the hotel entrance. 'They need some small change in the bar till,' he explained. 'I wish you well, Matt. Casey is a fine woman. I'm glad this has sorted itself out. I always said you were meant for each other.'

He left the couple to say their farewells and, loath to return to Eva, lingered in the bar. Yet his wife's words continued to nag at him. He couldn't push the manner of Joe's death from his mind. What had Eva meant? He'd got his come-uppance like the others. What others? Gradually realisation dawned, and with it horror. He stumbled blindly up the stairs, praying that he had got it wrong, that Eva was not capable of such evil.

When Rusty did not return, Eva sought out Casey in her sitting room. Her plans made, she was outwardly composed. Her cousin was standing by the window, staring dreamily out at the moonlit garden. Eva put the tray she was carrying down on to a table. She had brought a nightcap of hot chocolate for them.

'You must be very happy, Casey. There is so much to do and plan if your wedding is taking place so soon. You must have a special outfit, and of course we must get a bridesmaid's dress for Josephine. Shall we go to the West End shops tomorrow? We can be back before Matt returns in the afternoon.'

'Oh, Eva, I'm so happy.' Casey pirouetted as she hugged herself. 'Matt coming here today is the answer to all my prayers. I'd tried so hard to blot him from my mind. I'd even tried to convince myself that he was like Hardcastle. In my heart I knew that wasn't so. I couldn't forget him, or stop loving him.'

'We've seen enough of the war veterans here to know how many are mentally scarred from their experiences,' Eva commented with faint sarcasm. 'What a romantic fairytale to enchant your grandchildren. And now you have a new life before you.'

Casey moved towards her, her expression determined. 'Yes, and Josephine must be told the truth. Although we will move away from the Ringside, there is no reason why we can't see each other regularly. Josephine loves you, and Rusty. She believes Danny is her brother. She will miss him dreadfully.'

Eva looked away, her lips compressed and her knuckles white as she lifted the bone-china cup filled with hot chocolate. 'And I'll miss our nightcaps together, although they've become less frequent than when we were at the Britannia. I was so happy there, Casey. Happier than I've ever been in my life.'

'It was never the same after Dad died,' Casey answered softly.

Raising her cup to her lips, Eva said, 'Drink your chocolate. It will help you sleep. There is much to be done before Matt arrives tomorrow.'

'I can't see me getting much sleep tonight,' Casey replied dreamily.

Eva sipped her chocolate. 'We've been chattering on and it's nearly cold. Drink it quickly. It's like old times, but I doubt that we shall ever do this again.'

Casey drank the chocolate and pulled a face. 'Heavens, you put a lot of sugar in that. And it tasted a bit strange. How was yours?'

'Mine was fine. You've had too much champagne and excitement today.' To control her tension, Eva clasped her hands together. It stopped her raking her nails down her cousin's cheek. Her love for Casey had turned to loathing at the ease with which she would abandon her now that Matt was back in her life.

'But what a day it's been.' Casey was glowing with happiness and flopped down on to the bed. She raised her arms above her head with a purr of contentment. 'I must say you are taking it very well, Eva. I know it will be hard for you to give up Josephine. You've been like a mother to her.'

There was a sharp pain in Eva's palms as her nails broke the skin and drew blood. Did Casey think she would allow herself to be treated in this manner? Wasn't this how everyone she loved betrayed her? They used her for their own ends, then thought they could discard her like a broken toy. The only one who had ever got away with it was Goldstein, and that was because he was too powerful to destroy.

She watched dispassionately as Casey yawned, her voice

beginning to slur. 'Matt still wants us to have a white wedding, even though there will only be a few guests in the parish church. You'll be my maid of honour won't you, Eva? Rusty was so pleased when I asked him if he would give me away.' Casey put her hand to her mouth to stifle another yawn. 'I can't stop yawning. Perhaps I will sleep well tonight after all.'

Eva's eyes were cold and calculating. Finally she saw what she had been waiting for. Casey's lids were beginning to droop. When they closed and her breathing became even, Eva smiled. 'You'll sleep soundly all right,' she murmured, 'until the middle of tomorrow afternoon.'

Seeing her cousin so vulnerable, she was glad that she had only used enough of the sleeping drops to send her into a deep sleep and not kill her. There was another way to punish her.

Chapter Twenty-two

In the sitting room, Eva waited for Rusty to return. She regretted her outburst. The whisky had been a mistake. She had drunk it to give her courage. Instead it had disastrously loosened her tongue. She wasn't usually so indiscreet, but then she'd been frightened at the speed of Casey's plans and hadn't been thinking straight. When Rusty left the room she knew she had to deal with him on his return. He knew too much. It wouldn't take him long to put two and two together.

She rubbed her neck, the high frilled collar tightening like a noose. It made her spine prickle with foreboding. Fears long suppressed returned.

'Fer Gawd's sake, woman. Pull yerself together,' she berated herself, lapsing back, in her agitation, to the broad cockney accent of her youth. 'Yer must be turning soft if yer getting chicken-hearted now.'

She needed another drink badly, but she daren't risk it muddling her wits. Too much depended on her remaining sober and in control.

At the sound of Rusty's footfall on the landing she held her breath. The brass poker was warm in her hand from her tight grip. She regretted that she no longer had her pistol, but Rusty had sold it when they moved to the Ringside. She had dimmed the gaslight so that most of the room was in shadow. When she saw his silhouette in the doorway, she struck.

The poker juddered in her hand as it connected with Rusty's skull. With a cry he went down on his knees, his mouth gaping and eyes wide with shock as he faced her. She struck him twice more, mercilessly, while he was still stunned from the first blow, and watched his large body crumple to the floor.

Breathing heavily, she stood over her husband. She was unmoved by the spread of scarlet oozing from the back of his head. With brusque efficiency she put her fingers to his wrist. No pulse was detectable. After replacing the poker in its stand, she locked the door of their rooms behind her when she left. She had already packed the essentials she needed.

She looked at her watch. It was quarter past nine. There was no time to waste if she were to get clean away from the Ringside tonight.

First Eva ordered a taxicab to be outside the hotel in half an hour. She'd be far away before Rusty's body was found in the morning. She had briefly toyed with the idea of making his death look like another accident. He could have disturbed a thief who had clubbed him. She'd then inherit his share of the Ringside and be wealthy, but that wasn't why she had been so desperate tonight.

She was doing this for Josephine. Josephine was more her daughter than Casey's. Casey would not take her from her. And she couldn't if she couldn't find them. They would be far away where no one knew them.

Her face was grim with determination as she entered Casey's study and opened the safe. One good thing had come out of Matt's unexpected arrival. Casey had not banked the week's takings from the bar, restaurant and hotel. Unlocking the cash-box, a quick count showed her it contained over a hundred pounds. It was a start.

Swiftly, she moved through the private rooms of the hotel, selecting any items of value that were small and light enough to carry. The choice was limited as she had to avoid the heavier silverware, which was too cumbersome. But there were several silver and gold snuff-boxes and fob-watches, plus some rings and brooches that she had accumulated in recent years. Once a pickpocket, always a pickpocket, she reflected. The temptation and the skill had never left her. Seeing rich women with more money than sense had always made her burn with envy, and this was her way of redressing the balance.

Distrusting all men, she had been shrewd enough to secretly hoard these valuables. They were for a rainy day. They had been hidden in a pouch in one of her hat-boxes. There was also her own jewellery. She had insisted that Rusty buy her an expensive piece for her birthday, anniversary and Christmas. If she had to sell them she could get another three hundred pounds. She returned to Casey's room and, with only a cursory glance at her cousin who had not moved, she raided Casey's jewellery box. All told, she could raise several hundred pounds when the trinkets were sold. Money enough to start a new life. But little compensation considering how much the Ringside must now be worth.

And she had yet to claim the greatest prize of all.

'Josephine, wake up.' Impatiently she shook the child awake. 'You must get dressed and come with me.'

She swept aside the girl's sleepy protests.

'Hurry, we are going to arrange a very special surprise for Aunt Casey. We have to do it in secret tonight. Now don't make a sound, or you will spoil the surprise.'

Ten minutes later, all the doors to the private rooms were locked. Carrying two hastily packed valises of clothing, Eva helped Josephine into the taxicab and ordered the driver to take them to King's Cross station. It was quarter to ten. She felt a moment's panic not knowing what time the last train to her planned destination departed.

Matt arrived home to find all the people he intended to confront assembled in the parlour. Clementine had just finished a stumbling recital on the piano and was being praised by both Sybil and Millicent. Humphrey was dozing in his chair, his cheeks flushed by too much port.

'My darling,' Sybil cried as Matt entered the room. 'Where have you been? I phoned the airfield yesterday and they said you had come to London. I have been out of my wits with worry. Dear Clementine has been such a comfort.'

As she made to embrace him he stood back, his expression stony. 'I went to Richmond and have been reunited with my true fiancée, Cassandra Strong. I was appalled to learn how Casey has been treated by this family.'

Humphrey started awake, his glare belligerent as he rose to his feet. There was a gasp from Clementine who sank to the floor in a faint. Millicent rushed over to her.

'How could you be so cruel to her, Matthew?' his aunt screeched. 'The poor girl—'

'The poor girl was used by you because you wanted us to marry. She knew I didn't love her.'

He rounded on his mother, his voice hoarse with disgust. 'The way you tried to manipulate me whilst my memory was impaired was wicked. But what you did to Casey, knowing that I adored her, even suspecting that she was carrying my child . . .' He saw from the way that Sybil clutched at her mouth in horror that she had read Casey's letter to him which spoke of the baby. 'That was unforgivable.'

'I did it for the best. That woman has been spreading lies. She always was a schemer. Totally unsuitable . . .'

'Shut up, Mother!' Matt raged. 'You condemn yourself by your words.'

Humphrey jabbed a finger accusingly towards him as he stepped to his mother's side. 'How dare you speak to your mother like that! That woman was your whore. She got no more than she deserved.'

Matt grabbed his brother's lapels and flung him hard against the wall. A gilt-framed picture was knocked off its hook and crashed on to the floor. 'Say another word against Casey and I'll bloody well knock you senseless. This is Mother's doing, and you were too spineless to stand up to her. You're just as bad.'

He released Humphrey, who was trembling too much to retaliate. He turned to his mother. 'The petty-mindedness of this family sickens me. Casey has never said a word against you, or mentioned how vilely you treated her over her father's debt. In fact she insisted I return here tonight to make my peace with you.'

Sybil held her hands in front of her waist, her figure stiff with hauteur. 'She still has an eye on your family's money, I suppose. The common little strumpet was a fortune-huntress. She used the oldest trick there is by getting herself pregnant. She knew that you would be gullible enough to wed her.'

Matt inhaled sharply, knowing that there was only one thing he could say to put his mother firmly in her place. 'Is that how you got my father to marry you?' he accused. 'Humphrey was born only six months after your marriage. Or did you think we would remain ignorant of that fact? You've always kept very quiet about your family, except for your sister Millicent. But employees have long memories. Your father was the brewery foreman before he died. Not that you ever acknowledged his existence after your marriage. You made enemies by that, and they were quick to gossip. For whatever reason Father married you, that's your affair. But don't judge Cassandra Strong by your own standards.'

Sybil slumped down on to a chair, too shocked to speak. Humphrey put a hand on her shoulder, bristling at Matt. 'Get out of this house. How dare you speak such lies? You are no son of this house.'

Matt ignored his brother. He had known for years his

mother's background, and until now had never condemned her for it. 'I've no intention of setting foot in this house again until my wife is accepted as part of this family.' He looked at his mother's stricken expression and regretted his outburst. 'What happened between you and Father, I don't condemn you for it. Father loved you and I believe that you had a happy marriage. What pains me is that you are not prepared to give Cassandra and myself the same chance.'

He walked to the door before he spoke again. 'A wedding invitation will be sent to every member of the family. Your granddaughter is to be our bridesmaid. I would not like her to grow up without any grandparents. The choice is yours. Attend our wedding and we can begin to heal this breach you have created.'

As Matt walked out into the night, he could not bear the thought of being separated from Casey. He drew out his new pocket-watch. It was nine-thirty. Still time to return to the Ringside before the hotel closed for the night. He'd take a room there until the wedding.

The moment Matt stepped into the entrance hall of the Ringside Hotel he sensed something was wrong. It was just before eleven and a worried-looking barman had just come down the stairs leading to the family rooms.

He looked relieved at seeing Matt. 'You're the gentleman who came earlier, aren't you? I heard you and Miss Casey are to marry.'

Matt nodded.

'Perhaps you can tell me what to do,' the barman rushed on. 'I can't get no answer from them upstairs. It's not like Rusty to shirk his duty, but the till's got to be checked and I've no keys to lock up. No word was left that they'd all gone out. But I've knocked on every door and no one answers.'

'Could they have gone out?' Matt suggested.

'Not all three of them. Miss Casey and Mrs Chambers might have, but they make it a rule that one of them is here in case of an emergency. Besides, they'd not leave the boy or girl on their own; one of the staff always sits upstairs with them.'

Matt ran up the stairs to Casey's rooms. He tapped on the door. No answer. Trying the handle he found it locked. Ill-at-ease, he hurried along the corridor to Rusty and Eva's room. Again there was no answer to his knocking, and again he found the door locked.

A sleepy-eyed Danny wandered along the corridor, dragging his teddy-bear. 'Want Dadda.' There were tears on the child's cheeks.

'It's all right, Danny. Your father is in the bar. He'll be up in a minute.' Matt nodded to the barman to take the boy back to his room and was relieved when Danny followed him, although he was hiccuping tearfully.

Waiting until the boy was out of sight, Matt put his good shoulder towards the door and threw his weight against it. The woodwork shuddered but did not give. A second attempt jarred his body with agony, but still the door did not budge.

The barman returned. 'Danny has settled down, thank goodness.'

'It will take both of us to force this lock.' Matt indicated the door.

They rushed it together. This time the wood around the lock splintered. The door flew open, catapulting the two men inside. The room was in darkness. Matt struck a match and, locating a gaslamp, touched the wick. As the bluish light flared, there was a gasp from the barman.

'Blimey! It's Rusty and he's hurt.'

Matt saw Rusty's sprawled body. Blood from the wound to his head was spread in a dark pool on the Indian carpet. He swallowed against the bile which rose to his throat. He feared that his friend was dead. Kneeling at his side, he put two trembling fingers against Rusty's neck.

'Thank God! There's a faint pulse.' He glanced at the barman. 'Do you know how to use the telephone? I assume there is one installed here.'

'Yes,' the man answered.

'Ring for a doctor. And be quick about it, man.'

'There's a nurse on duty for the veterans. Shall I fetch her?'

Matt nodded. This was no accident. Something sinister had happened here after he had left. Casey's locked door also boded ill. Terror gripped him that she might also be hurt. There was nothing he could do to help Rusty for the moment, and he knew that it would be dangerous even to move him until the doctor examined him. He snatched a blanket from the bedroom, and covered him with it.

He was desperate now to find out how Casey was. With pounding heart he hurried back to Casey's rooms. At his fourth attempt at hurling himself against it, her locked door finally opened. His body had undergone a terrible hammering, yet he dismissed his pain, so great was his fear for Casey's safety. There was no sign of her in the sitting room; a cold sweat broke out along his spine as he limped to the bedroom. Her form was silvered by moonlight as she lay on the bed.

'Casey. Casey!' His voice rose when she did not respond. Alarmed, he gathered her into his arms, his heart wrenching with fear when her limp body lolled against his chest. At least she was breathing, but it was unnatural and shallow. He'd seen drug-induced sleep often enough to know she'd been given a powerful opiate. But how long ago? And could it have been enough to kill her?

'Wake up, Casey,' he shouted. 'Cassandra, sweetheart!'

Fear clutched at his throat when she did not stir. Dear God, what had happened here? Why were the doors locked? And where was Eva? The questions rapped through his mind as he tried to shake Casey awake.

There was the sound of sobbing and he swung round to discover Danny still with his teddy-bear in his hand, standing in the doorway.

'Want Dadda. Want Josie.' The boy burst into tears.

Matt groaned, powerless to leave Casey and comfort the boy. And if the child stumbled into the sitting room and found Rusty . . .

'Your aunt is ill,' he tried to explain. 'I have to stay with her. Go back to bed, there's a good lad. Someone will bring you some warm milk shortly.'

Danny sobbed louder. 'Want Josie. Josie not in bed.'

Matt had thought he'd reached the deepest pit of fear. Now he was plummeted into the bowels of hell. Everything fell into place. Casey drugged. Rusty attacked. Josie not in her bed. And there was no sign of Eva. Had Eva abducted Josephine? The woman was obsessive enough to do so.

''Ere Danny, what yer doin' out of bed?' The voice Matt recognised as one of the veteran's carried to him.

'In here, man,' he shouted.

The stocky figure froze in the doorway. 'Bloody hell! What's happened to Miss Casey?'

'She's been drugged,' Matt explained, hauling her to her feet, knowing that he had to try and rouse her. 'Rusty has been attacked. Get the boy back to his bed. The police have to be informed.'

To his relief the soldier did not argue. 'Name's Hodgekins, Bert Hodgekins. Leave the lad to me. Yer see ter Miss Casey.'

Matt was still attempting to rouse Casey. After seeing the brutality of Rusty's wounds, he prayed that Eva had intended only to drug Casey and not kill her.

The barman reappeared. 'Nurse Bell is with Rusty and Dr Mitchell is on his way.' Seeing Casey's unconscious figure, he groaned. 'No! Not Miss Casey as well. Is she badly hurt? Was it burglars?'

'She's been given a sleeping draught. And it wasn't burglars. Josephine has gone and so has Eva Chambers. This is a matter for the police. Can you ring the local constabulary?'

'To tell them that Mrs Chambers and her daughter are missing?' the barman queried.

Matt's reply was terse with impatience and fear. 'Just tell them about the attack on Rusty. That will do for now.'

Carrying Casey into the bathroom, he propped her on the side of the bath, her head hanging over the washbasin. Then he stuck his fingers down the back of her throat, pressing gently until he felt the muscles spasm and she began to vomit. A groan was torn from her as Matt held her and splashed her face with cold water. With her stomach emptied, he hoped that not all the drug would have been absorbed into her bloodstream, and that the cold water would rouse her.

'Casey, wake up. You've got to wake up,' he repeated with rough urgency.

Her eyelids flickered. He splashed more cold water on her face, and with a gasp her eyes opened, their gaze bleary.

'Casey, you must stay awake,' he commanded.

'Matt,' she drawled. 'Tired. So tired.'

Yawning, she tried to lie against him.

'No, Casey. You mustn't sleep. Wake up. Eva drugged you.' With each sentence, he splashed her face. 'Wake up. Eva has taken Josephine. They've gone and it's late at night.'

Where the water failed, his words pierced her drugged mind. 'Josephine! My Josie gone.' Her eyes were open, focused, and frantic with fear. Her hands clutched at Matt's shoulders.

'They can't have got far,' he reassured, although his own doubts were grave. 'It's twenty-past eleven. When did you last see Eva?'

'Some time after nine. She brought me some hot chocolate.'

Casey winced and clutched at her head. Matt filled a glass of water and held it to her lips. 'Drink this, it will help.'

She gulped it down. 'My head aches. Can't think straight. The chocolate. She must have drugged it. Rusty . . . He would have stopped her.'

'Rusty's hurt. I think it was Eva who laid his head open. He's unconscious. The doctor and the police have been summoned.'

'Eva did that?' Casey said stunned. 'I can't believe it.'

She tried to stand on her own and swayed. Matt put his arm around her and led her back into the bedroom. 'Sit by the open window,' he suggested. 'It will help revive you.'

Casey collapsed on to the chair, clearly having difficulty in channelling her thoughts. Matt hated having to press her so ruthlessly, but there was no time to waste if Eva was to be caught quickly.

'Would Eva have had much money?' he persisted. 'She couldn't have planned this. It must have been me turning up that made her desperate. She knew that finally you were lost to her, but seized her chance to keep Josie.'

Casey looked up at him, her eyes stark with fear. 'The safe had the week's takings in it. Over a hundred pounds.' She pushed herself upright and, clutching her head, swayed drunkenly. 'I'll have to check to see if anything else is missing. To get away she would have had to summon a taxicab. The local number for a company is in my address book on my desk in the study downstairs.'

A doorbell rang and the barman called out, 'It's Dr Mitchell.'

Matt held Casey close. 'Are you sure you're strong enough if I leave you while the doctor attends Rusty? Then he will see you. But don't let yourself go to sleep.'

She nodded weakly. 'I'm feeling stronger. The fresh air helps. Go to Rusty.'

Although he desperately wanted to stay with Casey, Matt knew he had to be with Rusty. He put a hand on the shoulder of the barman. 'I don't know your name.'

'Donald.' Matt saw now that he was only about twenty, and wore a leather glove to cover an injured hand. He guessed he was another war veteran whom Casey had employed; so many of the disabled soldiers found it difficult to find work.

'Will you stay with Miss Strong until the doctor can see her? She may ask you to run a few errands. There is information we need to find out.'

'You can rely on me, sir. Miss Strong is an angel. Reckon I'd have to answer to all the veterans if anything happened to her in my care.'

'Thank you, Donald. Will you show the police up when they arrive?'

Dr Mitchell was shaking his head as he bent over Rusty. He had lit an oil-lamp and placed it close to his patient on the floor.

'Nasty wound,' Mitchell observed. 'Lucky it didn't kill him. It'll need a dozen stitches and a few days in bed. Do you know how he got it?'

'I couldn't say. Though I guess he was struck.'

'A burglar?'

The doctor was a bluff man with receding hair and a large waxed moustache to disguise his fleshy jowls. He stood up and brushed down the pinstripe trousers of his suit.

'It wasn't a burglar,' Matt said. He glanced at the round homely face of Nurse Bell, who had returned from turning down the bedcovers in the adjoining room. 'His wife has gone and taken her niece with her.'

'You mean her daughter?' Nurse Bell corrected.

Matt shook her head. They could no longer keep Josephine's parentage a secret. 'The girl was her niece.'

Matt was saved from explaining further by the arrival of two police officers. Hearing their voices, Casey came in to the room and cried out at seeing Rusty's unconscious figure.

Dr Mitchell cleared his throat and addressed the policemen.

'Bad head wound, probably caused by a metal instrument of some kind. Three deliberate blows, I'd say. If you two gentlemen would be so kind as to carry him carefully to his bed, I will stitch the wound. Nurse Bell will stay with him all night. I want to be informed when he regains consciousness to give him further checks.'

He drew a small vial out of his bag and placed it on the table. 'When he awakes, give him a couple of drops of that in water. It will help the pain. If you will excuse me, gentlemen, Mrs Bagstock is having a difficult labour and the midwife has asked that I attend her.'

Once Rusty was settled and the doctor had left, one of the policemen took out a notepad. Matt answered his questions.

The older of the two men had a close-cropped ginger beard. He frowned. 'I'm Constable Rogers. Mrs Chambers has kidnapped the girl. She's not her daughter, then.'

'She is my child,' Casey said softly. 'For appearances' sake my cousin made it known that Josephine was her daughter. She is very attached to her. Today she learned that I am to marry Mr Frost, who is Josephine's father. Eva was very agitated at first. Then when she came to me this evening she seemed calmer. I thought she had accepted the situation.'

'Instead she drugged you and attempted to murder her husband,' the older policeman commented.

Casey nodded, too distraught to answer. Matt put his arm around her, his voice clipped with impatience. 'We are wasting time. She's been gone for two hours. It's the middle of the night.'

Constable Rogers drew his stout figure up self-importantly. 'We must know the facts, sir.'

'But couldn't we start searching?' he pleaded. 'Mrs Chambers can't have got too far yet. Whilst the doctor was stitching Mr Chambers' head and you were questioning the barman, I telephoned the local taxicab company. Mrs Chambers ordered a cab to come here and wait in the lane for quarter to ten. The driver had just returned. He dropped her off at King's Cross station.'

'She could be miles away by now,' Constable Rogers informed them. 'And trains leave from there with connections to the coast and the seaports.'

Casey stifled a sob. 'My cousin has enough money to pay for her passage to the Continent. She also took both her own and my jewellery.'

'I can't see Eva going out of the country,' Matt observed. 'She can't speak a foreign language.'

The older constable regarded them thoughtfully. 'Inquiries will be made at all the London stations. If she is that devious, she could have taken a second taxicab to another terminus. We'll telephone with descriptions. Don't you worry, Miss. Your daughter will be found.'

'I'm getting my coat and going to look for her.'

Casey tottered as she walked to the door. Matt caught her. 'Casey, you're in no fit state to go anywhere.'

Her eyes were bright with tears and she was trembling as she glared accusingly at him. 'Our daughter has been kidnapped. I'm not staying here and doing nothing. Bert Hodgekins will stay with Danny. They get on well, and someone will be here to take any message should the police telephone. I'm going to King's Cross. I'll take a photograph of Josephine with me. Someone must have seen what train they boarded.'

Eva sighed wearily and lay down in the hotel bed next to Josephine. Fondly she stroked the girl's dark hair. A secret smile played across her thin lips. So far her flight had gone really easily, with no hitches. She had taken the taxicab to King's Cross to throw up a false trail. From there she had taken a second cab to Victoria, and in the ladies' cloakroom had brought about a transformation in their appearances. She had changed into an old plain black travelling suit with a small straw hat over her auburn wig. What good fortune she had never thrown it away when she had finished working for Goldstein. But then she rarely discarded anything: even her old clothes were hoarded in the attic. She'd been poor too long, and hoarding possessions was second nature to her.

Without make-up, Eva would pass herself up as a widow of moderate means. If the police were looking for a black-haired woman with a girl they would not notice them. She had cut Josie's hair and changed her into the largest of Danny's sailor-suits. Thank goodness the child found the masquerade amusing. She thought it was a grand game. It was a distasteful disguise for Eva to accept that Josephine must dress as a boy, but the only one she felt would work. Time enough in the months ahead to move on and allow Josephine to be a girl again.

No one appeared to show any undue interest in them when she boarded the train, nor when she alighted at Clapham Junction and took the room in the modest lodging house overnight. Tomorrow she would catch a train to the coast and lose herself amongst the holidaymakers.

Eva smiled into the darkness. Again she had triumphed. Sid, Myrtle, Joe, Bertha and now Rusty – no one yet had got the better of her.

It was two in the morning and on their return to the Ringside, Casey wept inconsolably against Matt's shoulder. They had learned nothing. Eva and Josephine seemed to have disappeared without trace. No one had seen them at King's Cross or any of the main London stations. 'How could Eva be so cruel?' she sobbed. 'How could she take Josephine? She knew it would break my heart.'

'That woman only ever thought of herself!' Matt controlled his own rage, knowing that Casey needed his support and not his anger.

'It's my fault. I should never have agreed to Eva's idea to pass herself off as Josephine's mother. I may never see Josephine again. I disowned my own daughter. I don't deserve her. She will never know that I am her mother or how much I love her.'

'Casey, calm yourself. Josie knows you love her. You acted as you did because you believed it was for the best. It was to spare the child's feelings.'

'What if she believes that I was ashamed of her?'

Matt groaned and held her tight. 'It would never have happened if I had been there for you as I should have been. But what good does it do to blame ourselves? Fate took its hand to separate us. Surely it wouldn't be so cruel as to bring us together again only for us to lose Josie. Eva loves the girl. She is not going to harm her. Hopefully in a few days she will come to her senses and bring Josie back.'

Casey shook her head. 'No, she won't do that. She tried to kill Rusty. She won't come back. She'll know that the police are after her.'

She sat up, her face strained but determined. 'How could I have been so blind to the way she manipulated people? I felt sorry for her that she had lost her whole family. Never again. I know her for what she is capable of and I won't make the mistake of underestimating her. She will seek obscurity and want to make a new identity for herself. And she could be anywhere in England. However long it takes, I won't rest until I've scoured every inch of this country and found Josephine. And God help Eva when I get hold of her.'

Chapter Twenty-three

Sleet was slashing against the window-panes when Casey entered Rusty's room the next morning. She had been awake since dawn, the pewter sky as oppressive as her mood, the persistent rain on the glass drumming through her head. Matt stood up at her entrance. He had stayed with her until she fell asleep last night, then must have come to sit in vigil at Rusty's bedside. Matt's complexion was grey and the stubble along his jaw added to his haggard expression. Clearly he had not slept. 'There's been no change,' he said softly. 'I'd hoped that he'd have come round and we might get some idea about where Eva could have gone.'

Casey stared down at Rusty's broad figure lying so still beneath the bedclothes. He had been a part of her life for as long as she could remember. Half his head had been shaved when the doctor had sewn up the wounds. She moved to his side and took the large freckled hand that lay on top of the sheet.

'Don't give up, Rusty,' she urged. 'Keep fighting. Remember Danny needs you.'

'He can't hear you, Miss,' Nurse Bell said indulgently. She was middle-aged and plump, her greying-blonde hair pulled tight into a bun under her starched triangular cap. She was very matter of fact in her manner, a capable nurse who had lost both her husband and only son in the war.

'I wonder,' Casey answered. 'I can't see that there's any harm in giving him the encouragement he needs to fight for his life.'

'Happen not, Miss,' Nurse Bell stated with a shrug. 'You've performed miracles enough with some of the veterans here with your patience and understanding.'

Casey twisted a handkerchief between her hands, her voice low and crackling with anxiety, 'Come back to us, Rusty. Eva's taken Josie. We need your help. Danny needs you.'

Nurse Bell added, 'Right sorry to hear about the young girl. I always reckoned she were too sweet-tempered to be the offspring of Mrs Chambers.'

'I suppose it's common gossip now that Josephine is my daughter.' Casey tilted her chin defiantly. 'I'm not ashamed of it.'

'Precious few of us are as innocent on our wedding day as we would like others to think,' the nurse observed. 'Those who spread the blackest scandal are usually those who have more than most to hide. I'm sure you'll get your little girl back.'

Fighting against the tears which were threatening to destroy her self-control, Casey swallowed and lifted Rusty's hand to her cheek. 'Hang in there, Rusty. You've been a wonderful friend. Hang in there, for Danny's sake, Rusty.'

She repeated the words over and over again until Matt put his hands on her shoulders, saying, 'Come and get something to eat. You need your strength. It will be a long day.'

Reluctantly, Casey made to remove her hand from the barman's fingers and found them caught in an increasing grip.

'He moved, Nurse,' she exclaimed excitedly. 'He's coming round. We're here for you, Rusty. Danny is waiting to come to see yc

A faint moan rose from Rusty's throat, but his eyes remained shut. Matt put an arm around Casey's waist. 'Don't build your hopes up. Let Rusty rest.'

Casey turned her head into his chest. 'I don't want Rusty to die. He's always been there when I needed him.'

'He isn't going to die,' Matt said fiercely. 'He's as strong as an ox. Now come and have a cup of tea and try to eat something.'

'I don't want anything.'

'Then you'll end up getting ill. You've got to keep your strength up for Josie's and Danny's sake. There's going to be one very lost and upset little boy when he wakes up this morning.'

'He should be awake by now.' Casey conquered her own fears. 'What am I going to tell him?'

'Poor kid. How about saying that Rusty fell over and banged his head and Eva has taken Josephine away so that the hotel would be quieter, but Rusty wanted his son to stay with him? He'll accept that.'

She allowed Matt to persuade her to eat a slice of toast and drink some tea. Several times there was a hesitant knock on her door and one of the veterans would appear to express his condolences.

Sergeant Hodgekins shuffled uncomfortably as he entered. 'Young Danny looks rather lost. Miss Casey, would you mind if I took him into Kingston? There's a fair there at the moment. The rain has stopped and the weather looks to be brightening up.'

'Thank you, Bert. I'm sure Danny would like that and it would help us.'

'Miss Casey!' Nurse Bell hurried in. 'It's Mr Chambers, he's regained consciousness and he's asking for you. I've also put a call in to Dr Mitchell. The police will want a word with him too.'

Casey hurried to Rusty's side. He was propped up on a pillow, purple puffy bruises spreading all down the side of his face. Though he must've been in considerable pain, his eyes were anxious as he urged, 'You've got to stop Eva. The nurse won't tell me nothing, but she did this to me, didn't she? What else has she done?'

'You're not to worry, Rusty. Danny is safe. You've had a nasty blow to your head.'

'Don't fob me off with that,' Rusty said with surprising force considering his injuries. He looked at Nurse Bell. 'Will you wait outside? This is private business.'

When they were alone, he looked from Casey to Matt. 'Eva is evil. She were real upset about Matt turning up. All she could think about was losing you and Josephine. She's capable of anything.'

'She took Josephine and drugged Casey,' Matt intervened. 'The police have been informed. She tried to kill you, man. I hadn't realised she was that vicious.' He briefly explained the events of the previous evening.

Rusty closed his eyes, his voice strained. 'Eva is pure evil. To think that I wed her . . . She couldn't bear to be thwarted. I reckon she thought she'd left me for dead. And with you unconscious, I probably would have been, come the morning. I reckon Matt saved me life.'

Casey paled. 'Thank God he did. But it's hard to grasp that Eva is capable of murder. She must have cared for you, else she would not have married you, Rusty.'

'She wed me because I told her I was prepared to marry you and give your child a name. She only wanted me because it gave her a hold over you.' His eyes were bleak. 'As for murder, I suspect she had something to do with Joe's death. She taunted me that they were lovers.'

Casey reeled back, shocked by his words.

Rusty groaned and pressed on. 'I hate having to say this, Casey, but I reckon Joe would be alive now if she hadn't made a play for him. After what she did to me, I wouldn't put nothing past her. Even Joe's death. She must have realised that he would never marry her. I could never understand how someone as nimble-footed as Joe fell down the stairs – unless he were pushed. I were thinking about it whilst I were serving last night in the bar. I went over her life. She hated her father, Myrtle, and her little brother. Sid Bowman repeatedly raped her. She couldn't stand Bertha. They're all dead.'

Casey shook her head, stunned. Was Rusty delirious?

'I ain't out of me head,' Rusty continued. 'I know what I'm saying. After what Eva did last night, don't you think those deaths seem too much of a coincidence? The gas explosion which killed Myrtle and Sid needn't have been that Myrtle left the gas tap on whilst drunk. Could be that Eva turned it on before she left the house that morning. And young Charlie were in her care when he fell out of that window.'

'Oh Rusty, could she really be that evil?' Casey gasped. 'I can't believe it. The deaths were all tragic and unhappy coincidences.'

Matt cut in. 'I'm not so sure they were. There was always something odd about the way Joe died.'

'Matt's right,' Rusty continued feebly. 'There's two sides to Eva. She ain't no innocent. She were in league with Goldstein whilst we were at the Britannia. She acted as a fence for stolen goods for him.'

Casey shook her head. 'I knew nothing of this. It's like she's a stranger.'

Matt took her arm. 'You only ever see the good in people. Eva was a consummate actress when she chose to be.'

'She were that,' Rusty ground out. 'Happen you haven't seen the devil that gets into her when she don't get her own way. You always were her favourite, Casey. She always wanted to impress you. It weren't until I wed her that I realised that she hated men. But she could make herself irresistible to us when it suited her.'

'The bitch will have to answer for her crimes,' Matt burst

out. 'The police will be told everything.'

Casey shivered, gooseflesh breaking out over her skin. 'Josephine must be found. I'll never forgive myself if anything happens to my child.'

'Eva won't harm her,' Matt insisted. 'She cares for her too much. She is all she has left. And she loves her.'

Casey thrust a hand to her mouth, grappling to hold back her fears. Eva had proved more cunning than she'd thought her capable of. But Eva a murderess! Was that possible?

She was no longer sure her cousin was innocent. What sort of woman would callously drug her and then kidnap Josephine? Clearly she was capable of anything. It was beginning to look as though she had even got away with murder. Casey dared not succumb to her fears for her daughter. She had to remain strong. She had to think as Eva would be thinking.

'Obviously she's gone into hiding. Have you any idea where she could be?' Casey pressed, aware that the hours were ticking by and nothing had been heard from the police. 'We know that when she left here she took a taxicab to King's Cross.'

Rusty's face twisted with misery. 'Why didn't I suspect she would do something like this? It should have been obvious to me that she wouldn't let you and Matt take Josephine away. I was so angry when I twigged that she must have killed Joe that I didn't stop to think. I had to tackle her about it. I suppose I still cared enough for her to want her to prove that I was mistaken. What a bloody fool I was!'

'Don't upset yourself, Rusty. She duped us all.' Casey was worried at his pallor and feared he would suffer a relapse. 'You should be resting.'

'Leave it to us,' Matt agreed. 'Rest and get your strength back.'

Rusty groaned. 'Ain't no chance of resting whilst that cow is on the loose. She's too devious to leave a trail. Any idea where she could've gone?'

Casey shook her head. 'The only friend I know she has is that sculptress down the lane. It's too close for her to go there. I think she would go somewhere where there're crowds . A holiday town or city. She'd be noticed in a small village.'

'She could be anywhere,' Matt ground out. 'And if she feels cornered, she'll be dangerous.'

Rusty put a freckled hand over his eyes. 'She split me skull good and proper. It feels like the devil's doing a clog dance on it. Tell the police what I've told you. They'll make it a national hunt for her if they suspect Eva planned Joe's and the other deaths.'

As Matt led Casey outside, she leaned against him. 'Is it possible that Eva was so evil? She could be spiteful and had a temper, but to plan . . .'

She broke off. 'She never told me Uncle Sid abused her. Beat her, yes – but rape—' She shuddered. 'As for her and Dad. I can't take it in.'

Matt sighed. 'If what Rusty said is true, Joe would have been ashamed if you had found out. Perhaps he'd decided he didn't want you to have anything to do with her. If he'd told her to leave that would make her desperate. She was obsessive about being with you. I've always thought her a calculating creature. Looks like she's transferred that obsession to Josie.' He paused, his face taut with anxiety, and held her in his arms. 'Thank God you are safe. I've never liked the woman, but I hadn't thought her capable of murder. But after attacking Rusty so viciously and drugging you, I think she could have murdered the others. Your father included.'

Casey slumped against him, trembling violently. When she lifted her head, her eyes were glittering with the desire for justice.

'Eva must be found. Before she kills again. Dear God, let us find her before any harm comes to Josephine.'

Eva stared at her red-haired reflection in the train window as they steamed towards the south coast. Her auburn wig was the only splash of colour against the grey mist enveloping the landscape. At her side, Josephine slept soundly. There were only two other passengers in the carriage: a middle-aged couple who had embarked at Haywards Heath. The woman kept smiling at Josephine's sleeping figure. Eva was becoming nervous that the girl would wake up and say something that would destroy her disguise as a boy.

To avoid any eye-contact with the couple, Eva kept her head turned towards the window. A heavy lace veil draped over her black hat was secured under her chin to further obscure her features from curious eyes. She was uneasy that it had been impossible to make Rusty's death look like an accident as she had the others. The necessity of abducting Josephine had put paid to any pretence along those lines. Yet she had covered her tracks well. She was confident she would succeed. As she had succeeded before.

Those times it had all been so easy. Killing her brother Charlie had been so simple. The little sod was showing off as usual and hanging out of the window waving to his mates. Her back had been stinging painfully from the beating her dad had given her that morning. Charlie had told him she had been over the disused warehouse with Toby and Bob Sykes, the twelve-year-old twins. For sixpence she used to let them put their hands up her blouse and squeeze her tits, and the randy little bleeders kept coming back for more. It wasn't that her dad was angry at what she'd done. She'd been beaten for not handing the money over to him so that he could spend it in the Britannia.

She'd seen Charlie framed in the window, laughing at her pain and wiggling his fat backside at her. All it had taken was a push. The iron railings below the window had gone straight through his heart and lung. Charlie never made a sound, but she had screamed the street down, hysterically proclaiming that he had been dancing on the window-ledge and had fallen out. Without Charlie to dote upon she had thought her dad would be kinder to her. Instead he'd got worse.

Eva clenched her hand as the memory of her suffering gnawed at her breast. All she'd ever wanted was for her dad to love her. For years she'd endured his lecherous abuse, believing that it was his way of showing that he cared for her. That he loved her. But he hadn't. She'd caught him once humping one of her classmates in the outside privy. What had infuriated her the most was seeing Sid Bowman give the little tart a couple of pennies for sweets. He'd never given her money in his life. Just a beating if she protested. And how that cow Myrtle had enjoyed holding her down for the beatings.

That Sunday morning when she had turned on the gas taps of the parlour lamps, and walked out of the house to visit Casey, had changed her life. She'd done it because Sid expected to act the pimp for her. It was the final degradation, and she vowed he'd pay for every humiliation she had suffered. Again it had been easy. And again no one had suspected her.

Myrtle had been roaring drunk the previous night; she'd also been taking snuff for years and had lost her sense of smell. As soon as she'd struck a match to make a cuppa, she'd blown them both to kingdom-come.

Life was good after that. Eva had made herself indispensable to Joe and Casey. But Joe had never been easy to bend to her will. She'd underestimated him. When he threatened to throw her out and branded her a whore, then she'd had no choice but to kill him. She couldn't let him destroy Casey's affection for her. Besides, at that time, she had thought Joe was worth a mint, and that she and Casey would live comfortably off his savings.

It hadn't turned out that way, but Joe's death had not been difficult to achieve. After closing time, when she'd heard Rusty and Bertha leave the pub, she'd doused the hall gaslight and positioned herself in the deep shadows at the top of the stairs. Squatting on the floor, she'd waited. A short time later, Joe had cursed the darkness as he tripped on one of the stairs. Eva had braced her back against the wall and drawn up her legs. When his head and shoulders had come into view, she'd lashed out with both feet. In the moonlight she'd glimpsed the recognition on his face as her feet struck him in the centre of his chest. He'd gone down like a ninepin, tumbling backwards down the stairs to lie in a broken heap in the passageway.

She had followed cautiously, a poker to hand to finish him off if need be. But he was dead. His head had cracked open on the newel-post. To ensure that his death was declared accidental, she'd poured brandy over his clothing and trusted that the doctor would declare that, whilst drunk, Joe had fallen down the stairs. Returning to her room, she'd gone to bed and waited for her uncle's body to be discovered before acting the distraught and bereaved niece.

The memory made her smile to herself. The great Joe 'Strongarm' Strong, knocked out stone cold dead by a woman. Her future with Casey had been assured, until Bertha had started mouthing off. Fortunately by then Goldstein had come on the scene. One of his men had pushed her on to the railway line. Mind you, the Jew had made her pay for the privilege of having his men do the dirty work.

'Mama, where are we going?' Josephine asked as she sat upright, jerking Eva back to the present.

With relief Eva noticed that the train was slowing down. From the density of houses beside the track they must be approaching Brighton station.

'It's a treat for you, dear. We're going to the seaside. We're nearly there.'

'But why isn't Danny with us?'

'Danny is with Dadda. They've gone fishing. This is our treat.' Eva was struggling to keep her patience with the child.

'But Danny would have liked to come to the seaside,' Josephine persisted with the single-mindedness of the young. 'I want Danny. It won't be any fun without Danny. Or Aunty Casey. We never go anywhere without Aunt Casey.'

'I'm your mama. And you are with me.' Eva's voice sharpened but, aware of the middle-aged couple sitting opposite watching her, she forced a smile and addressed them. 'Children! You give them a treat and they do nothing but complain.'

'But Danny will be upset he's been left behind.' Josephine burst into loud tears.

Fearful that Josephine was drawing attention to them, Eva hugged her close and spoke comfortingly. Josephine would have none of it, struggling to break from her grip as, with a screech of brakes, the train shuddered to a halt.

She had forgotten how stubborn the girl could be. The last thing she needed was for Josephine to make a scene. She had chosen Brighton to lose herself amongst the August holidaymakers. It was still closer to London than she would have wished, but she knew it would be crowded here, and with crowds came anonymity.

She dragged Josephine out of her seat, her alarm mounting as the girl's sobs grew louder. 'I want Danny. I won't go without him.'

All patience deserting her, Eva swung the child round and snarled in her face. 'If you know what's good for you, shut up. Or you'll feel the back of my hand.'

Josephine eyed her sullenly, her sobs receding. 'I don't like you.'

Eva felt her heart clench. She flung her arms around the child. 'I'm sorry, my precious. Mama didn't mean it. We're going to have such fun and we will buy Danny a really special present. How's that?'

Josephine stopped crying. Not a moment before time as far as Eva was concerned. There seemed to be an uncomfortable number of police constables watching the ticket barriers. 'Come along, darling.' Eva forced herself to remain calm and sound confident.

With every footstep, Eva's heart thudded. Josephine was hanging back and dragging her feet and it wouldn't do to be seen dragging a reluctant child along. The policemen had sharp eyes. She must remain calm and not act suspiciously. They weren't looking for a dowdy redhead and a young boy. She must be confident that her disguises would fool them. Once Rusty's body was found, she'd be wanted for his murder as well as for Josephine's kidnapping. It was bound to be in all the papers.

Panic brought bile to her throat. She'd been a fool to lose her temper with Josephine. The child might be only four, but she had a strong will and a mind of her own, which Casey had always encouraged. The crowds of Brighton no longer seemed safe. Suddenly she felt as though everyone was staring at her.

Eva checked her thoughts. Don't think that way. If you look guilty, then they will nail you. She forced her tense shoulders into a more natural position and slowed her pace. She had risked everything because of the child. And Josephine with her dark hair, large hazel eyes and vivacious personality had always drawn people's attention. Even now with her hair short and dressed in a sailor suit, she looked as beautiful as a cherub. Josephine would be her downfall if she wasn't careful. Yet she was her reason for living. She could no more give her up than stop breathing. Josephine was her joy, her future. Without her she had nothing.

Two constables were up ahead. Eva speeded up her pace and deliberately dropped her case in front of a middle-aged man.

'Here, Madam, allow me to help you,' the gentleman offered as he picked up the case.

'That is very kind of you.' Eva smiled beguilingly. 'It is so difficult for a widow on her own.'

They were chatting naturally as they passed the two policemen, who took no notice of what appeared to be a married couple and their son. She was probably being fanciful to believe that the police were looking for her in Brighton, anyway. No one knew where she had gone, but it never did to underestimate the law. They stopped at nothing to bring a murderess to justice. All it would take was a telephone call to all the stations.

The thought filled her with dread. Damn Matt Frost for returning. He'd forced her to do this. She hadn't had time to plan this one like all the others. Even if she hadn't drugged Casey or done for Rusty to get Josephine away, kidnapping was a serious crime. Casey would never forgive her for taking her child. Eva's only chance was to start a new life with a new identity.

Chapter Twenty-four

Late that evening, Inspector Chapman called at the Ringside. He was a tall, ascetic, clean-shaven man with stooped shoulders and thick white curling hair. Casey and Matt were sitting beside Rusty's bed and he addressed them all.

'I'm sorry there's been no sighting of your sister-in-law and your daughter. A sketch of Mrs Chambers was in the late edition of all the papers and will be put in again tomorrow. There have been hundreds of calls informing us of sightings of lone women travelling with a child, but so far none really fits their description. Each will be investigated, though.'

'Could Eva have changed her appearance,' Rusty said thoughtfully. 'She's a cunning woman. When we ran the George and Dragon, I once caught her stuffing a red wig into her dressing-table drawer. Those days she occasionally had dealings with a man called Solomon Goldstein. Perhaps you know of him, Inspector?'

'What policeman in London did not know that villain? I had the pleasure of sending him down for a ten-year stretch last autumn. And not before time.' Chapman eyed him fixedly. 'What was your wife's connection with a criminal like him?'

'*That* she kept to herself. And Goldstein weren't a man you said no to if he wanted you to work for him. Unless you fancied being fishbait in the Thames. She said she wore the wig so that no one would recognise her. We moved to the Ringside to get away from the influence of such villains.'

'Is your wife still in possession of this wig?'

Rusty shrugged. 'She ain't had no dealings with Goldstein for several years now. Reckon she threw it out.'

The inspector scribbled in his notepad. 'Have you made a list of the clothing she may have taken?'

Casey handed it to him. 'She took very little, and for Josephine only the one navy dress which I described to the police officers yesterday.'

'Isn't that rather odd?' Inspector Chapman commented. 'Even though she had little time for packing. Are you sure that was all she took?'

'I know every article of my daughter's clothing. Only the navy dress is missing.'

'You have a son, Mr Chambers. Would anything of his fit the girl?'

Rusty looked at the inspector blankly and Casey answered for him. 'Danny is a year younger than Josephine, but he is big for his age. But Eva had no liking for boys. She would never dress Josephine as one.'

'These are exceptional circumstances, Miss Strong. But thank you for your time. I will keep you informed.'

Casey moved forward as the inspector made to leave. 'Is there nothing we can do? Have you no idea where she could have gone?'

'We are doing all we can, Miss Strong. The attack upon Mr Chambers was with intent to kill. In the light of that, and what Mr Chambers told us about the other deaths in your family, Mrs Chambers has some serious accusations to answer. This is now a murder inquiry, not just a kidnapping.'

Staring after Inspector Chapman's departing figure, Casey had never felt so helpless in her life. Every maternal instinct within her cried out to begin searching for Josephine. Yet that would be madness. Where would they start? It would be a wild-goose chase. She had no choice but to wait at the Ringside.

Each passing hour was riddled with anxiety. Her mind was unable to settle upon work, and sleep was impossible.

All the staff and residents were kind and understanding, which somehow made matters worse. It was a strain to make polite conversation. Inside she was feeling that her heart had been plucked out and lay exposed. The greatest solace she found was sitting in Josephine's room, staring at the rocking horse and doll's house on the floor. Matt was always at her side, his presence strengthening and comforting her. But even he could not alleviate her feelings of guilt. She could not forgive herself for repudiating her own daughter, and not facing the scandal that she had borne her out of marriage. She was convinced that this was her punishment.

'You are torturing yourself needlessly,' Matt said, embracing her. 'You have denied Josephine nothing. The child adores you. It's only been two days, Casey. Josephine will be found safe and well. Eva would never hurt her.'

As he spoke a boom of thunder resounded overhead, and the heavens opened to a violent downpour of rain. In the gloom Matt's face was shadowed, his eyes as darkly circled as her own from the strain of the last days.

'It's my fault,' she voiced her anguish. 'If I had told Josephine the truth she would have never gone off with Eva. I was so deliriously happy that you had returned, I thought only of myself. I should have known that Eva would resent my marriage. She doted on Josephine.'

Matt brushed his lips against Casey's hair. 'Don't blame yourself. Eva has duped us all. Why should Josephine not have trusted Eva, even had she been told that she was not her mother? And how would you guess that Eva would run away with her?'

Casey sank her head into her hands. 'I so completely misjudged my cousin. I convinced Dad to take Eva in. He never liked her or trusted her. Yet I insisted we gave her a home. He'd be alive now if I hadn't.'

Matt shook her gently. 'My darling, you must not think that way. You acted out of goodness. That can never be wrong. We've no proof that Eva caused Joe's death. And remember that Eva was also Sid Bowman's daughter. He was a nasty piece of work by all accounts. Joe never wanted his sister to marry him.'

A yellow flash of lightning lit up the room and Casey flinched. 'Is the storm as bad as this where Josephine is? She's frightened of them. I always took her into my bed if there was a storm at night. It was always me she wanted to comfort her. Eva was impatient with any sign of weakness. Is my little girl alone and frightened?'

The next flash was simultaneous with a cannonade of thunder directly overhead, making the panes of glass rattle in their frames. Casey pressed herself against Matt's body. 'Let our little girl be safe. I can't take this waiting. I should be out there looking for her.'

Casey twisted in Matt's arms and her gaze fell on the newspaper on Josephine's wooden desk which she had earlier discarded. The words glared up at her.

Hotel owner's daughter kidnapped by the woman who masqueraded as her mother to prevent a scandal.
Eva Chambers also wanted by the police for questioning about suspected family murders.

'My mother always said "Speak the truth and shame the devil",' Casey said heavily. 'She'd faced gossip enough in her days as an actress. How right she was. I've always hated lies and deceit. But Josephine was so tiny and precious, I couldn't bear the thought that she would be ostracised or ridiculed at school.

Now the whole of England knows of her bastardy. Yet I was never ashamed of bearing her. This report makes me sound like a scheming harlot.'

'Anyone who knows you well knows the lie of that,' Matt answered fiercely. 'More than one reporter hanging round the hotel who tried to imply that has had his nose bloodied by a resident.'

Casey laughed without mirth. 'And in the next edition of that reporter's paper, it was implied that the Ringside was little better than a bordello. That soon brought Inspector Chapman back here. He should have been trying to track down Josephine, not wasting time questioning the residents about my morals. Everything about my past has been dragged up. Even Dad's debt to your family.' Some of the strain in her face diminished as she put her arms around Matt's neck and added, 'I hadn't expected your brother to so wholeheartedly defend my father's reputation. He denied the debt. Said there had been an error in the brewery accounts some years ago, but the matter had been amicably settled. He upheld that my father had always been regarded as one of their most respected owner-managers.'

'It was mother's way of protecting the reputation of the brewery. She has also acknowledged that our marriage is inevitable, no matter how much the newspapers may try and tarnish your reputation.'

'My reputation is the least of my worries. I just want Josephine back. I want to hold her in my arms and hear her call me Mama.'

Matt kissed away a tear which rolled down her cheek. 'She will, my darling.'

There was a knock on the door and Rusty, with his hair sticking out of the bandage around his head, beamed at them.

'The inspector wants a word with you, Casey. He's in the parlour.'

'Has he word of Josephine?'

'He wouldn't say until we were all together. But from his expression I think the news will be promising.'

Casey ran to the parlour, her face alight with expectation. Inspector Chapman was standing by the fireplace. He had not removed his overcoat, and from the rain-drenched shoulders rose shadowy fingers of steam.

'Miss Strong, we have received several reports from the south coast that a red-haired woman has been seen with a child,' he stated without preamble. 'However, the child was reported to be a boy. But there was something about the child's manner which made these people suspicious enough to contact us. So far the Brighton police have been unable to locate this woman and child to question them.'

'I'm going to Brighton,' Casey declared. 'We can be there in three hours. I'll notify you of my hotel as soon as we arrive, Inspector.'

His expression was condemning. 'Is that wise, Miss Strong? So many of these reported sightings lead to nothing.'

'Brighton is the sort of place Eva would choose. Anything is better than just sitting here and waiting.'

Once the decision was made, Casey was packed and ready to leave within fifteen minutes.

'We'll stay at the Grand Hotel,' Matt suggested once they were on the train. 'But please, my darling, don't build your hopes up too high. There have been false reports of Eva and Josephine all over the country which have amounted to nothing.'

'She's at Brighton.' Casey was emphatic. 'Some deep intuition tells me. She's disguised Josephine as a boy. That's how desperate she is. Anyone who knows Eva knows she dislikes boys. She probably thought that we would never dream she would do that to Josephine, especially as she adored her girlish prettiness and loved to dress her in frills and ribbons. She can't keep Josephine hidden. My daughter is too active for that. She is capable of playing up if she becomes bored. We will tour every place of entertainment and amusement in Brighton suitable for children.' Her voice broke with emotion. 'We *must* find Josephine.'

'Bloody English weather,' Eva fumed. 'Will it never stop raining? It's August – the middle of summer.'

She turned away from the guest-house window to regard Josephine who was playing quietly with a wooden monkey on a stick. It was coming down cats and dogs outside, and the child was being difficult. When the storm broke in the night, she had thought Josephine would scream the house down. Nothing would pacify her. She had been shivering and calling out for Casey. In the end Eva became frightened that her screams would draw unwanted attention upon them. To stop them she had been forced to hold her hand over the girl's mouth. Finally when the storm abated, Josephine had sobbed herself to sleep. When she awoke, the girl had glared at her sullenly and demanded, 'I want to go home. I want Aunt Casey.'

Eva had never had any empathy with children. Casey had always been there to deal with Josephine or Danny when they became 'difficult', as Eva saw their moods or fears. Josephine's beauty had moved her and the girl could be enchanting when she was happy. Since coming to Brighton, Josephine had cried continually for Danny and Casey, until Eva was angry and exasperated. Yet her love for the girl was all-consuming, her thoughts all for their future.

A thin ray of sunlight penetrated the thin cotton of the curtains. If the day was dry she could take Josephine out. The child would enjoy a morning on the pier. There was a knock on the door and Mrs Monkton, the landlady, carried their breakfast tray inside. Eva had asked for all her meals to be brought to her room, declaring that in her recent widowhood she preferred seclusion. It was the first time that the landlady had seen her without the heavy veil obscuring her features. Mrs Monkton folded her fleshy arms under her large breasts and was regarding her with a scrutiny which Eva found disconcerting.

'Will yer be staying long, ma'am? Only, seeing as yer a widow like, me long-term guests get a cheaper rate than the fortnightly holidaymakers.'

'I haven't yet decided.'

'Mama, I don't want to stay,' Josephine piped out. 'I want to go home.'

The smile froze on Eva's face as she dreaded that the girl still dressed in a sailor suit would say something to betray herself. She moved to the door in a way which ushered the landlady out, her voice conciliatory. 'It's likely I'll stay for some weeks. My son doesn't understand that we lost our tithe cottage when my husband died.'

She forced tears into her eyes and dramatically dabbed at them with her handkerchief to gain the landlady's sympathy. There was something about the woman's stance, and the way she was staring over her shoulder towards Josephine that was making her uneasy. There was a shrewdness about this landlady which warned Eva that she missed little of what was going on in her boarding house.

Perhaps it was the red wig which Eva had always thought made her look tartish. It might be as well to move lodgings in a few days and change her identity again. Was this going to be the pattern of her life – always living with the fear of discovery?

On second thoughts, Brighton might not have been the best idea. She might be one amongst hundreds of holidaymakers, but landladies were notoriously nosy.

As the morning progressed, Eva's unease grew. Josephine kept insisting that they go home. Her constant whining made Eva's head ache. She was beginning to feel trapped. It was being shut in her room for so long, she reasoned. The sky remained overcast, but for the moment it was dry outside. Some fresh air would do both Josephine and herself good.

But once outside the boarding house, and even with the heavy net veil over her face, Eva felt vulnerable and exposed. Was she imagining it, or were people watching her and taking particular note of Josephine? The girl had lost all interest in pretending to be a boy, and too often her speech and manner was that of a girl.

Eva forced herself to remain calm. There had been nothing in yesterday's morning paper about Rusty's death or Josephine's disappearance. It was possible that Rusty had survived, but she couldn't believe that Casey would not report her daughter missing.

Deep in thought, Eva stepped into the road and, with a start, immediately jumped back on to the pavement as a tram rattled by. Her heart slammed against her breast. Though the traffic was less dense here than in London, the trams rattled past on their rails every few minutes. It was a sign of her growing distraction that she had been so careless.

Their boarding house was close to Victoria Gardens. She cut through them now, passing close to the smoke-grimed, oriental domes of The Pavilion, the palace Mrs Monkton had told her was built by the Prince Regent. They crossed the road by the Aquarium, and this time Eva was careful to watch for approaching trams at this busy terminus opposite the pier. The promenade was high above the beach, and crowded with people braving the showers to stroll and take in the sea air.

The breeze lifted Eva's veil as she paused to buy a newspaper from the ragged boy outside the tram shelter. He was sipping a cup of tea and for once silent in his raucous shouting of the headlines to attract customers.

Seeing a Punch and Judy Show about to start, Eva settled Josephine to watch it and sat down on a wooden seat to read the paper. Her hand shook at the headline which greeted her:

SUSPECTED MURDERESS KIDNAPS NIECE.

Her fingers lifted to massage her throat as she stared at the sketch of herself. Although it was not a good likeness, it was too close for comfort. Nervously, her hands twitched at the edges of her net veil which was thick enough to distort her features. She read on, her stomach contracting with fear. So Rusty wasn't dead and her attack on him had thrown suspicion on the other deaths. Her senses reeled. She'd been a fool to strike him. She should have drugged him like Casey. But he had angered her by his threats to sell the Ringside and set her aside. He was just like the others – her father and Joe – rousing the same murderous determination to be avenged upon him.

She gulped in sharp breaths of salty air to combat the queasiness roused by her fear of discovery. Striking Rusty had been a mistake. The police now suspected that those other deaths were not accidents.

With a furtive glance around her, she studied the holidaymakers on the promenade. Whenever one looked towards her, she quivered with alarm. Then the sight of a self-possessed figure in the throng made her cry out. Casey! How the hell did she learn I was here? Eva wondered in terror. All's lost!

She bolted out of the seat and snatched up Josephine's hand.

'Ow, you're hurting me, Mama,' the girl protested. 'I want to see the end of the show.'

'We have to go,' Eva snapped.

Immediately Josephine dug in her heels and hung back so that Eva was forced to drag the protesting child along the promenade.

'I want Aunt Casey.'

Josephine slipped on the wet pavement and grazed her knee.

With a groan of annoyance, Eva jerked the child upright and increased her pace. Josephine screamed louder. Heads were beginning to turn. A glance showed Eva that Matt, who was with Casey, had spotted her and had begun to run towards them.

Eva's skin was coated in a cold sweat which trickled between her shoulder-blades and breasts. It had started to rain again, the sudden shower heavy and stinging her face as she pulled Josephine towards the road. There was a tram at the Aquarium ready to leave. If she darted through the crowds, Matt might not notice them boarding it.

Her feet slithered on the wet road and she leapt on to the tram, hauling Josephine up behind her. At the same time Josephine yelled out, 'Aunt Casey!'

Then the girl jerked her hand free from Eva's. The tram had started to pull away and pick up speed. To her horror Eva saw Josephine overbalance backwards off the platform and fall between the tram rails as another tram was approaching behind them. The girl's mouth gaped open in terror as the vehicle bore down upon her, its air-brakes hissing. The motorman, his face porridge-grey beneath his cap, was frantically ringing the foot-operated gong in warning.

With a scream Eva leapt from the tram. She saw everything in slow motion – the cream and red paintwork rapidly advancing; the iron struts like a prison cage in front of the motorman, supporting the upper deck of the tram. The shocked faces of several male passengers peered over the top of the open upper deck, the protective rain-cover on the seat pulled up to their necks. She had even registered the poster for Tamplin's Ales whilst her heart pounded like a galloping horse. Sobbing, she picked up Josephine and shoved her roughly out of danger. Then there was a flare of agony in her back and head, and she was brutally buffeted sideways as the tram screeched to a halt.

'Josie!' Casey yelled. Her joy had turned to horror as she'd seen her daughter fall and lie frozen by fear between the tramlines. Even with her ringlets shorn and wearing a sailor suit, she had recognised her at once.

The approaching tram had been perilously close. The wet surface had slowed its brakes and it had seemed inevitable that it would run her down. At first she had not recognised the black-clad woman as Eva. When Josephine had been clasped and pushed to safety, she'd seen the tramcar ram her rescuer in the side, knocking her hat and red wig askew as she fell to the ground.

Josephine had burst into hysterical tears as Casey reached her and hugged her close, her tiny arms entwining around her neck. Across the top of her daughter's dark head, Casey gazed in stunned shock at the prone figure of her cousin. Blood was pumping from a large gash on Eva's temple. She wasn't moving.

'Is she dead?' Casey asked Matt as the motorman joined them in the road and ordered the crowds to stand back.

'This woman is the child's mother,' Matt informed the motorman, 'and the woman on the ground is her cousin.'

The motorman shouted for someone to call an ambulance. 'There was nothing I could do,' he explained, his expression haggard. 'The child fell off the other tram straight in front of me. Then the woman ran to save her. I did all I could. If it hadn't been raining, the brakes would have held faster. But she shouldn't be dead. The lifeguard at the front of the tram is designed so that, should anyone fall in front of it, the wooden struts come down and scoop the person along the track. It prevents them from going under the wheels. The only cases of accidents I've seen have escaped with bruising or an occasional broken leg.'

'She's not moving.' Casey nodded towards Eva. Holding Josephine close to her breast, she whispered soothing words to her sobbing daughter.

Matt put his arm protectively around Casey. 'Take Josephine back to the hotel. She needs you to protect her,' he suggested. 'I'll stay with Eva in the ambulance and hospital.'

Casey was trembling violently as she stood up, still clutching Josephine. The girl was crying uncontrollably. 'Didn't mean to hurt Mama.'

'It's not your fault, darling. Eva will be all right.' Casey stared from Eva's still figure to Matt. She was torn between getting Josephine away from the accident and needing to help Eva. 'I'll wait until the ambulance arrives. I can hear its bell ringing. It won't be long.'

Unmindful of the rain that was falling, she held Josephine tightly and pressed kisses against her cold face. Since Eva had taken Josephine, she had been furious at her cousin to the point of hating her, but seeing the way Eva had unselfishly risked her life to save Josephine had mellowed her anger.

She stared down at the parchment-white face of her cousin. Its beauty was marred by the scarlet rivulets of blood trickling from her mouth and ears. She knew that her injuries were serious, and suspected that she had hit her head on the side of the tram as she fell. The onlookers parted as the ambulance drew up and the two men placed Eva on to a stretcher.

''Ere, ain't that the woman in the newspaper?' a man shouted out from the crowd. 'Suspected murderess, weren't she? Looks like she's been spared the gallows.'

So wracked by fear for Josephine had she been, it had not crossed Casey's mind that, if Eva was guilty of murder, she would be hanged. But that was the fate of all murderesses.

There was a groan from her cousin and Casey moved closer. For a moment Eva's eyelids flickered open and her eyes, stark with pain and fear, held Casey's stare.

'Forgive me,' Eva croaked softly.

Casey staggered. The look in her cousin's eyes told her more than she wanted to see. It was not just forgiveness for kidnapping Josephine that she was asking.

Casey shook her head. 'I understand why you took Josephine. You also loved her enough to risk your life to save her. But my father . . . I cannot forgive you for that if you killed him. Did you?'

A quiver passed through Eva's figure as she continued to stare beseechingly at Casey. Then her eyes glazed, the lids shielding their expression as the ambulance men lifted the stretcher into the van. A policeman prevented Matt climbing in beside her. 'Is it correct that this woman is Eva Chambers, the woman wanted for kidnapping and suspected murder?'

Matt nodded. 'She is my fiancée's cousin. It was her child that Mrs Chambers abducted.'

'Then a police guard must be with her at all times. I'm sure you would prefer to be with your fiancée at this time. Besides, it don't look like there's much you can do for this woman now.'

Matt joined Casey as the ambulance, with its bell ringing, sped away.

'Will she live?' Casey asked.

'If she does it's likely that she will face the hangman's noose,' Matt replied too softly for Josephine to hear. 'She knew she'd have nothing to fear from us if she had been guilty of anything less than murder. So why did she run if she was innocent? Rusty would never press charges for her attack, and I doubt you'd allow her to be jailed for taking Josephine, especially as the child is safe.'

Two hours later, Inspector Chapman called at their suite in the Grand Hotel.

'Mrs Chambers died without giving a statement. She never regained consciousness. Two ribs were broken when the tram hit her, but as she went down she must have hit her head awkwardly. It was a freak blow which smashed her skull and killed her.'

Chapter Twenty-five

A month after Eva was buried, Casey married Matt. It had been a quiet affair, the reception held at the Ringside and attended by Matt's family. Only Millicent and Clementine were absent. Sybil and Humphrey were reserved, but at least they made the effort to be gracious, and Sybil had mellowed more when Josephine presented her with a bunch of violets. Casey had seen Sybil's expression soften as they rested on the child who resembled her son. Only when her stare lifted to regard Casey did the hostility return. Casey accepted the truce. Sybil would never wholly approve of her, but she was making the effort for Matt's sake and that was what mattered. Casey was prepared to do the same.

The wedding over, they had honeymooned for a week in Paris, Matt flying them across the English Channel in his biplane. It was the first time Casey had flown, and she could understand why Matt wanted to dedicate his life to flight. It was a wonderful experience.

As a wedding present to Matt, Casey had purchased a Model-T Ford. They were driving back from the airfield and were only a couple of miles from Richmond when they saw a portly, balding man, overdressed in tweeds and muffler on a warm September afternoon, anxiously pacing the deserted road. His large sleek Daimler was pulled over to the side, with the bonnet up and emitting a stream of smoke. From out of the window an equally overdressed woman, who seemed to be dripping pearls and gold chains from her fat neck, was shrilly berating him. Their four young children were jumping up and down on the seats, yelling their heads off.

'What a ghastly family,' Casey couldn't help commenting.

'I'd better see if I can help,' Matt said.

He stopped the car and Casey sank down into the seat, dreamily content with thoughts of her marriage. Paris had been bliss. Her body still glowed from Matt's ardent lovemaking that morning. She was eager to see Josephine again, who had remained with Rusty and Danny. It had been hard to be parted from her daughter so soon after her kidnapping, but she had known that Josephine was in loving hands. Matt and herself needed some time alone together.

Dimly she could hear a man's pompous voice cutting across the ceaseless nagging of his wife. She frowned and sat up to look more closely at the driver of the Daimler. His back was to her and did not look at all familiar, but his voice resurrected memories she preferred to forget. Matt had just emerged from under the car's bonnet. The engine was going but making an unhealthy spluttering noise.

'It will get you to the nearest garage, if you take it carefully,' Matt advised.

The driver's wife heaved her large bulk out of the car, diamonds glittering on her fleshy fingers. She was also heavily pregnant. 'Didn't I tell you that Larkin should have driven us? But you would insist on doing it yourself. What is the point of having a chauffeur if you don't use him? Now look at the inconvenience I have to suffer. And the children are hungry. Poor lambs. How far is the garage?' The last sentence was addressed to Matt, as though he were a servant, and without acknowledgement of his kindness in helping them.

Her manner angered Casey. The woman was rich and spoilt and expected everyone to come running to her call.

'The garage is about five miles,' Matt responded. 'But the Ringside Hotel which is owned by my wife is little more than a mile from here. If your wife would like to rest there, we have an excellent restaurant.'

'The Ringside? Isn't that the place which was recently in the papers about a child being kidnapped?' The woman sniffed disdainfully. 'We couldn't possibly stay anywhere so infamous.'

Matt had been wiping his oily hands on the handkerchief and he screwed it up and marched angrily towards the Model-T.

'I say, don't go and leave us stranded,' the man called. He hurried after Matt. 'I'm sure my wife didn't mean to give offence.'

It was then that Casey recognised James Hardcastle. His appearance shocked her. He was grossly overweight, his once-handsome looks lost amidst fleshy cheeks, his complexion mottled with the red veins of a heavy drinker.

Matt had paused and Casey knew that he would not leave anyone in difficulties on the road. As Matt began to retrace his steps to the Daimler, Casey got out of the car.

'I would have thought a word of gratitude for my husband restarting you car would be in order, James Hardcastle. And the Ringside is famous for its hospitality and cuisine. It's a favourite haunt of several members of the nobility when they are boating on the river.'

'Who is this creature, James?' his wife demanded. 'Is she another one of your floosies?' Prunella Hardcastle's thin lips turned down with disgust. Her contempt turned on her husband. 'Can I not even drive along the open road without being reminded of your infidelities?'

The woman's voice was rising in hysteria. Hardcastle had got the wife he deserved. Casey cut across the tirade.

'I have never been one of your husband's women. Though

I was a stenographer at the Emporium for a short time. And I am sure, Mr Hardcastle, that your wife had every intention of giving offence.'

He was looking at her in astonishment, his gaze taking in the details of her slender figure and elegant, understated peach suit and hat, which could only have come from one of Paris's top designer houses.

'Good Lord, it's Cassandra Strong, isn't it? Quite a scandal was stirred up over your cousin kidnapping your child – your bastard child.'

The salacious gleam in his eyes made her tilt her chin higher in affront. 'It's Mrs Frost now,' Casey corrected. 'And since I don't like to see any pregnant woman stranded in a wayside garage, your wife and family are still welcome to avail themselves of the facilities at the Ringside. The hotel has always been noted for its hospitality. And we have never turned anyone in need away. A room will be made available to your family, free of charge, if Mrs Hardcastle wishes to rest whilst your vehicle is repaired or you hire a taxicab to take you home.'

She saw Matt bristling at finally encountering the man who had tried to seduce her. Then suddenly, he grinned. 'Only a woman as generous and noble-hearted as my wife could make that offer in the circumstances. Good day, Hardcastle.'

'They were the last people I ever expected to see,' Casey said as they drove away. 'Is that how people will view the Ringside now – as notorious? I'd always wanted it to uphold my father's memory.'

'It will,' Matt said, smiling understandingly. 'Since the kidnapping, hundreds of people have flocked to the hotel. They were curious to see the place where a murderess had lived and wanted to see if what the papers said was true. But they go away praising the restaurant, and the men start reliving Strongarm's fights. He was a legend, Casey.'

He winked at her. 'And isn't that women's journal running

a story on how you helped the veterans in their convalescence? You must be proud of your achievements.'

She brushed the compliment aside. 'I only created a homely atmosphere for brave men who deserved something special. It's just seeing Hardcastle which has angered me. And the Ringside is important. Matt, I don't think I can sell it. It's more than just keeping Dad's memory alive. I would feel that I was deserting the veterans, many of whom I regard as friends. And there's Archie. He needs a home and work. These gardens are everything to him.'

Matt did not reply and her heart sank. They had just passed the black and gold painted signboard of the Ringside and, as he swung the car over the gravel forecourt to the driveway leading to the hotel grounds, she saw that the pub's sign had been taken down. It had simply stated the name of the hotel in gold lettering with the name of the brewery which supplied them underneath. Its absence mirrored the emptiness which had settled over her. Already it seemed the changes had begun. Had Rusty sold the pub whilst they'd been in Paris? Did the new owners intend to change its name? That felt like betraying her father's memory. Her loyalties were painfully divided.

She stepped out of the car. A lump of emotion knotted her throat as she stared around at the beautiful grounds which had meant so much to her. The willows swayed in the breeze and a family of swans were gliding regally down the river. The lawns were immaculate, the flowerbeds still colourful with roses and bedding plants. She suppressed a sigh. It would be hard to leave, but she had chosen to marry Matt and his life was running his air freight and passenger service. The sale of the Ringside would provide him with two new planes, and guarantee the success of his business

Why did nothing good in life come without sacrifice? And why did it have to be so painful? She felt that she was letting down the veterans and Archie by selling the hotel. Yet her support must be for Matt's new enterprise. He had waited so long to fulfil his ambition. And she loved him so much.

Matt had entered the hotel through the restaurant instead of the main entrance, and she could hear him calling her. Her step was slow as she responded, fighting hard to dispel her sadness. She could at least ensure that Archie always had a garden to work in, even if it was only her own.

On entering the restaurant her ears were suddenly blasted with the sound of a trumpet fanfare. She was surrounded by all the guests and restaurant customers who had become firm regulars. As the trumpet notes died, a loud cheer went up and several champagne corks popped.

'Here's to Casey Frost.' Rusty came forward to put his arm around her whilst Matt appeared smiling beside them. 'A toast to our much-loved proprietor and to my own dear partner. May the Ringside continue to prosper under her management.'

She looked askance at Matt who was grinning. 'I couldn't ask you to give it up as it meant so much to you. Rusty and I planned this surprise for your return. He doesn't want to sell up either, providing that you continue to work together. I don't have to use an airfield in Kent. I'll find something suitable much closer. This will be our home.'

Tears of happiness glistened in Casey's eyes. 'I couldn't have a more wonderful gift, or a more understanding husband.'

She turned to Rusty. 'I'm glad you are staying. Josephine will always think of Danny as her brother. It would be a shame to have parted them.'

His expression sobered. 'So Eva's fears were all unfounded. She'd not have lost you. It was her own obsessive nature which made her act as she did.'

'We will never know the truth about Eva. If she was a murderess, I mean,' Casey said heavily.

'She was guilty,' Rusty declared. 'I suppose for her sake it was best that she died the way she did. It was her one last redeeming act, saving Josephine. Hanging is a cruel end. At least this way Danny will be spared knowing the truth. Her death prevented her facing trial and the scandal that would have caused.'

Matt's hand was on Casey's shoulder. 'Don't let thoughts of your cousin spoil today.'

Casey smiled up at him. 'The past cannot be changed. It's the future which is important.'

'And that is ever-changing.'

'No more changes for a while yet,' Casey said with mock horror. 'I want to sit back and quietly enjoy married life.'

'But there is something,' Matt said with unusual seriousness. 'I'd like one significant change to be made with immediate effect.'

He stepped aside as Humphrey and Peter Frost appeared. Her smile was warm for Peter who, like his father, had always accepted her into their family. Humphrey was stiff and ill-at-ease, as though expecting her to slight him.

He held out a heavy board which was draped in scarlet silk. 'I hope you will accept this. It was Matt's idea, but it is wholeheartedly supported by our family.'

Puzzled, Casey drew aside the scarlet silk and put a hand to her mouth in astonishment. Humphrey was holding a newly painted pub sign. The image of Joe Strong in boxing shorts and gloves raised in a defensive pose stared back at her. At the top were the words 'The Ringside Hotel' and underneath the portrait was written 'Frost's Finest Ales'.

'We couldn't have the Ringside being supplied by anyone else, so we bought out the brewer's contract. Our family is proud to be associated with this hotel, and that it is dedicated to your father's memory.' She could see by Humphrey's stiff manner that he had swallowed his pride to say those words. It was another step towards a full reconciliation between their two families.

'Thank you, Humphrey. Frost's should be the only brewery supplying my hotel. And the pub sign is wonderful.'

She kissed both Matt's brothers' cheeks and, as she drew back, saw Sybil Frost watching her from across the room. She was holding Josephine's hand. Sybil inclined her head in formal greeting, but as Josephine pulled her grandmother into the garden to show her the swans, Casey thought she detected a greater softening in the woman's demeanour. Slowly Sybil Frost was also coming round, won over by Josephine.

'Happy, darling?' Matt asked, taking her hand and drawing her behind a large potted palm by a window which shielded them from the gathering. Suddenly his eyes widened and he went very pale. From the corner of her eye, Casey saw a large daddy-long-legs climbing up the plant leaves by her shoulder. She cupped it in her hands and gently set it outside the window.

His composure restored, Matt grinned. 'It was a spider which brought us together, so I recall.'

They laughed, remembering the incident in the solicitor's office. 'I fell in love with your laugh, Casey. Like everything about you it is natural, unaffected, and so full of life and energy.'

'I reckon we will always have laughter in our lives – and that's important,' she replied, her voice growing husky with desire. 'Laughter and love. They are the greatest gifts God gave mankind. Too often they are sadly missing in people's lives.'

'But not ours, Casey darling.'

'No, my love. Not ours.'